THE ANGEL SERIES COLLECTION

BOOKS 4-5

JO WILDE

CONTENTS

DEVIANT ANGEL

DEATH ANGEL

DEVIANT ANGEL

THE ANGEL SERIES BOOK 4

REFLECTION

$\mathscr{L}$ooking back throughout the short years of my twenty-two years of life, I, Stephanie Ray Collins, never dreamt that my journey would've ended at this very spot. Looking down the barrel of my enemies, I knew my demise was imminent. Even a genetically engineered angel couldn't have seen what was to come. I thought I had as much a chance as anyone, living a normal life, free to decide my own destination. I was dead wrong.

The Illuminati would never retract their ironclad claws from my flesh. I was their prized treasure and my sticker was far too valuable for them to ever let go of me. I may be a piece of property to the Family but *this* piece wasn't going down without an old fashion fight, but first… I had an uprising to go to.

The world had gone to hell in a handbasket. The system we once knew and depended on from the simplest task as getting the Sunday newspaper had come to a screeching halt. Every little minuscule part of our socialism, economy, and commerce had gone rogue. Famine blanketed the countryside like a frozen winter. Folks forced from their homes to the streets, banks closed and the almighty dollar suddenly crashed. People rioting and innocent ones shot in cold blood, left to bleed out onto the streets. As if in one sweep, the United Nations collapsed in less than one day.

The new authorities under the rule of National Socialism declared

The Order to be invoked, like martial law only far more sinister. Our old government had completely fallen. It was gone. Vanished in one night, just like the walls of Rome, our system collapsed, crumbling to the ground.

New rulers had emerged or maybe they'd been ruling all along, behind the shadows, in secret? Aidan was right. The Elite were always there watching, hiding, and waiting for their time to act. The populous were blindsided.

I recalled something that Aidan once told me–if people new the dark things that lurked in the shadows, they would go insane. At the time, I didn't understand. A lot had changed since then. Now I understood exactly what he meant. I wished I could go back to that time of ignorance.

As reality played its evil hand, the rulers had spread their poison like Hitler conquering half of Europe. Although this uprising was on a much larger scale, taking the world by sweeps and bounds.

The Illuminati had the world by its feet, but not me. I refused to give them my free will. Because of my threat and rebellion, they wanted rid of me. I reckoned, since I wouldn't join their political massacre, they viewed me as their enemy. I reckoned that any opposing threat had to be dealt with effectively… but I wasn't going down alone. *I planned to take some with me.*

It was going to be one hell of a Fourth of July in my neighborhood. This time, I was coming with my guns loaded just like the gunfight at OK-Fucking-Corral or at least that was my theory.

THROES OF CATACLYSM

I stood in the throes of cataclysm and the hard realization that I'd been duped once again ripped through me. My gaze dropped down to the ring that embellished his middle finger, the diamond eye that betrayed his identity as the faceless boy... *my beguiling adversary.* A deadly mistake on his part!

With complete certainty, I knew what I must do next. It was like the walk of doom. *Mine.* I scoffed.

Fuck 'em.

Aidan froze. Sweat beaded his forehead. My pendulous knives hovered dangerously at his throat. The cold blades obeyed my command. I narrowed my eyes at Aidan. He knew only one slight slip, and my knives would finish him off. I smelled his fear, and I reveled in it.

Rage surged forth deep within my core, and it obeyed. The winds whipped through as I unleashed my essence, an inauspicious place where I did not recognize myself.

As if we stood in amidst of a tornado, my powers soared and the tempest grew fiercer. Everything began twirling at warp speed. The winds howled encircling Aidan and me as if we were its prey. Trees snapped back and forth violently.

Focusing on my enemy, I reigned back my powerful essence as it gnarled in protest. I asked in a voice unknown to my ears, a voice of a true and deadly *Zophasemin.* "I'm going to ask you this once," my voice echoed. "Don't lie to me, druid," I warned in a calm, steel voice. "It was you and Sally all along. The two of you framed me!"

Aidan's mouth opened to speak, but it seemed the cat had taken his tongue.

"After all this time, you hid in the shadows of anonymity like a yellow-back *coward* with that damn needle, full of God-knows-*what*!" I hissed through gritted teeth. "I remember your diamond ring." My eyes fixed on his third finger, the ring glimmered in the sunlight, gold diamonds marking an eye. I nodded at it. "It's quite unique. Though, it's hideous." I snarled.

As rage embraced my internal war, I began to toy with Aidan. With a flick of the wrist, another knife appeared pointing straight at his groin. I taunted him with a wicked smile.

The glint in his blues confirmed his fraught. I knew that I'd never become a victim to *him* ever again and I delighted in that little insight. Aidan didn't dare flinch, not even a twitch. He was wise not to trust me. Hell, I didn't trust myself at this point.

I eyed him cautiously as the dark seductress deep within my core sang its wondrous song. Intoxicated, I craved the essence like a blood-thirsty vampire craving to feed. But I fought the urge and harnessed its desires.

Answers hung on the tip of his tongue and I needed the truth. I called to him in that strange voice. "It was your hand that was behind my suffering. It was your evil magick that compelled every lawman and judge in the state of Louisiana to convict me. You were the master-mind behind my fate, sending me off to an asylum where they left me lying in my own piss and vomit, under a constant drug induced stupor by *your* orders. As I laid unconscious for months on end, unaware, my child grew within me." My voice broke from the gut-wrenching pain that consumed me. "After I gave birth, you *ripped* my baby from me, denying a mother of her own child. You destroyed everything *I* loved!" Electricity coursed through my body as lightning struck a tree and snapped it in two. "Tell me *this* is not true!" I screamed with spittle spewing. My madness was more than a simple emotion. I was a mother aching to cradle her child, a child I'd never had the chance to know, a mother seeking justice.

Aidan stayed silent for a moment.

"Tell me, NOW!" I demanded. I wanted to rip his heart right out of his chest and set it ablaze. Yet, I held the essence back. I was in control... *not him.*

"Yes, it's true!" he admitted, his eyes wide with alarm. "It's all true!" Aidan bellowed. "Everything is true! Sally and I are married. We married two centuries ago. The girl lied to you. She's immortal," he rambled as if he was standing before a priest.

"Stop! I don't care, druid. Tell me why you framed me?" I stared at this stranger as my stomach winced from his atrocities. How could I have ever loved this man?

"Wait! I'll tell you!" Aidan exclaimed, losing what little courage he had. "Before you run your bloody knives through me at least give me the opportunity to explain." Without thinking, he flinched, and my knives inched closer. He pressed his head tight against the tree as he pleaded. "Wait! I'll tell you everything."

Unexpectedly, I heard a deep laugh. I tilted my chin sideways, catching the Cajun standing only a few paces behind me, smirking. He nodded to Aidan. "This one deserves death. He does not respect women, *non!* This pig murdered my sister!" The Cajun growled. "He got her drunk and had his way, this one did. That murderous bastard used his black magick on her. His puppets... the Law Enforcement claimed she committed suicide. It was lies! All lies. *My sister* would've never taken her life." The Cajun belted out; loathing filled his voice. "If you like... I will happily dispose of this filthy baggage for you. Gotta gator out back that's hungry." A wicked smile touched his lips.

Then, it occurred to me. "What did your sister look like?"

"A lot like me only a higher pitched voice." Sarcasm poured from his perilous voice. "Adaline was about your height, sixteen, dark hair, and dark skin... very beautiful. She was good. Never in trouble, full of life. She had plans, that one, college, husband, and children. Adaline was full of dreams." The Cajun's eyes moistened. "The police found my sister's body in the alley across from the Catfish diner. It was the last place she'd been seen alive. The authorities are liars. I spit on 'em!" The Cajun lurked forward and placed his hand on his gun holster, fingers tight around its hilt as he continued, "Funny how things bite you in the ass. My peeps thought they were doing a good thing. They wanted Adaline away from the thugs of the city." The Cajun's face

7

hardened. "They moved her to the small town of Tangi where that sociopath lived."

Emitting only a cold stone face, Aidan exhibited no remorse. The word *savage* came to mind.

I remembered the girl at the diner where my mother worked. She was wasted drunk hanging on Aidan. I had just had a huge argument with Sara. Aidan had caught me before I'd left on my bike. He'd arranged for Jeffery to pick the girl up and take her home. Could he have lied about that too? My incensed eyes cut back to Aidan. "Is this *true*?" I carefully eyed my captive. He lingered a moment as if he were conjuring up a lie. "I sent her home with Sam."

"Wait! I thought Jeffery had picked her up." Could he had been lying to me? Come to think about it, I didn't see Jeffery in the driver's seat. In fact, no one got out of the car.

My suddenly iced.

"The diner?" Aidan's brows pleated as if he had a sudden onset of amnesia. "I don't recall having Jeffery waste gas on a drunk girl."

I narrowed my eyes suspiciously. When did Aidan ever forget anything? "You don't remember?"

"Why would I remember such a mundane thing as some poor drunk twat's name?" His face carried no apology.

"Which one, Sam or Jeffery?" I spat out fighting against the fathom foot that pressed against my chest.

"Why the concern? She was merely a human girl." Finally, the villain revealed himself, emotions laced with arsenic.

I could hear the Cajun cursing a slew of words. "If you don't kill that bastard, I swear I will."

I craned my neck, eyes fixed on the Cajun. "Nick, back off! You'll get your turn!" I gravely promised. I whipped my eyes back at Aidan. "It looks like you have many enemies, druid."

"Get on with your barnyard trial. I have admitted to all my mishaps. You decide."

Nothing about him felt right. He exhumed the epitome of disgust. A far cry from the man I once knew and loved.

"No good deed goes unpunished, right?" I stared Aidan in the eye unlike that day he captured me. The essence rumbled deep within. I could feel the enmity begging to spew forth, and all I had to do was release its fervor on him. It'd be over just like that. Still, I couldn't do it.

8

Not yet.

Aidan spoke up. "You are aware as well as I am, the Family controls every living creature from the earth to the heavens, human and numinous. I've never belonged to myself. Nor do any of us, even you!" he paused. "Brave or perhaps witless, your father adventured down another path. He risked his life to leave the Family. If you ask me, he was a fool. Look what good his short-term freedom got him… buried six feet under."

"Shut up!" I stepped up, fist flexing by my side. "You don't get to speak about my father!"

"You mustn't get yourself in a tizzy, sweetheart. I am merely stating a fact." His arrogance superseded his common sense.

"Can the facts, druid! I haven't got time for your bullshit."

"Stupid, inbred! You think I'm wasting *your* time? Something you should know about *your* family… *our* family. If you defect from their sanction, you are as good as dead. The Family considers this apostasy, which is unforgivable. As you know, I make no excuse for my actions. I did what I had to do to survive. You can believe me or not, but I had no knowledge of where you were hanging your hat, so to speak. However, my uncle and the Family felt it was best I didn't have any contact. They claimed that a large sum of money had been exchanged for the baby. Shortly after, you disappeared with no forwarding address."

I spat at his elaborate tale. "You're *lying*! Money doesn't mean anything to me. You knew I would've never agreed to such bile."

"It's funny how fast a person can change their minds when he or she has no family and no means of support."

"You have yet to tell me why I took the fall for crimes I didn't commit."

"What does it matter now?" he shrugged. "You're free, aren't you?"

"Tell *me*!" I hissed.

Aidan exhaled a restless sigh. "Very well, if you insist," he said in a grudging voice. "The trumped-up charges were for show. It was only a front to the public's eye. We had to make it look legit. The Family wanted the heat off their trail. There were too many lives lost to sweep it under the rug. Therefore, they decided it was in the best interest for everyone if you took the fall."

"Fall? Your family murdered people and destroyed my life. It wasn't a fall. It was an atrocity. I lost my child!"

"Doesn't the end justify the means?"

There I had it, the worm in the apple. "No! Aidan, it doesn't," I bellowed.

"Look! Sorry to offend, but that's how my world operates. A few lives lost for the greater good."

I almost charged him, but somehow, I held my feet planted to the ground. "What about our daughter?" My voice broke, "Dawn?"

"What about her?"

"Did our child's death justify your *fucking* means?"

Aidan held his tongue for a brief moment, and then he answered. "I supposed she became collateral damage." A thirst for blood surged through me. I wanted him dead! To keep from unhinging my fury, I drove one knife through his right shoulder.

Aidan screamed out from the sharp stab. "You fucking bitch! If I get loose from here. I'm going to kill you myself!"

Silently communicating, I ordered my blades to still until further orders. They obeyed, hovering in Aidan's face.

Aidan was my captive now. He was pinned against the tree as blood trickled down his arms and chest. His once crisp, white shirt changed into a deep crimson and with each breath he took, his face deepened in agony.

Good! His heart may be a cold stone but at least, he was feeling pain. I flashed a satisfying grin. "I hope you bleed like the swine that you are."

"I had no way of knowing if you were in Tim-buck-fucking-two or at the Bahamas living it up with some fruity drink on the beach."

"You lie."

"You're right!" he threw at me like shooting bullets. "I should've looked further into your whereabouts, but I had to protect Dawn. I was backed into a corner, sweetheart. It's the truth. I swear!"

"If you cared for our child so much, then why did you let your family take Dawn's life?" I swallowed the lump that choked my pain. I wasn't going to cry, I wasn't going to cry. I repeated inwardly to myself.

"My uncle and the others in charge informed me that Sally and I would be raising the child. We'd teach her magick and our traditions. The family's long term goal had never changed. They wanted immortality.

I repeated my question. "If what you say is true, then why did they take Dawn's life?" I gritted through my teeth.

"It was not until I tried to escape with Dawn did the family turn on me. Sally ratted me out to the Family. I knew better than to trust that bitch." Aidan sneered.

"Yet, you trusted Sally enough to join her diabolical scheme to take me down."

"That's where you are wrong! I didn't get a say."

"Why are you still alive?"

Aidan's lips pressed tight and then he relented. "I remain useful to them."

"Like how?"

"The Family knows I can find you."

"They know your whereabouts?"

"My uncle bugged my jeep. Don't worry, Van or the Family won't come for you unless I defect or you murder me." His voice seemed stiff as if he'd been rehearsing lines for a Broadway play.

Holy geez! I'd put everyone into danger. I stared at him puzzled. "The Aidan I once knew would've never allowed this to happen."

"Don't blame me. Your lover boy has left a vapor trace that the Family can see miles away."

"You're lying!" I stepped closer. "Val would never be so careless. But *you*… coming here with a tracking device attached to your damn jeep takes the cake!" I wheeled on my heels, my gaze slamming into the Cajun. I shouted, as my voice spewed with panic. "Get under his jeep and find that damn tracker. Destroy it!" Then I shouted over at Jeffery and Dom. They'd gathered outside on the porch watching in silence. "Get your things. We gotta get moving *fast*. The Family will be sending their forces." I turned back to Aidan, our eyes locked. I had one more lie to uncover. "If you can track me, then why didn't you find me at Haven Hospital?"

"You may find this hard to believe, but it's the truth. The Family cast a spell. A recherché spell that blocks my sensory." His lies rolled off his tongue like sweet nectar. "It was not until you came to stay with Dom and Jeffery that I was able to find you. The Family used you as a decoy to pull me out of hiding. I underestimated them." Aidan jerked from the festering knife stuck in his shoulder. The old blood had dried his shirt as the fresh blood spread farther down his chest.

"Why should I believe you?"

"Because it's the truth!" He spewed, desperation marked his tone. "I want you back. Why is that so hard to believe?"

I scoffed. "And what? Sally, you and I all live happily ever after under the same roof?"

"I don't love Sally. I never have. I'd ditch her in a heartbeat to be with you. Besides, she's untrustworthy."

My brow shot up. "I could say the same about you."

"Like I said, I do have flaws." His voice seemed weaker. The pain was getting worse.

The soft Stevie wanted to run to him and throw her arms around his neck, but the hard Stevie preferred a daggered rammed through his lying, black heart. "Stop it! Stop saying those things to me. You do not get to whisper sweet nothings in my ear after you and your damn family destroyed my life. Everything that has ever meant anything to me, you have taken. The only thing I have in my heart for you is contempt." Calm rage poured from my voice.

Then I recalled a druid spell. One I inherited from Aidan when we had infused ourselves together. I began to chant, arms spread like an eagle's wings, calling to the elements, and demanding their powers.

"Est a tangle textu nos weave, oh quam nos decipio, nostrum pectus pectoris repletus per lugeo, nos must aufero is sceleris, a rutilus lux lucis mitis weaved, permissum suus subluceo take temerarious inter redimio him ut is nemus oh sic angustus si is wiggles retineo him anhelo!"

As my voice rose above the rising tempest, black, menacing clouds gathered. Thunder roared, and lightning streaked the sky. In the blink of an eye, a glowing rope materialized, snaking around Aidan's body, binding him to the tree. His eyes flew wide open. "Don't kill me!" he shrieked.

"You're not getting off that easily." I flashed him a dark grin. I thought at this point that I'd stepped off into the world of never, a land that had never been touched. I had to admit, there was something exalting about this all-knowing power. It made me feel alive, electrifying.

I spotted Jeffery and Dom embraced in each other's arms with the look of fear. Even the Cajun stood back eyeing me cautiously.

"What's wrong?" My eyes cut to Dom and Jeffery and then to the Cajun.

Jeffery spoke up in a worrisome tone. "Boo, go look at your face." His gaze quickly pulled away. "My face?" Alarm trickled over me. My hand shot straight to my cheek. Something was wrong. The strange texture of my skin was thick, like molten rock. The surface was hard and rough. I darted to the closest mirror … Aidan's jeep.

When I peered into the small mirror, hysteria seized my mind. I froze, astounded. Staring back at me was a hideous creature glaring at me in mock horror. Instantly, my hands flew to my face as bloodcurdling screams escaped my lips. "What have I've *done*?" I whaled.

My face had warped into a sick green with mounting wrinkles. My teeth had turned black as ink. My eyes were yellow. The creature in the mirror was as frightening as it was hideous. I collapsed to the ground, rocking back and forth sobbing. "I'll never use my powers again! I'll never wish evil upon anyone ever!" I ranted, through streaming tears. I didn't want anyone to see me like this. I tried covering my face with my hands.

Without warning, I felt a gentle hand on my shoulder. The Cajun had come to my side. Without a word uttered, he gathered me gently into his arms and carried me inside. He ventured down a narrow hall and into a dim bedroom, and gently laid me down on a bed, covered with a red patched quilt. I was in the same room before, dim lighting, a small dresser and a nightstand with a lamp setting on it.

As soon as the Cajun set me free, I shied away, with my back to him. The monstrosity that had consumed me repulsed my entire being. I couldn't stand for anyone to see me like this. I laid there heaving with painful tears while every regret I'd ever felt plowed its way through my mind. I wept not just for the ugliness that I'd become, but also for the loss of my child and for the abomination that resided within me.

All the rage.

I felt I was dying inside.

Then, out of the haze of my nightmare, a voice brought me back. "Look at me!" The Cajun spoke in a tender voice. "Come on *belle fille!*"

While dread twisted my gut, I eased up into a sitting position. I kept my face down and hidden with my hands and hair.

The Cajun's gaze felt like tiny needles stabbing me simultaneously. I despised him for seeing me like this, ugly and an abomination. "Don't call me that! I'm hideous!" Among other emotions, a deep sense of shame robbed me of any dignity.

"Don't hide your face." He tugged at my hands.

"Stop!" I jerked away. "Don't look at me!" I balled up into a fetal position with my back to the Cajun.

No matter how hard I resisted, he was relentless. "Your face has returned to normal. Look for yourself, you are still very beautiful." There was gentleness in his thick voice.

I flipped on my side facing the Cajun. My hand reached for my face. A burst of hope shot through me as I slid off the bed and darted down the hall to the bathroom. My heart pounded against my ears as I flipped the light on and went straight for the mirror.

Slowly, I reached up and lightly touched my cheeks while I stared blankly at the mock image. The girl with the green eyes, though frightened, stared back at me. Nick was right. My face had returned to normal.

I glanced up from the mirror and saw the Cajun leaning in the doorframe. A sudden rush of joy came over me as I rushed into his arms. He held me close to his chest, stroking my hair whispering soothing words in his native tongue. He held me tight for a good while, until I loosened my grip and the tears had dried. The warmth of his smile echoed in his voice. "Now you are better, *yes?*"

"Yes. Much!" I spoke shyly, dropping my gaze and pulling away from the comfort of his arms. His kindness reminded me too much of the old Aidan. The Aidan I once loved. I couldn't get involved with another man. Three wasn't a charm in my book. There would be no love interest here, not today or ever.

Giving him nothing more than a forced smile, I quickly skirted away, heading outside. I left the Cajun standing alone. He didn't like me, and I was comfortable with our toilsome friendship. It kept things simple. Right now, with everything toppling on my shoulders, simple was all I had to give.

GATOR DIVING

*J*effery and Dom had scurried about packing their personal belongings. I didn't have many possessions. I finished in less than ten minutes, throwing a few items in an army green backpack.

When I stepped outside, I noticed the tracking device laying on top of the jeep's hood. I went straight to the car and gathered the tracker in my palm, carefully examining it. The device was the size of a dime with a tiny, blinking red light. I assumed the light was the homing mechanism.

I began thinking that if we sent this thing in the opposite direction, it might buy us some time. I glanced over at Aidan. A spike of hope stirred. Luck might be on our side after all.

His eyes were fixed on me as he stood there, tied to the tree. If he so much as sneezed, the magick rope would tighten its grip like a python squeezing its prey. And for added protection, the knife in his shoulder kept him still. He wasn't wiggling out of that bind any time soon.

I reckoned that was the perks of being a genetically engineered angel. Though, I had no idea how I'd conjured up the rope. It was as amazing as it was frightening. I still preferred a bat. Much simpler and just as effective.

As much as I hated the notion, Aidan would have to remain as my prisoner. If his internal radars pinpointed my location, we all were sitting ducks.

I especially worried for the safety of Dom and Jeffery. If the guys landed in Van's hands, I didn't want to begin to think what he'd do. It seemed nothing had changed. Van was still hell bent on finishing me off. He'd stoop to any measure to draw me out.

That meant he'd use the guys for leverage. If Jeffery and Dom ended up hurt or worse, I wouldn't be able to live with myself. I had to get them out of the line of fire and to a safe place. The problem was, where?

Right now, anyone associated with me was in imminent danger. Even more of a reason why I needed to find a safe place for the guys. I'd figure it all out, but for now, we needed to get moving and find a new hideout and the sooner, the better.

In the break of silence, a twig snapped. In a deadly flash, I drew my knife. It hovered over my head ready to charge. When my eyes landed on the person approaching, I relaxed, sending my magical knife back to its sheath. I exhaled a tight breath. It was only the Cajun.

"Donnez-moi le dispositif!" (Give me the device!) He demanded.

"What are you going to do?" I asked, unsure if I should trust him.

"Ole Saint Nick has some tricks up his sleeve." His dark eyes glistened with mischief.

I snorted a short laugh. Someone really needed to talk to him about referring to himself in third person. "Oh *really*," I said. "This I gotta see."

The Cajun snatched the tracker out of my palm and off he went in three long strides to my one. Sprinting to keep up, I followed closely behind him, heading straight for the river at the backside of the house. A sense of dread came over me. I hoped he knew what he was doing. I might be able to throw a little magick here and there, but that swamp, bayou or hell water, scared the crap out of me.

In one swift motion, the Cajun pulled a knife from his hip, sliding it between his lips and tugging off his jeans, down to the bare. Without missing a beat, he dove into the murky water as if an Olympian swimmer had gone Tarzan. His masterstrokes were precise and fluid.

Jeffery and Dom had gathered beside me, watching in silence at the Cajun's head bobbing up and down, as he glided with ease across the steady stream.

Jeffery wedged his skinny ass between Dom and me to the front. "What the hell is that crazy hunk-of-loveliness doing in that nasty river?" Jeffery craned his neck, eyeballing the fully nude man. The three of us stood frozen, eyes glued to the Cajun. The starkness in our faces revealed our alarm.

I always had a healthy fear of the bayou. I respected its savageness. It was a haven to creatures of the dark. As for the rest of us, if we were smart, we keep our distance.

I had to admit, there was a part of me that felt enamored over the Cajun's dare-deviltry. Though, however brave he might appear, it was a reckless stunt that could get him killed.

I stood holding my breath, eyes glued to his glistening muscles flexing in the water. I watched in awe and horror as the water commenced splashing violently like an eruption from beneath.

All at once, a huge scaly tail emerged, following a white belly, churning in the roily water, thrashing this way and that. We caught a glimpse of the Cajun rolling under the water in a tug of war with the gator. His knife glinted from the sunlight as he clenched it between his teeth. I stifled a gasp, daring not to make a sound. Jeffery was doing enough screeching for all of us.

The gator fought furiously. Yet the Cajun clung to the back of the beast, riding it like a bronco in a rodeo. With each death-dealing spin, he held the creature's snout tightly shut as he and the long-tail reptile pirouetted in a fierce battle.

"Uh-huh, it's not every day you see a naked man battlin' an alligator." Jeffery stretched his neck over Dom's shoulder to catch a look at the Cajun's glimmering backside popping from the water.

"Jeffery, shut up!" I nudged him with my elbow.

Dom flashed him a warning, but remained quiet.

"Oookay!" he threw his hands to his hips. "I'm just sayin'." Jeffery pursed his lips, giving me the evil eye. I snorted a laugh and turned my attention back to the commotion in the water.

We watched helplessly from the bank as the Cajun continued wrestling the mighty creature. With no warning, a dead silence swathed the forest. Even the birds stopped chirping. Not even the soft hum of a Cicada among the trees. The river calmed, and a soft trickle meandered downstream.

All at once, movement stirred. Two perfectly round eyeballs peeked the surface of the murky water. It was the gator drifting aimlessly down the river stream as if he'd had a lazy day sunbathing.

We all three gasped in fear as alarm hit me like a head on collision with a freight train. The Cajun hadn't surfaced. In a fit of fury, I tossed my boots off and started stripping off every stitch of clothing down to my underwear.

The white of Jeffery's eyes nearly went to the back of his head, "What the hell are you doing?" he shrieked, grabbing my arm.

"I don't want my clothing to hold me down. I have to save Nick!"

"Stevie, the alligator!"

"Dom, I've gotta go after him!" The Cajun was an idiot, but he doesn't deserve to die. Yet, I wasn't letting his rash decision slip past me, either. I couldn't promise that he'd remain intact when I got my hands on him.

Just as I started to plunge headfirst into the foul water, the Cajun's head popped up with his knife still gripped between his teeth, swimming toward us.

A rush of relief came over me. I was happy to see him and the thought of jumping in the river didn't seem like an unthinkable task.

When the Cajun pulled himself onto the bank, my mood quickly shifted to a boiling stew. "What the hell were you thinking? You could've gotten yourself killed!" I shoved his chest hard. "We don't have time for such recklessness!"

"Ah, how sweet!" Water dripped down his face as he flashed his white pearly smile. "I had no idea you cared so much, Red."

My face blazed as I fired back. "You arrogant son of a " The Cajun interrupted.

"*Non!*" he wagged his finger, tsking me. "You leave *mon mère* (my mother) out of this." he snarled. "I solved the *problème*. The device is deep in the belly of the alligator. It should keep those *bâtard* busy for hours. Perhaps days."

"You-you wrestled that six-foot-something beast."

"*Oui!* Just call me the gator whisperer." He slapped me on my back as if I were one of the boys. "See… Saint Nick is smart. Yes?" The Cajun tapped his temple with his finger.

We all stood there gaping at him. I thought I was impulsive. The Cajun had me beat.

"We need to leave *now*! Got any ideas?"

"*Oui*, we can go to my place. Tie your boyfriend up in the jeep and you ride with me." As his eyes slowly roamed over my body, my face blistered. I'd forgotten about stripping down to my bra and panties. In a huff, I snatched up my clothes and stalked off with a slew of curse words trailing behind me.

LIES UNVEILED

*S*itting on the back of his damn bike and clinching my arms around his waist had not been my idea. In fact, I despised it. The Cajun reeked of swamp water. It had been bad enough for me to cling to his half-naked body. Granted, with the dirty water slapping my face, I was at the end of my patience. I preferred eating bugs over coughing and gagging on the stale water that tasted like rotten fish.

Watching the Cajun snorkel at my uncomfortable plight only escalated my pissy mood. The man detested me. His bold grin across his face proved my suspicions.

Dom drove the Jeep and Jeffery sat in the passenger seat, doing his usual directing. I had battened down Aidan in the back with the magickal rope. He was nicely snug, and knew better than to attempt breaking free. My knives hovered evenly with Aidan's neck.

Despite everything, my heart tugged at my decision. I tossed a glimpsed over my shoulder at my prisoner. I no longer knew this man. Where did that Aidan go? The man who risked his own life for mine.

That Aidan was gone, and in his place, a soulless monster resided. I mustn't forget that the present Aidan had proven where his loyalties lie. The Illuminist had their poisonous claws in him. I realized that Aidan inherited his family's traits.

Setting aside my guilt, I had to keep my family safe. Perhaps giving myself up would get the Family off everyone else's tail? The guys would be fine with the Cajun. They were no threat to the Family, but staying with me, I feared would put a target on their backs.

I desperately wished Val were here. He'd know what to do. I was more helpless than a toddler. Just because I had the ability of a powerful angel didn't mean anything. The few tricks I had up my sleeve weren't enough. I didn't have the supernatural smarts to get us through this. I was no match for the Family. None of us were.

Strange now that I thought about it. I'd give away every bit of my magickal birth to be an ordinary girl again. Looking back, struggling for food and a roof over my head and even having my crazy mom by my side, sounded like a little piece of heaven compared to now.

I wished I could go back to blissful ignorance, thinking I was human, benighted to the harsh world's reality.

In my world, fairytales weren't for the faint hearted. It was far too sinister and far too deadly. I shuddered. Gosh, how I wanted my dad right now. Nevertheless, I knew that wasn't going to happen, and yearning for the impossible meant disappointment and a huge distraction. It was time that I put my big-girl panties on and got with the program. Impulsive Stevie had to die, and strategic, warrior Stevie had to step up to the plate and take charge.

I turned back facing the Cajun's head. Thankfully, from the wind drying him off, he wasn't slinging mud in my face any longer.

My mind began to trail back to Nick's grandmother, Mable. She hit the nail on the head and was right about Val. He never was my true boyfriend. I thought he was the one. Then he left me here, earthbound, and defenseless.

Val really thought the Cajun could protect me. I didn't see how. Yet what other choice did I have right now? I had to give him credit. Regardless of how much he despised me, he'd stuck to his word helping us. No wonder Val depended on him.

Loneliness swallowed my sigh. I was alone with no back up from any one of my kind. Even after Val and I had broken up, I somehow felt he'd find his way back to me. We'd work through the issues of the Zophasemin's prejudice. I now knew how wrong I was. Chances of that happening were zero. Val had left this realm, abandoning his human body and returning to his natural form, a spiritual creature.

Strange how I was the same race as Val and his mighty warriors. Though, I couldn't materialize into a spirit form like the rest of the Zophasemin nation. Unlike my fellow brothers, Val explained that I was earthbound. I'd already felt like an outsider looking through a plate glass. His words confirmed my beliefs. But where did I go? Whom could I turn to for help? I didn't belong to the human race no more than I belonged to the Zophasemin.

Artificial was the term Val used. I supposed the Zop leader viewed me as unnatural and impure as his own kind did. How could a nation accept diversity when their own leader could not? If Val had stood up for me, perhaps his race would've accepted me.

How ironic. I bled just like any extant creature, human or not. I was as real and genuine as the best. I resented the term, synthetic.

I finally came to a hard realization that Val's absence was for the best. If I hadn't pushed myself through his men to take one last look at him before he left, he would've vanished without so much as a good-bye. He knew he wasn't coming back and that I'd never see him again. Whatever we had was final. I wasn't his first priority and never was. If I was going to keep my family safe and survive this uprising, I had to keep my head on straight. Forget these men. They had brought nothing but misery to me and if I didn't get a grip, they would be the death of me and possibly the death of Dom and Jeffery. That, I couldn't fathom.

It seemed every road we'd traveled was paved with dirt. Deep craters marked the way with erosion by previous high waters. Good Ole Saint Nick hit every pothole in sight too. Thank God for my death grip around the Cajun's waist. He seemed not to mind. An interesting observation, I thought. I wondered how he was breathing with my hands tightly latched around his lungs. He didn't complain, and I didn't plan on letting go either. I wasn't going to die today. I'd save my death for a better cause.

I tossed another glance over my shoulder. Dom was tailgating us. The area here seemed to host some sketchy characters. I reckoned that Dom didn't want to get lost in this neck of woods and especially with Aidan.

The closeness the boys once had with their employer had dissipated. It was understandable considering the change in Aidan's behavior. The only one who could stand to be around him was Sally. I hope she didn't come looking for him. The last thing I needed was another captive.

I planned to kiss the ground once we reached our destination. This ride was torture and with *rápida Diablo* (speedy devil) flying down the byway, hitting every freaking hole, I expected my butt to be bruised tomorrow. To top it off, my lungs would be hacking up dirt for the next month. I hated the woods and the rough outdoors. I hated the swamp, the bugs, snakes, and gators. I wasn't too fond of the Cajun grinning every time he flew over a bump either.

After what seemed like an eternity, we finally pulled up to a clearing surrounded by Cypress trees down in the basin. I could see that the land was not prime soil and living down here had its hardships.

A small house stood nestled in the middle of the clearing. The cabin was built from pine with white stucco pressed between each log and stood high on pier and beam. Steep steps led up to the large wrap around porch. There was no grass, only dirt in the yard. I reckoned there was no point in planting greenery when the floods killed everything in its path.

I noticed at the side of the house a boat flipped over, tied to a post with an anchor dropped to the ground. My guess, it was to keep the boat in one place when the floods rushed through. Farther down, toward the back of the house, a ramp led up to the house, I assumed it was for his bike.

It was apparent the work of love that went into building the home. The cabin was solid, most likely sturdy enough to withstand the frequent storms in this God forsaken country.

When we came to a halt, I climbed off the bike and made a beeline for the sanctuary of the front porch. I climbed the steps and went straight to the rockers. I flopped down in one, and immediately a sigh of relief escaped my lips as comfort enshrouded my badly beaten backside. I smiled as my hands rubbed against the smooth arms of the chair. The wood felt cool, and the chair rocked with perfect precision, an ingenious design. I leaned back, taking in the wonderful solace of the chair and smiled to myself.

Suddenly, I heard footfalls approaching. Startled, I whipped my eyes open and my gaze landed on the Cajun. He was as bad as a little puppy, following me wherever I went. I exhaled. He was very easy on the eyes, just a little rough around the edges, which worked for him. Too bad, he didn't have a personality. I scoffed as I watched him climb the stairs, one stomp at a time.

"Must your face sour whenever you look at me? Most ladies enjoy my company," Nick bragged tossing his crooked smile at me.

"Those women are paid by the hour," I mused. I couldn't resist the jab.

"If you keep that nasty attitude no one will ever care about you," he sneered.

"Don't worry, I'm as cuddly as a porcupine!" I smiled back. Deep down, I feared he might be right.

"You are one bitter woman. I suppose if you got with him," The Cajun nodded at Aidan. "I'd be bitter too. The problem with you, is you have never had a real man. One who is willing to stick up for you and stay by your side when times get rocky. Your choice of men is no good."

"Val would be here if he could!" The Cajun had a point, but my pride got the best of me. I didn't want to admit he was right.

"*Moi*! However, he was not a man. He was a celestial being, an angel. Even if he wanted to stay, it would have never worked between the two of you. His kind does not permit such …."

I halted that damn coonass right then and there. "Stop it! What do you know about me? You've known me for about one hot minute. Until you do, don't be so quick to judge me." By then, I was on my feet and in his face. Or somewhat. He was an astounding six foot five and I barely reached five-five.

"*Pas de problème*! (No problem) I was only trying to be nice." The Cajun threw up his palms in surrender. "I really do not care about your lovers. You probably lie still like a stump." His scornful eyes locked with mine.

"Let's get something straight, Saint Nick. As soon as I can find us a place to go, your sorry ass is relieved of duty," I hissed in his face.

"Red, I'm going to give you the same advice you have been so kind to have given *moi. Take a bath.* You stink. There's a towel and soap in the shower. It's on the back porch. Enjoy!" He smiled, but it didn't touch his deep brown eyes. I stared at him for a moment as faint laughter drifted from Aidan who remained tied to the Jeep. With a deep throaty growl, I twirled in my shoes and headed for the back porch. Nothing like a cold shower to wash off the dirt and angry steam. I had a strong hunch that this wasn't going to end well. Between the Cajun and Aidan, my nerves were grating fast. *What was Val thinking?*

~

I sent Jeffery off to find my bag of clothes. Luckily, he found them in the nick of time, as I'd finished showering. "Thanks, Jeff!" I reached up over the wooden enclosure, snatching up my backpack and smiled.

"Hurry up! I want to shower too. I hope you didn't take all the hot water," Jeffery mumbled, stomping off and disappearing around the corner of the porch. I shook my head, laughing.

Though there wasn't a hot and cold valve, the clean water was amazing. The shower was enclosed with crafted wood, attached to the side of the house with plumbing connected to the outdoor pipe and a wide showerhead hanging above. It was like a regular indoor shower only it was on his back porch. "Rats!" I fumbled through my bag. Just my luck, no bra. Great! No bra around a bunch of men and only a thin tee shirt to wear. Crap! No Wal-Mart to remedy that problem either. I had my dirty bra that reeked of swamp and sweat. Geez, I missed the comforts of the modern world's conveniences. Nothing I could do about it right now. I did what any woman would do, I sucked it up and decided to keep my arms folded.

In a rush, I slipped on my cut off shorts and doubled up on the thin tank tops. I figured if I wore two tops, no one would notice. I ran a hand through my hair and felt the matted tangles. My hair was a mess. I didn't care. It was the least of my worries. I grabbed my cowboy boots and slipped them on. My old western boots couldn't have been a better fit. They pretty much reached my knees. Out here in the bayou, I doubted the old leather would protect me from a gator, but it might stave off a snakebite.

Once I stepped into the house, I caught sight of a cozy fire radiating the fireplace. The sound of the kindling crackling brought back memories of a time I didn't care to revisit. I quickly started to exit the house but stalled. I'd unknowingly walked upon a conversation that appeared heated. I eavesdropped listening to the Cajun and Aidan. I knew I shouldn't be snooping. The last time I'd listened in on a private discussion, it didn't turn out well for me. Even still, I couldn't peel myself away. A deadly habit, I reckoned I had.

"You should be ashamed of yourself, rich boy." The disdain in the Cajun's tone was blistering.

"You'd be wise to mind your own business," Aidan's aversion matched the Cajun's.

"I am a good judge of character. You, ami (friend), are rotten from the inside out. Did you take this young girl's virginity?"

Aidan answered with silence.

I heard the ire in the Cajun's words. "Of course, I should've known. You had to go and ruin this innocent girl. I have a mind to horse whip you."

"What do you know about family and duty?" Aidan snarled. "Bet you've never had to do a thing in your whole pathetic life except run your mouth and snort a keg of beer down." The narcissism in Aidan's voice was startling.

"You think you know me well," the Cajun laughed darkly.

"Don't worry about the girl. She received an ample settlement for her services."

"One thing you forget rich boy."

"And?" Aidan growled.

"All the money in the world will never bring her child back."

"She will move on." Aidan's voice resonated with a coldness that turned my blood cold. I bit my lip, reeling in my own anger.

"Are you that conceited?" the Cajun snarled. "It is your family's selfish greed that has brought mayhem to this girl. She's a fugitive because of you!"

Aidan scoffed, "Must we be gloomy?"

The Cajun spoke a calm cold voice. "I'd much rather take a Benelli M4 semi-automatic rifle to you. Maybe before the uprising is over, I will have that opportunity."

"Get over yourself," Aidan dismissed him. "I believe my family has improved her life," Aidan contended proudly. "She can grow old and weary, never having to lift a finger ever again with her wealth."

"Setting aside the little fact that money is useless right now. You think money can erase the bad deeds you and your family have committed. You're *wrong! She's only twenty-one. She has yet to live her life, and you once again have taken that from her. No wonder she is bitter. If I were her, I'd be throwing knives at every man's balls that came in close contact of me. You are a hypocrite, and you call me trash? In my book, I'd much rather be my kind of trash than yours. It is not the material things that makes men. It is the good deeds men do that makes a man. You hide behind your tainted magick."* I heard feet stomping and stopping short. I peeked around the corner. The Cajun had gotten in Aidan's face. *"I say come out like a man with your fist up. Let's see how long you last then, yes?"* The challenge in the Cajun's voice was grave.

I doubted Nick's blows would be as fast as Aidan's. I knew far too well how deadly Aidan could be if pushed. I had to admit, the Cajun defending my honor took me by surprise. Aidan's cavalier attitude was expected.

I needed to break this scuffle up before the Cajun got himself skinned alive. I stepped out onto the front porch. My eyes landed on the Cajun. He stood up from Aidan who was sitting in one of the rockers. My eyes drifted to Jeffery standing on the bottom steps tapping his foot nervously. Dom stood by the Jeep, pulling out his and Jeffery's bags.

All eyes fell on me. Talk about uncomfortable! The tension in the air was heavy. I blew out an awkward breath. Instead of reacting, I pretended I didn't notice and directed my attention to Nick. "Hey, what kind of vittles you got around here? I can get dinner started."

The Cajun stood up as his eyes lingered a little too long over my tank top while Aidan sat quite full of piss. Jeffery kept wiggling as though he might pee in his pants. The smartest one of all, Dom, had kept his distance from the volatile situation.

The Cajun answered, "You look good enough to eat." He flashed his crooked smile, perfect white teeth, openly flirting with me.

"Do you mind if I go through your kitchen and see what you got to eat?" A terse smile toiled at the corner of my lips. I ignored the Cajun's compliment. He was only taunting the prisoner. I had no plans to join his little spar. I caught a glance at Aidan. Noting his angry blues, that Cajun better watch his step. An immortal druid brawling with a human, the odds were stacked against the Cajun and

I wasn't too keen on the idea of having to step between those two big jugheads.

The Cajun caught my attention, disrupting my train of thoughts. "Don't worry about cooking. We're having guest coming later. Barbeque and beer. We're having a social gathering. I know some bedfellows who can help. Go rest. I'll watch the prisoner for you." The Cajun flashed a far too confident grin.

"Nick, I'm not sure that's a good idea." My lips twisted sourly.

"Damn woman! You take the joy out of a little fun for Saint Nick."

There he went speaking in third person again.

"Sorry to be a killjoy." I smiled, even though I didn't feel it in my eyes. "Okay, a nap sounds great, but I have to do something first."

I turned to go back inside, and a few minutes later, I returned with a glass of cold water. I had no idea the last time Aidan had anything to drink and I couldn't rest until I knew he'd at least had some water. I recalled how courteous he was to me when I went to stay at his castle. I felt I owed him that much.

Standing at the last rocker, I leaned down, low, in order for our conversation to be more private. "I thought you might be thirsty." I held the drink to his lips. He sipped slowly. I hoped we could have an amiable discussion, "Aidan," I started. "I hate holding you hostage. But you leave me no other choice. I can't trust you." If I appealed to his selfishness, he might ease up. I furthered with my discussion, "If we could free our bond, I'd let you go unharmed."

I held the glass to his lips again, but he pushed his lips away and glared up at me through murderous eyes. "Sweetheart, I'm really getting tired of repeating myself." His Adam's apple bobbed. "I'm afraid you're stuck with me."

"Why do we have to continue this union when we both want separation?"

"Sorry, toots! Death is the only option we have to break the bond."

Did I hear him correctly? I fell into the rocker beside Aidan. My body went numb. "We're bound to each other forever?" I looked at him with shock, remembering his spurn.

"I suppose our bond takes a whole new meaning to ball-and-chain." His implacable expression was unnerving.

"Stop with the jokes. There has to be some way to break the curse."

"Not unless you wish to die." A satanic smile pressed against his lips. "You might as well give it up. Embrace our dark bond and accept your destiny."

"Destiny?" my brows shot up. "What destiny are you referring to?" his cocky attitude was starting to grate on me.

"Did I not explain to you or are you just too stupid to catch on?"

Aidan was pushing my buttons. His taunting was futile. I wasn't going to take his bait. "Gee, after all that angel dust you so kindly bestowed upon me, I can't say for sure. But why don't you humor me and tell me anyway. I'll be sure and take notes this time."

Aidan laughed. Disappointingly, I found his laugh flat, not the usual infectious laugh that I once adored.

"I can't do or undo the impossible. But I'm a fair man." An expression of satisfaction showed in his eyes. "Leave with me now and all will be forgotten. Your friends will be pardoned of their treason. Save your friends and save yourself. We both know you belong with the Family, *our* family. Live like the princess you are by my side, ruling the world."

I stared into Aidan's bloodshot eyes. The sparkle had vanished. Even his skin appeared gray and pallid. "Look, I'm not leaving with you." I shook my head. "I don't want any part of the Family." I looked off into the stand of trees. "Do you want anything to eat? You're looking ill."

"Of course, I look like shit! This rope is siphoning the life out of me." Suddenly an attack of coughing came over him, wheezing, straining for breath as his face blistered. He finally managed to gain his composure enough to choke out. "I need a cigarette."

Shock stole my breath. "Since when do you smoke?"

"Never mind about what I do," he choked out. "Since you plan on keeping me tied up, go ask the basin trash for a smoke."

"You can ask him yourself. I'll get you some food."

"Fuck food. I want a cigarette!" he practically screeched.

"Whatever!" I jumped to my feet. "Starve for all I care, but I won't get you a cigarette." I turned to leave but stopped.

"Why do you torment yourself? You have the power to stop all this running and hiding."

I slowly turned to face him. "What do you mean?"

"Surrender and your friends will go unscathed. They can go free," he flashed a weak smile. "I miss us. I still love you?"

I stared at him for a moment. Repulsion churned my stomach, taking everything I had not to vomit, "I refuse to do that to Sally."

"She's simply a distraction," Aidan refuted. His smooth talk paled in comparison to the hold he once held on my heart.

"Sally thinks the two of you are a couple. You are sleeping with her."

"A man does have needs."

"Does Sally know that she's scratching your need?" I glowered at his opened decadence.

"Don't be such a rigid bitch! You once liked my affections lying in bed all day between the sheets?"

"Your memory must really be slipping from your old age. That's not how I remember it."

"Oh yes, we mostly fought."

"You can sleep with the Dalai Lama for all I care. I want my life back. Just break the curse."

"You think our bond is a curse?"

"Look! Curse or not, does it matter? You and I have changed. Or maybe I'm the one who has." Cutting ties was the only thing that made sense. "We've grown apart," I pointed out. By the disdain tainting his face, I knew he loathed my rejection even though he no more desired me than I did him.

"You forget too easily," he accused.

"I only wish that were true."

"Don't you remember our conversation about our infusion at your house?" His smile became voracious, "The spell keeps other men away. It works much like a bug repellent."

"I repel men?" I thought he was just trying to hurt me. I didn't realize he meant it literally.

Aidan smirked. "Why do you think Val never went through with sealing the deal?"

"Come again?" All at once, it was like the bell of clarity sounding off in my head. All the times that Val held back, I blamed him for not taking it to the next level.

"That's even more reason I want this curse broken," I snapped. "You better figure out a way to break this curse or else I swear, I'll take your life myself." In the heat of the moment, I threw the rest of the iced water in his face. "Get your own damn water!" I twirled on my heels and stalked off into the house. I glimpsed up, and there stood Nick leaning against the door jam. I expected him to be laughing. To my surprise, sadness glimmered behind his eyes. As we stood briefly holding each other's gaze, neither one of us uttered a word.

At this point, I didn't have the strength to rehash this thing between Aidan and me. It was too complicated and disturbing. Rather, I brushed past him and went straight to the room with the biggest bed. Guessing from the Cajun's size, I assumed that would be his room.

~

After a couple of hours of sleep, my eyes popped open. My head swirled with murk, and my body ached like an old woman with rheumatoid arthritis. I blamed it on my angel magick. It had taken a toll on me. My strength felt depleted.

When my eyes drifted down to my feet, I gasped. The last time a person sat on the edge of my bed, it turned out to be a ghost, Ms. Noel. Then my eyes landed on the tear streaked face and I eased a breath.

Jeffery sat with his shoulders slumped, sobbing. I right away sat up with alarm. "Jeff, what's wrong?"

"Oh, I don't mean to wake you," he sniffled.

"No. You're fine. What's wrong?"

"What isn't wrong? We've lost our home. We all may die. That vicious Family is coming after all of us. Dom isn't well. He has heart problems, and I'm afraid he's going to drop dead. Boo, I can't lose Dom." Jeffery's tears poured. My heart dropped, and I took Jeff into my arms and embraced his quivering body. After a minute, he pulled himself together and straightened up, wiping his tear stained face.

"I know this isn't easy. I've been racking my brain trying to think of a perfect hideout for you and Dom until this uprising is over." I chewed on my bottom lip, thinking. "I'll talk to Nick and see if he has any ideas. Right now, we have no defense. We haven't a clue to what's going on out there. We have no outside sources to update us on the current situation. Hell, we don't even have our cell phones anymore. I don't know if we can even drive through town without getting killed."

"It's the not knowing that is worrying Dom and me." Jeffery choked through tears.

"I'm terribly sorry for bringing you and Dom in the middle of this mishap. I've put you in danger."

"Stop that! Don't blame yourself." Jeffery wiped his face with the back of his hand. This ain't your fault, boo." Jeffery squeezed my hand, "Those mofos had this foolery planned eons ago. Gurrrl, don't you blame yourself for one minute. Dom and I will stand beside you no matter what. We love you like a daughter, and I knows that love is returned," then he paused, shaking his head. "It's different with Aidan. Don't get me wrong, Dom and I love Aidan. But we knows to keep our distance and our opinions to ourselves. And this new Aidan, actin' like a fool, I see now that we never knew him at all. We hate every nasty thing he's done to you. For that, we is mad as hell at him."

"Don't go wagging your finger at him. He's dangerous and unpredictable. He's not the same, Jeffery." I tightened my lips, feeling an urge of ire. "Why is that? I don't get it."

"Gurrrlfriend, Dom and I have been wonderin' the same thang," Jeffery huffed out a long breath. "It's like some stranger has stepped into Aidan's skin. I don't recognize this man."

"I know what you mean. If Sam was alive and knowing Sam's cloning abilities, I'd be asking questions. But Sam's dead. I witnessed his death with my own eyes. That theory of cloning Aidan died with Sam." I raked my fingers through my hair.

"Dom and I've been talkin'." Jeffery jumped up and shut the door and quickly returned, sitting back down on the edge of the bed with me. "If we didn't know any better, Aidan's actin' a lot like his uncle, Van."

"Van? No way!" My breath stalled.

"I knows how ugly his uncle can get. Dom knows it too."

I bit my bottom lip. "There's no way Van could be masquerading as Aidan. I overheard the old man say to the brotherhood that he's mortal and doesn't have any special abilities. Van is not Aidan's actual uncle. They're not blood relative nor does Van have druid magick."

"Dom and I figured that out real quick. Van always seemed different. You know, cut from a different cloth."

"I think you're right, but I think Van has a hold over Aidan. Maybe that's why Aidan's acting so strange."

"Maybe? Van is sneaky as a snake. I wouldn't put anything past him."

"We're wasting time speculating. I need to find a safe place for you and Dom. The sooner the better too!"

"You is comin' with us, right? It ain't your fight either." Jeffery knew how to make a good argument.

My brows wrinkled, and my heart tugged. "Jeff… it is my fight. I'm fighting for my freedom, for *our* freedom. I don't belong to myself."

"You talk like you is their property!"

"Think about it, Jeff," I paused. "The Family created me. I don't even have a biological mother. I'm not human!" I sucked in a deep breath. I was stuck between a rock and a hard spot. No one could save me. Not even God, if there was such a person.

"Now you're actin' cray-cray! You is more human than most!"

I smiled, but only to ease my friend. "You're sweet! I might look human, but technically, I'm an experiment, a genetically engineered creature to fit whatever mold they intended for me. I have no rights. The Illuminist has ownership of me."

"What?" Jeffery shrieked.

"I haven't told anyone about this, but the Illuminist tagged Mom and me."

"What you mean tagged?" Jeffery's eyes bugged.

"It's alien technology known as implants. I can't be certain, but I think during the lab trials, the scientist inserted a tiny alien micro-magnetic device in my mom and me. The Family has been keeping tabs on us all my life. I fear the microchip is still active. If I'm right, no matter where I go the Family can find me."

"Oh lord, have mercy! *Jesus* take me home! We gotta get that thang out of you."

"You can't without killing me."

"Sweet Mother of God! We need to bring in the cavalry." Sweat dotted Jeffery's forehead as he patted his forehead with the end of the blanket.

"If the device is still working, then it's pointless for me to hide. I'm like a beacon in the middle of a shit-storm. Even if Aidan and I break our bond, his family might still be able to detect my location." Chills bristled my neck. "Aidan once told me that the tags have dissolved. I have a gut feeling he lied and if so, that means anyone hanging around me is at risk."

"Gurrrl, there's got to be another way."

"I don't see how," I shrugged. I jumped up and stood in front of the window. The worried expression in Jeffery's face was too much for me to bear.

"Damn, Val! He ought to be 'ere for you." Jeffery's anger and frustration came through loud and clear.

I looked over my shoulder at Jeffery. "No need to blame Val," I said. "It's not his fault. His priority is to the Zophasemin nation."

"Isn't that your race too?"

"It's different for me. I was man-made. The others came from divine creation. Anyway, that doesn't matter now," I shrugged. "The Zops consider me impure. That's not ever going to change."

"Impure, my sweet ass!"

"It's complicated." Revisiting the memories were so acute, it was like physical pain.

"Boo, Dom and I are not abandoning you."

"I know you want to stay with me to protect me, but let's be honest. We're not going up against just ordinary people. We might be facing a nation of supernatural demons. So, you guys staying with me would be suicide and I can't let that happen. That's non-negotiable." I'd put my foot down to that.

"Gurrrl, I ain't arguing with you. We're not leaving you!" Jeffery pursed his lips and folded his arms. He was stubborn as a jackass and cuddly as a puppy. I loved my Jeffery. "Let's change the subject!"

Jeffery's eyes lit up. Oh lord! "Okay." With Jeffery, one never knew what was going to come out of his mouth. "Don't be hatin' me for saying this, but I like Nick. He may be human and rough around those delicious edges, but I think that's what you need. If there's anything that I know best … is when a man is juicy for another. And boo, that man is thick pulp-juicy for you."

I burst into laughter, and it felt good too. A nice change. "Oh yeah, the Cajun's juicy alright. He's so juicy, he'd like to feed me to the gators."

"Now I didn't say you didn't rub him the wrong way. I don't think he's accustomed to women like you. Have you got a real good look at that man? Uh huh, he is one tall dark drink."

"Jeff!" I held my palm up. "Please!" I rolled my eyes.

"Don't be ridiculous. That man is fine! With that deep chocolate hair and his yummy brown eyes gleaming at you and have you seen the six pack he's packin'?" Jeffery nearly started drooling.

I tried stifling a laugh, but I lost the battle shamefully. "Jeffery don't be getting bugged-eyed over the candy Cajun. I don't want to whoop his ass on your behalf."

"Don't worry gurrrl. I've been a butler for more than half my life. I knows how to look without really lookin'."

"Jeffery, that's too much information!" I giggled as I swatted my friend's arm. Then the mood shifted like the wind on a stormy Sunday.

"Jeff, with the way the world is going right now, the last thing I need is a boyfriend." I exhaled a long breath. "I'm still trying to get over my feelings for Aidan." I shrugged, feeling so lost in this mad world.

"You ain't meaning that Aidan out there tied up?"

I gave a curt laugh as I joined him back on the end of the bed. "Hell, no!" I paused. "No, it's the old Aidan I miss. There's a part of me that hopes and prays that maybe this is all a bad dream or maybe the man I keep staring at comes out of a trance and *my* Aidan returns."

"I thought you and Val had something special."

"Val couldn't offer me anything long term. Our relationship was doomed. His first alliance was the Zops and since I'm an outcast, his race would never accept me. For the sake of his nation, Val had to let me go."

"He should've stood up for you."

My stomach twisted into a knot.

"We can debate on this forever, but the bottom line is that Val picked his race. It's over," I shrugged.

"It's gonna get better and you is gonna find someone. You see there's a silver lining waitin' for you." Jeffery patted me on my shoulder.

I smiled back. "Listen, I'll talk to Nick tonight. I'm sure we can think of some place for you and Dom to go." I reached over and hugged my dear friend.

Jeffery went back out to find Dom. I stayed back for a minute to gather my thoughts. I had so much weighing on my shoulders and there was no room for mistakes or acting impulsively. Not my best attribute.

Jeffery was a mixture of things to me, a boy-girlfriend, sometimes a mother and a father as well. Dom was straight up a father figure. And I loved them both with every last breath I had. All the more reason why I had to separate myself from them.

Before I could make any decisions, I needed to find out what was happening outside our hideaway. It didn't take a genius to figure out that the uprising was going to get worse before there was light. My bones sensed it.

THE LAND OF YONDER

*S*tanding at the sink in Nick's bathroom, I turned on the cool water. Thanks to his generator, we had clear running water. I splashed my face a good three times, letting the water sooth my heated skin. I didn't bother toweling. I let the water drip from my face as I paused in the mirror. I stared back at a face filled with despair and something I recognized from my past, emptiness. My throat ached with defeat. After everything I'd gone through, I stood in silence staring at a hollow face. I was lost.

What if I screw this up too? What if I let my temper get the best of me, and I acted before thinking? How many times did I have to act hastily to learn my lesson before another person died?

If I hadn't acted so foolishly and arrogantly, Dawn might still be alive today. I was faster than Mustafa. I could've outrun him. I could be holding Dawn in my arms right now, singing to her, rocking her, and reminding her everyday how much I loved her.

Suddenly, a wave of pain ripped through me and I covered my face, sobbing to the floor. I drew my knees up to my chest in a fetal position and wailed in silence.

I wasn't feeling sorry for myself. No, I didn't deserve that kind of self-indulgence. Terrible mothers didn't get to pity themselves. My daughter deserved the right to have a loving mother, one that coddles her and keeps her safe. But she didn't get that chance, and it was all because of me.

My fault.

I didn't save her. As if it was yesterday, I was standing only a few feet from her side, staring into her sweet pleading face. Dawn's angelic face would haunt me for the rest of my life. I didn't save her, and I deserved eternal punishment. I should just turn myself in to the Illuminati. Let Van do to me whatever he wished. Dom and Jeffery would be better off without me. Hell, even Nick would be better off. I brought nothing but trouble and pain to anyone who came around me.

I could end the pain right now by taking my life. No longer would I have to look in the mirror and see the face of failure. Even still, I didn't deserve taking my life. Killing myself was the easy way out. No. I deserved to suffer. I owed Dawn that much.

I didn't know how long I'd lain on the floor, but I knew if I didn't get up and make an appearance that someone would be looking for me. I didn't want anyone to catch me like this, in my moment of weakness.

I peeled myself off the floor and splashed some more water over my face, washing away any signs of tears. Even though my eyes were a little red and puffy, I hoped no one noticed.

∾

I stepped into the small kitchen. I glanced at both guys and thought to myself that some things never changed.

Dom was working kneading bread and Jeffery sat at the small breakfast table reading an old newspaper.

"Hey, guys!" I said as I held a light note to my voice. "Dom, can I do anything to help?" I clapped my hands together, hiding my edginess.

Both Dom and Jeffery jerked their heads up in my direction.

"I hope you had a good rest, yes?" Dom flashed a bright smile.

Jeffery's nose wrinkled as he eyeballed me. "Dom, she ain't been restin'. See those big puffy circles under her eyes?"

Oh, snap! I didn't want anyone to notice my eyes. I could strangle Jeffery. I glowered at him. "Last time I saw you, you weren't resting very much either."

Jeffery wiggled in his chair and quickly moved on to the next subject. "I'd sure been drooling over that outdoor shower. A cool shower sure would be a nice break from this unusual heat." He fanned himself with a page from of the paper. "But I don't want anyone peekin' at my lovely body. You know how shy I is." Jeffery pursed his lips, fanning the paper a little faster.

I joined him at the table. "You could wait until everyone goes to bed." An impish grin tainted the corners of my mouth. "Of course, I reckon that's when the snakes come out."

"Gurrrlfriend, watch your mouth!" Jeffery's face drew into a frown, not missing a beat, fanning himself at near warp speed. "I knows the harshness of this yonder land. That's why I stays in the city. Now city folk, I can deal." Jeffery bobbed his head.

I smiled to myself as my attention fell on the stack of potatoes in a large basket. "Dom, I'll peel the potatoes." I rose from the table grabbing up the basket and slammed it down on the table with a jolt. I tossed Jeffery an evil eye like a pissed off sibling. Jeffery jolted, glaring at me from the rim of the newspaper. I spoke up, irately. "It wouldn't hurt for you to pitch in. I peel half and you peel the other half."

Dom turned to face me with two peelers in his hand. I took them both and then tossed the other one to my friend whose head went back to viewing the newspaper.

When the peeler hit Jeffery's chest, he yapped like a pig caught by his hindquarters. "AAaiiee!" He grabbed the peeler, cutting his eyes at me. "Gurrrlfriend, you have lost your damn mind!" Jeffery stuck his lips out, eyeing me like he wanted to throttle me.

"We all need to pull our weight around here. Those days of you sitting on your lovely caboose are over, pal." I slapped my hand on his shoulder. "We all pitch in. *Comprende*?" I arched a brow.

"Fine!" Jeffery grumbled a slew of colorful words under his breath.

Dom and I shared a laughable glance. It seemed that Jeffery might have some struggles with the new arrangements. He was going to have to toughen up a bit, get some calluses on those soft caramel colored hands of his.

I didn't mind reminding Jeff either. A little ribbing might be fun and could lighten up the mood around here. We all could use a good laugh.

On a more serious note, we needed to have a meeting of the minds and figure out an ironclad plan. What should we do with Aidan?

Where to hide the guys? Should we join a militia? Could human rebels and manmade weaponry work? It was no telling what the Family had conjured up. If they had the technology to create, Sam, half-fey and creatures like me, genetically altered angels, it was anyone's guess what other monsters they might have created next.

I reckoned the first thing we needed to do was find out the advantage our enemies had and more importantly their weaknesses. Spying was in order and time was of the essence.

There was a moment of silence as I stared out the window, slicing the peelings with more force than necessary. The sun was sinking behind the trees. Sunlight glinted off the river. Everything seemed peaceful. The river stream flowed with ease, the birds chirped gaily, the sun set. Nothing appeared affected by the collapse of this system. Regardless of how bad things seemed, the order of nature didn't change. We could learn a thing or two from nature.

I hated breaking up this pleasant moment, the three of us like it used to be, sitting around our kitchen table at the house. I inhaled a wry breath. I might not get another opportunity to speak with Dom. Regretfully, I broke the silence. "Dom, what do you think of all this craziness? Should we be afraid? We don't even know really what's going on out there." I picked up a new potato and began peeling it.

Dom inhaled a long breath, tossing a small towel over his shoulder. He continued chopping up potatoes, though, I could tell his worry weighed heavily on his mind. "I think Monsieur Nick is a better person to answer that question. After all, he served two tours in Iraq. He's seen combat at its worst. What do I know about war? I'm merely a cook." He tossed a smile over his shoulder.

My face soured as I threw down the peeler and potato. "I'm afraid none of us are really prepared. This isn't a war of guns and bombs, man against man. We're dealing with a fight against supernatural forces. We can't even begin to speculate what's to come." I raked my fingers through my hair, roughly.

"We can't get too worked up over things we are unclear about. We will investigate what we are dealing with and then we will decide from there." Dom placed the ball of dough in a bowl and covered it. He wiped his hands on a towel and joined Jeffery and me at the table. He rested his elbows on the table and gave way to a long sigh. I knew what that meant.

"Stevie, you must prepare yourself for the unexpected. The Illuminati is looking for you. You are a threat to them. I think if we go deeper into hiding, perhaps somewhere in the bayou, you will be much safer," Dom paused. "Don't think you can fight them. You might have special powers, but they are many and you haven't a chance in hell against them. It would be like suicide. Staying out of sight is your best ammunition."

I'd never seen Dom's brown eyes so solemn. It was startling. "I don't know if Jeffery has had a chance to mention this to you, but I think it's best if you guys and I part ways." Dom started to speak up, shaking his head, but I held up my palm halting his protest. "Listen to me! Anyone near me is at risk. Look at that man out there that once was your friend." I nodded over my shoulder. "He's unrecognizable. Who knows what the Family has done to him! They have him under some sort of mind control. Who's to say they can't do the same to me." I swallowed the knot in my throat. "It's not safe being here with me."

Jeffery intervened. "As much as I hate sayin' it, she's right."

Dom shared a glance at his lifelong partner. I saw the love in his eyes as he and Jeffery paused silently for a moment. Then Dom slid his gentle eyes back to me. "I can't bare the idea of something happening to you. You are our child." Dom's voice nearly cracked.

I reached over and gathered him in the folds of my arms, clinging to him for several minutes before I pulled away. "I get you're scared. I'm scared too, but I have a better chance of staying alive than you out there on my own. I may not be able to fight off an army of freaks, but I can hold my own in most cases. I want you guys safe away from me until this uprising is under control or we find a place that we all can be together and remain safe."

Jeffery reached over and placed his hand on his partners shoulder. "I didn't want to leave Stevie at first either. I don't like it any more than you do, but I think our girl is right. We don't stand a chance if we stay. What are you gonna do to protect yourself? Beat some mofo with your bread? We hide until our girl comes for us."

I spoke up. "Dom, he's right. Neither one of you can stay here with me."

"Do you have an idea where we can go?" Dom asked.

Looking at the disquietude in Dom's eyes, I knew I'd made the right decision. It was settled. "I'm going to speak with Nick tonight. He knows the ins and outs of this strange land better than anyone," I reassured him. "I'm not going to let you guys down. I promise. You're going to be safe and so am I. We just need to be smart and levelheaded."

Dom's thin mustache stretched across his face. "I know you will do your best and that's good enough for Jeffery and me. But you stay safe even if it means we don't make it."

Jeffery shrieked! "Dom what the hell is you sayin'."

Dom glanced at Jeffery giving him the hush-your-mouth, look. Then he focused his gaze back to me. "You might be an angel, but there is only so much you can do. So… save yourself. You are so much more valuable than Jeffery and I will ever be. We are mere humans. You have gifts that can help the masses. People are going to need your help."

I sat there listening to Dom, shaking my head. "I don't want to hear that kind of talk." I grabbed his shoulders. "I'm not leaving you and Jeffery behind." I stared into his deep browns forcing the full meaning of my intent.

Jeffery interjected. "Whew! I'm glad to hear that. For a minute, I thought you meant for Stevie to leave us to hang."

"Jeffery!" Dom scolded. "We have to think of the greater good. We are not part of this grand scale. Though Stevie can't do this alone, the world still needs her if the human population is going to survive. There are millions depending on her leadership."

"Guys, please don't argue over me." I held my palms out. "I am a lab experiment. What can I offer these good folks? Feed thousands by making one fish into a meal for everyone?" I exhaled. "I throw knives. That's my gift." There was a faint tremor in my voice. Their belief in me touched me, but it terrified me even more.

"You have more to offer than you realize, chéri. Did you forget how you handled Aidan? In all the years I have known him, there has never been anything to frighten him as you did. I felt your strength. The electricity in the air was mighty powerful." Dom's soft voice touched me.

I let out a long audible breath. "My abilities are not reliable. I never know when they're going to work. Besides look what happened to me when I released my anger on Aidan. I turned into a hideous green monster." I shivered, hugging my waist.

"Now don't beat yourself up for that," Jeffery chimed in. "You weren't *that* ugly. I heard from the fat lady's society that green is the new trend."

I rolled my eyes at my friend. "Really?"

"Jeffery!" Dom snapped.

"I'm just sayin'" Jeffery shrugged.

A FEW GOOD MEN

J stepped outside onto the front porch and spotted Aidan still tied up in the same rocker. Aidan's head slightly nodded my way. His eyelids were heavy. He appeared drained and his face carried the color of agony. I didn't notice any blood lining the magick rope or his white shirt. A good indication that the rope wasn't cutting into his skin. If I didn't know any better, I'd think the druid was ill. Yet how was that possible when he was an immortal?

He started a violent bout of coughing. His face paled and his lips changed to blue. He was choking, struggling to breathe. I huffed a loud sigh and spun on my heels, heading back inside.

When I returned, I had a glass of tap water and a cloth for the blood he just coughed up. I wiped the blood that drooled from the corner of his mouth and then tilted the glass to his lips as he drank generously.

"Why are you coughing up blood? Are you sick?"

Aidan cut his heated eyes at me and then back at the glass for his second gulp. He kept drinking greedily as though he'd traveled a desert for days, deprived of water.

After he'd drained the glass, he gnarled. "I'm fine! I'm not use to inhaling all this damn dirt." His voice was sharp, but he was short winded. I slipped my eyes over him. Even under the twilight, his skin looked pallid. This was new to me.

"Since when does a little dust make you cough blood?" I eyed him suspiciously.

Aidan cut his harsh eyes back at me. "Since when do high school dropouts become doctors?"

My first impulse was to slap him. How ironic of him to say such a thing. My education was abruptly disrupted when he decided to frame me for murder. I held my tongue though and replied in a calm voice. "Since I became a serial killer." I paused holding the glass at my side, tapping it against my thigh. "You want some more water?" My voice was remote, void of emotions.

Aidan's bloodshot eyes lingered on my breasts a moment too long, and then he lifted his gaze to me. "I'm good on the water part. You offering any other services?" If I didn't know any better, this Aidan would've never treated me like a whore. I was starting to believe more and more that the Family had altered his brain.

I merely shook my head, setting the glass down on a small table beside Aidan and walked off. I didn't stomp or stalk. I simply walked away.

I was getting better at controlling my temper. Good thing too because I would've ended his life right then and there.

I hopped down the stairs and made my way over to the Cajun's side. "Hey!" I forced a smile. "It looks like we're having quite a crowd." My eyes dropped to several meat pans spread over a wooden table next to the grill. I didn't dare ask what kind of beast he'd butchered. Some things were best left alone. With food shortages, I reckoned I best get use to eating unsavory meals.

"*Oui!* It seems that way, doesn't it?" The Cajun briefly looked up at me with a condescending grin.

I rolled my eyes. "Who's coming?" I swiped a quick glance over my shoulder at the porch where Aidan continued to sit. His gaze stayed fixed on me with a heavy dose of loathing.

"A few fellows. They are tough as nails. I think we can use their help."

I blew out a whistle. "You do know that humans don't really have much of a chance, right? Could he be that blind or was he speaking from pride? "It's gonna take superhuman powers if we're going to have a fighting chance. You don't happen to know a super-soldier militia, do you? We don't need to risk anymore lives!"

"*Oui!* I agree. These men are not your run of the mill kind of men."

"Yeah! Well, they bleed, don't they?"

"Do you bleed, *non?*" The Cajun cut his eyes at me, challenging.

"I'm not exactly like Val, a Zophasemin."

"So, what! *Si vous êtes un ange!* (if you are an angel) Like I said, do you bleed?" He looked at me with reaching eyes.

"Yes, I bleed just like any human," my jaw tightened. "I'm a synthetic angel. I was created in a lab."

"Excusez-moi!" His brow shot up. "How did they create you?"

I crinkled my forehead. "That's an interesting question. I'll have to get back to you on that one when I find out myself."

The Cajun nodded at Aidan. "Did that bastard's family have anything to do with your creation?"

I clasped my hands together, rocking on my heels. "Yep, and that's a huge problem."

"Gul, if you know something, you best spit it out." The Cajun snarled as he gathered a slab of meat in his tongs and dropped it onto the grill. Flames hissed, licking the air in protest.

I reckoned I needed to fess up, "We might have a problem. I mean, *I* may have a problem," I huffed, kicking the dirt with my boot. "The Family might be able to trace me."

His brown eyes hardened. "Why do you say that?"

"Aidan mentioned that the Family may have implanted a tracking device in me. He also claimed that when Sara sealed the contract, delivering me to Aidan, the implant had been deactivated." I shrugged. "At the time, I believed him but now," I wrinkled my nose. "I'm not sure."

The Cajun looked at me and then his gaze lifted to Aidan and then back to me. "We can't be certain much of anything right now other than we are confronting hell. We will decide as a collective. If they come, we'll be ready."

"I think we need to find the guys a place to hide and fast. Do you have any friends who live on the bayou? The deeper the better."

"Let's not do anything until we have a plan in motion. If we are being watched, we need to act as normal as possible. If their spies are watching and we do anything that might give them alarm, they might come at us with God knows what."

"Don't forget we have one of their most prized members, Aidan," I half-whispered.

"Yes, and I think he just might be our meal ticket for getting us out of this shit-bath."

"I'm not sure I follow you."

"Our prisoner could be a spy for them. He sits and listens to everything and watches our moves. You've heard that saying about keeping your enemy closer?"

"Yeah, but I don't think the person who said that was thinking of a supernatural Holocaust?"

"Don't worry about it. My men know what they are getting themselves into. We may be mere flesh and bone, with more liquor than blood, but our experience and know how makes up where we lack," he flashed an arrogant grin. "Now hand me that tray over there on the table. We need to get this *barbe à queue* cranked up."

I hated when this human tried to make light of the situation. I shoved the pan in his chest, though he didn't flinch. His pride was going to get him killed and all of us with him. He had no idea what dangers were embarking upon us. No one did.

The Cajun took the pan from me and suddenly my attention veered at the bloody slab of meat he'd dumped onto the hot charcoal. "That-that's a… !" I stammered, gaping.

"*Oui!*" the Cajun concurred. "You like gator, yes?"

"Are you *crazy*? I'm not eating that!"

The Cajun burst into a howl of laughter that could've broken the sound barrier.

"Look! This might be your usual diet, but I'm not the Wild Man of Terrebonne of the bayou. It wouldn't hurt you to give me time to adjust to your strange palate."

"You better hurry, then." His deep browns sparkled in the fire. "We may not have any other food than what is graced to us from the swamp. Did your pampered ass ever think about that?"

"What happened to fish?"

"Tsk, tsk!" he wagged his finger. "You are going to have a difficult time down here in the basin, *visage d'ange!*" (angel face)

"Don't call me that!"

"If you wish." His eyes danced with mischief. "*Très bien,* (very good) you might prefer it to other names I could call you."

"Get over yourself, Saint Nick! My advice to you is don't piss off an angel." I matched his mirthful eyes with snarky green darts.

"*Excusez-moi.* I like to tease a little too much."

"I'll go get more barbeque sauce." I wasn't in the mood for his nonsense.

When I returned outside with my arms full of bottled sauce, the whole front yard sounded like motocross speedway. The roars of motorcycles had drowned out the usual gentle hum of the cicadas. Apparently, the party had arrived as the revving bikes parked to a dusty quiet; several deep male voices meandered from the stand of trees. I quickly spotted several heads of men encircling the Cajun, giving bro hugs and popping beer bottle tops.

Standing on the top step, I glanced back at Aidan. Still battened down in the rocker, he'd nodded off to sleep. His head dropped to the side and his chest moved faintly from breathing. A pain of guilt licked through me. Maybe I should lay him down on one of the beds. Even in his sleep, his face appeared strained. We couldn't keep him in that chair all night. I needed to speak to Nick about this. Maybe he had a cot that we could put Aidan on. At least he'd be lying down.

Exhaling a deep sigh, I made my way down to the burly guest huddled in a circle.

The Cajun's head popped up. His grin flashed briefly, dazzling against his olive skin. He was in his element, obviously happy. "Come Stevie, let me introduce you to these losers," he shouted, laughing

Yep! He's in his comfort zone, alright. Men insult each other when they're buddies. A tradition that I'd never understand.

I walked up beside the Cajun and he gently placed his hand in the small of my back. I quickly stiffened. A bit taken aback, I didn't see that coming from Ole Saint Nick.

The Cajun commenced with the introductions. He slapped his hand on the stocky guy's shoulder and said, "This son of a bitch is Toe. Don't let his size fool you. Despite what he says, he can't eat a whole gator." An eruption of male laughter wafted in the air. I nodded at the man and smiled. Toe wasn't as tall as Nick, though much thicker, and packing a bulging mid-section. I wondered if the man thought his beard, long to his waist, hid his jutting belly? Like most bikers, Toe wore a leather vest at least two sizes too small with a skull on the back and tattoos that embellished his meaty arms.

The Cajun continued. "This is the one and only Dopy." The long-haired man smiled, flashing broken teeth as the Cajun clapped down on his shoulder. "This poor bastard can't hold his liquor." Guffaws followed. The men seemed to enjoy the Cajun's taunting. I gathered they were all close friends, a bond one rarely saw. I waved my hand at Dopy and smiled. He politely nodded. "Next," the Cajun moved on, "This is Titan," he snorted. "He can whoop every man in the parish except me, of course." The men roared, "But he can't whoop his old lady." The Cajun teasingly shoved his friend's baldhead. The man was a giant. He had to have been seven feet tall. Just his size and height alone could be intimidating. "That fella over there," the Cajun pointed to, "Is Slim. Now that spindly bastard *can* eat a whole gator!" Laughter poured into the air once more. The Cajun moved on to the following, "Last, but not least." He moved to the last man, standing on the outs. "That there is Scrubby with a goatee. It's safe to say he came from a long line of sheep!"

The laughter floated into the night air as I spoke up. "It's nice to meet y'all," I smiled, giving a light nod. My hands were stuffed in my pockets, uncertain if I should shake hands or slap 'em on their backs. I decided to keep my hands in my pockets.

My gaze drifted off to where several bikes with sparkling chrome sat parked. Harleys, as far as I could tell. That was a sure sign that these men were proficient bikers. Setting aside their scary appearances, they all seemed harmless enough. They were strange looking with nose piercings, tattoos and hair longer than mine. I didn't mind. I felt right at home among them.

Though, I worried how they might receive Dom and Jeffery. I hoped Jeffery would hold his tongue. I didn't want to think what he might ask one of these grungy men.

The Cajun spoke up, "These men and I go back a few years. We are former military. Special Operations. Army soldiers."

"Wow! That's impressive," I smiled approvingly.

"These men are my brothers," Nick spoke proudly.

"Where were you men stationed?" I asked.

The Cajun slipped a sideways glance at the men and said,

"Afghanistan. I was the baby of this ugly bunch! They hated me at first, cuz I was prettier."

Shrubby interjected, "Yeah! You might have been the prettiest, but you were the stupidest little wiener."

"Don't worry about my *wiener*! I save that for the ladies."

"That's not what I heard," said Titan. "Some of those gals were disappointed."

"*Non!* They wanted more of me and I turned them away. Of course, they are going to bitch. If you'd had me, you'd want more of me too." The Cajun wore pomposity like his Sunday church clothes.

Titan flashed a wide smile. "Nah! You ain't my type. I hate whiskers on *women*." Laughter encircled the men like a domino effect. I found myself laughing too. The Cajun snorted and didn't have much of a comeback after that shade. Come to think about it, he had looked a bit peaked. I imagined only few could taunt him about his manhood.

Later that night the whole gang and I had settled around the blazing campfire, eating gator. Surprisingly, it was tasty. I found it had a lingering taste between catfish and chicken. I didn't even need the barbeque sauce. *Go figure!*

After we finished our meal, talk started to rumble. My ears were perked and ready to hear the latest events that had transpired since we took underground. I felt cut off from civilization, like a blind person standing on a cliff. I needed a heavy scoop to remedy the bothersome tick that twisted my gut.

Toe began the conversation. "I've been snooping around. Asking my peeps what they know about our city. Man, I have to tell you, it's pretty fucking bleak."

I jumped in, "What's happening?"

"To start, the United Nations has been seized and the Order has declared martial law. This ain't just local. It's worldwide. Curfew is enforced. Anyone outside roaming the streets after eight p.m. will be gunned down. No questions asked. My informant said two neighbors of his got shot down in cold blood. They got caught pillaging through a busted-up grocery store for food. One fellow was looking for baby formula."

"Damn! Can we help these families?" The Cajun's voice was tight with anger.

"I don't know. There's regulators at every corner."

"Regulators?" Titan asked.

"Yeah, they are some strange looking fellows what I've heard. They're the enforcers of peace. Some cold-blooded bastards, I hear."

The Cajun interjected. "Are they military forces?"

Toe squinted his face like he'd eaten something rotten. "I hadn't seen 'em, but my sources say they sound like robots but look like reptiles, scales, and all. They ain't human. The street has it that they are alien. Spaceships and shit. They come from Bellatrix." He tipped his head back and pointed to the sky at a yellow star. "You can't see it all the time, but tonight the planet's brighter than normal. I looked through my telescope earlier today and you can see small streaks coming from it. My redneck guess is that they're coming in their ships. Mostly thousands headed to earth."

Curses spewed among the men.

"What has your source seen?" The Cajun asked, rubbing his bristled jaw.

"For starters, those fuckers," Toe nodded at me, "Pardon my language ma'am."

I caught Toe's gaze, "It's fine. Go on, please," I wanted to hear as much as anyone.

Toe continued. "The creatures move faster than any human. Hell, my source saw one jump a building like superman. Only this creature wasn't pretty or friendly. He threw a man off the top of a building, killing the poor man." The tensing of Toe's jaw betrayed his trepidation. "I tell you, man, my source doesn't get scared that easily. But the white in his eyes were far too wide when he finished his story. Those regulators had him spooked!"

The look on Toe's face gave me shivers. No doubt, we were all in over our heads. And the worst part, I had the feeling we'd just grazed the surface.

"Merde!" The Cajun blurted out. "What else do you know?"

"It ain't good for us po-boys." Fear laced Toe's voice. "The uprising has shut the city down. Everything is closed banks, grocery stores, any thriving business. Even the bars have closed. The streets are filled with

51

hungry people and dead bodies with their guts hanging out as they bleed out onto the street.

"What? Is the government pulling a Hitler regime on us?" Titan asked.

"I suspected the same thing myself, *man*!" Toe resumed. "Word is going around that our old system has fully collapsed. Riots have been going on downtown. In fact, the whole world is a massacre." He gave pause, rubbing his eyes briefly. I reckoned he was trying to keep from losing it. After a bucket of minutes, he lifted his gaze back at us and finished. "Hell, its history repeating itself. Hitler and Castro forcing working folks from their homes. It's just a matter of time before they come take our land too." Toe shook his head. The blunt of shock, fear for an uncertain future hung on his burdened shoulders.

The Cajun butted in. "It sounds like a Marxism–Leninism socialism. They intend to convert our country into a one-party socialist, under Communist Party rule. These animals seek dominance, a one government over the people. Strip folks of their possessions. Force people to surrender and follow the bastards just for food." The Cajun summed it up in a nutshell.

"These new authorities are fucking cowards. Too afraid to show their ugly mugs." Toe's whole demeanor boiled with raw anger.

"Seriously?" I clamored in shock.

The Cajun broke in, "Sorry, Red. Looks like your poor again." He had flopped his unwanted butt down beside me.

I just smiled. "Money isn't important to me. Besides, I'm glad to be rid of it. It was blood money."

The Cajun reached over and squeezed my hand. "I'm sorry. Bad joke, y*es*?

I replied. "Yes, very!" I caught a quick glimpse of regret behind his dark browns. I nudged Nick with my shoulder to make light. I didn't have the tenacity to keep up with his tough jabs. My head felt weighed down with sand. I couldn't wrap my head around the reality of my surroundings. The world was changing, and it was scaring the hell out of me.

"How are folks getting food?" The Cajun asked Toe.

"Funny, you should ask. People are forced to stand in long lines, hours at a time. In order to receive food, you have to get inked on your wrist like a tattoo. You can only detect it with a special monitor." Toe went on to say. "You won't believe what the number is, *man*." Toe shook his head, clearly shaken.

"I'm not sure I want to know." Dread swirled in the Cajun's voice.

With no warning, sleeping beauty had awaken. Aidan bellowed. "Let me guess! Would it happen to be the numbers six six six?"

"What do those numbers mean?" I asked, though, I knew it wasn't anything good.

"It stands for man's reign has come to an end. It divides the imperfect humans from the supreme humans. Imperfect man. The stamp contains a tracking device. It's how the NWO keeps track of citizens." Aidan seemed to have regained some of his steam as he leaned back in his chair, gloating.

Slim called out among the stir. "What the hell is NWO?"

With a heavy sigh, I answered, "New World Order." I cut my ireful eyes at Aidan and then back at Slim, "It's a conspiracy. The Illuminati have been planning this for centuries."

The Cajun cut in, "Slim, they're the bastards that are behind the curtain," the Cajun grated. "They're like those radicals in Afghanistan tying bombs to children. Those *sac à foutre* (scum-bags) can fuck off!

I spoke up before World War III started in Nick's front yard. "I think we need to keep our calm. We have someone who can give in-depth details of what's happening." Everyone followed the line of my gaze.

"Yeah, but will he tell the truth?" Toe stared menacingly at Aidan.

With this different Aidan, it was hard to say. "What do we have to lose?" I dragged in a biting breath.

DEED OF TRUST

*B*y the blood-curling screams of Jeffery, I'd thought someone had skinned him alive. How that man lived in New Orleans all his life and never had eaten gator, would baffle my mind forever. That was like a Texan never eating deer. I think Jeffery was in his own genre.

A sudden dead silence fell over the crackling fire as all eyes snapped up at my good friend. Shortly following, there was a chorus of laughter. Obviously, Jeffery made a big hit with the bikers as they enjoyed a friendly slap across his boney back.

Jeffery pursed his lips and held his head high as he walked prissily over and sat down next to Dom and me without so much as an utter.

Slim nodded over to Aidan as he directed his question to me. "Since you think it's a shot… ask that fella what he knows. If he won't talk, we have ways of making him." In his deep baritone voice there was a minatory tint.

My gaze jolted sharply at Slim. I might not like my hostage, but for some reason, I felt protective of him. I wasn't ready to let any of these bikers work him over. I remembered when Aidan could've taken any one of these men and not bat an eye. Now, by the ragged look on his face, I wasn't so sure. Even still, I didn't want to find out if Aidan could hold his own. I needed to keep the peace.

Before I answered Slim, Aidan erupted. "Ask me!" he bellowed.

"No need for torture." His conceit grated me. "I'll tell you anything you want to know. First, I want some food and an ice-cold beer before I divulge any information."

"I'll fix him a plate." Dom exhaled as he started to his feet.

I placed my hand on his shoulder. "Dom, *no*. Let me take care of Aidan. He's too unpredictable and dangerous."

After I stacked the plate full of gator and potatoes, I swiped a cold beer from the ice barrel and marched up the steps.

Standing directly in front of him, our eyes met. His eyes were flat, hard and passionless. I knew this was going to be tricky. I had to stand my ground. I slightly shifted in my feet. "You go first, my friend. No negotiating." I stood, chin tilted slightly upward.

Aidan fumed for a second as his eyes locked into a gun-down stare at me. "Ah, she commands!"

"Cough it up!" My patience was running thin.

A smirk curved the corner of his mouth, "There's really not a lot to tell. The almighty Illuminati have destroyed the old system as you have some idea already. However, this uprising will make Hitler look like a saint. First, those deemed contaminated will be extinguished." He snarled.

"What do you mean extinguished?" I asked.

Aidan lifted his red eyes at me and smirked. "I understand why you didn't finish school. Don't you know that history repeats itself?" He then cut his eyes at the men and rose his voice. "People who do not honor the Omniscient God, the true leader, the Illuminati, and denounce their useless religions will be executed. They can meet their delightful maker who doesn't give two shits that they are suffering.

I took a step back. I was shocked over his words. "You can't expect people to lay down and surrender to your Order. They will rebel as I recall history accounts." My hands began to tremble. He was talking about mass destruction.

Aidan turned his disdainful eyes at me. "You'd be surprise what a person will do for a little food and a warm place to sleep."

I gawked at him as my stomach churned. I looked down at the plate of food and the cold beer in my hand. "Strange that you should say that." I nodded over my shoulder to the men. "You brazenly brag to these good folks about starving people to get them to bend to your will and yet these folks are willing to feed you for just a little information."

My lips curled into a scowl. "Go screw yourself!" I threw the food over the rail. "I'm tired of your bullshit!" I spun on my heels and headed inside the house. I'd had my limit with Aidan, but I had to finish hearing what else he had to say. I halted in the doorframe listening.

"Your friend is correct." He nodded to Toe. "The government has declared a state of emergency. If you resist, and you will, the regulators will shoot dissenters on sight. You're defiant. And you will not conform to the *New World Order*. You are the bottom of the barrel and are only good for slaves."

The men began to stir restlessly. Murmurs of curses wafted in the night air.

I flinched when the word slave came out of his mouth. I could only imagine what he meant. The only explanation I could see was that the Family had Aidan under mind control. What else could it possibly be? I swallowed down the pending dread and asked, "The regulators are the police now."

"Yes," Aidan went on to explain, "They are the new law enforcement. All citizens must be contained to keep the peace."

"What do you mean contained." My neck bristled.

"The regulators are ordered to do whatever it takes to keep the populace calm. Anyone who is opposed to our cause will be shot down in plain sight."

The Cajun scoffed. "I suppose killing innocent women and children is keeping the peace."

A hunted look came over Aidan's face. "The Order will do whatever it takes to keep the compliance."

"So, we don't get a vote?" the Cajun asked.

Aidan laughed. "Of course not! The Order is not a utopian society. Freedom will be stripped from every living soul."

The Cajun stood up, stalking his way to the porch. He stopped at the bottom steps.

A breath of relief eased from my chest. I was glad the Cajun didn't come any closer. Aidan, with a mere thought, could've snapped the Cajun in two. I didn't want to have to step between a 300-year-old-druid and a big-headed human.

"You do realize the old leaders and the people will rebel. You're asking for war." The Cajun's voice came off tight and ready to blow up with rage.

Aidan sneered. "Neither the officials in the White House, including the president, nor the CIA, FBI, or even the NSA, have ever actually been in charge. That's why it has been a breeze taking over. The old system you once knew no longer exists. Out with the old and in with the new."

"Are you saying other countries are under siege?" By the twitching of the Cajun's jaw I could tell he wanted to pounce on Aidan.

"That is correct." An insidious grin abraded Aidan's face. "We, the Illuminist are the supremacy. We are the only hope you have. Not your weak government nor the UN can help you now. It is *we* who have ceased all wars. Soon we will claim peace and security. Only those who subject themselves to our authority will reap the benefits of our pardon."

The words fell out of my mouth before I could stop myself. "What happens if we resist?"

"Freedom Fighters will die," he paused with a scowl welded to his face. "For you, sweetheart, your days are numbered regardless."

With no warning, my eyes ignited as a faint gasp settled among the men. "What do you *mean*?" I asked as I stepped onto the porch, forgetting that the men didn't know about my druid gifts. I wasn't sure how I'd explain this either. It was a gift I'd inherited from Aidan when we'd sealed our fate as one. Funny, I had yet to have seen Aidan's eyes flame. I wondered if I'd taken the ability from him.

"Do you think they are just going to let you get off scot free?" Aidan didn't wait for me to respond. "My uncle, our Grandmaster, is determined to have your head on a silver platter. He has ordered for you to be hunted down and destroyed. He claims you are a danger to the New World Order. You must be eliminated."

My mouth flew open. "Oh, really! They're going to have a tough time bringing me down, buddy!" I promised with fist to my side, white knuckled.

"I didn't assume otherwise," Aidan scoffed. "Don't you think they have prepared for your little bag of tricks?"

"Speaking of tricks…" My eyes narrowed with suspicion. "Where are yours?"

Aidan's body tightened. "When I'm drained of energy, my powers are depleted," he snarled.

"Is that why you're spitting up blood?"

"I haven't spit up any blood," he lied.

I gawked at him for a minute and then with a heavy sigh, I replied, "You're lying, but if you want to save face, that's fine. I don't care if you're coughing up your dick!" An explosion of laughter burst into the night's dew. I was sure that I'd scored a few points for that jab.

"You really should be more concerned for yourself," Aidan gravely advised.

"What are you saying?"

"You don't know, do you?" His laugh assaulted my ears.

"I wouldn't have asked if I knew."

"Well, let me enlighten you, sweetheart," he paused flashing his smile. Was I imagining things or was Aidan's teeth starting to decay? Perhaps his druid years were catching up to him. I pulled my eyes from his smirk and crossed my arms over my chest.

"Thanks to your DNA, they have cloned an army of soldiers with your same novel capabilities," Aidan continued. "You have multiple blood relatives. We refer to you as the new age Eve. Though for you, it will be a short celebration. I'm expecting your family reunion will be a huge bang!"

"Have you gone mad?" I knew with certainty this was the beginning of the end. Aidan confirmed my suspicions. I was a liability. Anyone around me would face the same fate. *Holy crap!* I ripped my fingers through my tangled hair. We were doomed. I slid my gaze at the Cajun. When our eyes latched, I instantly knew he realized the peril we were in.

Then, Aidan distracted me from my nightmarish thoughts. "Your friend is right. The Order has eminent domain. The change will be a feudal society. A military hierarchy in which the ruler will have control and say over the land. Only those worthy of such a privilege to possess land will receive deeds of trust. However, the Order has the right to revoke the tenant's ownership and kick his ass to the streets if he breaks the *Order of Solomon*.

The Cajun's eyes flashed a grave look at our captive. "I'm sick of hearing this Euro's trash talk! Too much talk." The Cajun darted up the steps heading toward Aidan.

Since I'd made the druid my responsibility, I stepped in front of the Cajun. He grasped my arms and lifted me to the side. "*Non!*" he barked. "Let one of the men get him."

58

"Fine!" I stepped back, palms in the air.

The Cajun nodded to Titan.

Moments later, Aidan found himself face down in the dirt in the center of a circle of men. He was nearly kissing the Cajun's boots.

My magical rope still clung to Aidan's body, but it didn't stop him from rising on his haunches as he raked his baleful eyes over the circle of bikers as if he were memorizing their faces.

I cringed, fearing for their lives. These humans were tough, but I feared if Aidan had only a mere smudge of his powers, they wouldn't stand a chance.

When my eyes gravitated to the Cajun's face, my breath stalled. His taunt expression reminded me of a lion inching closer to its kill. "Start talking or else I'll cut your tongue out, *yes*?"

For a minute, I pitied Aidan. He looked beaten like a dog kicked to submission, but he still had some fight in him as he spoke with audacious pride. "My family is many." Aidan's voice was raspy as sandpaper. "We have a far reach beyond what your pathetic minds can grasp. This planet is only a speck of our scope compared to the range of our supremacy. We are in the folds of profound change and not one of you simpletons can appreciate the magnitude and benefits of our rising."

"I have a mind to run the girl's dagger through your black heart right now!" The Cajun's jaw was set in steel.

Aidan broke into laughter that seeped of venom. "Watch what you threaten, lowly one. I can take every one of you in one swift sweep."

If Aidan's threat had worried the Cajun, he didn't show it. Rather, he went on with his interrogation. *"Vous ne me fais pas peur avec votre visage dans la boue."* (You do not frighten me with your face in the dirt.) The Cajun grated. "Tell me why your people want the girl."

"Why do you care? She's a useless whore!" The acidity in his voice was prolific.

The Cajun interrupted with little tolerance. "Don't talk about the girl that way. After all, she was the mother of your child. Get on with what you know. And make it quick before I lose my patience."

Aidan flashed a fiendish sneer. "A little scared there, human?" He carefully shifted on his knees as he glared at the different faces staring down at him, "You are fools if you take this lightly," he bellowed. "If you are willing to set aside your differences, The Order will pardon your crimes. Join in our takeover and pledge your allegiance to the

New World Order. I will see to it that you are each given a unit of land in exchange for your military services. Nothing short will be acceptable. Failure to do so will result in death."

I couldn't listen to his vile any longer. I stormed down the steps and pushed my way through a couple of men until I reached Aidan's side. I spoke out against his fanatical babble. "You're describing a monopoly, but really in truth, we will be slaves to your damn family." I raked in a shard of breath and knocked Aidan down into the dirt, face grinding against the ground. I dug my foot into the nemesis's back. "You mentioned an army like me. *Elaborate!*" I gritted my teeth.

"Since you were not in compliance with the Family, we went to plan B."

"Plan B?" I hesitated briefly, then it hit me. I flung into action, flipping him on his back. "You son of a *bitch!*" I throttled him, pressing my dagger to his throat. The Cajun caught me by my waist, pulling me back as I barely missed Aidan's jugular. Still, I fought to get at him. "You gave our daughter over to that beast, Mustafa. And in return, that monster gave you his DNA!" The Cajun had a death grip on me. "Forget this shit!" I ordered my dagger to ram through his collarbone. I heard bone snap and immediately following, Aidan howled. The next knife loomed evenly at his eye level. "You are nothing but a black hearted *monster!*" I spat in his face.

Aidan's grin transformed into something unrecognizable. Pure evil, I speculated. "I am a survivor, my dear. I follow orders and I stay alive. Hate me if you wish. Where I stand, I have no choice. The Order wanted your DNA. For the exchange of your daddy, Mustafa's DNA, we bargained with the child," he gnarled. "If you ask me, we got the better deal."

All this time, Aidan had looked me straight in the eye and lied to me. He was in on the plan with Mustafa all along.

Unable to contain myself, I snapped. Blinded by rage, I dove for Aidan. But before I had a chance to squeeze my fingers around his throat, I felt a sudden sharp force to the back of my head and all at once, everything went blank.

FREEDOM FIGHTERS

$\mathcal{T}$he morning came as a thin beam of light hit me straight in the face. I slowly opened my eyes. With my head full of cobwebs, I skimmed the surroundings and my memory came flooding back. A throbbing ache resonated from the crown of my head. My fingers grazed the spot but I flinched, regretting my move. It stung like a *mother*. I had a good hunch the huge goose bump on my noggin came from a blunt object. And the force behind the strike could only have been one person… *the Cajun*.

"Ouch!" I mumbled. "Damn that hurts!" Did he have to hit me so hard? I get why he needed to stop me. We needed to keep the prisoner alive. I couldn't believe I almost killed Aidan. He was our only connection to *the Family*.

Whata nightmare! We were helpless. Innocent people were going to die. And those sociopaths didn't care. Self-entitled *pricks*! I covered my arm over my eyes, trying to will my mind to go blank. Yet old memories gnawed at me. I remembered a time that seemed so long ago. A time when Aidan stayed by my side to comfort me. A tear escaped and I quickly wiped it away with the back of my hand. I missed *that* Aidan. The one who saved me many times from the harsh fate of death. Even the underhanded things he had done seemed tenable. But now, not a glimmer of the old Aidan I once knew. I wondered if *that* Aidan had ever existed? Whether or not he was a figment of my imagination, he felt real to me. How I craved to feel his arms around me. I still ached for our child. My child that I'd never been able to cradle in my arms. I knew wishing wasn't going to bring Dawn back or the man I once loved. I had to focus on surviving in the present. A daunting task I feared.

I worried over the Cajun and his men. Even though they had fought in a gruesome war, it didn't prepare the men for this catastrophe. They should lay low, live off the swamp.

To add to the heap of woes, I worried about Jeffery and Dom. They wouldn't make it in the wild. They were accustomed to a pampered lifestyle. They had no survival skills. Maybe, the men could teach Dom and Jeff some survival skills. That might not be a bad idea, but did we have enough time? After all, it was only a matter of time before the Illuminist found us.

Val came to mind and a spurt of anger smacked me like a coconut dropping from a tree. Why did he leave us to fight this battle alone? How could I fend off these monsters with no proficient back up? Humans were defenseless against the Illuminist's army of super-freaks. I needed angel power. If there was a fleet of genetically engineered angels coming for me... how the hell was I to fight them off? An impossible endeavor.

I couldn't lie here all day and do nothing. I needed to speak with Nick.

I threw the covers off and gently swung my legs off the bed to the floor. I sat for a moment letting my head stop spinning. I inhaled a few heavy breaths to ease the pain and settle my stomach. As my sickness lessened, I scanned the room for my clothes. I had only my tank top and panties on. I didn't even want to think who undressed me. I had enough on my plate as it was already. This one, I'd let slid. I spotted some clothes laid out over a chair in the corner. I raised off the bed and padded over to the folded clothing. I'd never seen these threads before. It was army combat gear. A cap, khaki pants, tee shirt, a black sports bra, go figure on that one. And boots my size. I grabbed up the pants and they were my size too. I guess these items were meant for me. I tied my hair up in a ponytail with a band I'd found on the nightstand. Then I covered my hair up with the cap, letting my ponytail hang out. I stood in front of the mirror. Not too bad, I thought as I eyed myself carefully.

Moments later, I stepped outside and noted right away that the boys had moved Aidan to the large oak tree just off to the side of the porch. My breath eased when I spotted the magick rope still intact, wrapped around him like a tight rubber band.

Aidan and I swapped glances and neither one of us bothered with pleasantries. I think after last night, we'd exchanged enough insults to last a lifetime.

I combed my eyes over the grounds. Everything had settled. I saw no signs of the bikers. They must've left last night after I got knocked out. The sun was climbing the blue sky and the heat was following quickly after.

Judging by the high sun, the morning was almost over. I quickly spied the Cajun making a bunch of ruckus inside his storage building, set high off the ground like the house. I made my way to him, climbing the steps. When I stepped inside, my eyes instantly landed on a metal table stock-piled of guns and grenades. The Cajun was dismantling his rifle. I cleared my throat. "Good morning."

Nick turned to me, combing his eyes over me. "You gotta good bump on the head there, yes?"

"Yeah," I half scoffed. "Did you have to hit me so hard?" My fingers touched my forehead and I flinched.

"When you act *coo-yon*, I do what I must." The corner of his lip twitched.

"Coo-yon? I'm far from foolish." I could feel the onset of irritation starting to sizzle.

"Maybe, maybe not. But I can't have you ruining the only leverage we have." He nodded at Aidan. "Without pretty boy, our ass is cooked." The Cajun's dark eyes collided with Aidan's withering stare.

I decided to change the subject as my eyes swiped over all his arsenal goodies spread about over the table in a nice neat line. "Wow! Looks like you've been stocking up for a while. Is it legal to carry this much weaponry?" I thought David Koresh, a notorious cult leader in Waco, Texas a few years back, had some serious ammo, but the Cajun puts that dude to shame.

He nodded toward the back of the building. "Go see for yourself."

When I reached the back, my chin hit the floor. I whistled, "Damn! You have a serious hobby!" It quickly came to mind the collection of weapons that Val stored in his gym. They were more magical than manmade but very effective.

"Is it even legal for you to carry so much arms?" I slipped a sideways glance at the Cajun and then back at the rows of tubs full of every kind of gun one could possibly imagine.

"At one time, it was illegal. Now, I don't give a shit. I fight for my rights. That's the only law I honor."

The conviction in the Cajun's voice was impregnable. To be honest, I agreed. Yet I feared he might be fighting a lost cause. You didn't bring a knife to a gunfight. His collection of weaponry might be quite destructive to the norm, but I had a sneaky feeling it was nothing more than a water gun up against the Order's artillery.

As I made my way back to the Cajun's side, my stomach twisted in knots. I had to get this man to understand that his weapons were useless. "If Aidan is right, those soldiers are super-soldiers. You think mankind's arsenals will serve your purpose?" I didn't want to douse the Cajun with despair, but I had to be real.

"Nope! I don't." The Cajun answered while he cocked one of his rifles back and looked down its barrel. I stared at him baffled.

"Then what's the point?"

The Cajun finally glanced up at me. "It might not kill 'em but it might slow them down long enough for us to get away."

He went back to cleaning his gun.

I stood there chewing the inside of my mouth. Then a thought popped up. "Homemade bombs might be more effective."

The Cajun snapped his head up, glaring at me like I was 'Jihadi John'. "What's going on inside that pretty head of yours?"

"I'm just saying… if these creatures are not of this world, they may be sensitive to certain human products."

Out of nowhere, Aidan burst into cackles.

The Cajun's eyes blazed with murder. "What's so funny, druid?"

"Nothing will defeat our super-soldiers. Freedom fighters!" Aidan crowed.

"You over there shut your trap! Unless you want to eat turpentine." By the scorn on the Cajun's face, I gathered that he wasn't making an idol threat.

Strangely, Aidan regarded bitterly, simmering to a quiet. The old Aidan would have never backed down.

The Cajun cut his eyes back to me. "Exactly what do you have in mind?" He kept his voice just above a whisper.

I whispered back. "Like common household items."

"*Non!*" he shook his head. "We can't test it on any of those bastards. We'll be wasting our time." He returned to his gun cleaning.

I bit my bottom lip, thinking. "Hmm, you can use me." I shrugged. "Who else would be a better lab rat?" I feigned a smile.

That was the first time I'd seen the look of shock on the Cajun's face. "Come again?"

"Well, someone has to test the product. The only way we're going to find out if the chemicals work is testing them on me. We don't have to use a full dose." I stood there silent while the Cajun stared at me as if I'd lost my mind. Maybe I had. Still the same, what other choice did we have?

All of a sudden, he uttered a slew of curse words, "Gul, what is wrong with you?"

"You got any better ideas?" I stood at an impasse with my arms folded with a lock down stare at the Cajun.

He rubbed his two-day-old stubble. "What kind of homemade bombs are you talking about?"

"If we used household goods, we'd have ourselves an arsenal of bombs far more effective than your most mighty guns." I nodded at the trash bin and under the house, "All these beer bottles and any plastic bottles laying around, will come in handy. Got any balloons?" I crossed my arms, staring the Cajun dead in the eye.

"You're not kidding, are you?"

"Nope, but it can get tricky. If you shake 'em they can explode."

"How do you know these things?" The Cajun's eyes glazed with shock.

A wicked grin skirted across my face, "I paid attention in chemistry."

The Cajun paused with a look of death on his face, and then suddenly he blurted out, "*Non!* I don't think so!"

"Look we can use a little on a small spot of skin." I rolled my sleeve up showing bare skin.

"*Non!* It could be fatal."

The man was more stubborn than a barnyard of mules, but I

couldn't back down now. "If it kills me, then we know it works." I glared back at him, hell-bent.

"You are *couyon* (crazy), yes?"

"Yes." I said flat, staring into his black opal eyes.

He stomped his foot and raked his fingers through his disheveled hair. "*Assez!*" (Enough) He let out a huff in his heavy French accent. "Only a drop on your skin. You got that, gul?"

"*Oui*, Saint Nick!" I snapped my heels together and saluted sharply with a broad smiled.

"Grrrr," the Cajun rumbled. "Don't use my name until you survive the test. I hate being on first name basis with someone on her deathbed," he grumbled.

Eight hours later and I looked like someone who stepped into a hornet's nest. The welts were red and full of pus. Although, it was painful, we now had bombs that might take down a few super-soldiers.

No matter how pretty the sun looked dipping behind the horizon, another concern picked at my gut. How would we identify the super ones from a regular human? They could look like anyone on the street, blending into the crowd. It was going to be tough dividing the humans from the unhuman. Unless they wore a stamp across their forehead, we were going to have to take our chances. That meant we were going to have to be alert of every person out in the open and even those lurking in the shadows. I raked in a fretful sigh. The odds were against us and yet we still stood to fight. Freedom fighters or suicide idiots?

BOMBS AWAY

"*J*effery, I understand that you're afraid." He followed closely behind me into the kitchen like a puppy dog. I tossed over my shoulder as I headed for the coffee pot. "Despite the risk, I have to do this." I grabbed a cup from the cupboard and poured myself a cup of coffee. I took a seat at the small table by the window as Jeffery stayed on my heels. I sighed, thinking what I'd give for a little sugar and cream. "Don't worry." I lifted my gaze at my pestering friend. "I'll be with the Cajun," I shrugged. "We have to see what's out there."

"Let Nick and one of his buddies go scope out the city! For once in your life let the men take the lead." Jeffery raved, standing over me with determination etched in his sour face.

"My friend," I reached up, grasping my fingers around his hand, "I appreciate your concern, but this is what I was made to do. I'm just like one of those super-soldiers. I'll be okay. Stop worrying your beautiful head over me."

"My beautiful head and all my other lovely *isn't the point*!" Jeffery's voice went up an octave.

I blew out an irate sigh. "I can hold my own with the best." I wasn't wavering on my decision.

"One on one, gurrrl! Not no hundred clones like yourself. You go out there it'll be like walkin' out naked to a firing squad." I stifled a giggle. Only Jeffery could use nudity in a situation daring as this.

I'd placed the guys in a dangerous position by mere association. For that reason alone, I needed to step up to the plate and protect them. That meant I needed to see what was going on in the city. I might not know combat, but common sense told me that before any of us could make any strategic move, we needed to see for ourselves what was going on.

I gulped my hot coffee down, feeling the sear down my windpipe. I didn't care. I needed its boost last week. I didn't have it in me to argue with a damn grasshopper, much less Jeffery. "Look!" I sighed deeply. "I don't have the answer for everything. We have to go into the city and check out what's happening. I might be able to speak to some of the locals. Maybe they can give us some insight." I took another gulp of coffee, somehow the burn kept my mind from going AWOL.

Dom came into the kitchen greeting us with a tired smile. *"Bonjour!"* he started shuffling through the cabinets and fridge to see what to fix for his usual morning breakfast.

Jeffery and I both mumbled, "Morning," in a half-hearted way. Neither one of us were in the best mood.

Though considering our current dilemma, we were in pretty good shape. Fortunately, Toe had been kind enough to bring us a few dozen eggs and he'd butchered a nutria, a bayou rabbit. At least we'll be eating, even if the food was less than desirable.

When I first laid eyes on that furry varmint, I nearly choked. I swore it was an over-sized rat. Yet in this strange land of Louisiana, I found myself often surprised.

After Dom had skinned it and made it into chili, it turned out quite tasty. Of course, Dom could make anything taste good. To add to the list of worry, with little food supply, we might be eating a lot more of those critters. The bayou had plenty of nutria to keep us fed. On top of that, the fur might be good for trade.

Soon Dom busied himself with breakfast. It didn't take Dom long before he began rolling out dough, making his simple rolls. I hoped he planned to make some gravy from the milk that Slim brought us, fresh from his cow. Dom showed me how to make butter from the cream. I reckoned in times like this, having a little know how of nature was a priceless tool to have in your back-pocket. It could be a matter of life and death.

Jeffery decided to bring Dom into our lovely discussion. "Do you think it's safe enough for Stevie to go into the city while Aidan's family's lookin' for her? She's gonna get her head chopped off."

"I think it is dangerous for all of us," Dom sighed. "Unfortunately, it might be a necessary risk."

"See! he agrees!" I stuck my tongue out at Jeffery like an annoying sibling.

"Gurrrlfriend, don't get your panties in a bunch just yet. He might change his mind when he finds out what you plan to do!" Jeffery pursed his lips and straightened his shoulders back, snapping his fingers in my face.

"Children!" Dom scolded. "Stop!"

Jeffery chimed in. "She's gonna throw homemade bombs at those mofo monsters!"

"I'm not going right up to a regulator and yell… hey, nana, nana, boo, boo, you can't catch me!" I sang, pushing Jeffery's buttons.

"Gurrrl, you ain't too big to slap!" Jeffery twisted his lips into a snarl.

"Stop worrying! We plan to blend in with the crowd. We're merely going to observe. That's all. I swear!" I slapped Jeffery on the back and flashed a grin.

"Then why is Aidan's Jeep gettin' loaded down with homemade bombs?" Jeffery crossed his arms, bobbing his head like the cat that ate the canary.

"*What*?" I sprung from my chair and darted out the front door and made a beeline to where the Cajun and Titan were gathered.

Once I reached their side, I stopped, gaping at Aidan's Jeep. They'd taken the top off and were making more than minor changes to the car. "What are you doing?" I washed my eyes over the once bright yellow Jeep and cut my gaze at the Cajun and Titan. "The Jeep looks like green vomit." I walked around the car, inspecting. "How did all these dings get here? Even the front bumper is banged up and twisted." The Frenchman ignored me as he moved to the back of the Jeep, squatting down with a screwdriver in his hand. I stalked over to his side. "This car looks like crap!"

The Cajun cut his eyes at me briefly, answering curtly. "*Oui!*"

"And may I ask why?" I glimpsed over at Aidan shooting blue shards my way. I reckoned he didn't appreciate the minor adjustments to his Jeep either.

Titan spoke up. "We can't drive around with a brand-new Jeep that's bright yellow and with the same license plate. They'd see us coming."

"After you've smashed it, this thing doesn't look like it'll get us out of the driveway." I noticed a sledgehammer laying in the dirt.

"That's the point!" Titan grinned underneath his gruffly beard. We'll look like po-folks beggin' for handouts."

After changing the plates, the Cajun came around the car to Titan and me. He raked his eyes over me like he was summing me up like I was the new dog to the pack. "You need to dirty up a bit. It wouldn't hurt to tear some holes in your shirt and pants." He studied my hair, fingering a strand in his fingers. "Keep that cap on. Your red hair is distracting."

"Whatever!" I slapped his hand way. "What about the bombs? I noticed you got 'em loaded."

"*Peut être.* (Maybe)" The Cajun flashed a mischievous grin.

"Holy hell! I didn't intend for you to use those unless we were under attack," I gawked at the two men who seemed far too confident.

The Cajun stepped up, looming over me. "We're headed into hostile territory. I'm not taking any chances."

Titan spoke up. "It's best to expect the unexpected, Ms. Stevie."

I glimpsed at the back of the Jeep. I spotted several crates that were used to contain mudbugs or crabs. "Why crates?" I went to move a lid and the Cajun snatched my hand back.

"*Non,* gul!" he said sternly. "Don't open those crates unless you intend to lose a finger."

"What's in there?"

The Cajun snarled with pride. "We put snappers in the crates in case we get searched."

A smile tugged on the corners of my mouth. "Aren't you full of surprises!" I didn't think about disguising the weapons. Such a clever idea, but I hoped they didn't think I was throwing the bombs.

"We aren't as green behind the ears as you think," the Cajun smiled brightly. War seemed to suit him as if he thrived on it.

Then our pending reality struck. "Fools, you are!" Aidan yelled out.

"When they have you blindfolded, lined against a wall with guns aiming at your heads, be sure and tell them where to find me," he bellowed with mirth.

The Cajun shouted back. "You should worry about yourself. You're the one tied up," he gnarled. He cut his hard eyes back to me, "Rub dirt on your face and clothes. We need to get going."

I grabbed his arm before he stalked off. "Wait! What about the guys? We can't leave them unprotected."

"Don't worry," the Cajun nodded at Titan. "He's going to stay. Your friends are safe." He turned away climbing in the driver's seat.

I felt a sudden heavy hand on my shoulder. Startled, my gaze flew up at the person with the hand. "Don't worry Ms. Stevie," Titan smiled, missing a front tooth. "I'll take real good care of your friends." Titan nodded to Aidan, "That son of a bitch over there won't move an inch unless he wants a belly full of lead," he swore. "I got this!"

I smiled at the gentle giant and rubbed his arm. Then my attention focused back to Aidan. "Hold on!" I called out to the Cajun as he juiced the car's engine. I trotted over to Aidan. Just for peace of mind, I wanted to check the rope. I sat on my heels and tugged on the golden fire that encircled his body. I whispered a few words, solidifying the bind.

Once upon a time, I would've never worried about Aidan harming the guys. This *Aidan* was as trustworthy as a cottonmouth. There was a stir in my gut that gave me unease.

Titan might be tough as nails, capable of taking care of himself in any bar brawl. But he was no match against a perfidious druid. Dark magick had a way of gaining momentum even on the most fiercest.

If only I could be in two places at once. I bit my bottom lip, indecisive. What other choice did I have? I had to trust Titan and the magick rope. My gaze collided with Aidan. "If you hurt my friends, I will hunt you down to the far corners of this earth. You got that!" Ice rolled off my tongue.

Aidan's lips flat-lined and his eyes displayed blatant contempt. I stood up, hesitating, then with an abrupt sneer, I spun on my heels, kicking up dirt in his face.

Before I had a chance to climb in the Jeep, the Cajun leaned over to the passenger's side, cutting a firm gaze at me. "I'm in charge. You follow my orders and we live. *Comprende?*" Veins in his neck stood out in livid ridges.

I scoffed at his arrogance. I reckoned he didn't think a woman could handle herself. Or maybe, he felt he was the better man for the position because he'd fought in the Middle East. "Okay, Commander!" I saluted, snappy. "Whatever you say."

"*Bien*! I'll drive first," he barked. "I know how to navigate around all the potholes on the backroad. When we get out on the paved highway, you take the wheel. I'll take watch and handle the bombs."

The reality of the peril we were about to encroach upon was starting to sink in. I took a deep nervous breath and exhaled. "Okay, let's get rolling." I climbed in the passenger's seat and buckled up, clenching the grab bar and grinding my teeth.

Once we neared the outskirts of the city, I took over the wheel.

As we slowly rolled into downtown, I cut the lights so that we might slip past anyone looking for trouble.

The streets were nearly empty, only a handful of folks walking down the sidewalk. It was startling. All of them seemed in a trance, walking mindlessly, faces void of expression. It iced my bones. I thought of the patients at Haven Hospital. Walking and breathing but no light upstairs.

When we turned onto Bourbon Street, my heart squeezed. Only a block ahead, in plain sight, stood three regulators heavily armed. Their weapons were like nothing I'd ever seen. The foreign guns glistened with a weird metal, some sort of clear shield covering it. The barrel had to be the size of a small cannon. A sense of the willies rushed over me. We were screwed. Their advanced arms against our meager guns and homemade bombs were like bringing sparklers to a nuke war. The worst part I couldn't protect us. My unstable magick was useless against their technology. I eased out a prickly sigh.

These fat cats were not your typical police. A staggering seven foot or better in height and massive bodies, these regulators gave advanced science a whole new freak-on. They were clothed in gray uniforms that shined like metal. I couldn't get a good look at their faces. They wore a tinted bubbled shield over their heads. It was weird, the shield shifted, moving to the form of their head. Like nothing I'd ever seen. If I were a betting gal, I'd wager that our atmosphere was incompatible to their environment. If my hunch were right, having that little juice in my back pocket could give us an edge. Smash their helmets and watch 'em suffocate. Cruel, but effective.

Suddenly, my eyes locked onto three silver spheres, hovering a few feet above the regulators. An unnatural humming resonated from the silver balls. They zipped back and forth, turning and twisting. I think they were communicating. I first thought they were drones. Though, the spheres didn't resemble a drone at all or what I imagined, comparing them to Hollywood's version. Apart from popular belief, this was different, a new technology, my guess. The strange spheres were like liquid metal that glinted similar to a mirror, yet they moved like liquid, changing its form from a ball to a flat wafer of paper. Sci-fi movie of the fourth kind, I called it. Not taking my eyes off the strange metal, I whispered. "Nick, look up," I nodded curtly. "In your entire military career, have you ever seen a drone like that?"

The Cajun's eyes followed my fixation. "Damn!" he gasped. "*Non!* Drones do not look like that." He blew a low whistle.

I think for once, the Cajun and I were on the same page. We both knew we had underestimated the hostiles. This uprising placed eerie on a whole new platform.

We didn't utter another word, keeping our eyes glued. Any second this could go bad. I think the Cajun sensed it too by the clench in his jaw.

My eyes caught his, silently cuing for further instructions. The Cajun nodded, urging me to keep driving forward. Adrenaline coursed through my veins as I slowly crept along. My palms were sweaty, gripping the wheel as we slowly rolled past one of the regulators standing guard at the corner. We acknowledged his presence with a curt nod, hoping not to stir suspicion. Sweat beaded across my forehead and began to drip into my left eye. My first reaction was to wipe it off, but I withdrew. Instead, I kept my hands on the wheel with one clear eye.

Despite our caution, I had a whirl of doubts that we had managed to stay under the guards' radar. Blending was the plan, yet I think we made a huge mistake. We were the only ones with a vehicle and our eyes still had life. The locals I saw were on foot. As if marching to the same tune, they all parroted the same slow step and expression.

One of the regulators yelled out to us, "Halt, humans!" Fear stifled my breath. Without so much as a flick, I slipped a sideways glance at the Cajun. He remained poker faced.

I tapped the brake and rolled to an easy stop. My hands were white knuckling the wheel as my heart protested. I sat quiet, not uttering a word, keeping my face emotionless. Sweat poured from under my cap and it itched like a mother. Even still, I didn't make any sudden move. I waited for my cue, anticipating the worst scenarios possible.

The regulator loomed over the Jeep, investigating the contents loaded in the back. Without warning, he drew to attention, speaking sharply. "State your destination." His gruff voice hummed, like he was breathing through a trach tube. I slipped a sideways glance but all I could see was my reflection off the shield of his helmet.

The Cajun spoke, no detection of alarm in his deep voice. "We want to trade goods for food. You like crabs, yes?" the Cajun flashed his pearly whites, keeping his hands raised, as he slowly eased out of the Jeep, making his way to the back. He lifted one of the crate's lid revealing a large catch of snappers. The sound of splashing in the water and claws clicking wafted in the air.

The regulator peered into the crate, and then suddenly leaped backward, shrieking like a banshee. I reckoned it was the alien universal sound of fright. He mumbled something in his native tongue, quickly wagging his weapon at the Cajun, shouting, "Keep that closed! Pass earth-dweller and don't return," he muttered something in his own tongue. Strange enough, his language sounded similar to clicking his tongue over a loud mic. The Cajun jumped back in the Jeep as he slipped me a quick wink. His glint beamed with pride. I'd have to hand it to him, that was a smart move.

Getting past the regulator made us both breathe a little easier. Although, we came to a quick conclusion that we were not out of the alien corral just yet.

Around the corner in the French Quarter, I blinked, doubting my own eyes. The street was completely barren. No lights, no music, not a soul stirring. The once thriving street laid in total darkness. I couldn't believe my own eyes as I combed over the dark buildings. I was just here at *The Royal Café* eating dinner with Dom and Jeffery a few weeks ago. Now, it was gone. All of it was gone! The street was deserted like a long-forgotten ghost town.

Trash and broken glass splayed the street. Most of the buildings had broken windows. I stared blankly as the wind tossed an empty can across the street as it echoed in my ears. Other than our Jeep's engine, the can was the only noise.

I inclined my head slightly, speaking low where only Nick could hear. "I can't believe this is happening." My eyes darted wildly back and forth from one side of the street to the next.

The Cajun touched my shoulder and whispered pointedly. "Hush!"

I nodded, drawing my words to myself. Freaking out while we were in the middle of hell zone wasn't an option. I inhaled a ragged breath and I nearly gagged. The stench in the night's sultry air smelled of decayed, dead bodies. I held my hand to my nose. This took me back to the time when Sam nearly raped me in a field of bones and decay. All those bodies of women that Sam had viciously murdered. I was lucky then, Aidan swooping in and rescuing me from his psycho cousin. I inhaled a despairing sigh. How I wished that Aidan were here now. I shook the memory from my brain. I couldn't afford memory lane right now.

Especially now.

The Cajun tapped my thigh. I glanced down at a red bandana. I took it and parroted him, tying it around my neck and slipping the cloth over my nose and mouth. I nodded to him with a silent thank you.

As we ventured farther down, we spotted more zombie like people, creeping along, dragging their feet, clothes soiled and torn. Sadly, I knew that expressionless face far too well. They were homeless. I rolled past them, watching one by one, as they made their way down the street, heading in the same direction.

I spied several folks ahead, falling in line, farther down the street. I reckoned they had come for food rations. The Cajun and I shared a quick glimpse at each other. If his face mirrored mine, we were both sharing the same horror.

At the front of the line, a regulator hovered over an elderly woman. The creature was holding a small metal device over the woman's wrist. I had my suspicions that he was looking for the number Aidan boldly bragged about the other day, the digits, six six six. A sneaky feeling crept down my spine that it was more than just a mark. They were tagging people. Inserting implants to keep track of every soul or worse, using the tags to control. A sudden sharp twist to the gut made me flinch and I turned to the Cajun, "Nick," I whispered. "Whatever you do don't let them ink you. I think it's affecting the people." I glanced over at him, my eyes brimmed with worry.

Keeping his eyes steady ahead, he barely whispered, "I was thinking the same thing," he exhaled softly. "I think we've seen enough."

Nodding in compliance, I took a sharp turn down Pirate's Alley. The alley was a 600 foot long cobblestone, pedestrian street that ran between St. Louis Cathedral and Cabildo and was one of the most fabled streets in New Orleans, full of wild stories of the infamous, Jean Lafitte. As time passed, the alley seemed more suitable for tourists on foot. Jeffery and I used to grab lunch at the little café, named after the street, *Pirate's Alley Café*.

When I coiled the corner, alarm surged through me. I let up off the gas, gaping in silence. "Nick," I barely mumbled. The Cajun drew in a sharp gasp, though not uttering a word. His eyes held to what laid ahead.

As if it had never existed, the alleyway was in complete ruin, burned to the ground, left only with the stench of feces floating in the night's air and a charred heap scarfing the cobblestone. "They're destroying our city."

"*Oui!* This sickens me too," the Cajun grated, "Let's get out of this hell."

Before Nick and I could pull ourselves together, three regulators stepped out from behind the corner building at the end of the alleyway into plain sight, guns aiming and blocking the exit.

My foot hit the brake, "Nick! We got company."

"Back up, slowly," he spoke low as tension fostered his face. I slowly shifted the gears into reverse and pressed the gas, backing up. Two more regulators stepped from the shadows, barricading us in at both entrances. I knew we were in deep crap up to our necks, maybe more. Hell, we didn't even have an escape plan. Luckily, my daggers laid safely tucked underneath my clothes, sheathed and ready to go into action. Their light hum soothed me.

All at once, Nick snatched a jug of moonshine from the back and hung half his body over the grab-bar of the Jeep, taking a sloppy swig. When he came back up for air, he wiped his mouth with the back of his hand and waved the gallon in the air at the regulators. His words slurred as if he'd polished off the whole jug. "*Hey*, you *b-b-boys* want some *gud* old corn w-whiskey, *yessss?* It will w-wet your whistle and make the ladies spread their legs!" He staggered, taking another big gulp. It was clear to me now that the Cajun was sidetracking their attention from us to the whiskey.

The regulators paused as confusion eddied their stride. Heads snapping amidst each other, and then back at Nick and me.

Our engagement must've startled them. That was a no brainer. I doubted any local was capable of a simple *"hello"*.

I watched, not making a move as they slowly etched forward. Mistrust dabbled the humid air as they approached us, keeping their weapons drawn, pointing straight at our heads. Slowly they etched closer. It seemed his boozehound manner eased the regulators, making them more curious than trigger-happy.

Trapped in the alleyway, Nick and I sat helpless like chickens caught in a hen house with a fox.

Alarm bristled my spine as I hissed under my breath. "Whatever you're doing, it better work!"

The Cajun ignored me as if he'd forgotten that I was sitting in the driver's seat. I stiffened, waiting for the next move either by the Cajun or the regulators. At this point, I wasn't sure which was worse.

Nerves squeezed my gut as I sat there silent, hands clenching the steering wheel, white knuckled and sweaty palms.

I flinched slightly as the regulators corralled the Jeep, banging their weapons against the rear. A downwind draft shimmied up my nose, nearly causing me to lose my cookies. I held my breath to avoid vomiting. I didn't know if it was an alien thing, but their smell reminded me of rotten eggs.

The Cajun was playing the juicehead far too well. I prayed that his acting skills worked. "You soldiers like some of the best homemade moonshine in *New Or-lins?* Gotta jug with your name on it." The Cajun patted the large glass jar as he sloppily leaned over dragging out a couple of bottles and offering them to the regulators.

At first, the creatures hesitated. To my surprise, one regulator snatched one of the jugs from Nick with lightning speed. I stayed quiet while I watched from the corner of my eye, avoiding eye contact. The regulator held the glass jug up looking at the white liquid. He spoke to the others in that strange tongue-clicking dialect.

The large regulator kept shaking his head trying to knock the jug out of his comrade's hand. Finally, the smaller creature holding the jug shoved the larger one back and appeared to be possessive of his new discovery as he raised his voice at the other four. The shorter one lowered his shield, opening his large mouth, tipping the jug to his mouth.

I nearly choked on my breath trying to stifle a gasp. His features were human like, but his skin was scaly, and his eyes were almond shape and cold black.

The short regulator immediately started gasping. He pulled it together and cut his black eyes at Nick. A smiled stretched his scaly face, revealing sharp jagged teeth. He tilted the jug and took another gulp. Nick nodded with approval urging the creature to drink up. "*Gud!* Yes?" he encouraged, smiling.

In the next second, the larger regulator grabbed the other jug from the short one and lowered his shield revealing a very similar face. The bigger one tipped the jug to his cracked lips and wrapped his brown scaly lips around the mouth of the bottle, downing the moonshine.

At that point, they all seemed to share deep interest in our drink. After the ticking of a few moments, the five regulators had lowered their shields, passing the moonshine around. Strangely, their behavior reminded me of humans.

I understood now what the Cajun was doing. He was diverting their attention and it was working. The moonshine was taking effect on the creatures and fast too. Even in their own hideous language, their words were slurring. One of the regulators aggressively leaned into the Jeep shouting at Nick, "Give us more of this strange liquid!" He demanded as he commenced shoving the crates around and nearly knocking over a few.

Nick jumped in the back before our cover was blown, grabbing up more jugs, "Here!" He held two jugs in each hand. "Compliments, please!" It seemed to appease the creatures' burst of anger and appealed to their greedy thirsts. It wasn't long before they'd forgotten about us. They huddled together, guzzling down the corn liquor, laughing and patting each other on the back.

Without delay, the Cajun motioned for me to punch the gas. I gladly put the Jeep in gear and accelerated, burning rubber down the alleyway.

The regulators didn't even bother looking up. I took a sharp turn down Anne Street and hooked it onto Decatur.

But we weren't out of the woods yet. I spotted a regulator heading our way, chasing, and shouting something incomprehensible. I wasn't sticking around to find out what he wanted. I gunned the Jeep picking up speed. Besides, there was nothing I hated worse than a seven-foot alien throwing a temper tantrum in my rearview mirror.

The creature was gaining on us at an inhuman speed. The Cajun shouted, "Floor this damn Jeep!"

I peered in the mirror to see if we were gaining momentum. Unfortunately, our Jeep had nothing on this creature. Just when he grasped the back of the Jeep, the creature hoisted himself up on the cab. With no time to spare, the Cajun slammed a balloon into the creature's face.

The homemade bomb exploded knocking the Cajun off his feet and tumbling on top of me. Lucky for us, the regulator had taken off his shield and the fluid spattered across his face and into his eyes. He screeched like something out of a horror movie. For the Cajun and me, it confirmed our hopes that the bomb would work. The creature fell backwards hitting the hard pavement, face first. The Cajun and I bellowed with triumph, high fiving each other.

STEAL AWAY

*O*nce we got back to the Cajun's house, I wanted to kiss the ground. After I cut the engine, the Cajun jumped out of the Jeep. I slid out of the driver's seat and ran after him. "Wait!" I called to him. "Are you okay?" Not one word uttered between us the whole trip back. I didn't know about the Cajun, but my body was trembling.

The Cajun stopped in his tracks and turned abruptly to face me. A wide smile plagued his face. "*Oui!* That got my motor revved."

"You're kidding? Do you have any concept of what just happened?"

"I do! Aliens are running amok." His dark eyes glistened.

"I think it's a bit more than creatures running haywire. Our world is under siege by freaking aliens!"

The Cajun raked his fingers through his sable waves. "One thing you must know about me," he pointed to his chest, "I know war better than most. I even received a medal of honor. But it meant nothing." His face grew pinched with anger.

"Have you ever fought against creatures such as these?" I stepped up closer, meeting him toe to toe, forcing him to look at me. I had to make him understand what we were up against.

The Cajun's jaw twitched. "War is war, *babé!* I've seen my men who trusted me with their lives get blown to pieces and none of those high-falutin officials cared. My men died for a senseless war. A war that wasn't ours to fight. You say Freedom Fighters. I say there is no freedom in fighting. Those young men didn't have a say. So, in my opinion, it doesn't matter who we fight. We do the best we can with what we have and pray there's a God to deliver us from the Devil himself."

I stood there lost for words. How could I argue? He was right. We didn't fight for *our* freedom. Innocent people gave their lives for leaders that were setup to fail while all along the Illuminati had full sovereignty. Those in the forefront were merely puppets on a string. I inhaled a sharp breath as I replied, "I'm sorry." I jerked my cap off and wiped the sweat from my face with the back of my hand. "You're right." We both stood there in an awkward silence, our eyes glued to each other.

Then my heart lurched. I skimmed the grounds. A strange sensation rushed through me. Everything was too quiet, not even the stir of birds chirping, the cicadas cricking, and the house inside, not one light, just darkness. Something was wrong. The Cajun kept the generator running. And Jeffery didn't like the dark. Even Titan hadn't shown his face. I thought someone would've came out to greet us by now. But there wasn't a peep.

An eerie breeze blew through my damp hair as my blood iced.

"Oh my God, Dom and Jeffery!" My alarm soared to the moon as I sprinted for the house. I called for my knives as they followed my commands, unsheathe, resting on my shoulder, waiting for word to attack. I stepped into the darkness as the Cajun followed closely behind me with his gun in hand and cocked, ready to fire. We padded quietly without a sound throughout the house. No signs of anyone! But all of Dom's and Jeffery's clothes were still here. My pulse raced in my throat as my worse fear began to sink into my skull.

The Cajun called out to me as he switched a light on. "Come here!" he shouted. I followed his stressful voice. The Cajun was standing in the kitchen by the table holding a note. Quickly, I snatched it from his hand and read it out loud.

Sorry to leave before saying my good-byes. I'm taking the boys with me. If you want your little gay friends, you know where to find them. Don't wait too long. They may end up like your friend.

When we meet again,

Before I took my next breath, the Cajun had charged out the door, heading straight for the storage. I raced after him as my gut roiled every step of the way. I sensed this wasn't good. I could smell Titan's fate wafting in the air.

When the Cajun threw open the doors, the stench struck our nostrils, jolting us back. I gagged, covering my mouth. The unusual heat had sped up the decay making the fetor more than insufferable. Holding back vomit, I tugged my bandana over my mouth and nose.

The Cajun slowly entered the storage, dropping to his knees, his face stricken with grief.

I gasped realizing the ferocity of what length Aidan would go to was terrifying.

Titan's body hung on two heavy oak limbs, tied with my rope into a cross, nails driven into his hands, legs, and one large stake pierced through his head.

As if frozen in time, Titan's face was the poster of horror. His mouth stretched wide into an O as if he'd been screaming at the top of his lungs. I had a strong suspicion that Titan's death was a slow torturous one. His missing eyeballs were now an empty cavity brimmed with blood. As if he'd been dipped into a bucket of scarlet red paint, his whole face and beard were saturated. Shear black fear pummeled through my skull as my eyes raked over Titan's body. Guts dangled from the gaping hole in his stomach and by the deep indentions that wrapped around his neck, my guess was that Aidan had slit his throat.

I spied bloody handprints over the cross and Titan's body. I suspected the handprints belonged to Aidan. Footprints, large and smaller ones collected around Titan's body. It was clear to me that two people were involved. One being a *woman.*

If I were a betting gal, I'd bet it was Sally. Who else would come to rescue Aidan and assist in a gruesome murder? *His uncle, Van?* Possibly, but I doubted it. Van would've sent for one of his MIB, *men in black.*

I had to admit that this murder didn't seem like the work of Aidan. It was too messy for a 300-year-old druid. To put it candidly, Aidan didn't do sloppy. Everything about Aidan was precise, right down to the last detail. Keeping that little tidbit in mind had me muddled. The details about this murder screamed volumes to look deeper.

The untidy letter came to mind. Whoever wrote the letter had unsteady hands. Like someone nervous. Aidan didn't do shaky.

Nothing made sense. My brain told me Aidan murdered Titan, yet there weren't any telltale signs that this was his doing.

For example, I noticed the trail of blood through the yard, up the steps, leading to inside the storage room. Obviously, they had dragged Titan's body. That seemed odd to me.

They called him Titan for a reason. The man outstood most with a height nearly seven feet and his belt size most likely had to be special ordered.

Why would a druid do such a human task? Aidan could've killed Titan with the flick of his hand and conjured up a cross with Titan's body nailed to it, not getting even a drop of blood on himself or anything else. He certainly wouldn't need assistance. It was clear Titan's death had a meaning, definitely a sadistic one, but this wasn't the work of a druid. It was more like a human with tons of strength.

I saw how easily Aidan had taken down a fey, Sam, and disposed of his body in a matter of minutes. I inhaled a ragged breath. My eyes combed over the murder scene as I shook my head, puzzled. I didn't see the consistency in the two murders.

I glanced over to the Cajun. He was taking his friend's death hard. Understandably. Tears swelled. This was my fault. If I'd just gone off on my own, Titan would be alive, and the guys would be safe too. Aidan only took Dom and Jeffery because he knew how important they were to me. What a fool I'd been, thinking that my rope would've kept him captive. Aidan had tricked me and now I had cost human lives.

My stomach started to erupt as I darted for the deck, stopping in the nick of time, puking up my guts. I'd seen gruesome things in my life before, but this was incomparable.

After I finished, I wiped my mouth with my sleeve and collapsed on the steps. I buried my head into my palms as my body shook, racked with sobs. I reckoned that was the human in me.

I heard the Cajun murmuring curse words and feeble prayers in French as he pulled out the nails from Titan's body. My heart ached for him and I wanted to console him. Despite my good intentions, I knew he blamed me for this tragedy. I was sure that my face was the last thing he wanted to see.

"God!" I shivered trying to make sense of this monstrosity. That poor man was tortured to death. This murder or more appropriately, butchering, was a message. Aidan had left that especially for me. He meant to frighten me, and it worked. Any humanity that Aidan once possessed had been totally depleted, leaving him nothing short of a monster. He had taken my family. I feared the worst. I had to pull myself together and get Jeffery and Dom back before Aidan hurts them like he did Titan. I hoped as long as they remained a bargaining tool, Aidan would keep them alive. "Geez!" I raked my fingernails over my face. How would we all survive this devastation? I hadn't a clue what I should do next. How was I supposed to find them? I might have angel blood, but I didn't have a GPS. I didn't even have wings.

Heavy footsteps startled me. I stiffened as my eyes froze on the Cajun's face, his eyes blazing murderously. With no warning, he grabbed me by my collar and jerked me to my feet. His deep inky eyes glistened with raw odium as he snarled in my face, "I thought you said that *couillon* (scoundrel) was tied down. Obviously, your magic rope didn't work. Or did you loosen it so he could get away?" The Cajun dropped his grip, shoving me backward, twisting my feet into a near stumble, but I caught the railing.

I shot back. "I did check the rope! Do you think I wanted this too?" My tears swallowed up my last word.

A swift shadow of rage swept across the Cajun's face. "*Non!* Stop crying!" he leaned closer. "You didn't do a good enough job! My *ami* is *dead* and most likely your boys are too!"

I shoved the Cajun out of my personal space, "I know better than anyone what Aidan's capable of *doing*! I'm-I'm sorry for your friend." Tears rolled down my cheeks as I wiped them with my sleeve.

"What kind of fucking creature is your ex-lover?"

"Stop calling him my ex!" I shouted. My shame quickly turned into stabbing anger.

"There's something unearthly about that boy. That upside-down cross is suspended in air! Floating! No wires dangling it. Can you explain that to me?"

"What?" I was caught off guard. "What are you talking about?"

84

The Cajun grabbed my arm, dragging me along with his deep stride. "Come see for yourself!" he bit out through gritting teeth.

Standing in the doorframe, the Cajun dropped his grip abruptly. I glared at him as if he'd lost his damn mind. "Tell me what you see."

I studied the cross up to the rope that tied the cross to the beam. I turned to the Cajun. "The cross isn't floating." I pointed to one of the high beam. "Don't you see the yellow rope?" I stared back at him.

The Cajun sputtered, bristling with indignation. "Are referring to *your* rope?"

My brows dipped into a scowl. "No! I mean the rope hanging from the beam."

He stared, complete disgust on his face. "*Non!* I see only your magical rope. *Vous devez être aveugle!* (You must be blind!)"

"Me blind!" I shouted. "You're the blind one here!"

By the lines of his tight face, I could see that we both were on the brink of insanity.

"I don't see a rope!" he grated.

Then as it hit me, my eyes orbed like golf balls. "I think I know what's happening here."

"Spit it out!"

I looked up at the rope and then my eyes locked onto the Cajun's face. "It's not real, Nick! What you are seeing is an illusion. The kind of illusions fey create."

"I am not imagining things!"

"What you are seeing is something like a mirage."

"Are you saying Titan is not dead?"

"No, no! I'm sorry, but Titan is gone. I think Sally came to help Aidan escape. She has to be fey." My eyes kept shifting back and forth to Titan's body and then to the Cajun. "It makes sense."

"Maybe to you but not to me." The Cajun threw his hands to his hips, shooting bullets at me.

"Listen to me!" I demanded, wishing I could slap some sense into him. "Your grandmother had the gift and you know that Val and I are angels."

The Cajun didn't deign to answer.

"Look, I know how crazy it sounds but think about it. You know humans are not the only creatures. The night before Aidan and Sally took me away, Sam had tricked me into believing that he was Aidan.

Sam had taken me to a field of lilies. Only it was an illusion. Fey cannot conjure up tangible items. Underneath the glamor, I was standing in a field of bones and decay." I pointed to the yellow rope. "What you are seeing is a Fey's glamor, an *illusion*." I gave pause. "I think Aidan's partner, Sally, is fey."

"Huh! Like little fairies with wings, yes?" The Cajun made a mocking gesture with his fingers.

"Nick, that's fairytale stuff. Fey are vile and evil. They are notorious for their skullduggery." I suddenly felt my stomach roil once again. In a snap, I spun on my heels and headed out to the deck. I needed fresh air.

I stopped at the steps and bent over, hands on my knees to brace myself for my next purge. Guilt, loathing, and sorrow weighed heavily on my chest. I hated myself right now.

The Cajun startled me when he came up from behind. "Are you, alright?" His gentle voice pierced my thoughts.

I squared my shoulders, standing up, wiping my mouth with the back of my hand as our eyes locked. "No, I don't think either one of us are going to be okay. Not after today."

"It sure is looking that way, yes?" The Cajun quiet for a moment. "What is this creature you once loved?"

"Aidan's immortal and he draws dark magick from his druid heritage," I said. "He's invincible."

"I remember you calling him druid." The Cajun exhaled a raspy breath, "I thought that was a nickname. And he can't die!" the Cajun half yelled at me. "How could you have forgotten to mention this little piece of information to me?" The insolence in his voice was sharp as a razor.

"Honestly, I don't know why!" I swallowed hard. My throat ached from sheer guilt. "I thought I had Aidan contained."

"What else are you not telling me?" Nick's face darkened like a thunderstorm. "Don't hold back!"

I couldn't look him in the eyes. His dark eyes glistened with pain and enmity. I held my gaze to the tree line. "I think Aidan's trying to draw me out from hiding. That much I am certain of. Why else would he have taken Dom and Jeffery?"

The Cajun stood there gawking at me with the look of wanting to throttle me. Under the heat of his blaze, I felt like crawling under a rock. But I knew that checking out wouldn't make any of this go away. I had to be accountable for my mistakes even if it meant my death.

The Cajun spoke through clenched teeth. "I have to bury my friend. Then we need to get the hell out of here. It's not safe." He stalled for a moment as if he wanted to say something else. Then without another word, he stormed off.

I watched as he disappeared behind the back of the house. I whirled on my heels, not sure what I should do next. I needed to help, to be useful.

Nick had a right to be angry with me. I had cost him his best friend's life and possibly Dom and Jeffery's too. I should've stayed behind to guard Aidan myself. Titan should've gone with Nick. Why didn't I listen to Jeff?

I struggled, fighting off a meltdown. Tears were pushing to the forefront. Instead of letting go, I bit against the burn.

My eyes stalled on the chopped up oak that once held Aidan captive. I stared at it as a gentle breeze rustled through my hair. Curiosity jump kicked me into action as I stalked down the steps and over to the once thriving tree.

As my eyes skimmed the ground, I spotted tracks... *Aidan's*. Somehow, he'd managed to cut himself free of my magickal rope but not without injury. Scarlet red churned in the dirt. Lots of it too.

I spotted a procession of footprints mixed with a lot of blood. Three different sizes circled the tree. The soil and bloodshed disturbed the ground as if Freddie Krueger had driven a John Deer tractor through a crowd of bystanders. Apparently, there was a struggle. It looked like Titan had given Aidan a good fight.

The night was embarking, and a strange chill hung in the air as I shivered. I spotted the security light. It was out. From what I could tell, someone had thrown a rock, busting the bulb. Tiny pieces of glass pooled around the pole and a large rock laid only a couple of feet away. I scratched my head, baffled. Taking in account of a bloody brawl and a light bulb busted, which none of this made any sense. Why would Aidan get into a physical altercation with a human? Come to think about it... since Aidan's return, I hadn't seen him do one magick act. More missing pieces to add to the puzzle.

I turned around and found more footsteps leading to the house. I could quickly pick out the sizes and the kind of tread on the bottom.

Aidan's footprints were easy. Jeffery's and Dom's too. I squatted to get a closer look. By the shuffle in the dirt, it appeared that the guys were forced against their will. It was as though they had been dragged out of the house. Fear dug into my chest.

Suddenly my eyes landed on tire tracks. These set of tracts belonged to an unknown car. On the left side of the tracks, I spotted a female's footprints. Small though wide, like a chubby person. The same bloody footprints in the shed. My suspicions were confirmed that Sally was somewhere in the mix of this crime.

I noticed the flurry of footprints stopped, ending on the right side of the tire tracks. It appeared the wheels sped out, kicking up a huge cloud of dirt. Obviously, they were in a rush.

I found that strange. If Aidan were in a hurry, why would he wait for transportation when he could've materialized to any location in seconds?

I inhaled a sharp breath, biting my bottom lip. It didn't matter that Sally or Tom Dick and Harry had helped Aidan escape. The height of my worry was that Aidan was free and unpredictably dangerous and all the more reason why I had to find him before he killed Dom and Jeffery.

THE LION'S DEN

J stood quietly as the Cajun threw on the last shovel of dirt. He marked the grave with a couple of plyboards nailed together. He carved into the wood Titan's legal name,

John Mack, CPL US Marine Corps, Afghanistan War 2012-2015
Born: July 15, 1986, Died: July 9, 2020

It was short and to the point. The Cajun whispered a few words to his dear friend. I stood back a few feet, quiet, feeling like an intruder. I gulped down the knot lodged in my throat. I didn't have a right to cry. So, I swallowed the pain and didn't dare utter a word.

Once Nick finished giving his respect, our eyes locked for the first time since he'd left me to go bury Titan. "We need to get going. The boat's loaded with supplies." His words were cold, and all emotions depleted. I knew better though. Inside, the man was broken over the loss of his friend. I admired his strength and hated his condemning eyes that singed my heart. Though the blame was all mine. I'd carry that blame for the rest of my life, too.

"The boat?" I was taken aback.

"You have a problem riding in a boat?" He brushed the remaining dirt from his hands as a faint line appeared between his brows.

"We have to go looking for Jeffery and Dom!"

"Are you *crazy*?" the Cajun growled. "Those boys are dead!"

"Don't say that!"

"We go back to town and we are as good as dead, gul!"

I stood my ground, determined. "Fine! I'll go without you."

The Cajun stood silent for a moment, staring a hole through me. Then he said with a huff, "You don't even know where to look."

"There's a good chance that Aidan's holding the guys hostage at his mansion on the outskirts of town. We can take the backroads. It should be safe enough."

The Cajun's face took on the look of an angry bear. "Past the sugar cane fields?"

"Yes."

"Are you that naïve or just stupid?" his voice grated harshly. "You're walking into a trap."

"I still have to go!"

The Cajun stepped up even closer, looming over me. "Do you think he's going to hand over your love ones?" his lips tightened as his hands flexed into a tight ball. "That *le diable* (devil) is too fucking evil."

My eyes tensed, no flinching as I held my stance. "He might not have a choice if I kill him."

"You think you can kill that bastard?" Doubt laced his voice. "*Non!* You won't." he flashed a seedy grin.

"Where's your faith in me, Nick?" Any kindred feelings for Aidan had been long gone. I blamed him for the loss of my child. And now, he'd taken the only two people in the world that meant anything to me. "You've underestimated me." I spoke in a mere whisper but there was nothing calm about my words or my intentions.

"You might have angel magick," he said as he fingered his two-day-old stubble, "but it's not going to do much good, gul. *You* still love him." The Cajun's words stabbed me viciously.

"Listen, Cajun!" I jabbed my finger into his chest. "The Aidan I once loved is not in that animal that killed your friend and kidnapped my family. The Aidan I once loved is dead!" I clenched my teeth. "Dead! *Il est mort* (he is dead)! Got that?"

"I heard you the first time!"

"Good! Don't get it confused." I stormed off jumping in the Jeep. I tossed over my shoulder, not looking at his face. "You coming or staying? Either way, I'm going after that son of a bitch!"

He hesitated kicking at the dirt. "Fine!" he grinded out. "Give me a minute. I need to radio the others and warn them." He swiftly spun on his heels darting into the house. I laid my head on the steering wheel and let out a scream of frustration. How the hell did I get myself into this mess? The world was crumbling around me. My family was gone, taken as hostages. I'd give anything to go back in time to a much simpler life. I wished I were eight again and my dad was alive. I wished Sara hadn't fallen prey to greed and I'd been born an average child. Rather than a freak created in a lab by the Illuminati's scientist. Boy, I didn't want much.

~

The Cajun insisted on driving. I didn't have it in me to argue. So, I gladly gave him the wheel as I slid to the passenger seat. We were off down the dirt road and on the major highway before the Cajun struck up a conversation. The Cajun cleared his throat. "I apologize for accusing you of …"

I butted in, stopping him in midstream, "Nick! Don't! I should've stayed behind. Titan's death is my fault. I was wrong not warning you or Titan about Aidan's magick." I let out a painful sigh. "You were right." Our eyes met briefly, and I saw pity in the Cajun's eyes. I hated it too.

For the remainder of the ride, we didn't talk. Although, I felt torn about the Cajun coming, even still, I was glad. He may be human, though he proved his usefulness. I only hoped I didn't get him killed. Too much bloodshed had been spilt already.

When we got on the edge of the city, the Cajun drew me from my thoughts. "Where is the bastard's mansion?"

My face twisted, lips squeezed, full of apprehension. I knew he wasn't going to like what I had to say next. The truth was sort of tucked away in my pocket. "Hmm, I wasn't entirely honest with you." I said feeling unease. "Aidan's not holding the men at his mansion. It's actually on Bourbon Street at Val's bar."

"You got to be fucking kidding me!" he clenched his jaw.

I shrugged.

"You purposely lied to me!" A slew of French curses paraded from his mouth.

I eased a sharp sigh. "I did. I had to!"

"*Non!* I'm not dying for you!" Swiftly, he cut the steering wheel to the left, heading back.

With no time to waste, I went into action. My angel powers kicked into gear. Before he knew what had happened, I'd thrown him to the back of the Jeep as I swiftly slid into the driver's seat. With my foot on the break, I twisted in my seat, staring back at him as he lay wedged between two crates. "Look!" My voice rose. "You promised Val you'd protect me! Are you a man of your word or not?" I was wearing determination like an armored suit. The Cajun was going with me whether he liked it or not. In my book, a promise was a promise.

The look of shock veiled his face for a minute. Grumbling to himself, with more French curse words, he managed to wiggle himself free from the two crates. Sitting up, he sneered. "True. I promised Valor. *But* I didn't sign up for this!" The exasperation in his voice came out like a swift, left hook. "While serving my country, I saw enough death that I wish I could erase from my mind. Every time I close my eyes, those images haunt me." He glimpsed away, pain colored his face as if he were reliving the atrocities. His gaze returned back to me. "Good soldiers blown to pieces with their intestines hanging out. Or their bodies ripped in two, lying in their own pool of blood." He raked his fingers roughly through his brown hair. "But this has me breaking out in a cold sweat. Not because I fear death. I've kissed the face of death more times than I care to count. What I fear is those poor people. They're getting slaughtered for nothing. It's like the Holocaust all over again. Only this time, it's every human being regardless of race. And the worst part, we've lost the fucking battle before it's begun. Our world isn't ours any longer. The human race is an endangered species. How can we fight that?"

It was hard listening to him. I felt his pain and shared his pessimism. "Those are my concerns too," I pushed. "If we don't fight, they'll surely win. Isn't it better to at least give it our all?" My eyes pleaded with him.

His deep browns softened. "Those two boys mean a lot to you, yes?"

I held my breath for a second. That damn knot in my throat again. I swallowed. "I'd give my life for them." Tears collected, burning my eyes.

The Cajun half teased. "*Only your life*? I thought you loved these boys?" his lip tipped up, almost into a smile. Then a cold silence fell between us. He went on to say, "We're headed straight for the lion's den. Those little bastards better appreciate me risking my ass."

I smiled back, half laughing. "They will be but be easy on the skinny one. He's just full of piss and vinegar."

The Cajun laughed shaking his head. "Hell, let's get this party started. I hate being late to a fight," he leaped into the passenger seat. I put the stick in gear and punched the pedal to the metal.

It was well after midnight when we slowly rolled onto Bourbon Street. Strangely, the stars weren't out and as far as I could tell, there wasn't any cloud coverage either. The sky was a vacuum of blackness. Farther down the street, there was a heavy cloud of fog. Right away, I sensed an eeriness that lodged in my throat. I didn't like the look of this one bit.

I cut the lights, hoping we'd go unnoticed. The street was vacant. Not even the locals were to be seen. The air felt nulled as if the atmosphere suffered from depletion of oxygen. Sulfur lingered in my mouth, along with the stifling humidity. Not the usual Louisiana sultry heat, but something else, something *unnatural*.

Once we reached Val's bar, I spotted the sign that once lit the sidewalk with its bright neon lights. Now only one bulb flickered. An annoying buzz skidded down my spine as the sign squeaked on its last hinge. Just like every other establishment downtown, Val's bar lacked the vibrant life it once formerly possessed. A sense of loss washed over me as I quietly inhaled a sharp breath.

Jarring me from my thoughts, the Cajun nudged me to park under the stairwell. I nodded in compliance. I eased the Jeep up on the curve and parked it under the stairwell. It was a tight fit, but I managed to pull it off. The shadows promised safety rather than parking the Jeep in the street. With the streetlights out, the Jeep camouflaged into the darkness.

With my magickal daggers following closely behind like faithful pets, I jumped from the driver's seat and started for the stairs. The Cajun swiftly grabbed my upper arm, halting me. One of my daggers swiftly dropped between the Cajun and me, hovering right in his face, ready to deliver a fatal blow to the head.

He raised his palms surrendering, slowly backing up. "I mean no harm. I simply want to take the lead," he explained, agitated. "Do you mind calling your dog off?" he whispered angrily, nodding to my dagger.

"Sorry! She's trained to attack upon any aggression."

"That's why you should keep your puppies in an ironclad lockbox."

At a flick of the wrist, my dagger returned to her previous position.

The Cajun cocked his pistol, quietly advancing up the stairwell. I followed just as light-footed. I nearly laughed at his little gun. Looking at our visitors' weaponry, I'd reckon around this neck of the woods, his choice of protection was useless. I hoped luck was on our side that he wouldn't have to use it.

Without making a sound, we halted at Val's apartment door. The Cajun leaned in, putting his ear to the door, listening for any signs of life. He raised his gun up to his shoulder. Our eyes locked as he nodded for us to proceed.

Obviously, he didn't detect anything alarming. He may have felt the close was clear, but if I were right about *this* Aidan, the silence meant trouble.

The Cajun gently jiggled the doorknob. The knob didn't budge. He glanced back at me and whispered in my ear, "Do you have any suggestions?"

I paused, biting my bottom lip. I had to get inside Val's pad. Aidan could've left a clue.

Funny, how things just came to me. It was like breathing. I didn't know how I knew but I just did. I quietly stepped past the Cajun and stood in front of the door. I placed my hand around the knob and whispered a few druid words, twisting my hand a certain angle, snapping my wrist. The door crept open. I smiled to myself. At least, something good came from my infusion with Aidan.

The Cajun blinked at me in disbelief. The starkness in his eyes painted a vivid picture. We stepped inside. The pad was empty. No sign of life. The Cajun grabbed a chair setting it under the doorknob. It might secure the door for a minute, long enough for us to draw our weapons. Even then, I had my doubts. Judging by the size of one of those creatures, it wouldn't take much of a shove to jar the door open.

The Cajun pulled out his flashlight, giving us a steady stream of light to scout out Val's place. As my eyes combed over the dusty apartment, a swirl of memories came to mind. A touch of sadness struck me as I flopped down on the couch. I felt jilted. Val left us here alone to fend for ourselves. His race meant more to him than the guys and my safety and the safety of these poor people who were defenseless. The sting of disappointment grated against me and all I wanted to do was lay my face into my hands and have a good cry. But big girls didn't cry. I pushed off the couch and said to the Cajun, "Nick, there's nothing here except dust and empty memories."

"Let's move on to his bar," I huffed. The Cajun ignored my suggestion and started dragging out Val's frozen food from the freezer.

"What are you doing?"

"Val left all this food, beef, ribs, TV dinners, pot pies. The food's still frozen. It's wasting here."

I stood there blinking, just staring, mouth gaping. Then I yielded. What did I care? Val had left and no hope of him ever returning. "Go ahead!" I waved my hand. "I reckon your right."

"I don't recall needing your permission," the Cajun flashed a seedy grin. "But thanks anyway." He grabbed a trash bag from under the sink and raked the frozen foods inside the bag, tying it up. He shouldered the bag as we exited the apartment. It tugged on me taking Val's food. I didn't know why it bothered me. I reckoned it hit home knowing that I'd never see Val again. I suddenly stopped. Thinking about a past that no longer existed was only punishing myself. I had to get my head in the game. So, I pushed my feelings down to the dark place where forgetful memories lie. I had enough to worry about than fretting over some stupid food and a man. Tomorrow would be a brand new day and a whole set of different problems. Life sure was grand, I laughed to myself bitterly.

After leaving Val's pad, we eased our way down to the bar. When we reached the entrance, we stopped abruptly. The Cajun and I shared a brusque glance as suspicion between us went red alert. Someone had been here, leaving the double doors open.

My breath hung in my throat as the Cajun calmly eased the door wider. The door creaked, taking me to some horror flick. With his gun cocked, the Cajun went first. I stayed on his heels with my trusty knives hovering close to my shoulders.

When we stepped inside, we were quickly doused with blackness. The Cajun flipped on his flashlight and carefully combed over the establishment. I shook my head, disgusted. "This has to be the handy work of the regulators. They ransacked the place!" The chairs were disheveled, and thrown about, along with the broken and dismantled tables that were not much more than splinters of wood.

"*Baise-moi!*" the Cajun cursed softly. "These regulators are grimy bastards."

"Let's check out the storage." I nudged the Cajun.

"You lead."

To our surprise, nothing had been disturbed. Liquor bottles were in order in the showcase behind the register. "*Nous sommes de la chance! De l'alcool!* (We are in luck. Alcohol!) the Cajun mumbled with glee. Wasting no time, he made a beeline for the shelved liquor, snatching the bottles down, stacking them in an empty crate.

I stood there glaring at him. "Have you lost your damn mind?" I held my stance with my hands resting on my hips. "This isn't a looting party!"

I ordered my knives to return back to their sheath. I felt safe enough to put my girls back. There was no immediate threat of any intruders in the bar.

The Cajun gathered a box in his arms and pointedly replied, "*Oui!* I remember well and I might as well make the best of this lousy search and rescue," he grinned heading for the Jeep.

I rolled my eyes, but I didn't try to stop him. Let him have all the liquor in the world. He might be easier to deal with perhaps. I spotted a bottle of Jack Daniels and snatched it off the bar. I opened the fresh bottle as my mouth watered for the soothing gold liquid. Hell, a little liquor might lift our spirits a bit. I threw my head back and guzzled down a strong gulp. It burned all the way down as I coughed up air, but the numbness soon kicked in and all I could think about was drinking myself into a stupor. I needed a moment to check out just to reboot.

I found my way to the back. The walk-in cooler was still cold and soothing against the sultry heat that had been astronomical. I wanted to bathe in it. The coolness gave my skin chills, but it felt so good against my singeing skin. I pulled my cap off and wiped the sweat off my forehead. I blew out a relaxing sigh. "Whew! I'd forgotten how good air conditioning felt." I closed my eyes and took another swig of the liquor. I couldn't remember the last time I had a good night's sleep. Then I thought about Dom and Jeffery. A pain stabbed at my heart. I needed to think where Aidan could've taken the guys. My mind just drew a blank as I gulped down more whiskey.

When the Cajun returned, he found me sitting on the floor leaning back against a shelf. He paused for a brief second, and then joined me on the floor. Not uttering a word, the Cajun reached over taking the bottle from my grip, turning it up to his lips, taking a long swig. "Too sweet!" He drew the bottle from his mouth, scowling, and passed it back to me.

"My mom liked Jack Daniels."

"Where is your *mère* (mother) now?"

"Dead," I stated as I took another drink and passed it back.

"How did she die?" the Cajun asked, taking the bottle.

"She was poisoned by angel dust."

"Angel dust?"

"Yeah, it's crushed up fey gems. It's very potent and deadly."

"How did your *mère* find such a rare concoction?"

"The dust belonged to Aidan." I never was one for beating around the bush.

No more than my admittance, the Cajun started coughing after he'd swallowed a huge gulp of liquor. I reckoned he wasn't ready for that shocker. "Your boyfriend poisoned your own *mère*?!" he choked out the words.

"I once thought it was my doing. I had Aidan give her just enough for her to forget the death of her boyfriend, Francis. I didn't want her to suffer." I grabbed up the bottle and guzzled down a healthy dose.

"Instead, it killed her?" The Cajun finished my sentence.

I grinned bitterly. "I was told by a questionable source that it was Aidan's adopted sister, Helen, who finished my mother off. But that little fact didn't help my case any. I still got charged for three deaths. My mom and two of her boyfriends.

"Merde! Did you do time?"

"Yep! They sent me up the river to an insane asylum."

The Cajun began coughing again over his drink. Finally, when his scratchy voice returned, he asked, "Are you guilty *and* insane?" Surprise siphoned the color from his face.

"Nope, I'm innocent. Van, Aidan's uncle, and a legion of Illuminist, set me up. Once I gave birth to my child, they didn't feel threatened any longer. So, they released me."

"*Merde*! You are mighty young to have been through such a turbulent life."

"I'm a survivor," I shrugged. "What about you? What do you do for a living before our world was jerked out from under us?"

"*Moi*!" he grinned to himself. "Contrary to popular belief, I happen to be a doctor. My *grand mere* instilled that in me. She practiced medicine in the unconventional way. She worked with herbs and magic potions for healing."

"Really! My neighbor dealt in the same stuff. She once read my future." A sudden sting of heartburn struck. "My neighbor warned me about Aidan.

The Cajun laughed. "Hell! Even I could've seen that coming."

I smiled but it was burdened with sadness. "Yeah, I was easily fooled back then." I shifted my eyes away. "I liked your grandmother. Even though I had met only her ghost. She was very intuitive and seemed to know things before I had a clue," I smiled.

"*Oui!* I was taken aback when you delivered her message. I'd been a bad grandson. I should've painted her house." A faint light twinkled in the depth of his black eyes.

"I remember," I laughed softly.

Then the Cajun abruptly changed the direction of our light conversation. "He's your first, yes?"

Why did he go there of all people? I answered begrudgingly, "Yes, first of everything. In the beginning, I fought my feelings. I knew he'd break my heart. I just didn't realize the magnitude. It's quite terrifying when your life is taken away and you've lost everyone you ever loved."

His mouth curved into an unconscious smile. "I can't imagine you afraid of anything."

"Are you kidding!" I snorted. "I'm afraid of my own shadow. In fact, I am petrified." I grabbed the bottle back and took a huge gulp.

"That sounds pretty human to me."

I grinned, wiping my mouth with the back of my hand. "Yeah, that's what I keep telling myself."

For a minute reticence fell between us as we passed the Jack Daniels between us.

Then I asked, "That night at the barbeque when we first met... why did you kiss me?" I glanced down at the bottle. My cheeks flushed.

"I thought you needed to be kissed by a real man," he laughed to himself. "*Non!* The real truth is that I thought you were beautiful, full of fire that I couldn't resist the temptation."

When he handed the bottle back to me, I paused gripping the bottleneck, "And now you hate me?"

"*Non!*" he shook his head, brows colliding into a furrow. "I don't hate you," he smiled. "I rather admire you. To be so young, you're a brave soldier. I'd be proud to serve with you."

"Really?" Suddenly, I glanced up meeting his eyes.

"You have heart and courage," his soft browns searched longingly into my gaze. I sat there still in the moment as the Cajun leaned toward me, his eyes filled with tenderness.

I froze, uncertain of what to do.

Startled by a loud clatter from outside. We both froze. Robotic voices sounded angry and agitated. The Cajun and I both vaulted to our feet and sprinted to the front door. He leaned against the wall by the door and I stood across on the other side. He'd cocked his pistol, gripping it in both hands. My magickal daggers were out, hovering over my shoulder and ready for attack. We both listened intently. Neither one of us at that moment dared to breathe.

After a few seconds, we heard heavy footsteps. My horrified eyes locked with the Cajun's. With alarm strapped to our boots, we didn't have to guess who was making the ruckus. The *regulators* were pillaging through our Jeep. *Crap!* If they took our ride, we were screwed.

In a blink of an eye our dilemma exploded. The Cajun decided to do a James Bond move. Without warning, he hit the doors, ducking, and rolling, firing his gun.

I lurched to my feet, staying on the Cajun's heels with my daggers ready for action. I ran for cover behind the light post. In a flash, gunfire went off... *Bang! Bang! Bang!* Shots blasted in my ears.

Unable to see past the dark smoke and shadows, the Cajun's voice pierced the murk, calling my name. Then silence devoured all sound. An eerie silent shifted the air. Before I knew it, three regulators were right on top of us, firing back at both Nick and me. The creatures' weapons far surpassed our technology. The Cajun and his small pistol didn't have a chance against their high-power weaponry.

All of a sudden, I heard a loud humming like a swarm of bees. I looked up to the dark sky and spied three objects that appeared to operate on their own cognizance, intelligence of the fourth kind. They appeared similar to the drones we saw earlier. They were made of some unknown substance that reminded me of molten metal. The strange drones had no solid form. They were clear like a bubble and their shape kept changing like liquid.

One spotted me and hummed to the other drones. It was communicating. In less than a blink, its silver shine grew into a flaming ball of fire. One of my knives shot up and pierced the center of the thing. It sputtered with a fight, fluttering like a butterfly dipping up and down. It finally lost its power, crashing to the ground, exploding, and shooting sparks in every direction. I ducked behind a trashcan but ended up struck as I cried in silence from the sheer burn.

I no more caught my breath when I spotted a speedy missile soaring straight for me. I hit the ground, but the missile still charged at me. It was as though it had some kind of sensor. Quickly, I bolted for cover as the missile stayed hot on my tail. It was only inches from blowing me to smithereens. I dove into the alleyway right before the missile crashed into the corner of the building. A huge chunk of brick and mortar exploded, shattering into a powdery dust. I hid behind a bin that spilled with decaying trash. I was in luck. I think the stench threw off the missile as it returned to the regulators.

I sat there for a second trying to calm my trembling nerves. As much as I wanted to find cover and hide, I knew I had to get to Nick.

Trembling with unsteady legs, I got to my feet and carefully peered around the corner. *Damn!* The regulators had the Cajun, kicking him viciously as he lay there on the concrete sidewalk helplessly. Those damn bullets he fired only irritated the creatures. I watched as sweat beaded across my forehead and my hands shook like a three-day-old drunk. I couldn't just stand here and watch. The regulators were brutally torturing the Cajun, leaving him in his own pool of blood while they took turns kicking the crap out of him. With each forceful blow, his body rose up off the ground. If I didn't act fast, he wouldn't last long.

I had my knives tucked behind me. I didn't want them spotted. Taking a deep breath for courage, I stepped out into the wide open. "Hey!" I yelled sauntering down the sidewalk encroaching upon them. "It's not fair three against one!" A smirk played across my face as I spread my arms a part daring them. "Come fight a Zop!" I taunted. Funny, when they heard the word " Zop" they all three stopped and turned their reptile eyes on me. They knew my race and a sense of pride came over me. "That's right you, *circle-jerks*, I'm part of the Zophasmin race." I flashed a seedy grin.

The big one spoke out, "It's because of you, angel, that we lost five of our kind," he snarled. "You must pay for your crimes!" The three regulators started growling and hissing like animals. Eeriness ignited through me.

I acted on instinct, calling to my essence and it answered with glee. The regulators pointed their weapons at me and fired. This time, I deflected the deadly missiles, thrusting my palms out. To my disbelief, the bombs ricocheted off me as if an impenetrable barrier stood between me and the missiles.

The regulators halted, reptile eyes widened with astonishment. That was when I swung into action. Quickly, I ordered my magickal daggers to attack. Upon command, they soared through the air, whizzing past me, hilt over blade, with perfect precision until they stopped with fatal impact, ramming its deadly blade through each lizards' skull. The sound of skin and bone cracking wafted into the humid night. Immediately following, sulfur filled my nostrils. I reckoned that was the stench of their blood.

They all spewed blue toxin and screeched like hyenas dropping to the ground with a loud thud. Their bodies seized, limbs thrashing nonsensically and then they stilled, bodies went limp. I counted my lucky stars that they were down. With all the blue liquid puddling around them, I presumed if they weren't dead, they soon would be.

My attention shot to the Cajun as I raced to his side. Fear pulled through me, terrified that I might be too late. I slid to my knees, urgently placing my index finger and my middle finger over his carotid artery. He laid too still on the concrete with his knees drawn to his chest in a fetal position. "Nick! Get up! *Now!*" I shook him. His eyes popped open and started to swing at me, but as soon as he realized it was me, he calmed. "Come on we have to get moving," I tugged at him.

"*Non!* You go. I'm dying. I'll slow you down," he insisted in a faltering voice.

"Like hell, soldier! Get your ass up!" I commanded. I reckoned that I'd made a believer out of him. Even though I saw the consuming pain in his face, he managed to get to his feet with my assistance, leaning heavily on me for support. Half dragging the Cajun, we made it to the Jeep. I helped him into the passenger seat, belted him in and with no time left, I dove for the driver's side. I snatched the keys from my pocket and motioned for my daggers to return to their sheath.

In a matter of seconds, I floored that Jeep in reverse, wheels bouncing off three large lumps. They were still down from the knife wounds and hopefully the tires would flatten their faces. We wasted no time hauling ass heading for the outskirts of the city.

Every minute counted. No telling how many regulators overheard the commotion. I could hear their cannons miles away. And even worse, those three knew who we were. I had a strong hunch the others knew about us too. The odds weren't in our favor.

The moonshine and homemade bombs had a fatal reaction to their internal organs. Ultimately, we were the cause of the regulators' death. I reckoned after our baleful act of rebellion, the Illuminati would be sicking their posse on the Cajun and me. One good thing that we knew for certain was that our homemade concoctions worked. That brought a smile to my face.

Since the stars and moon weren't out, we were steeped in darkness. According to Toe, there was a curfew. The regulators patrolled the streets at night. I felt like we were rolling into a minefield. I took extra care to keep my eyes open as we tore through the city heading for refuge. Wherever that might be. One thing I did know was that we needed to find shelter and fast.

By the Cajun's pale face and pasty lips, he was in serious trouble. I think he had passed out rather than fallen asleep. I could tell he was still breathing by the slight rise and fall of his chest. But his breathing was shallow, meaning he was growing weaker by the minute.

I had high hopes that certain abilities that Aidan acquired might've been bestowed upon me. *His healing*. I didn't know how to activate that skill, but I had to find a way to tap into the ability. I couldn't let Nick die on my behalf.

I bit my lip to feel pain. *Anything but the guilt that riddled my entire body.* If I'd listened to Nick, he wouldn't have gotten hurt and we wouldn't be running for our lives. I had tunnel vision. All that pummeled my mind was saving Jeffery and Dom. My one-mindedness caused harm to the Cajun. The sting in my eyes stole my breath. I shouldn't have played the moral card on him. It was unfair of me to hold him to his promise. I think that after I heal him and he gets back on his feet, we should part ways. I'd search for the guys on my own. I made a wrong call coercing the Cajun to come with me. I needed to apologize, but first, I needed to get us out of the city and on a dark backroad where we would be out of harm's way.

All of a sudden, an idea struck.

RESPITE

*B*y the skin of my derrière, we made it out of the city limits without a hitch. Well, not entirely. The left tire whined against the road as it grew flat. The turbulent ride burdened me with dread. Regardless, we were pointed straight for Aidan's place. Hell or high water, I wasn't giving up. I kept telling myself that we had only a little farther to go.

Sally spoke of Aidan owning a historical mansion down on the river road. She described it as a shroud of trees lining the drive that led to a huge white plantation.

I reckoned that I'd stay with the Cajun until he was strong enough to fend for himself and then I think we should separate. But first things first, we both needed food and drink and sleep. Alcohol wasn't my idea of nourishment, but the Cajun might beg to differ.

Another thing to add to the list was finding gasoline. The Jeep was running on fumes. If I didn't find some, the Cajun and I'd be walking. I hated to think about being on foot and trying to stay out of sight. It was hard enough out running a regulator in the Jeep. When my angel abilities worked, my chances were slightly higher escaping the regulators, but my powers were unreliable.

The Cajun seemed quite agile on that attack earlier, but he wasn't fast enough or strong enough to out fist them. God forbid that we get gang-banged by several of those dirty bastards. The Cajun and I on foot would be like committing suicide. I'd worry about that after I get him well. That was if I could invoke that power.

The uprising had just begun, and I dared not to think about how bloody our world would become. The Illuminati didn't care about the afflictions they were imposing. Mankind, had nowhere to escape. The human race was doomed. No clean water or medicine for the sick. Food was scarce. And there was no one strong enough, fierce enough that could stand up against them. This world as we once knew it was facing distinction. Hell, the dinosaurs, and Neanderthals all perished. Mankind could face the very same ending too.

I saw exactly what was going on here. The Illuminati intended to take the world by sweeps and bounds, letting innocent people die a slow agonizing death. This heinous act of ridding the world of the underprivileged and replacing those poor souls with super-humans, superior genetic humans, made me ill. They were creating a perfect race. Historians say that history repeats itself. This sounded much like a worldwide *Hitler on steroids.*

I glanced at the Cajun and my heart sunk. He came to protect me. Boy, did he bite off more than he could chew! Now he lay quiet, dying. And if he expired, I had only myself to blame. He was a noble man even with his flaws. I understood now why Val entrusted him. Sadly, Val didn't think about how dangerous it was placing me in the care of a mortal. Anyone who hangs with me was facing a death sentence. What was Val thinking?

I threw my cap off my head, tossing it in the back of the Jeep and raked my fingers roughly through my dirty hair. Geez! What I wouldn't do for a hot shower and a cold beer? I snorted to myself. I hated beer. Yet it seemed so... *normal.* Crap! I craved normal. My gut told me this was the new norm. Running, starving, dirty, dressed in rags, destitute and homeless. A new kind of indigent.

This was no life for anyone. My heart ached for the people and their families. The *children.* Oh my God! What about the children? I needed to find a way to fight this atrocity. I couldn't give up. If I was supposed to save the world because, after all, I was a genetically altered angel, I should have the ability and a sound plan to take my world back! But the truth was I was useless and that made me furious. If that wasn't being human, then what was?

My mind went back to that day on Bourbon Street. The people

standing in the food line. Their faces withdrawn and void. No expression, just blank. They looked more like the walking dead than the living. No glimmer of light or twinkle in their eyes, brain-dead at its best. I knew there was a connection to that ink number six six six stamped on their wrist. I felt it deep in my gut that somehow the Illuminati concocted a way to control the masses of people by inserting a mind-controlling implant through the ink. How else were they keeping people under their dominance? The thought of how far the Illuminati would go disturbed me on so many levels. I knew this uprising promised only havoc and bloodshed. The Illuminist, sadistic, cold murdering bastards, was seizing the human world. Mankind didn't have a chance against their advance technology. Humans were sitting ducks.

As we came around the bend, I spotted the house just ahead, a huge Victorian house with towering pillars and the house painted white as snow. This had to be it… *Aidan's plantation*. I glanced at the Cajun. He hadn't made a peep since we made our get-away. I saw that he was still breathing. Relief washed over me. I still had a chance in healing him. I felt hopeful.

I came to a slow speed and turned down the long drive. In spite of our dire situation, I gasped at the unwavering beauty. Sally didn't exaggerate. The drive leading up to the mansion offered a thick green canopy of majestic oaks. The land was an endless carpet of plush green. The home sat front and center commanding attention in its glory of the old South. It dominated the graceful grounds just like any master. It had huge columns connected with wrought iron. Long narrow windows covered with plantation shutters lined the front porch and balcony. Black wicker chairs sat elegantly on the porch as if they were waiting for guest to arrive. The home had to have been over a hundred years old yet, it stood just as mighty. I didn't expect anything less.

We cautiously rolled down to the end of the drive, halting at the front steps of the mansion. After I killed the car, I waited for any signs of life. The old place was as still as a haunted house. The cluster of trees rustled loudly through the warm breeze and a faint smell of crepe myrtle perfumed the air. I drew in a deep whiff. God, how I missed that scent.

The house was pitch black. No porch light or the flicker of a candle inside nor out. Most locals didn't have electricity but then again this was Aidan's house. As I spied over the grounds, it suggested to me that we were the only living souls at this grand home. But I wasn't quite sold on that just yet.

I went straight for the door taking two steps at a time up the stairs. I stopped at the entrance staring at a brass bell off to the side. It looked like it was attached to a mechanical device leading into the house. I reached up and pulled down on the rope and off to the side of the door. I stood there against the wall as the bell sounded off. I made sure it was loud enough for anyone in the house to hear. The echo of the bell assured me it made its rounds throughout the house announcing our arrival. Still, the house remained silent.

I decided to check the back. I jumped off the side of the porch and headed in that direction quietly. The backyard was just as lovely as the front. Azaleas and sweet smelling crepe myrtle embellished the yard with lawn chairs placed about the garden. Several windows lined the back of the house. I peeked through one window that appeared to be the kitchen, in another window I spotted a long table with chairs. Still, no sign of life. Good! The easiest way to break in would be through the sunroom. I looked around double checking if the coast was clear. I held my hand to the knob and concentrated. The door gave just as it did at Val's apartment.

To my surprise, there was no alarm sounding off. A sigh of relief hit, and I thought just maybe we might be safe here. Or at least for the night. I cautiously stepped through the threshold holding my breath. I decided to do a final walk-through just to be safe. One could never be too careful.

After I felt confident that we were alone, I went out the front to get the Cajun. He hadn't awakened but he still was breathing. I nudged him to try to get him stirring. I knew I couldn't carry him up those stairs. "Hey! Soldier, wake up!" I demanded. I slightly shook him. I knew the pain would stir him enough that I could get him awake and on his feet. Finally, he started to move. He groaned gritting his teeth. "Where are we?"

I figured the less he knew the better. "Come on! I need to get you in the house."

"*Non!* Leave me!" he grumbled nearly passing out again.

"Soldier, I'm not asking. Get your ass up! You can do this," I promised.

Slowly, he moved one leg at a time and after a few French curse words flying from his mouth, he was standing on his feet. I threw his arm around my neck, we ventured our way up the steps and into the house.

I lay him down on the sofa in a room to the left. It looked like some sort of fancy parlor with a grand piano in the corner. The sofa looked like it came from the same century of the house. The whole house with its high ceilings and crystal chandeliers carried the same Victorian vibe, even the wallpaper. Strange, I thought. This room didn't fit Aidan at all. Of course, there were a lot of things about him that didn't seem like him.

Once I got the Cajun settled and comfortable, I rushed to hide the Jeep. I didn't want anyone spotting us from the road. I raised the garage door that was on the backside of the house. To my surprise, a Hummer sat parked nicely polished as if it were ready for a long trip. In spite of the size of the truck, the centuries old garage had enough room for the Jeep. I thought after I took care of the Cajun, I'd come back out here and check this place out. No telling what I might find useful.

Once I'd tucked the Jeep away and closed the garage door, I rushed back in the house to the Cajun. I checked his pulse and felt relieved that he was still breathing; but his condition was becoming dire. His breath was stressed, and his coloring had grayed. I glanced around looking for a lamp but then I remembered we couldn't use any lights. The last thing I needed was alerting unsavory characters to our presence. I had to do this magickal task in the dark. I just hoped I didn't slice him in two since I'd never performed this procedure. That was if I could figure how to get my hand to glow. But if my memory served me right, whatever magickal talents Aidan possessed, I too carried through my veins.

I looked down at his swollen face. I didn't have to be a physician to know that time was running out. The Cajun wasn't going to make it through the night unless I intervened. I took a deep breath trying to calm my trembling hands. I kneeled down beside the Cajun as he lay flat on the couch. I eased my hands on his chest and closed my eyes focusing. My mind wouldn't settle. It felt like a freight train going from zero to ninety. And worse, my essence appeared empty. I sensed nothing. My heart rate kicked up several notches like a fluttering hawk clawing to escape.

I stretched my neck and eased my breathing for the second time. Slowly, I exhaled and inhaled. I did this for several seconds to rest my mind and body. Then I called to my essence and with promise, it answered. This time as I had never experienced, it appeared gentle and soft as a white dove. Slowly, it feathered its way to the surface. I opened my eyes and surprise consumed me as a bright glow radiated from my hand. It was warm like a blanket spreading its mystical caress throughout the Cajun's body.

I focused on its soothing touch and after a few minutes, his eyes popped open with a gasping breath. Startled, I jumped back, gaping at my glowing hands then back at the Cajun, jolted to a sitting position.

"What did you do to me?" he demanded as his voice came in short pants and raspy as his eyes flew open gawking at my hands.

"I-I'm not sure. How do you feel?"

"Better!" he half-laughed, raising his shirt and rubbing his stomach. "The pain is mild." his eyes were gentle but confused.

"Okay, that's good!" I slowly breathed. "Let me finish." I sat up on my knees, back in position. "Hold still." I reckoned since my hands were still glowing and he wasn't completely out of pain, I still needed to do some more work. I steadied my hands on his stomach as I held my eyes on the focal point. The glow coursed through me as well and spilled over onto the injured area of the Cajun's abdomen.

After the glow faded, I sat back pulling my hands to my chest. "All right, all done, I think." I held my breath fretting that I might've over done it.

The Cajun slowly opened his eyes as our gaze met. "I'm better." He started to rise.

"No, don't get up!" I urged with my hand pushing his shoulder back down.

"You truly are *moi ange!*" (My angel) The Cajun stared at me with awe.

"I-I guess so." My face flushed.

Our eyes locked and his fingers clamped down on my trembling chin. The expression in his current black eyes seemed to plea for something that I'd never seen in him before. "Thank you," he half whispered.

It felt as if he could see every rotten last bit of me. I didn't deserve his gratitude. His near death was my fault. "I don't deserve your gratitude. You nearly died because of me."

"Why do you say that?"

"I coerced you into coming. If I'd not been so determined to go back, you'd be off on the river safe."

"Gul! You didn't trick me into coming. I came because I'd rather be with a beautiful woman than alone with the mosquitoes and gators," he flashed a weak smile. "Now I got to witness a miracle. It was worth the injury."

"I'm happy you're going to live," I smiled back. Taking a deep, unsteady breath, I quickly changed the subject, glancing down at my hands. "Wow! I have the gift," I giggled staring down at my hands, amazed.

He leaned back on the couch, fitting his fingers together, resting them over his chest. "You didn't know?"

"No," I shook my head. "I never had the opportunity to test it."

"Do angels like you usually have this gift?"

"Val has the ability. He used it on me once but not at this magnitude," I paused, as pain wedged in my throat. I hated memory lane. "This might sound bizarre but I think I inherited this power from Aidan."

"Aidan!" The Cajun nearly croaked on his words.

"Can you be still?" I snapped, taking my hand, gently pushing him back down on the couch.

"*Désolé.* (Sorry), I am stunned. How did this happen?" His brows drew together in disbelief.

Oh geez! I wasn't sure I wanted to drag out my whole life. I had enough demons to fill my brain already. I sighed. "It's a long story." I fiddled with my hands, avoiding eye contact.

"I got time. Tell me," the Cajun insisted.

"Hmm, before I was born, our families made arrangements for Aidan and me to marry."

"*Merde!*" the Cajun snarled his lips. "Marriage with the devil himself? I thought those kinds of arrangements were a thing of the past, *no?*"

"One would assume," I grimaced. "I'm not sure how to say this but my father was once a member of the Illuminati."

The Cajun's glint held incertitude as his mouth opened and closed. Before he uttered a word, I protested, holding my palm up. "Let me explain," I said. "My father left the Family, leaving behind their political beliefs, their harsh traditions. He left behind that world and everything in it including the wealth."

"That had to be hard, leaving behind his entire life." The Cajun marveled as if it was some impossible feat.

It almost was.

"My father was more of a humanitarian. He didn't approve of the Illuminati's sadistic ways. So, I reckoned that he rebelled by taking a shine to a worldly person, an outsider, my mother, Sara. As the story churns, he eloped with my mom."

"Ah, nothing like young love, yes?"

I flinched, remembering how Sara told her side of the story, the viciousness in her voice. It was worse than hoards of rocks hurling at my body. "Well, their marriage wasn't exactly a fairytale."

"Your *mère* must've had great admiration for your father standing up to that sadistic family, yes?"

"No, Sara wasn't the type to think outside the box. Instead, she had an ulterior motive. My mom agreed to marry my father because of his wealth. Sara wanted a life of luxury. Her dreams soon were shot down on the night of their honeymoon. It was not until then that my father revealed his truth; he was penniless for the first time in his life. Sara hated him for that. And for his betrayal, she decided she would get revenge. Sara stayed married to my father, but she wasn't exactly a model wife."

The Cajun laughed bitterly. "Eh, loose women! They take from you until you have nothing else to give and then poof!" He brought his fingers to his lips, making a kissing sound. "They leave," he smirked.

"It sounds like you're talking from experience," I half laughed.

"*Oui*! I am twenty-nine. I have a few bumps in the way. I loved a girl once. She damn near broke my heart." His eyes drifted off as if his thoughts were revisiting a past he'd forgotten.

"I'm sorry to hear that."

"It was a long time ago. I am over it. Maybe a scar or two, eh!" he shrugged.

"It seems that getting jilted by a lover runs strong in my family," I huffed before I continued. "Unfortunately, my father didn't see Sara for her true self. As the miscarriages continued, Sara pretended that she was devastated over losing a baby. It was all a con."

"This just gets worse."

"That's not the half of it. The Family had a watchful eye on my parents and knew about Sara abusing herself. Someone from the Family approached her offering a deal."

The Cajun scoffed. "A deal with the devil, yes?"

"Yup. That's how I came into the picture. To sum it all up, the Illuminati's scientist, with the assistance of alien technology, was able to use a celestial being's DNA and my human father's to create me… *a genetically engineer angel.*"

The Cajun rose up on his elbows, gawking at me before he'd found his tongue. "That's impossible!"

I dragged in a wary sigh. "Alien technology has mankind beat hands down. I'm the proof," I smiled bitterly.

"That is very interesting. So, how did your birth and the Illuminati come into play?"

"That's the easy part. My parents signed a blood contract with the Family. There was a two-fold agreement to the contract that my mother and the Family made together in secret. She would exchange me to my betrothed once I turned the ripe age of eighteen. That's when my mother and I moved to Tangi."

"What happened to your father?"

"Dad died by a hit-and-run driver, my mother. She managed to hide that little fact from me until after I'd met Aidan. He was the one who sprang it on me."

"Mère! That must have shattered your world."

"It did but that was only the tip of the iceberg. Aidan kindly took the time to explain the history of my family, and he's the one who told me about myself. I didn't believe him at first, but it all made sense in a really crazy screwed up way."

"*Non*! You mean to tell me that you trusted that sociopath at his word. He's a murderer!" the Cajun grinded his words between his teeth.

"Hmm, it wasn't like that in the beginning. Aidan was very different. He was dashing, strong, tender, and intense." I shuddered inwardly remembering the past. "He was protective of me and I fell in love with him." I shrugged, unable to say any more.

"He doesn't sound like the jackass I know."

"The Aidan I once knew, and the present Aidan are polar opposites." I licked my dry lips. "That's why I think his family has him under some sort of enchantment."

"How did you inherit his powers?"

"I was being hunted down by his uncle, Edward Van Dunn. He wanted to extract my powers for himself."

"The same pervert that asshole, Aidan bragged about?"

"Yup, that would be the same psychopath that wanted my head on a platter," I sighed. "Anyway, to protect myself and to keep Aidan safe, I offered myself to him. It involved me losing my virginity."

"Damn! He tricked you!"

"Yes, it seems so, doesn't it?" I forced a smile. "I thought he cared." I scoffed, remembering the pain of betrayal.

"Did he have anything to do with you going to that insane hospital?"

"I believe so. He didn't come completely clean. He has selective amnesia. Aidan has a problem remembering certain things that went down back then."

"It doesn't matter. He's a monster." The Cajun's face soured.

"I have to agree." I shook my head, frustrated. "Could I have been that blind?"

"Love is a funny emotion. You could fall for an axe murderer and not see the truth."

"I reckon you're right."

"Pardon me, but I overheard you say something about a girl named Dawn."

Tears welled into my eyes as I quickly dabbed them dry with my sleeve. "Yes, Dawn is mine and Aidan's daughter. She was murdered by a dark angel that I share the other DNA with, and I have a blade with his name on it." I swallowed down the vile that threatened.

"You lost your child! No wonder you are bitter."

The Cajun had me pegged right.

"First chance I get, I'm going after him too. He will pay for what he's done." My lips tightened into anger.

"This is the angel you are related to?"

"I share only Mustafa's DNA. Nothing else."

"I certainly can relate to that emotion. I wish revenge for my friend too. But first comes first."

"Meaning?"

"Meaning, you don't show up for a gun fight with a knife. You be patient until you get the upper hand. Then you attack."

"That sounds like you're speaking about your tour in the middle East."

"*Oui*! I lost good men." Quiet settled between us, and then he switched to another uncomfortable subject. "What happened to Valor and you? I thought you two were tight."

"Oh, Val!" I half laughed. "Yeah, it didn't work out."

"I apologize if my kissing you caused you to part ways."

I laughed. "Don't flatter yourself, Cajun. No. I'm afraid there were other factors that played into our breakup." I looked down at my hands, feeling heavy hearted. "He was the leader of my kind, Zophasemin. Although I am the same race, I'm marked as an impure and an outcast."

"Ouch! That must've hurt?"

"It did hurt very much and is still raw."

"I gather he chose his kind."

"Yep! You gathered right."

He drew his brows down into a puzzled gaze. "Why are you an outsider?"

I huffed, feeling the bite of ire. "I'm not a creature of divine creation. I was created by a team of scientist that were handpicked by the Illuminati."

"*Merde*! That explains why those bastards are hunting you."

I shrugged, looking down at my lap. "Yep, I'm not even my own person," I sighed. "That's why Val and I broke up. I'd never be accepted by the Zop."

The Cajun snorted. "It's his lost, yes?" his lips tipped up, hinting at a smile.

"Perhaps. I don't know anymore. I thought I loved him but when we broke up, I wasn't that unhappy. Of course, I didn't like him leaving earth's realm. When I heard he was leaving, it was like a cold slap in the face. I thought I stilled loved him but then…"

The Cajun jumped in. "You don't miss him so much?"

114

"No, I'm more upset at him for leaving the people than for myself. He should be here protecting defenseless folks."

"He's doing what he thinks is best."

"Maybe or maybe not." I rose to my feet. I'd had a belly full of my past. "You need to eat and no liquor tonight. You need your strength."

"What? I'm perfectly fine. See?" He raised his shirt. The deep bruises had faded but I remembered how I felt when Aidan had healed me from a fatal wound. I was putting my foot down. "Sorry! One night doing without liquor won't hurt you. I'm going to find us something to eat." I threw over my shoulder as I headed for the kitchen. "Don't move off that couch!" I ordered before I disappeared to the back.

The kitchen felt like a mixture of old and contemporary. Chrome shelves with an old wooden stove and a stack pipe going through the ceiling. Exposed stone embellished the mantle and fireplace. When I spotted the stainless-steel fridge, my eyes lit up.

Good question if the house had electricity. If I flipped on a light switch, it could be a beacon in the dark. Drawing attention to ourselves could get us caught. We were already on borrowed time. No point in pushing the bounds of luck any further.

I reached around the back and felt for the plug. Once my fingers band around the cord, I gave it a brisk tug. "There!" I huffed, tugging the door open.

My breath stalled as I stood there swooned with crisp cold air caressing my face. Surprise and glee surged through me as my mouth began to water. I hadn't eaten since yesterday morning. It seemed luck had our backs for now.

Right off, I spotted orange juice, milk, eggs, and cold cuts for sandwiches with all the trimmings too, tomatoes and pickles. I overloaded my arms with all the goodies and placed them on the counter. Then I went to the pantry and my eyes widened with delight. I spotted bread, cookies, canned soup, and bottled water. I figured when we got ready to leave, I'd help myself to the staples that didn't need refrigeration. Too bad all that food we'd gathered at Val's apartment got wasted. The regulators ruined all our findings, smashing it all over the sidewalk. They knew it was food. I reckoned the New World Order only allowed folks to eat food they provided. Whata bunch of dickweeds. The cynicism of this new world grated on me furiously. But for now, we had shelter and food. That was more than what most had. I was grateful.

I opened a can of chicken soup for the Cajun. I hustled about the kitchen as though it was my own. A few minutes later, I came out with a tray of sorted foods.

The Cajun was sitting up, but he still looked a little under the mend. I fretted if I'd completed the healing process completely. Now that I knew I had the touch, literally speaking, I'd keep my eye on him. Apart from his slight paleness, he looked pretty good. Maybe we both can get a few hours of sleep.

I set the tray on the floor next to the sofa where the Cajun sat. I grabbed up his bowl of hot soup and eased down next to him. "The soups hot." I blew a moment and raised the spoon to him. His eyes gleamed with amusement. I stopped in midair, I asked, "What?"

"Nothing. Just never expected to see you feed me. That's all."

"Do you want to feed yourself? Or better, you could wear it?" I replied letting the scorn flavor my voice a little too heavy.

"*Non*. It's fine. You do it." Sarcasm dipped in his deep throaty voice like a cookie to coffee.

I hesitated a second and thought what the hell, he'd nearly lost his life for me. I owed him a lot more than a spoon-feeding, but I did have my limits. "Alright, but you can't tease me." I shot him a smothering look. I raised the spoon back to his lips and he took the sip.

"Good!" he whispered and flashed a devilish smile.

Time ticked away as an old grandfather clock chimed throughout the mansion. We sat there in the dark not speaking. By the drained look in the Cajun's face, I was certain that my face parroted his. The night had devoured us both. Despite the odds, he was going to live or at least for now. I put myself in the same statistics as well. Nothing was stable and any hope of a future in this new system was bleak.

After tonight, the Cajun and I should part ways. I couldn't have him lose his life for me. Though my angel gifts were unreliable, I had an advantage. That was more than the Cajun.

Nick knew the land. He could hunt or trap just about any wild creature on the bayou. He was a survivor. I knew if he went deep into the back woods, down the river, he could hide, and no one would ever find him.

Then again with alien technology and those eerie drones, no telling what sort of satellite they had spying on us lowly ones.

Regardless of the advanced tech, he had a better chance surviving in the bayou than hanging with me. I, on the other hand, didn't have that luxury. I had to find the guys. Then after they were tucked away in a safe place, I was turning myself over to the Illuminati. The Cajun and his friends along with Dom and Jeffery, didn't need me hanging on their shirttails. I was a liability. Besides, it was only a matter of time before the Illuminati's dogs found me. My going off in the opposite direction might throw off the Cajun's scent and make it easier for him to get away. It was a theory, but it was all I had for the time being.

After we'd finished eating, the Cajun grumbled about the OJ. "What no liquor in the juice?" he scowled with uttered contempt.

My furrowed brows met his scowl as I responded, "Will you just shut up and be grateful you have a full belly? You don't need liquor with every meal!"

"I'm a big boy. I think I can decide for myself," he shot back with his nostrils flaring.

I dragged in a long sigh and figured it wasn't worth blowing up over. Instead I said, "If you want to destroy your liver, I reckon that's your right."

The Cajun's face dropped, full of regret. "I'm sorry. That was rude of me."

"You, rude? Never!" I flashed him a seedy grin.

"Okay, I deserved that," he paused, "You and me, we're gonna make it, yes?"

"Your guess is as good as mine," I said. "But I think it's best that we part ways after tonight." I suddenly felt a tug of sadness.

He eased himself down to the floor next to me. His body moved stiffly as he grimaced. I avoided his eyes. I just didn't want him to see me fragile like this. We both had lost so much, his best friend, my mother and Dawn, my child, now the guys. How much more torture did we have to bear?

For a moment, we didn't say anything to each other as we leaned against the sofa taking in the darkness. I stared off at the empty fireplace remembering the inviting warmth. On cold nights, Dom would throw in a few pinecones on top of the burning wood. I'd never forget that wonderful scent of pine floating throughout the house. I wished I could go back in time. If I had a day to choose, I'd pick a time before Dawn's death. Maybe I could've prevented it. Then I sighed. She'd be growing up in this terrible mutiny. The world as it was, certainly no place to raise a child. Could death have been a blessing? My eyes suddenly felt the onset of tears. I fought the sting. No parent should ever have to lose a child. What was wrong with this world?

"Are you crying?" the Cajun's voice roped me back in.

I released a wary sigh. "No." I avoided his penetrating eyes.

"I have a nice shoulder to cry on."

I almost giggled. Why did the Cajun have to be nice to me of all nights? While focusing on a flaw in the plank flooring to keep my eyes from finding his, I retorted, "It doesn't matter now!" I swallowed hard. Damn knot wouldn't go away.

"You and I will find your boys, and everything will be fine."

Sorrow spilled from my smile. "Nick, I can't have you tag along anymore." He opened his mouth to protest but I stopped him, holding my fingers to his lips. "Look, I know you're trying to comfort me and," I swallowed. "That's sweet but we both know it's too dangerous. I have a target on my back."

"I think after trip 2 to downtown, I'm pretty sure I have the same target, yes?"

I could feel the heat of his eyes on me. "Not like me. I think you can stay under radar, deep in the bayou. I can give you directions where to find Val's cabin. It's completely enshrouded by cypress and gators. Right up your alley."

"I'm not a man that runs from my enemies. You forget that bastard killed my friend. I want to strangle him with my bare hands."

"A minute ago, you said you never go to a gun fight with a knife. Now you're flip flopping," I accused.

"I didn't say we go running into an enemy territory without a good plan, gul! We strategize, then we go in when they least expect us."

I shook my head. "How do we map out a plan against a druid?" His arrogant tone sparked my frustration. "Look! Your pride is going to get you killed. Aidan can snap you like a twig."

"I know I wanted to hide out at the river. But I was wrong. I gave my word to Valor and I am not backing out!" A chill in his voice stabbed the darkness.

"You saw what he did to Titan. I can't let you risk your life and I don't think your friend would want that for you either."

"I think I know what my friend would want!" The Cajun snapped.

"Okay, you win!" I huffed. "We stay together, then." Geez! There was no reasoning with him. Still, I couldn't blame him. I had my own demons to kill. Mustafa being on the top of my list. One sadistic angel that needed to die. Next on the list was Aidan. I planned to torture him.

∼

The Cajun insisted on taking first watch. We stood at an impasse over who watched first. I reckoned it was a man's thing. I didn't argue. Who was I to burst his male pride? I went off scouting out the mansion.

Upstairs, I found the master bedroom at the end of the hall. The room didn't lack in its exquisite décor, a stark white. Although no matter how heavy the price tag, the room felt cold and void. I stood in the center of the large bedroom peering through the darkness. I didn't see anything that had Aidan's stamp on it. Not even that woodsy scent I'd once loved. Instead, the room smelled of rubbing alcohol that stung my nose and eyes. Apparently, someone went to great lengths to sterilize the room for an ill person. There was nothing personal in the bedroom. No pictures of family, no clutter showing evidence of a person using this room, everything was in perfect order. Why would a Druid need his room sterilized? Come to think about it, I'd never seen his private boudoir. A heaviness centered in my chest. I reckoned he reserved that part of his life for Sally.

My eyes fell upon an interior door. I gasped, padding my way through the dark. I stopped at the door and reached for the knob. Slowly, I eased the door open. I peeked inside as I let out a soft whistle. "A shower! And I'm bettin' there's hot water too." I gasped at the white marble. Suddenly my mood lifted.

I quickly peeled off my clothes and stepped into the massive shower. It took me a moment to figure out all the gadgets. "Dang! Why does one need so many knobs for a shower?" I grumbled to myself. Not wasting one moment, I started twisting all the gold knob. Right away, the water heated, shooting warm beads of water. Only moments later, the aroma of gardenias had swept me away. Soon my body was lathered in suds and my world didn't seem as bleak. I stood there letting the pulsating streams beat the dirt and grim down the drain. The tension in my shoulders eased. I stood there breathing in the delicious warmth.

Then my emotions hit me and I suddenly dropped to the floor huddled, racked with sobs. My sense of loss was beyond tears. What had happened to my life? It never really was my life to own. The Illuminati owned me before birth. But there had been so much pain. The loss of a child that I'd never had the privilege to embrace or get to know. My father, murdered before I had a chance to know him, a mother who never truly loved me. And now, my dearest friends, my adopted family, had been kidnapped by a sociopath. Because of my careless mistake, they may be dead. And poor Titan tortured on that satanic cross flashed before my eyes.

Then I thought about Dawn. The tears flooded even more as my whole body shook. I wanted nothing more than death at this point. Maybe if I didn't exist, the world would be less chaotic. The Order wouldn't have someone to chase and others wouldn't be endangered by merely knowing me. An invasion was forced upon our world and I dared to think what the Order planned next. How many innocent lives would have to suffer or die for their greedy rulership? Yet, the worst... I had no power against these fiends. Not only was I useless with my limited magick, I was defenseless against the great mighty and powerful Illuminati. I laid there sobbing until I started choking on my tears. The water had turned cold and I still remained huddled under its icy flow. Chills spurred over my body. Unaware, I heard the shower door open and the cold water ceased. I was shivering, teeth chattering. A shadow moved swiftly as he picked me up with a towel wrapped around me and gently lifted me into his arms. Once I sunk into the cushion of the soft bed, my eyes collided with the Cajun's face. He quickly covered my bare body with the dry covers. Our eyes locked and I suddenly felt a deep appreciation for him. "Did you hear me crying?" I asked.

"*Oui.*" his deep browns glistened in the dark. "Like you... I couldn't abandon you."

Tears began to swell again as my teeth chattered.

"Now take this. You need sleep. I'll continue to watch."

I looked down and the Cajun had a glass of OJ and a tiny pill. My brows furrowed. "What's that?"

"It literally is a chill pill. Xanax. It will help you relax." he held the tiny pink pill up in his hand.

"A narcotic?" I panicked.

The Cajun grinned. "Don't worry. Have you forgotten, I'm a doctor. It is a very low dose. It won't hurt you. I promise."

"Where did you find it?"

The Cajun grinned, "In your bathroom."

"Oh!" I hesitated. I didn't like drugs. Especially after my stay at Haven. Then I thought what the hell. I could use a peaceful rest. I sat up slightly and took the OJ and the pill in my hands. Not wanting to argue, I flipped my head backward, chasing the pill down with the orange juice. "Thanks." I said in a drained voice handing the glass back.

The Cajun smiled, "That's my gul." he paused, "You can't take the whole world on, *non*! You can only save one person at a time. Your heart is good. In my book, that's pretty, damn human!"

I pushed myself to smile but failed miserly. The Cajun seemed to understand and he just patted my foot and left me alone to myself. Once the door creaked shut, I closed my eyes and the tears started flowing once again.

❧

I didn't know how long I'd been dozing, but something jarred me from a dead sleep. I jumped to a sitting position. I let out a sigh of relief when I realized it was only a tree scraping the window. A faint shaft of light peeked through the sheer curtains. Daylight was nearing.

After combing the dim room, it came back to me that we were still in Aidan's house. A frown crept across my face and dread spiked my stomach. I didn't cotton to the idea of staying in his house, even though it was for only a night.

My grogginess had subsided as I sat peering over the room. I tugged the cover off and began to slip out of bed until I realized I didn't have a stitch on. I needed to find something to wear. I imagined Aidan had a belt or two in his closet. I didn't care if the clothes were baggy. A belt could hold the pants up. As long as it didn't fall off my body and it was clean, I'd be happy.

I went straight for the armoire and swung the doors open. Wow! I hit the jackpot. Women's clothing to the galore. "Eureka!" Then a sharp bite slug me in the gut. *Sally!* Could these garments be hers?

A prestigious stock of designer clothing with the tag still attached.

My eyes washed over the various brands, Vera Wang, Gucci, Dolce and Gabbana. Strangely, I didn't see any men's clothing. Maybe Aidan stayed in separate quarters. Oh, well! I shrugged it off.

The closet took me back in time when my mother was alive. Sara had a closet very much like this one. I gave way to a somber sigh. Oh well, no time for revisiting the past. It was better buried. I quickly pushed the clothing around trying to find something that was less formal. "Ah, found it!" I pulled out a pair of jeans with holes through the knees and a simple white blouse. I found a pair of black riding boots. I guess this person spent her leisure time riding horses.

I checked the size, a five! Then I thought of Sally. These couldn't be hers unless she'd lost forty pounds. Oh well, like I cared.

I went to the chest of drawers. If Sally or whoever was anything like my mom, she might have undergarments that still had tags. I opened the top drawer and sure enough, I was right! This girl had a ton of panties and bras with tags hanging on the garments. I grabbed up a pair and a pink bra matching. I was in luck, it was my size and brand new. I quickly got dressed. In the bathroom, I found a brush and a hair band. I didn't waste time trying to run a brush through my wild mane of hair so I threw down the brush and tied my hair up in a ponytail.

After a moment of admiring myself in the mirror, I made my way to hallway. Slowly, I creaked the door open, cautiously checking if the close was clear. The house was still dark and quiet. I had no idea the time, but I imagine it would be light soon. We needed to get the hell out of here before anyone noticed us. I tipped toed down the hall opening doors looking for the Cajun.

When I came to one room, I stopped in my tracks. Through the dim light, I recognized the room. It was as if I'd stepped back in time. A time I didn't want to relive... the *principal's office*. I gaped at the room. "Holy crap!" I mumbled barely above a whisper. I shut the door behind me and I made my way to that same ornate desk that I remembered well. Even the scent of tobacco lingered in the room. My gaze combed over the room as if in slow motion taking in every inch of the office.

When my eyes landed on that same ornate desk, I made a beeline for it. I began jiggling the drawers checking for any one unlocked. To my disappointment, the owner had locked it up before leaving.

Then I recalled unlocking Val's apartment door. I wrapped my fingers around a long narrow knob to the master drawer. If I could get into it, the other drawers might automatically open too. I closed my eyes, concentrating. I give it a tug and nothing. It didn't budge. "Dang!" I grated through my teeth. This time I put more will-power onto essence. I tightened my fingers around the metal knob. A light from my palm glistened in the dim light. I tugged harder this time and almost knocked everything off the desk but the knob, itself. It remained steadfast.

Locked!

I flopped back into that god-awful chair. I felt so tiny leaning back in it. I blew out a huff of frustration. My eyes squinted, determination seethe as my mind roiled with ideas. I was breaking into the desk if I had to take a hatchet and chop it into a million pieces. My eyes washed over the top of the desk hoping to find a sharp object. I'd thought about a hair pen. I scratched that idea. If my magick couldn't break it, a thin wire wouldn't work for sure.

I started to swipe everything off the desk in one sweep until my eyes caught the cup holder. A letter opener with a folded note clung to the sharp point, standing erect in the cup.

A seedy smile crossed my face as I jolted up in my seat. I leaned over and snatched the note. My hands were trembling. On the fold, my name was hand written. I froze staring at it. It was the same writing from the note the Cajun and I found lying on his kitchen table from Aidan. Yet, this writing like the other one was sloppy and looked more like a girl's writing. It had to be Sally's.

I jerked my head up skimming the room. Chills washed over me as if a pair of eyes were watching. Panic seized my breath. The only thing I could hear was my pounding heart. I glanced back down at the folded note. Crap! How did Aidan know that I'd be snooping in his office? My mind flooded with questions that threatened to send me into a tizzy.

I couldn't stand it any longer. I unfolded the note. My hands trembled, barely able to hold the paper steady enough to read. The paper felt soft as a baby's bottom. The color was a starch white with swirls of what appeared to be an eye in an abstract marking, circling the edges of the paper. With a nervous sigh, I began to read:

Dear Stevie,

It is so lovely of you to drop by and visit my home in the country. However, it pains me greatly to inform you that you missed your love ones earlier. Unfortunate for them, you missed a spot. Retract your steps. However, you must hurry. Jeffery and Dom don't have much time left. They're having a difficult time breathing, I fear.

Sincerely,
Aidan

Son of a *bitch*! This time I swiped my arm across the surface of the desk, knocking everything off to the floor, crashing. A loud crash burst disturbed the whole house.

I had to find the Cajun! We needed to get the *hell* out of here and fast. I charged out the office with the letter clenched in my hand, yelling down the hall, "Nick! Where are you, *goddamnit!*"

I flew down the stairs darting from room to room searching for him. I halted in the kitchen staring at the coffeemaker brewing. "Well, at least I know he was here a minute ago." I stood resting my hands on my hips huffing in the door jam. Normally, I'd be jonesing over a hot cup of java but my chest was already taking a beating from my heart. I didn't need the caffeine boost.

Obviously, the Cajun was nowhere in the house.

Outside!

I tore out the front door and I spotted the garage door slightly open and a gentle light spilling from underneath. I sprinted toward the garage hoping I'd find the Cajun alive and alone.

I stretched my neck, peering around to see if we had any visitors. I saw nothing out of the ordinary. A slight relief flickered through me, but I remained alert to any surprises just in case.

When I reached the garage door, I needed to make sure the close was clear. One could never be too careful these days. I pressed my back flat against the corner of the building. I stilled, listening over my erratic heartbeat for any signs of the Cajun or unwanted visitors. I heard faint footsteps scrapping across the concrete floor and sounds of metal rubbing against another metal like someone tinkering with a car.

I summed it up in a nutshell and went into action.

I bent down, lifting the door as it squeaked in protest. The Cajun jumped with a start aiming a cocked rifle straight at my head. Looking down the barrel of a gun wasn't what I'd expected from my partner.

As soon as he saw me, curses fell from his mouth, "Gul, I nearly shot you!"

I ignored his canter and blurted out, "We have to leave now! We've been setup. Aidan knows we're here!" frantically, I shoved the letter in his face, "Read this!" Hysteria was banking on the edge of my last strand of sanity. It took all I had to hold myself together.

The Cajun set his rifle down, grabbing the letter from my hand and unfolded it. His eyes quickly scanned over the writing. Dark snappy eyes shot back at me from his sun toughen face. "What does he mean retract our steps? What did we overlook?"

I shifted in my feet and blew out a deep sigh, "Val's gym."

The Cajun stood in silence. His flat unspeaking eyes prolonged the moment. With no warning, he snatched up a screwdriver and hurled it against the wall. It hit the old wood with a vibrating bang, bouncing off and landing on the concrete with a loud ding.

Okay, this was going better than I thought.

"If that no-balls bastard knew we'd end up at his planation, then don't you think us going back to Val's bar is bat-shit crazy? We'll be walking into a trap!" The Cajun shook his head. "*Non!* I think I wish to live, *yes?*"

"That note changes everything! Can't you see that? Dom and Jeffery are still alive. You can stay here if you want, but I'm going back!" Anger had nipped at my heels as I crossed my arms holding my stance.

"I'm not going back there!" the Cajun's voice hinged on the verge of shouting. "And neither are you!"

"Look! I understand your reservations but… "

Abruptly, I stopped in the stream of our argument.

"Phew! What is that awful smell?" I crunched my nose.

The Cajun's glint fixed on an old building farther back on the perimeter of the land. It was such a far distance from the house. I'd over looked it when I'd been scooting out the place last night. There was nothing to it, tattered boards that looked like the wind could knock it down. It was in desperate need of a paint job. Faded red, chipped, exposing boards that were black and rotten. I assumed that it had served as an outhouse back in the day during the planation's early beginnings.

The Cajun as if he'd forgotten about our heated debate, became deathly silent as he stomped off heading for the direction of the shack. His face took on a hunted look and I knew our troubles had changed for the worse.

As we neared the shed, there was a loud buzzing coming from inside. I felt the color drain from my face.

Suddenly, the Cajun stopped right at the door. He'd quickly jerked his bandana over his mouth and nose. When I reached his side, I gagged, quickly covering my mouth. The smell reminded me of decay and lye.

It didn't take a Brainiac to know what laid behind that door. "Oh, my God!" I dropped to my knees. "Nick, please tell me that's not Dom and Jeffery!" Icy fear tore at my insides.

Without a word, the Cajun opened the door. Swarms of buzzing flies flew into his face as he stepped back swatting. The stench of decay attacked the air as we both gagged, covering our faces. Brusquely, the Cajun shut the door and then turned to me. His sorrowful eyes sought mine and sheer panic roared in my eardrums.

"NO!" I screeched. "It's not the boys!" Tears clouded my vision. Sheer black terror charged through me. "*Please*, not them!" I pleaded.

"*Non!*" the Cajun rushed to my side, gently lifting me to my feet. "Shush, shush, *cheri!*" I eased in his arms. "*Non!* It's not the boys." His voice was tender. "The body is a woman."

My eyes flew up at him. "A woman?" I asked in a tremulous whisper.

"*Oui!* A young woman."

Suddenly I had to see for myself. I jerked free from the Cajun's embrace and bolted for the door, swinging it open. I quickly stepped back covering my nose and mouth from the horrific stench. "I-I know her!" I stuttered as shock poured over me. Maggots covered her remains, creeping through every crevice, severed body parts tossed into a pile like dog scraps, and thousands of flies blanketed her decomposing body. It was more than sick. It was pure evil.

In a flash, I spun on my heels darting to the side of the shack, bending over, choking up my insides. I swore that I'd coughed up so much vile that my belly was rubbing against my spine. I had no more to give.

The Cajun shut the door to the shack and rushed to my side. I felt his hand pressed against my back, gently stroking. "Who is the *gul*, Stevie?" his voice pierced my madness.

I straightened up tugging out my bandana from my back pocket and cleaning my mouth. Tears came at me again as I forced the words out. "*Sally!* My cousin and Aidan's wife."

"*Merde*! That psychopath killed his own wife. If you go after him, he will do the same to you or worse."

"Not if I kill him first!" I hissed, squaring my shoulders.

"Did you see her body? He mutilated the gul!" the Cajun flung his arm out, pointing to the shack's door, "I bet that sick fuck had sex with her when he slit her throat."

My stomach roiled over the vision of Sally, now burned forever in my retina. Another death to add to my growing list. "She didn't deserve this!" I looked off staring at the far stretched land. I didn't spot a house in sight. We were in the middle of nowhere. It would've been easy to murder someone here. The screams would've gone unheard. My gaze shot back at the Cajun. "I have to find him!"

"*Non*! You're not going after that cold murdering psychopath!"

"Look! I appreciate your concern. But don't you see the message here?"

The Cajun scoffed. "*Oui*! We get the hell out of dodge."

"I don't have the luxury that you do, just run?" I charged.

"I pick my battles." He grated. "This one is suicide, gul. Your friend, Val, put me in charge. And I decide for you!" He stepped closer glaring at me intensely.

"Oh, you think you can exert your authority?" my hands flew to his chest and shoved him hard, my voice just below a bellow. "Val doesn't own me nor do you!" I paused, calming my tone. "Sally's body is a message. If I don't go after Jeffery and Dom then they are as good as dead."

The Cajun roared, throwing his hand on my shoulder in a possessive manner. "They are already dead! That's why this wild goose chase is a waste of time."

"That's not true!" I refuted. "If they were already dead don't you think Aidan would've left their bodies instead of Sally's remains?"

"I can't say. It is very hard gauging a maniac." The Cajun bit out through his teeth.

"I know you don't want to hear this, but if there is a chance in hell that the guys are still alive, I have to try. I owe them that much. This is my entire fault!"

"How is this your fault?"

"The Illuminati owns me. I am their slave. I will never belong to myself and as long as I run from those insidious bastards, anyone in a five-mile radius of me is not safe."

A shiver of uncertainty glinted in the Cajun's dark eyes. He stalled capturing my gaze to his. "If you go, then I go with you!"

"This idea isn't any better than me running. I can't have you risk your life too. Right now, you are all I have. I don't want to lose you too."

"All the more reason I should go with you, *yes?*" He retorted with determination that forbade any further argument.

THE POINT OF NO RETURN

*O*ff we rolled in the hummer loaded down with our homemade bombs and even jugs of moonshine. Since we were looking down the barrel of advance alien weaponry, we needed as much muscle as we could muster. If it could kill the regulators, then I wanted to stockpile every cleansing chemical underneath the sink and moonshine to the heavens. It's like a skinny man sparring with a heavy weight boxer on steroids. We had to fight dirty. Personally, I never knew a fight that wasn't.

We'd grabbed up can goods and other foods that didn't require refrigeration. I found in the pantry a large box of beef jerky. We hit the jackpot with that. Dried jerky didn't spoil. We could eat on it forever.

To add to our survival list, we collected every empty container that we could find and filled them with clean water. For now, we were okay. I reckoned that was as good as it gets these days. All we could do was count our blessings and stay alive.

~

The honeycomb sun had crest the horizon. There was promise of another unusually hot sultry day. The atmosphere was taut, unyielding.

This time I felt a bit more protected in this huge tank. The tinted windows gave us a sense of protection. And the renowned symbol, the knowing eye, on the plates, I felt hopeful that we'd pass for Illuminist, slipping past their dirty noses. Of course, this was all in theory.

The Cajun insisted on driving. I wasn't up for the challenge to argue, so I didn't put up a fight. In fact, I actually felt relieved when he took over the wheel. He knew the town better than I did and he'd had experience, during his tour in Afghanistan, driving heavy-duty tankers similar to the Hummer.

The wheels churned in my ear as my heart joined, pounding my chest when we entered Bourbon Street. A stark silence lingered between us.

My teeth were on edge as I gripped my seat. The Cajun's gaze was as intense as a mountain lion hunting for prey. He kept combing the street for any signs of trouble.

Not much had changed since last night. Similar to the day after the Mardi Gras, the street was cluttered. The only proof of life left was the tons of debris, scurrying in the wind and collecting at the curbside. The air had a pungent odor of garbage, feces and something else that I couldn't put my finger on. It was almost as bad as Sally's decaying body.

Almost.

I wringed my hands, feeling like a cat in ice water scrambling for a dry surface. I glanced at the Cajun and then back to street. I felt responsible for him. I blamed Val. He should've never given Nick the burden of protecting me. Having me for a partner was like sitting on a live grenade. You knew it was going to explode, you just didn't know exactly when. I wished he's gone his way but he was too bullheaded to listen to reason. So here we were about to bite off more than we could chew.

Another frightening thought, knowing how much the Illuminist loved experimenting, creating genetic freaks like me; I feared the regulators were small fries compared to a much larger picture. I recalled how Aidan boasted about super-soldiers. No telling what kind of monsters the Illuminist planned springing on us. I didn't want to think about the peril that awaits. I was already on the ledge ready to jump. Despite my frail mind, I had to face the possibilities and prepare myself for the worst. The Illuminist had the control, and we were the roaches that they intended to exterminate.

We rolled into downtown on Bourbon Street, a line of locals had started to gather on the sidewalk. They must be getting food rations. I spotted stacks of brown boxes against a brick building.

My pulse lurched when I spotted two regulators. One stood at the front of the line, checking each person's wrist. Another regulator was herding the growing crowd, aiming his weapon and shouting at them to form a line.

An elderly woman suddenly emerged from the line. She appeared lost. I watched as she clenched her cane for support, creeping across the street. Just like the others, the woman had the same dazed expression.

Suddenly the regulator cut his attention to the woman. He shouted at her, but she continued edging her way to the other side of the street.

Angry fowl words spilled from the creature's mouth as he abruptly aimed and fired his weapon, shooting the elderly woman in cold blood.

Her body went limp, crashing to the pavement headfirst. Like a watermelon bursting, a loud thud pierced the air. Crimson blood pooled around the crumpled body.

My hands flew to my mouth unconsciously, eyes wide.

In the next breath, drones exact duplicates of the ones that attacked me, swooped in and hovered over the woman's limp body as if they were collecting data. Seconds later, they zipped across the sky vanishing behind a strange gray cloud.

I stuttered in horror, "H-h-he just shot her!" out of my mind, I half shrieked rushing for my door. The Cajun swiftly grabbed my upper arm, his fingers biting into my skin.

I snapped my eyes back at him and hissed, "I have to stop that creature from killing anyone else!" Tears filled my eyes.

"*Non*! You can't help her or any of those people." His voice lulled me back to my senses.

I settled back into my seat, giving him a curt nod. Once he dropped his hand, I swiped the tears from my eyes. He was right. I couldn't save her. I couldn't save any of them.

The Cajun and I shared in an icy silence as we eased down the street.

Chills spiked down my spine as I watched from my side window. Not taking another glance at the old woman's body, the regulator stalked back to the line. He displayed no concern, not even giving it a thought to his injustice, murdering a defenseless old woman. He left her there for the birds to pick. I wanted to vomit.

Chills slithered across my neck as my eyes spread over the crowd. They all stood with blank faces, staring at the front of the line. It was as if the crowd was void of any natural emotions. Not one person acknowledged that an execution had just befallen.

Shock, fright and anger pummeled me. The regulator's deliberate cruelty didn't make sense. The woman wasn't resisting. She was merely confused.

In fact, everything about this picture left me disconcerted. They all wore the same far-off-distant, blank face as if they'd had a lobotomy or underwent one too many shock treatments. It became evident to me just how sickly these people were. As I noted the black circles that embellished their dull eyes and their pale skin that sagged off their bones, I knew that they were only a breath away from death. The worse part was the children. Large eyes sunk back into their small skulls, staring absent-mindedly, cheeks hollowed, no more than an empty shell of the children they once were, jumping and running, little voices full of laughter.

At that moment, I'd never felt more useless, watching innocent men, women and children getting treated worse than animals. I was furious with myself and enraged at these monsters that called their barbarian justice.

My heart was breaking knowing I couldn't do anything to help. Could anyone save the suffering? No one had the power to fight against this atrocity. Not one person! Not even a genetic angel! I sighed with overwhelming grief.

While we edged closer to Val's place, I kept my eyes on the increasing number of locals piling in line and stretching several blocks down at this point. Geez! I got the impression that the whole city had depended on the food rations. I didn't like this one bit.

I noticed that several folks wore the same tattoo on their wrist. When we rolled by a man making his way to the line, I got a good look at his mark.

When I realized what was happening, I gasped with a start. "Oh, my God!" I mumbled. The Cajun's friend, Toe, was right. The Illuminist was inking everyone with the mark of the beast. Numbers 666, mankind's imprisonment. Of course, the Order took away all food sources forcing the people to become dependent on them for stables and clean water. But only those who receive the ink would be given the free rations. My stomach roiled just thinking about the lengths these devils would go. The Order is sweeping the world by medicating humanity through their most basic needs.

I rushed my words at Nick, "I think I know what they are doing."

"What are you talking about?"

"The Illuminati are using the ink to control the people!" My words heightened.

"Shush! Keep it down," he growled in a low voice.

"Those numbers on the wrist are implants, tags. They use the implants to hinge these people into a state of hypnosis!"

The Cajun stiffened. "*Merde*! I wouldn't put anything passed those fucking bastards."

"They're killing the people by poisoning them with the food." I crossed my arms, eyeballing the regulator that had shot down the old woman. I wanted to murder him with my bare hands.

The Cajun rubbed absently at his right arm, "How can you be certain? It's possible that they are starving, yes?"

I jerked my gaze to his, "Nick, think about it!" I did a mock thump to his forehead. "What better way to wipe out a civilization than poisoning their water supply and food?"

The Cajun shifted in his seat and blew out a disparaging breath. "Even if you are right, it makes no matter? We can't help them. They're already dead. Look at them." The Cajun nodded to crowd. "They are not much more than ghost in human flesh. That's all the more reason why we need to get what we came for and get the fuck out of here."

I think at that point, we both sensed an unfathomable end, terrified for what was to come and this was only the beginning. The beginning of the apocalypse.

∾

We parked at the curb in front of Val's place. Unlike the Jeep, the Hummer was too burly to fit under the stairwell. I reckoned it was a risk we had to take. Thank goodness, the Hummer looked like one of the vehicles the Order used.

I reached for my door when the Cajun halted me with an iron grip on the wrist. My gaze caught his and I paused, confused.

Dipping his head closer to my face, he spoke in a low voice. "You need to pull yourself together. We can't show any emotion or our cover will be blown. Moi je comprends-vous? (Do you understand me?)" his jaw clenched, his eyes slightly narrowed.

"I've got this!" I shrugged, withdrawing my hand.

One corner of his mouth tugged into a smile. "C'est ma fille! (That's my girl!)"

With my knives strapped underneath my clothes, hidden, I followed the Cajun's lead, sliding out of the car and casually made my way to his side. Our eyes stayed alert to any possible threat.

When I stepped into a downwind, I instantly picked up a pungent odor. Disgust hit me as I spied the side of Val's bar where splattered piss decorated the building, along with clumps of feces soiling the sidewalk.

I cupped my mouth, gagging involuntarily. The Cajun grabbed my elbow roughly, as he leaned into me. He smiled against my ear, whispering in a low harsh voice. "Pull your shit together before you get us both killed."

I dropped my hands to my side and smiled back at the Cajun as if we were lovers. I hated that he was right. Any natural reaction to the creatures' insidious behavior would bring unwanted attention. I needed to be more careful. We couldn't afford any more slipups.

I swiped a quick glanced back down the street where we'd drove past the two regulators and the increasing crowd of locals. The two guards were plenty busy passing out food-boxes to the locals to pay any mind to our presence. A little spurt of hope bristled my neck. We might pull this off after all.

We stopped at the door to Val's gym. My pulse erratically pounded in my ears. It was the only part of me that wasn't numb. I shared a terse glance with the Cajun.

He brusquely nudged my shoulder. "Use your magic. Open the door."

I nodded, stepping up and wringing my fingers around the door handle. I first turned the handle, hoping that Val might've left the gym unlocked. To my disappointment, the handle didn't budge.

Realizing we had only minutes left, I began to invoke my essence. I closed my eyes focusing on the lock. A sudden spark of warmth shot through me, reaching my tingling palm. In the next half breath, the handle gave under my grasp.

I smiled up at the Cajun as he pressed the small of my back for me to move inside.

Blood rushed to my head as I eased the door open. With caution, I stepped inside. Alert to any surprises, my knives hovered above my head cocked, ready to spring into action. The Cajun stayed on my heels, eyes watchful to any signs of trouble, fingering his pistol, sheath to his hip as he shut the door behind us.

Plunged into darkness, we paused just passed the entrance. The Cajun pulled out of his pockedt a small flashlight and flipped it on, shining the small stream of light out into the vast gym. The light only reached a small distance, but it was better than groping through the dark.

The Cajun leaned in my ear. "Do you even know what you're looking for?" He grated.

"I'll know when I see it," I snapped in a hushed voice.

"You better hurry! Time is running out," he whispered over my shoulder.

Frustrated, I snatched the flashlight from the Cajun's hand and ventured my way to the very back where Val had his collection of sorted weapons cased.

When I stopped, I shined the light on the wall, but Val's collection of swords were gone, only a blank canvas. I didn't know why I was surprised. Val wouldn't have left his valuable collections for the regulators to destroy.

I twirled on my heels facing Nick. "There's nothing here!" my voice broke. Did I risk both our lives coming here?

The Cajun grabbed the flashlight from my hand and swiped the room over and stopped on a glass case sitting off by itself. "What about this?"

My eyes followed the dim light and a burst of excitement struck. "The spear!" I half mumbled, running to its side.

Nick followed shortly behind me.

I stood with my palms on the glass peering through to the spear. "That is so strange for Val to leave this behind."

"It looks old. What's so great about this?"

My eyes hitched to Nick's. "It is ancient. It's called the Sword of Destiny." I swallowed. "It's the same spear that pierced Jesus Christ."

"What a sick fuck to keep such an evil thing." Nick blew out a harsh sigh.

"No! Val was keeping it safe and out of the hands of the Illuminati. Do you know if this spear ever got into their hands, they would be unstoppable?"

"All the more reason we should destroy it."

"We can't. It's cursed with dark enchantments."

"Merci! Ne jamais s'arrêter cette folie? (Mercy! Will this madness ever stop?)" The Cajun flurried a string of French curses.

I brushed the stream of light over the spear and stopped.

"Nick!" I could hardly breathe. "I found our next clue."

The Cajun stepped up and followed the light. "Another note!"

"Yes!" hope charged through me. "Give me your gun." I held out my palm, but keeping my eyes on the note that laid at the base of the spear.

"*Non*! No way are you going to fire a gun and alert those shit-dropping regulators."

I turned to Nick, facing him. "I don't want to fire the gun. I want to break the glass." I hissed.

The Cajun paused, soaking in my stern gaze. "You don't want to touch that spear."

I huffed. "Just give me the gun." I glared at him as I held out my palm.

The Cajun grumbled to himself. "Move! I'll do it." he pulled out the pistol and gently shoved me to the side.

He struck the glass with the grip of the gun. Glass went shattering, smashing onto the concrete floor into tiny shards. Nick reached in and drew out the note. "You read it." he shoved the note into my hand.

A quiver in my stomach seized my breath as I paused for a brief moment, staring at the note. Dragging in the air born dust, I opened the note and began to read,

Dear Stevie and your comrade, Nick,

I hope you both had a wonderful stay at my home. I hope it wasn't too

disturbing when you found Sally. I'm truly sorry for the mess. I
simply no longer needed her services.

By now, I am quite certain you must be wondering if your love ones
are safe and alive. I assure you they are still breathing. Although, I
regret to inform you that your friends are in a place you cannot reach. I
am sure you have heard of its existence… the floating castle.

I understand you have rather a difficult time traveling out of your
dimension. It will be very interesting to see if you can hurdle this task.
Hope to see you soon, for time is of the essence. No punt intended.

Oh, yes. Just to make things more interesting, I decided to throw in
another challenge. You are in the throes of an attack. I fear my sweet
darling that you and your Arcadian friend have walked into a trap.

Sincerely,
Aidan

The Cajun raked his fingers through his disheveled curls, more curses streamed from his mouth. "Let's get out of here and now!" he half shouted.

"Wait!" I called out. I reached in and snatched up the spear. "We can't leave this behind."

"*Non*! It's cursed. You said yourself."

"I'm not leaving it!" I bit down on my words. I'd take my chances with the spear than risk it ending in the wrong hands.

"Come on! No time to argue with you, gul." He tugged my arm, dragging me along with him.

The Cajun stopped at the entrance and pressed his ear against the door, listening. I stood beside him waiting for him to signal to go.

After what felt like an eternity, he waved his finger for me to proceed.

I eased out the door, combing my glaze over the street. The Cajun was right behind me. I could feel his warm breath on my shoulder.

We paused under the stairwell, checking if the close was clear. Neither one of us spotted possible trouble as we scurried for the Hummer.

The Cajun had the keys in his hands ready. He punched the remote, unlocking the Hummer. Not wasting a beat, I dove in on his side and swiftly climbed over to my seat. I rushed to buckle up as the Cajun slid behind the wheel, slamming the key in the ignition.

In one quick motion, Nick turned the key but the motor stalled. "Damn!" he grated curses. He pumped the gas and turned the key. The motor dragged, slowly churning.

"It sounds like the battery's dead."

"*Merde*! Someone fucked with the motor while we were inside." Nick pounded his fist against the wheel, French curse words spewed.

He threw the door open and started to step out but he halted. The street began to rumble. Not like an earthquake but like an army of heavy feet stomping.

Nick and I shared a wary glance as the sound increased.

Then the reality of our peril reared its ugly head. A rumble stronger than the one before vibrated the Hummer. I grabbed the handle above my head to hang on.

When my eyes lifted, sheer panic iced me to the bone. Approaching fast coming around the corner where we entered Bourbon Street, I saw marching men in gray uniform.

Soldiers!

These men were not your run of the mill troopers. They were massive in size, ten feet or better with weapons that equally matched their size.

Each synchronized step they took, the vibration grew stronger. The Hummer began shaking, bouncing off the curb. I compared it to the Great Chilean Earthquake.

I knew with certainty that Aidan had been sending me on a wild goose chase, and I had myself to blame for this. I had led Nick into this insidious trap.

"Nick! We've got to get this car moving!" my voice carried over the stepping feet.

"What the fuck you think I'm doing!" he bit back.

Think Stevie, think, I said to myself. "Nick let me in the driver's seat!" I urged.

The Cajun glared at me like I'd lost my mind. Maybe he was right.

"Nick! Give me the wheel *now*!" I insisted. Time was running out. The infantry of men were approaching upon us fast. I knew exactly what we were about to confront...*the Nephilim*. Hybrid giants of their ancestors. Aidan had warned me of such and now I wish I'd listened.

"Nick! I can start the car."

After a sour glare, the Cajun snatched me up and slid me over him as we swapped seats. "I hope you know what you're doing." The Cajun scowled.

I ignored his comment, "Be quiet. I have to concentrate." I placed my hands on the stirring wheel and closed my eyes. I pushed for my essence and slowly it rose. Soon my hands were glowing and I felt the warmth from my hands to the wheel as it continued to weave its magick throughout the metal of the hummer.

"You better hurry! Or else we're going to become those giants' fucking meal." The Cajun growled as he gathered more grenades from the back.

"I know! I know already!" I repeated, as fright surged through me like ice. I pushed my essence even harder as the engine started to kick. Churning and churning and finally the engine turned and the Hummer was purring like new.

"*Merde*! Let's get this baby rolling!"

He didn't have to ask me twice. I put the petal to the metal and peeled out. The Hummer's motor revved as I gunned it down the street heading in the opposite direction.

Nick kept his eyes peeled, if the giants or anything was gaining.

Then suddenly, my heart stopped. I hit the brakes as we went into a tailspin. The hummer hit the curb and nearly flipped over but it managed to land back on its wheels with a hard thud. "Dammit!" I cursed. The Cajun and I gaped at the sight before us. "Those cold heartless bastards did the unthinkable. Innocent men, women and children stood as a barrier blocking our path!"

"I've seen this before. They're banking on your humanity. Those sick fucks will stoop to whatever it takes." Nick sneered.

I glanced back to go the other way but the giants and regulators had other folks barricading the other end of the street too. "I can't run those people over!" I shouted at the Cajun.

"Give me the wheel!" he commanded.

"*No*! I won't let you hurt these people."

"*Non*! We don't have time for debate! Give me the fucking wheel!"

I glared at him.

"Come on! We ain't got time to argue, gul!"

I paused biting my lip hard. "Fine! Take the wheel." I opened the door and started to step out.

The Cajun halted me by clasping his fingers around my arm. "What the fuck are *you* doing?" His face said it all.

I was one crazy bitch tempting fate.

"I'm going to distract them while *you* escape."

"*Non!* I can't let you commit suicide." his jaw twitched.

"It's all we got. Look! I can handle it. Whatever they dish out, I can dish back. That's what I was designed for… *to fight!*" I reasoned.

"You can't fight a whole army, gul!"

My voice calmed, "I don't plan to. I'm giving myself up."

A trail of curses flew from the Cajun as he ran his fingers through his thick hair. "Why would you want to do such a cuckoo thing?"

"It's the only way I can save you and these people. Besides, if I can get inside, I have a chance of finding the guys."

"I don't like this one damn bit!" Nick growled.

"You knew we were going to part ways sooner or later." I glanced back at the encroaching troops. For every second we stalled, the soldiers drew closer. There was no time to argue. I expected any minute now that they'd take us hostage and it'd be too late for the Cajun. They'd kill him and maybe kill me too.

Then I did something that had not crossed my mind or entered my heart. Maybe it was his soulful eyes pleading, or just the craziness of facing death, but I reached over weaving my hands through his thick curls and laid one tongue thrashing kiss right on him. At first, he stiffened, and then soon he returned the kiss with as much passion as I gave him. When we pulled away, we both were short of breath. Our eyes connected as we shared a golden moment of farewell. No words were needed. We both knew this was the end of the line.

With a smothered groan, the Cajun let go of my arm and I stepped out of the Hummer. My hands raised above my head, I sauntered over to the encroaching giants and their comrades, the regulators. I halted in the center of the street.

Behind me, I heard wheels peeling. The smell of rubber burning assaulted my nose. Then I heard glass shattering and the crashing of a building crumbling. I smiled to myself. The Cajun did exactly what he said he'd do. A calm sense came over me knowing he'd gotten away. They didn't want him anyway. The Order wanted me.

Yet I was disappointed that Aidan wasn't leading the pack. What I'd do right now if I could get my hands on him.

I tried not to flinch but I couldn't stop myself as I closed my eyes waiting for my fate.

The next thing I heard was harsh murmurs. Several ironclad hands accosted me roughly, pulling me a part like a medieval rack, ankles and wrists bound, stretching my limbs until they snap.

Then the unfathomable pain stopped after a sudden blow to the back of my head and my world went black.

DEATH ANGEL

THE ANGEL SERIES BOOK 5

LOOKING BACK

hough born as a genetically engineered angel, I'd made many mistakes. But I swore I'd never become a victim of deception ever again.

I discovered that Aidan was the man assisting Sally in her abduction. He was behind my incarceration, forcing me to take the rap for murders I didn't commit.

Witnessing Aidan's betrayal, there was a nagging feeling deep inside of me that nothing was what it seemed. Could I have been that blind to his tricks? Did he ever love me or was it all a lie? I recalled the riddle Aidan had given me before he'd disappeared.

"Believe in only half of what you see and none of which you don't."

What did he mean? Could all this be a vicious nightmare?

I hoped in the end, I'd learn the truth.

A spiritual war broke out in the heavens. As a result, Val had forsaken me, leaving me in the care of a mortal man while he and his heavenly army left earth to fight for the greater good. Though I understood his duties, his leaving left me feeling abandoned and angry.

The world crashed and the Illuminati took over the system bringing in forces of another kind, aliens, called the regulators. They were the peacemakers, but nothing about them was peaceful. They murdered innocent people and destroyed everything in their path. Starvation blanketed the earth like a frozen winter. No one was safe.

The Illuminati was gunning for me. I was a threat to their cause. Forced to seek safety with the help of the Cajun, the guys and I had to go underground. The Cajun promised Val that he would watch over us. We took cover at his grandmother's house but it didn't take long before Aidan found us.

Realizing Aidan's vile betrayal, I seized him, taking him prisoner. I feared he'd alert Van, his uncle, to our whereabouts, who sought to take my life.

Despite the precautions I'd taken, Aidan escaped and kidnaped Dom and Jeffery. He left a note behind with a clear threat and an example of how far he'd go… leaving behind the dead body of the Cajun's best friend, Titan.

Now I must hunt down Aidan and save the guys before he carried through on his threat.

Just as luck would have it, the Cajun and I parted ways. We'd been found and the regulators were coming for me. No point in both of us going down. I had a better chance of surviving. The Cajun didn't. While I distracted the regulators, the Cajun escaped. I wasn't as lucky. I was captured and paid a heavy price.

THE GENTLEMEN'S CLUB

$\mathcal{I}$ had awakened with a splitting headache. Punching through the throbbing pain only made my head hurt worse. I touched the crown of my head and flinched. Memories of my capture slowly crept through my skull, and I jolted, sitting up. The sudden urge to vomit struck hard.

My eyes fluttered open as I caught a trashcan beside the bed. I threw my legs over to the side just in time before I hurled. As I wiped my mouth with the back of my hand, I wondered if all angels had a sensitive stomach. I reckoned that was the human in me.

I placed the trashcan down and drew back into bed, drawing my knees to my chest. I eased out a wry sigh. There were worse things. They could've killed me.

The last vision that repeatedly circled my brain was the pleading expression on Nick's face as I darted out of the Hummer. Most likely our last glance forever. It was for the best. The Cajun alone slipping under the radar of the authorities would keep him safe. Hanging around me meant his chances of living were zero. I had to believe he made it out of the city safely and unharmed.

I swallowed down the knot that seemed to have cemented in my throat. As my eyes adjusted to the dim light, I skimmed over my surroundings. To my surprise, I wasn't stuck in a drafty dungeon or restraint in a mental hospital. Nothing like my last capture. The room reminded me of a fancy hotel: a king-size bed with monogrammed pillows, sheets that felt like Egyptian and royal blue carpet. Not the sort of grand treatment I'd expected. Nevertheless, I was still a prisoner.

Of course, Aidan came through with his threat. The coward didn't even bother showing up for the show. I questioned if he was the one that set me up in this cozy suite. That had me more worried than if I'd been sitting in a dank dungeon cell. At least I'd know what to expect. This exquisite suite pestered me like a pus-filled boil ready to pop. Whoever was keeping me hostage went through great lengths to spare my life. I should still be on guard. I wasn't out of the woods by any means.

What did the Illuminati want from me? I figured there wasn't much I could offer. After all, I'd infused my essence with Aidan. They couldn't extract my powers and they had taken my child. Dom and Jeffery were mortals. And my powers were unpredictable.

Yet as I'd said before, I would never belong to myself. I wasn't born like a normal person. There wasn't anything about me that was ordinary. I was a product of my environment, a genetically engineered angel that turned out to be a dud, a useless mistake.

If anything good comes out of this, I hoped Aidan would make a gesture of good faith and free Dom and Jeffery. Surely, considering their history together, Aidan would have a soft spot for them. He no longer needed the guys to bait me. He wanted my capture and now he had it. Yet if that wasn't enough, I'd gladly give my life in exchange for the guys.

I'd caused a lot of pain to those I loved. If I'd just turned myself in before now, the Cajun and the guys wouldn't have been thrust into peril. Because of me, the Cajun nearly died and because of me, Aidan kidnapped Jeffery and Dom. I blamed myself. A creature like me didn't have the right to walk freely. This planet belonged to humans. Not a freak created in a lab. I shouldn't have ever been born. I wasn't feeling sorry for myself or expecting anyone to take pity on me. It was the truth.

Despite my resolve, I wasn't going to sit still and allow them to do whatever they wanted to me without giving them one hell of a good old southern ass kicking.

I knew what I had to do next. My eyes gravitated to the door. With a little help from my essence, I was fairly certain that I could break out of this joint. I reckoned I had the advantage there. What worried me was what might be lurking on the other side of the door. Did I have enough strength to fight any attack?

What if I used the same exertion that I'd used on Aidan and I turned back into that green-faced monster? Chills spiraled down my spine. Morphing into a monster was something I preferred to avoid. But was there a way I could balance my powers without turning into some hideous creature?

If Val were here, I could've asked him if my green face was normal for a Zop. Then again, this problem could stem from my creation. After all, I was a lab experiment. It wouldn't be much of a stretch that the scientist made a mistake mixing a celestial being with a human's DNA. There could be a hundred and one reasons why I had morphed.

One thing for sure, I wasn't going to find answers sitting in this suite. I had to do what I had to do and worry about the effects later. I had to escape. It was that simple. First thing on the list after I blew this coop was finding Jeffery and Dom. I'd like to think that Aidan had the guys stowed away in one of these rooms here.

Wherever here was.

Still, it made sense. He staged my capture, knowing that I'd follow the guys anywhere. What other place did Aidan have to hide them?

Then I remembered the note. He mentioned another dimension. I didn't see how he could carry the guys to another world. They were mortal. Aidan had mentioned that their oxygen was running low. What if he were merely trying to scare me?

What if Aidan were telling the truth? I remembered how the castle had magically vanished at his place in Tangi and then when I met Mustafa at the castle for the first time. We were in limbo. An empty forsaken land of darkness. The castle must be enchanted, traveling from dimension to dimension.

I lost Dawn in that castle to Mustafa. My chest tightened as the visions pummeled through my mind. That was the worst moment of my life. I drew in a sharp sigh. As much as I wanted to curl up and have a good cry over my loss, I needed to keep my head clear.

I threw my legs off the bed as the pounding ache in the back of my head sharpened. My whole body throbbed. I pushed past it and focused on that mahogany door, the barrier blocking my freedom. In four strides, I had my ear against the cool wood listening. It was quiet. "Okay, so far so good!" I mumbled.

I dropped down to the floor and peered through the space under the door. I spotted a shadow, pacing back and forth. I gathered to my feet quietly with a scowl on my face. "Ugh… a guard!" I bit my bottom lip wondering if I'd be encountering a regulator or a Nephilim? First, I needed to weigh out my options before making a move. I glanced over the room. Nothing but four walls. No windows. I checked the bathroom. It was nice but nothing out of the ordinary, monogram towels, a separate shower with white marble and blue rugs and no windows either. It made sense why they put me in this room. It wasn't an easy escape. I huffed an exasperated sigh. It looked like the only way out was the door. And I'd bet my life on it that it was heavily guarded.

Then I thought about the element of surprise. If it were going to work, I had to attack swiftly, with no hesitation. I lifted under my blouse feeling for my blades. A smile spread wide across my face. Ms. Noel once taught me an invisible spell. Good thing too! It sure came in handy. They didn't spot my sheath of knives.

It was a shame the spell only worked on inanimate objects. If I could cast the spell on myself, I'd walk straight out of this place and no one would know the better. Sweet idea, but an impossible feat. Too bad I couldn't shift like Aidan. That was a trick I'd kill to have. So, I had to go to plan B. Whatever the hell that might be.

I drew in a deep breath and walked back to the end of the bed and stretched my arms out focusing on the door, pushing the limits of my powers. The energy in the atmosphere sizzled. I could feel my magick boil like a pressure cooker, climbing to the surface. My essence expanded, shooting forth with mighty force like a mini volcano obliterating the door into a million wooden splinters, knocking the massive guard off his feet. A loud clunk echoed down the hallway as blood oozed from the beast's head. How about that? I giggled, staring at the large stiff scaly body. It was a giant Nephilim with a shard of wood penetrating his thick skull lay sprawled on the floor.

I jumped with triumph, confident that the beast was dead as I spun on my heels to make my get-away. But when I felt my feet rumble, I stopped and turned. The beast had risen to his feet, standing a good seven feet tall and gnarling at me. He shook his massive head, knocking the splinter free from his thick skull. Sheer black fright swept through me as I gawked. He pointed his hell-hot eyes at me and with lightning speed, he wrangled me by the neck and slammed my body onto the floor. The impact knocked the breath out of me, but I had to act fast or else die. I scrambled to my feet and shot my hands out, expecting to blast the beast to Timbuktu but nothing happened. *"Shit!"* I shook my hands trying to ignite the magical fire but all it did was sputter. *"Freckin' magick!"* I stomped my feet in a tantrum, *"Can't depend on it for nothin'!"* Swiftly moving on to the next line of offense, I commanded my steel knives to attack the beast, aiming between his black eyes. This rascal was one tough *mother*. The giant was ready to fight to the death. He swatted his burly fist at my blades, sending them crashing to the wall. Continuing his attack, he twisted his dense body and then like a wrecking ball, his massive fist collided into my stomach, sending me sailing several feet into the air and falling to the floor with a hard whomp. Before I could catch my breath, the Nephilim wrapped his meaty fingers around my neck and lifted me to eye level as drool dripped from his long, sharp snappers. *"Holy shit!"* Staring back into his hungry, baleful eyes, I came to a haunting realization that this fat bastard intended to eat me!

I reached out for my knives commanding them to attack. The deadly blades shot forth, piercing his left eye. I could hear cartilage snapping as the bloody eyeball dropped down his face. Like a domino effect: the giant dropped his grip, staggered backward, fell flat on his back, shook the floor, and knocked me off my feet.

But the creature was like a cat with nine lives, springing to his feet and charging. His speed was incredibly fast that I hardly had time to think. He flew in the air and pounced on me with all fours. As I ducked and rolled underneath him, clenching my fingers around the hilt of my dagger, raised above my head, I thrust the deadly blade between the Nephilim's legs, swiftly sliding out from under him.

This time, I hurt the beast as his loud squealed burst my eardrums. *"Damnit!"* I had to stop him before he brought down this whole place. I leaped into the air, taking my knife to his throat. The blade sliced his vocal cords stopping his screams. Crimson blood splattered the wall and my face and clothes. The giant fell like a fallen tree crashing to the ground. His body jerked as he lay on his back as blood pooled around his whale body. Gurgling sounds emerged as he suffocated from his own blood. Seconds later, he stilled.

I stood raking in air as my eyes washed over the giant. How much I'd changed in these last three years. I was turning into one cold bitch. I felt no remorse. Strangely, I delighted in his kill. That was one less evil bastard hurting innocent folks.

Moving along, I coiled the corner, noticing a black cape and mask on a small table. I smirked. Anonymity wasn't such a bad idea. I quickly snatched the items and slipped them on. I pulled the hood down over my head, trying to hide my hair. The mask would take care of my face. The disguise might work. I could blend in with all the other cloaks. I needed to act fast and get as far from this area as possible.

Then it hit me that I couldn't leave the bloody Nephilim for everyone's eyes. Once a guard spotted him, he'd alert the whole house that I'd escaped. I went back to where I'd left the giant now saturated in his blood. Judging by his monstrous size, he was too heavy for me to drag. Then my gaze dropped to the crimson saturated carpet. Blood was everywhere, streaking the walls and ceiling.

My mind began to churn… if an inanimate object could become invisible, then a dead person had to be considered as one of those stiff objects. I looked in both directions of the hall. No sign of anyone coming. I leaned over the smelly creature, not touching the blood that enwreathed him. God, he reeked!

I took a second to relax and I spoke a soft flow of words, *"Let this object hide from sight, veiled behind the light, where it might go unnoticed passing through the night."* I repeated the same spell on the blood that had grown cold and still and the broken door.

After I finished all three objects, the Nephilim, the blood, and the door, there were no visible signs of a disturbance. The wooden door looked as it had before. An illusion. Though, it wasn't forever. Any minute someone could walk down this hall and stumble over the giant's body or try to open the door, my illusion would be discovered. I planned to be gone by then. With any luck, I hoped the spell would last long enough for me to find Jeffery and Dom and blow this joint.

I hurried along down the hall, listening at each door. I softly whispered out Dom and Jeffery's name but no one answered. I remembered the doors were soundproof. I dropped to my knees looking under the door for a shadow, any movement at all. But I came up empty-handed. Desperation was starting to get under my skin.

I turned the corner and entered a spacious lobby. I paused for a second recovering my shock, raking my gaze over the room. One thing f'sure... money didn't buy class.

The room reeked of cigars and sex. Glowing Candles flickered heavily in the swirl of gray smoke. It had man-cave stamped all over it. Deep Mahogany wood, crystal chandeliers, and topless women wore nothing but a thong while parading trays of flutes filled to the brim with what looked like champagne.

Adorned with their black mask, the men hid their faces. A nice feature to their costume or lack of. I continued to walk through the establishment. Each room looked like the next, men smoking cigars and taking liberties with the women. The men didn't seem to care if others watched.

Depraved much?

I made a point to look the other way. Not a sideshow I particularly wanted to watch. Why would any woman subject herself to such degradation? Did they do this for food or a position among the elite? Whatever their reason might be, I hoped it was worth it. I'd rather die than let any one of these disgusting pigs put their paws on me. I reckoned the women might not have a choice. Perhaps they were like me. Captured and held captive against their will.

When I entered another open room, one girl caught my eye. She stood out among the rest with long, blonde hair, glistening in the candlelight. The way she carried her shoulders seemed familiar to me. Then she glanced at me and I gawked. I knew this girl... *it was Gina! Holy shit!* She was a prostitute! Gina didn't have the cleanest rep in school, but I knew she had too much pride to stoop this low. Now I had to somehow get these girls out of here. That wasn't going to be easy. They were mostly naked and if I counted correctly, there had to be at least twenty girls. Guards were standing at every exit too. *Crap!*

I had to get Gina's attention. The last thing I wanted was to stir the nest. I casually walked up, hiding my face, and whispered in her ear. "Come with me." I tried deepening my voice like a man. I did a pathetic job at it too. Luckily, only she could hear me.

She replied as if she was reciting lines from a bad play. "Yes. Shall I invite any of the other girls, sir?"

Damn! Had The Family turned her into Robo-chick? "No. Just you," I whispered curtly. I started for another room and she followed behind me. The girl's movements reminded me of someone under a trance.

Though her cheeks were not hollow like the street people, she carried that same empty stare as they held.

I hoped she snapped out of it. I wasn't sure how I'd manage to get her out safely. I reckoned I'd figure it out as I go. Not a soundproof plan but it would have to do. Rescuing one girl was tough but twenty would be impossible without reinforcement. And where I saw it, I was the only reinforcement left. Boy, us girls were screwed.

I found an empty room down a long narrow hall. I quickly ushered her inside and shut the door. Strangely, she went straight for the bed and began to tug off her thong. Gross! I sprinted to her side, "No, no! I didn't call you in here for *that*! Put your... *that* cloth back on." I lowered my eyes, totally grossed out.

"Have I disappointed you?" She stared at me blank-faced.

"You are not disappointing me. I'm a friend." I pulled off my hoodie and mask, hoping I'd jarred her memory.

Her eyes orbed in sheer fear and she started to scream. I lunged, slapping my hand across her mouth to muffle her protest. "Shush! I'm here to help you." I waited a moment to let it sink in her thick skull. "If I take my hand away are you going to scream?"

She shook her head no, but her eyes remained glossed with fright. I had to talk to her and I had to trust that she trusted me even in her state of mind. I eased my hand off and she stood there quiet but trembling. I pulled my cape off and wrapped it around her, sitting back down on the bed. Gina sat there staring off into space. What had these devils done to this girl? It wouldn't be hard to guess that the other women were in the same state of fog.

Then my eyes dropped to her wrist. The *ink*! Gina was under some sort of mind control through that ink. Then I remembered the people in the food line. Gina had the same void look. I knew it! Son of a mother *fucking bitch*! I ran my fingers through my hair wanting to pull it out. I wasn't angry I was enraged! I had to stop this barbarity.

I sat on the bed next to Gina. I took her inked hand into mine. I'd never seen one of these up close. I gently ran my fingers over it. Nothing by sight seemed unusual. But the Illuminists were masters of deception. My senses were high on alert. Those tainted numbers 6.6.6. swam in black magick. The implant's purpose was poisonous.

I lifted my gaze to Gina's dull eyes. She sat there on the edge of the bed staring blankly. Creepy as hell. "Gina, I'm going to try a little experiment. I want to help you feel better. Will you let me do that for you?"

"Yes, I want to feel better. Shall I lie down on my stomach?"

Ugh! "What? *No!*" I sucked in a bristled breath, "Just hold still. This might hurt."

"Okay," she said, flat with no emotion.

I placed my right hand over the ink and held her hand firmly with my left. I could feel its vibration under her skin. I closed my eyes. I exerted as much essence that I could muster up. I needed the heat to penetrate below the skin, underneath the ink. The numbers had a strong resistance. I pushed through its fortress and kept focusing on the ink and that damn device that vibrated under the skin. My hand began to glow and the warmth intensified. Then it got uncomfortable.

Hot steam began curling to the surface and the smell of burning skin attacked my nostrils. I hated doing this to her. Strangely, she didn't flinch or show any signs of agony. Though, if I managed to draw the implant out from under her skin, she might come alive hurling a lamp at me. Pain was good, though. It meant she was still alive. And hopefully back to her old self, fully aware of her surroundings.

After a few moments, I began to see the ink fade. I felt the tiny metal device wiggle underneath my palm. That sucker was coming out even if I had to go in after it, I swore under my breath.

The implant moved similar to a worm, inching its way to the surface. Soon the ink would completely disappear and the implant would be clear of her skin. A pair of tweezers would've come in handy right now.

Finally, the implant peeked above the surface of the skin. I gave it a good tug but it tried to resist. I didn't let go and after a good grip and tug, the device slid out into my hand.

I'd forgotten about zombie Gina. She perked up and started screaming. Swiftly, I stamped my hand across her mouth as I pressed my finger to my lips. She settled down, but her eyes were wild with terror. "Gina, it's me, Stevie! I'm trying to help you. I'm going to get you out of here. Okay?"

Gina nodded her head sharply. A deep glint of mistrust gleamed in her eyes. The poor girl was in shock.

"Do you remember me?"

"Yes," she barely whispered.

"Good girl!" I smiled, "Do you know where you are?"

Her face twisted. "I'm not sure. Everything's a blur." Tears swelled in her eyes.

"You've been under a trance by a device like this." I picked up the tiny implant off the floor. It wiggled in my palm as if it was looking to nest. Eerie had a whole new meaning as I watched the small metal jump like a flea. I extended my palm to Gina. "This is what I removed from you."

She leaned forward but jumped back when it leaped at her. It was as though it knew her. Chills grated against my spine. "Get it away from me!" she shrieked as fright flickered in her brown eyes.

"Don't worry. It can't hurt you anymore." I grabbed it up and closed my palm tightly. I wanted to take it and have it analyzed but I feared if I got caught with it, who knows, one of those bastards might use it on me. I quickly dove for the bathroom and flushed it down the toilet. I watched and made sure it flushed. I couldn't have that little bugger floating to the top for someone to see.

When I returned to Gina, she was curled up next to the headboard on the bed. I sat down on the edge. I wanted to comfort her, "I can take the pain away. May I have your hand again?" I reached out baring my palm.

Gina snapped out of her muffled dilemma as she hauled off and slugged me across my face. "You bitch!" she hissed. "Don't touch me!" She clasped her injured hand and scooted to the other side of the bed.

I rubbed my face but remained calm. I understood her reaction. I spoke in a whisper, "I get why you don't trust me. But you're out of options. I'm your only hope of getting out of here. Do you know what happened to you?"

She shook her head no, holding her bleeding wrist. Her whole body shivered and her face, tight with fear. I felt stifled like a ton of bricks toppled upon my chest. I wanted to help her, but unless I get her to trust me, the chances of us escaping this vile place were slim. And time wasn't on our side. Sooner or later, the Regulators were going to start looking for their missing pal, and I had no idea how long that spell would last. I spoke up, "Gina, you've been hypnotized with an implant." I bit my bottom lip, pausing. "Did they ink you in the food line?"

"Yes, I was hungry."

"I know. I don't blame you. But when the Regulator inked you, an implant was inserted below the skin. That's how the elite controls you along with everyone else."

She eyed my wrist. "How come you didn't get one?"

"I reckon I got lucky," I shrugged. "I need you to trust me and cooperate with me. I want to get you out of here."

Gina scoffed. "You help me… *my ass!* You hate me."

I raked in an exasperating breath. "Our squabble is water under the bridge." I looked down at the floor. I didn't want to rehash that day that Gina called my father roadkill. The bunt of her cruel words still stung, but I'd to push past it. I lifted my gaze back at her. "Will you let me help you?"

"How are you going to help me?" Her tone was full of mistrust.

"First of all, I just dug that implant out from your wrist. Five minutes ago, you were acting more like a robot than a human. You even made a pass at me." I made a circle with my finger pointing to the ceiling. "It's no telling how many people in this gentleman's club has been all up in your grill." I huffed. "*FYI*, the elite had turned you into a sex slave. If it weren't for me digging that implant out of you, you'd be screwing some fat, bald man right now. You can thank me later once we're free of this God-forsaken place." I glared at her.

Gina flinched. Then she eased over to me still keeping a distance. "That little thing you gouged out of me… w-w-was controlling me?" She stammered over her words.

"Yep! That's what I said," I spoke bluntly.

Gina's brows smashed together. "They're not controlling you?"

I smiled to myself. "I'm a little different. But I can help you if you let me. I can heal your wrist. I can stop the pain." I nodded to her bleeding wound.

"Yeah, you burnt my wrist and now you want to heal it! No thanks."

Difficult Gina was back.

I grimaced, "Sorry, but I had no other option," I shrugged. "That little piece of shit controlled every move you made. It can tell you to stop breathing and you would've obeyed its command. This new system, the New World Order, and the leaders are killing people with implants and poisoning folks with the food. This gentlemen's club is by no means a gentleman. They had you parading around here almost naked."

"What?!"

"Look under your cape."

Gina immediately opened the robe and gasped as her head snapped back up at me.

"Do you believe me now?" I arched a brow.

She shook her head, yes.

"Then will you give me your hand and let me heal your wrist? I promise it won't hurt." I stared at her with a solemn face. She had to trust me, or we were doomed.

Gina hesitated and then she scooted to me and opened her wrist to me.

The wound was deep. I'd barely missed the ulnar artery. Good thing too. The last thing I needed was an actual murder on my hands. I examined the injury more closely. I reckoned that if a doctor had examined her, he would've given her stitches. But then again, she seemed too numb to feel the brunt of the actual pain. I was grateful for that.

I suddenly thought about the Cajun. If he were here, he'd likely take care of it in the normal way. I think normal is good. The people needed normal and yet, it was so far from reach.

With a deep sigh, I placed my hand over the wound and closed my eyes. Soon my essence powered forth and my hand began to glow a bright light. At first, Gina jerked back but when she realized I meant no harm, she relaxed, allowing the gentle light to soothe her.

At the moment, I was appreciative that I had inherited this gift from Aidan. A minute or two passed and her hand was as good as new. Gina glanced down at her wrist and there wasn't a scar or even a trace of the ink. She gasped, "How did you do that?" Astonishment coated her voice.

This time I felt like smiling. "It's a little trick I picked up." I didn't have time to explain the whole story. I had to get her out of here. "We got to move!" I stood up and pulled my shirt and pants off. I was keeping my boots. "You put this on and give me the cape back." I tossed the clothes to her.

"Okay! I was feeling a little draft." She smiled.

I think I just witnessed Gina joking. I smiled back.

Gina hurriedly threw on the clothes with no protest.

Soon we were standing at the door ready to spring into action. I tossed over my shoulder, "Any chance you know where the exit to this place is?"

"Maybe, but I can't be certain." She shared a wry glance.

"What do you remember?"

"I recall a hallway and foyer leading to double doors and bright light. I don't know where it's located. Sorry, that's all I remember," she whispered back.

"No, you did great. We have something to go on," I grabbed up the mask off the bed. "Here, put my mask on. Don't take it off until you are long gone from this place."

She nodded in silence.

"Okay, follow me," I smiled tightly. "Whatever you do, don't speak out. They'll know right away you're no longer under their control. Understand?"

"Yes," Gina nodded.

I placed the hood over my hair and down over my eyes as I cracked the door open, peering down the hall. It appeared empty for now. We eased out of the room and shut the door behind us and headed the way we came.

There was a large gathering room off to my left and to my right I spotted a foyer. Gina and I shared a quick glance and we went for the double doors. I thought this seemed too easy, but I didn't have time to investigate it first.

Right as my hand touched the doorknob, I heard the click of a gun, several followed. Gina and I both slowly pivoted on our heels, facing a line of Regulators. And behind them all, one person stood out from among the other unknown black capes... Aidan's uncle, Edward Van Dunn. I instantly grimaced. I pulled Gina behind me shielding her from any outbreak.

I raked in some air for my lungs and spoke up as cocky as I could have mustered, "Hello, Van! So lovely running into you. I must apologize though. We were just leaving. Surely you can understand," I sneered.

"Well, as usual, I see you're trying to steal my property." Van didn't even acknowledge Gina. But he didn't have to.

"Come on, Van! What's one less girl?" I flashed a cocky smile.

"I might be more inclined to let this one go but for you... *never*," his eyes flared with hatred.

"Van, since the fight is with me, let the innocent go and you and I can duke it out. Just like back in the day when you wanted to strangle me."

He laughed with a deeply depraved cadence.

I needed to act fast and get Gina out of here. This was where I had good use for the gifts that had been bestowed upon me.

Swiftly, I acted, shoving Gina out the door. I screamed at her, "*Run!*" Without hesitation, Gina darted down the street not looking back. I took a deep breath of relief. A sense of glee flickered through me. At least one girl got away.

Back to the present, I quickly cut my aim back to Van and his dominions. My chances of surviving were slim to none but at least they'd know they'd been in a fight. With murder in my eyes, I shot my arms out calling on my knives to attack. In the next breath, I blasted fireballs at the Regulators, knocking them off their feet. Some caught fire and shrieked running as the angry blame engulf them.

One Regulator tried to catch me off guard, charging at me from my right side. I reacted immediately, ducking, and thrusting my dagger into his gut. He dropped to the floor with a loud clonk.

Another Regulator charged me from behind. He landed a swift powerful leg kick to my ribs, sending me crashing onto a table. Splinters of wood shattered as pain shot through my body. For a minute I was knocked silly.

Before I could recharge, swarms of Regulators closed in on me, attacking me with great force. Helpless and defeated with each striking blow, my mind filled with murk and as a result, my daggers fatally fell to my side. They were coming at me so hard and frequently, their assaults began to blur. A vision fluttered through my mind of Gina escaping. I smiled to myself. At least I saved her.

THE COUNCIL

*A*bruptly, I gained consciousness. The Regulators had doused me with a bucket of icy water. I shivered, gagging, and coughing from the stench. The smell of fish and decay lingered in my throat.

Before I could fully gain awareness, the same two Regulators ripped me off the floor, dragging me to the center of a circle. Pain shot through my entire body as they roughly dropped me. With my one good eye, I peered through a strand of sopping hair at an assembly of scarlet cloaks seated around a table that was similar to the Senate Chambers.

The two Regulators forced me onto my feet, placing me on a steel plate that lit up like a Christmas tree. A low buzzing hummed beneath my feet. It was astounding how I could stand on my own two feet after that horrific bashing. I thought my ribs might be cracked and perhaps internal bleeding as well. My bottom lip stung like a *mother*. My whole body screamed in agony. If I'd been human, I doubt I'd be breathing. Then I thought about the Cajun and how much pain he'd endured on my account. Guilt hit me worse than my injuries.

With hindered one eye, I scanned the dim. My swollen, shut-eye throbbed like hell. As far as I could tell, I counted thirteen cloaks sitting around a table, all scowling at me. I tried to twist around to get a full panoramic view but the neon plate had some kind of magnetic force.

My feet felt heavy as if I cemented to the ground. I didn't like this feeling, a sense of being trapped and defenseless.

All at once, my gaze landed on a familiar face. I knew with certainty that my fate had just been sealed. Our eyes locked and we both glared at each other with equal disdain. Mustafa! Of all creatures, he was sitting right next to my favorite adversary, Edward Van Dunn, Aidan's uncle. "What a wonderful family reunion," I blurted wearing sarcasm.

"What a pleasure it is seeing you once again, my daughter." A smile broke across Mustafa's face. It was so eliminating that it sickened me. The dark angel was as beautiful as he was contemptible. And I had no intentions of falling prey to his charms. *"I. Am. Not. Your. Daughter!"* I hissed through clenched teeth.

Van spoke up, "My, such rebellion you are harvesting, young lady. Most would be dead after the lashing you received. Yet here you stand full of audacity." Van nodded to his companion seated next to him, "That one you best watch. She'll run a knife through your back."

Mustafa glanced over at me and just smiled like a proud father. Though rage washed over me in waves, wishing I could band my fingers around his neck and strangle the dark angel.

"Do you know why you are here?" Mustafa asked.

"No. But I have a feeling you're going to tell me." I wasn't in the mood to hear his reasons. If they planned to kill me, I'd prefer they get on with it. Of course, they had to gloat first like a hunter trapping a deer before the kill.

"Why do you resist us? The Family has made great efforts in creating you, they wish to preserve your life rather than end it so abruptly," Mustafa pointed out.

I replied snidely, "And your point?"

Mustafa paused and then smiled, never taking his baleful eyes off me. "We wish for you to join our crusade. You could be a great service to us and we would grant your freedom and full range of your magick."

"Freedom and magick?" I scoffed. "I've never been free of your clinches and I will find my own way to my magick without your help." My fist tightened at my side.

Van interjected making known his hatred for me. "You are such a selfish little bitch. We have given you unimaginable abilities and you

162

throw it back in our faces. How ungrateful you are!" He leaned over his desk as hostility rolled off his shoulders.

"Ah, Van are you still harboring resentment that I wouldn't let you slaughter me?" I ignored his scowl. "You look like you could use an anger management class. I hear they work wonders."

Van repeated brusquely. "You are in contempt of this council!" He rose to his feet, beady eyes shooting fire at me.

"My respect went down the crapper when you murdered my child!" I hissed.

"Your child is the past. There are bigger matters that beseech our present attention. We are the masters of a new age. The old system is gone. The New World Order is at hand!" His anger escalated. "You have a choice, either you are a part of the new Order or you are an enemy."

I scoffed, "I think you know my answer. How could I be a party to any leadership that murders innocent people, or forces them into slavery?" My temper was barely contained, my fist clenched to my side, nails digging into my palm.

"My, what a clever girl you have become in these last three years. Then surely you see the mercy we have granted you? Is that not momentous to you?"

"Momentous!" I choked out a course laugh. "I'd rather starve before I let you ink me!" I spat, darkly. "I have no use for your new world."

"Don't be so pigheaded. If you join us," Mustafa's musical voice probed further, "You'll experience an eternity of blessings."

Their lies only fueled my rage. "Blessings? The only one I recollect having favors is you! When you took *my* child's *breath*!" I swallowed hard trying not to lose control. "I recall a time when I asked you to spare my daughter's life and take me instead." I pounded my chest with a balled-up fist. "You refused my offer then and now you desire the very thing you rejected?" I glared at Mustafa. "Sorry *Daddy*, that offer no longer stands." My fingers ached for my knives but they had been confiscated.

"Yes," the dark angel sang. "At the time, your offer didn't fulfill my purpose. Sadly, but a fact that you must accept is that Dawn collateral damage. Even Jesus gave his life for a higher power. Why can you not see this?"

"Collateral damage? *A higher power?*" I roared. "You depraved sick bastard!" His words tasted like venom. "You murdered *my* child! That is a reality that I am forced to live with for the rest of my life. I promised you once and I'm promising you now, you will pay for taking her life. You have my word, wicked one." I leered at him with burning, reproachable eyes. For a second, I swore I saw a flicker of *fear*. A tug pulled at the corner of my lip. He *should* fear me.

Suddenly, Van joined the party. "I see your powers are growing. Though, they have yet to excel to their full potential." He flashed his tobacco-stained teeth. "I wonder if you are defective."

A smirk rose from the corner of my lips. "Why don't you tell me, Van?" I noted that he appeared haggard more than usual. "Van, you're not looking too good these days," I smirked. He'd dropped a good thirty pounds. But it seemed strange to me that he had aged so rapidly. He was in his early fifties, yet by his leathered skin, he looked like seventy.

His eyes hardened. "Don't worry about me. You should be more concerned over yourself," he hissed.

"Van, don't flatter yourself. I hardly ever give you a thought," I shot back.

Van smirked as if he'd won. He leaned back in his seat obscuring his face into the shadows. "Perhaps you will think about our offer. I think we can convince you to come to our side," he brazenly boasted.

I burst into bitter laughter. "I'm not joining your stupid Order, Van, and partner up with a bunch of psychopaths. You're not any better than Hitler." I tilted my chin with clear defiance.

All at once, laughter ricocheted off the panel of cloaks throughout the chamber. A sick dread stirred my gut. I knew my pride had over-stepped its boundary.

Mustafa leaned forward smiling like a fat cat that just ate the last canary. My gut told me I was in over my head. "My child, don't under-estimate the almighty."

I crossed my arms over my chest. "Do you plan to ink me?" I snarled at his underlying threat.

Snickers echoed, sounding similar to acoustics; every little sound seemed amplified. The corners of Mustafa's lips curled upward for a flash and then his lips dove into a tight lip. "The ink doesn't work on you. Only humans. We have something more appropriate for you."

Then before I took my next breath, I heard a loud clicking and chains rattling underneath me. With no warning, the metal plate dropped.

Like a domino effect, the magnetic force holding me prisoner abruptly released its grip. Unable to brace myself, I dropped like a heavy brick, plummeting down some sort of tunnel into blackness.

Sharp stone grated my backside as I slid down the wall. Several seconds passed before I hit stinging ice water that felt worse than a thousand needles. The water was polar cold. I gasped as my body pierced the brutal water, swallowing gulfs of fishy ice.

Disoriented, I didn't know which direction was up. *Shit!* If I fought the water, I'd surely drown. I calmed my panic, holding my body still and letting my body drift toward the top. When I found my bearings, I started paddling to the top.

Once I pierced the surface and felt the frigid air burning my face and eyes, I sucked in oxygen, choking up water. My lungs felt on fire.

Horror saturated my mind as I tried adjusting my eyes to the darkness. Lighting wasn't any better at the surface than the bottom, no glimmer, not even a faint shaft of light. I didn't have long before hyperthermia would set. I knew I had to crawl my way out of this tunnel or I was as good as dead. I doubted even the strongest angel could tolerate these conditions. My limbs were already getting numb and stiff. My body temperature was dropping fast. I tried to keep moving, but it was getting harder with each second that passed. My whole life flashed before me. I'd never imagined my life ending so brutally. So many unanswered questions still hung in the balance.

Aidan came to mind. The Aidan I still loved. The one that no longer existed. I ached for his touch, his soothing voice, his salty kisses. The reality of my first love was gone. My mind was languid, without hope.

Jerked back into my current peril, something in the water caught my breath. I stilled to listen. The smooth swish of the water trickled in my ears. I concluded right then that I wasn't alone. Hairs bristled my neck as I recalled that same sound from the bayou, a soothing stream gliding down the river and headed my way.

An alligator! I gasped.

"Shit! Think Stevie, *think!*" I needed to see. Then it hit me, the glow from my hands! I closed my eyes trying to calm my erratic heartbeat. I slowed my breathing and just when I felt my essence bubble, I lost control as my whole body slammed violently against a sharp boulder.

For a second it knocked me silly, but when I gained my where-abouts, the beast rammed its scaly body into me with such a force that it nearly made me into mincemeat pie. This time swift and accurate, the beast latched its teeth onto my upper arm. I felt its teeth sink into my flesh, down to the bone and a crackling sound quickly followed. An intense pain struck, sending me to hell as I screamed until my voice broke.

Once the creature released his powerful grip, I swam to the surface, gulping air. I prayed for someone to rescue me, but I knew death was a breath away.

My instinct took hold and I started kicking and swinging with my one good arm. I wasn't in any shape to fight the beast. The Regulators' friendly welcoming made sure of it. I was lucky to breathe.

I pushed again for my essence. Once more before I had gained my powers, abruptly, the beast sunk his teeth into my leg, plunging my body back down into the subzero water, shaking me like a dog shaking a mere cloth.

The beast had the advantage. Fighting such a strong creature was futile. In my desperate attempt, I called to my daggers, hoping they'd sense me.

Yet nothing, no signs of help.

From shock to loss of blood, my strength was waning fast. My mind was losing focus. I was so cold that my body stopped shivering. It was shutting down. Soon the inevitable was sure to come... *unconsciousness*.

I welcomed a beating compared to this... the frigid water torturing my mind was by far a thousand times worse. How I craved restfulness. I closed my eyes waiting for death to take me.

Just when I'd resigned myself to defeat, I felt a sharp jolt. It was apparent that I'd been strapped in a harness all this time. I let out a teeth-chattering sigh as they eased my limp body from the bowels of polar hell. For just a second, I was free. Free of the vicious attacks and free of the panel of cloaks. I closed my eyes and let myself go.

I must've passed out. When my eyes fluttered open, I was back on the metal plate lying in a puddle of icy blood.

Weak from the brutal gator-attack, I held my broken arm, clenching the insidious pain. I managed to lift my gaze at the silent panel and stopped on Mustafa.

If I didn't agree to their plan, I knew they'd drop me back down the tunnel. Once again, I had to confront death. Did I save myself and possibly the guys and give the Order, the Family, the Illuminist…whatever the hell they called themselves, what they wanted. Or should I meet my maker now? And send the guys to their death as well. I shivered breathlessly, holding my gaze at Mustafa.

"If I agree to your terms will you let my family go unharmed?"

ANGEL OF DEATH

I'd awaken in a hospital bed dressed in a soft blue cotton gown. A quick prick alerted me to my hand. Someone had administered a drip as I stared blankly at the syringe attached to my taped hand. A bag of clear solution hung beside my bed on a pole.

A heart monitor ticked annoyingly nonstop in my ear as I noticed thin-white wires trailing from the monitor to small flat disks stuck to my chest.

The perfume of antiseptic wafted in the room and burned my eyes. Typical of a hospital. A shaft of light filtered through the drawn curtains covering a small window. Apart from the monitor's light, the thin stream was the only light in the room. Howling wind kept rattling the windowpane. Louisiana was the central station for thunderstorms.

Sleep was out of the question, not that I wanted any. I might be toasty up in this bed feeling like my old self, but that didn't mean I was out of the woods by any means.

As my mind began to process everything, I noted that my swollen eye was almost back to normal. I gently pressed my finger to it. To my surprise, it was mildly tender.

My eyes drifted to my arm as I nearly came off the bed. I ran my fingers over the smooth skin unable to believe my own eyes.

My mangled arm was back to normal.

Only a faint bruise was left in its place. I wiggled my fingers. The feeling was back and a warm pink colored my arm, not the deep red and blue bruises. Even the punctured wounds from the beast's teeth had vanished. A faint smile tipped the corners of my lips.

Then alarm struck me like an avalanche.

That could only mean one thing... someone took the initiative to heal my wounds. Only a particular kind of creature could manage such a task at hand. An angel or a druid. Neither likelihood made me feel warm and fuzzy. My eyes swept over the room once more. I bit my bottom lip.

All at once, an onset of fright punched my gut. *Holy crap!* I was back at Haven!

I had to get the hell out of here. I'd die before I'd let them lock me back up at Haven. I wrapped my fingers around the cord of my IV but before I could rip the needle out, the door crept open.

My eyes snapped up and I froze.

Mustafa!

A warning voice whispered in my head as I sat there staring at him. It took everything in my power not to lunge at his throat.

Mustafa closed the door and made his way toward me. He wore a bright smile, cradling a bouquet of daisies and a box of chocolates that made me almost barf. I reckoned the gifts were for me.

Blech!

I thought how human-like he appeared, wearing military clothes and army boots, nothing like the majestic angel that I recalled back at Aidan's castle. Just by his arresting beauty alone, one would never see him for his true self... *a monster.* Judging by his age, I'd say he was no more than thirty. No one would guess that he was hundreds of years old. His skin, perfect as if he'd been air brushed in a magazine. Undeniably, Mustafa was beyond breathtaking. His compelling green eyes, the charismatic step in his walk revealed a grandiose arrogance. A self privilege he was not entitled to.

Despite his magnetic lure, I didn't let any of his angelic features fool me. Inside, down to the core, he was as evil as he was beautiful.

He casually sat down on the edge of the bed as if we were long-forgotten friends. His pearly smile didn't ease me. I watched in silence.

"Ah, she awakes!" He paused for a brief moment. "I hope you don't mind, but I took the liberty of healing you." There was an icy touch to his tone. "I see that you are as good as new." He nodded to my arm.

I remained quiet.

"Here, I thought you might like a little something to brighten your day. Flowers and sweets for the sweet." His face glowed as if he prided himself for the gesture of gifts as if his meager attempt of generosity was renowned and special. I reckoned it was a peace offering. What a douche bag to think flowers and candy would be exoneration for the death of my child. I'd never forgive him. Not in this lifetime, not even in death.

Not taking my eyes off him or making a move, I remained still like a lifeless doll, not accepting his gifts.

Mustafa gave in to an acidotic sigh as he leaned closer. "I understand your hesitance. However, you will find that I am not so bad."

I abided my silence, yet, I narrowed my eyes.

"I heard you calling out Aidan's name in your sleep. You must still care for the druid?"

What the hell?

I didn't like Mustafa hovering over me while I was unconscious. Biting my tongue, I swallowed hard, trying not to reveal my loathing for the fallen angel.

"It is fine," he patted my foot. I stiffened, shooting daggers at his face. "We will talk later after you've rested and are stronger. I will explain your duties then." He laid the flowers and candy on the tray beside the bed and made his way toward the door.

"What about Jeffery and Dom?" I croaked. My throat burned like a red-hot branding iron.

Mustafa cut his eyes back at me. "Why, yes. Your family. I recall," he simply replied.

"That's right, my family. Are you even aware that Aidan Bane Du Pont has kidnapped my family? I believe you are acquainted with him."

"Yes, quite." His voice went up a notch.

Holding my cool by a mere thread, I asked, "Then you know the whereabouts of my family?"

"I am aware." His angelic face held no telltale sign he was an accomplice to their capture.

Okay, were we going to play with our words now? "You gave me your word that Dom and Jeffery would go free."

"No, I agreed that they would be unharmed." A lack of empathy tampered with his voice.

Murder entered my heart.

"The way I see it, you want me more alive than dead. Torture me all you want but unless you free Jeffery and Dom, you will get nothing from me." I crossed my arms, glaring at him. *"And I want proof!"*

"Proof?" He appeared surprised.

"Yes! You don't expect me to believe a cold-blooded murderer, do you?"

Mustafa tilted his head sideways. A spark flickered in his eyes, suggesting he was pleased. "You are not one to hold back your tongue." Our eyes latched. "Very well. You shall get your wish *and* proof," his musical voice darkened. "However, I get to bargain as well." He paused. "If you do not cooperate, our agreement will be in breach and your family will pay with their lives for your failure. Do we have an agreement?" His eyes were hard and cold.

"Yes," I hissed.

"Very well." Mustafa proceeded to the door.

"Wait! One more thing!"

He halted, turning his eyes back at me, "And?"

"Am I in a hospital?"

"Yes, the medical unit."

"A military hospital?"

"Something similar to one, yes."

I sat straight up, dread squeezing my lungs. "Does New Orleans have a military base?"

Mustafa laughed. "No. Not New Orleans."

"If we're not in New Orleans, where are we then?"

His vibrant-green eyes danced with mischief. "We are at one of our undisclosed sites."

"You don't mean Haven Hospital?" A shiver of fear whipped through me.

"You must know that I'd never allow anyone to send you back to that dreadful place." There was a faint glint of pride in his eyes. "It was I who saved you from that filthy asylum."

I stared at him gaping. Did he expect a thank you?

After a moment, he spoke, "Very well." The left corner of his lips twitched brusquely. "Get some rest. I'll be by to check on you in the morning." Without another word, he left shutting the door behind him. The last thing I heard was keys jangling. He'd locked the door.

"Great! I'm locked in this freaking room." A frown veiled my face as I dropped back in bed, flinging my arms to my sides. I blew out a huge sigh, blowing a strand of hair off my face.

I was relieved to hear that I wasn't at Haven. I wasn't sure how I felt about Mustafa getting me released. The lesser evil was a fine line to discern. Haven hospital or stuck at some secretive covert? Which was worse? I had a hunch that both places were as equally as bad. Not one thing about Mustafa settled my unrest. Hell, I was stupid if I believed the words of a cold calculating narcissist.

I buried my face in the palm of my hands, trying to wrap my head around all the unrequited questions that haunted me. Not knowing was killing me. I couldn't trust Mustafa to keep his word. I trusted him like I trusted a rattlesnake.

Then there was Van. What involvement did he have in this triangle of duplicitousness? And, where the hell was Aidan? What if Mustafa was lying about the whereabouts of Jeffery and Dom? Was it possible that he was using the one thing that mattered to me the most to bend me at his will? I shook my head in frustration.

For all I knew, Mustafa, Van, and Aidan could be separately double-dealing. Each with their own agenda. I reckoned I'd burn that bridge when I came to it. The only thing I was certain about was my headache. I rubbed my temples, trying to ease the throb.

What should I expect next? *The duties!* What sort of duties did he have in mind for me? I scoffed. Mustafa's intent could be only one thing… *malice.* I saw through his facade. I glowered at the door. Never trust a polite psychopath. Then in a rush of anger, I hurled the flowers and candy across the room.

I must've drifted off to sleep when my eyes fluttered open. Taking in a quick sigh, I noticed the IV and heart monitor had vanished. The nurse must've taken it down while I was sleeping. Not waking up during a stranger's visit, I reckoned I needed more rest than I thought. Chills iced my skin. Though I didn't cotton to the idea of a stranger freely roaming in my room while I was sleeping.

I propped myself up on my elbows spotting a pile of fresh clothes in a chair by the window. My guess, it was put there by the same person who'd been overseeing my care. My eyes dropped down looking at the wrinkled hospital gown. Seeing the clean clothes made me crave a hot shower.

I spied a second door off to the side. I assumed it was the bathroom. I threw my legs off the bed and gathered to my feet. At first, my legs felt a little wobbly like stiff legs on a turbulent boat. No telling how long I'd been passed out. I stalled for a moment getting my balance. After a minute, I felt stable enough and padded over to the chair.

I held up the clothes against the light. They were army green, military-style, heavy, long-sleeved, and thick material. Even the underwear seemed to be military standard, a tawny sports bra and matching cotton panties. I shrugged. I didn't care. It was clean. I spotted a pair of army boots and a pair of heavy socks inside one of the boots beside the chair. "Hmm, this must be the latest trend." At least I'd blend. That was a plus. Easier to go unseen.

I made my way to the bathroom. It wasn't the Hilton, but rather plain and ordinary. It didn't matter. The small bathroom was clean with fresh towels and a hot shower. That was good enough for me.

It only took a second for the hospital gown to hit the floor, and I was stepping into the hot shower. I grabbed one of the paper-wrapped soaps that laid in a small soap holder. It smelt like hospital soap, but I didn't care. Its fragrance was vitalizing and it lathered up generously.

After I finished, I toweled off and wrapped the white towel around me. I paused in front of a long mirror attached to the door. When was the last time that I'd looked at myself in a mirror? I paused, studying myself. My hair was disheveled, copper ringlets, tumbling carelessly down my back. I remembered not too long ago, on a whim, I'd chopped it off before meeting with Val for my first day of training. It had grown since. My skin was a bit more sun-kissed too. Since my stay at the Cajun's, I'd been spending my days in the sun. Until then, I never really was an outdoorsy girl.

I saw that I'd dropped a few pounds. Not much of an appetite these last few weeks. I brushed my eyes over the curves of my body. I noted a slimmer waist that flared into agilely rounded hips, long, lithe thighs. I sorta liked the new version of me. Then I frowned, my boobs were still the same. Pebbles. I twisted my body where I could get a better look at my bum. *Crap!* Some things never changed. I still had junk in the trunk. I huffed, covering myself back with the towel.

After I dressed, I didn't know what to do with myself. I didn't want to lie down. I'd had enough sleep to do me for an eternity and I couldn't leave my room. Mustafa had locked my door. If I blasted the door down, my actions might cause serious problems, jeopardizing my agreement and putting Jeffery and Dom in worse danger than they already were. No, I needed to be patient which wasn't one of my best attributes. So, I paced the floor.

My mind began to revisit all the events that transpired in the last few weeks. I thought about Gina and hoped she'd made it to safety.

Then there was Nick. At times, I hated him, but in the end, he'd gained my love and deepest respect. There was an unspoken friendship between us. We had never voiced it, but I knew he didn't hate me any more than I hated him. If I ever saw him again, I'd like to thank him for his help. I missed old Saint Nick. I suspected that he'd made it down to the bayou, off the grid, and setting up camp. He knew better than anyone how to live off the land. Nick was born and raised in the basin. Hell, any man who nosedived after a ten-foot gator had skills that I'd never be capable of conquering. Now that was a he-man! I laughed to myself.

I then thought of Logan, my sweet Logan. My first crush. Gosh! That seemed like light-years ago. So much had happened since then. I sighed, biting my bottom lip. I hoped Logan was safe. I thought of Beck and Laura. I couldn't bear the thought of anything happening to those two.

Knocking me back to my plight, I stopped cold in my feet as I heard keys rattling on the other side of the door. My heart kicked my chest as Mustafa, with his lame smile, stepped inside. "I am glad to see you are up and dressed," he paused, still holding the door open. "Come! You must be hungry."

I glared at him without saying a word but followed his lead. I suddenly realized that I was starving. My belly was starting to rub against my spine. Even more importantly, I wanted to scope this place out. With any luck, I might stumble onto where the guys were celled. Chances were slim but I still held on to my hope.

I followed Mustafa's long strides down a long bright corridor, rolls of closed doors leading to God knows where.

Everything was bleached white, a blinding white that hurt my eyes. The ceiling down to the floor was like milk, shiny as glass and too clean. A strong aroma of rubbing alcohol mixed with some other type of chemical irritated my eyes and nose.

After a few corners, we passed two soldiers going the opposite direction. I tossed a glance over my shoulder wondering where they might be heading. The short man out of the two, winked at me as we caught each other's brief gaze. He wasn't much older than I was. I wondered if he'd volunteered or if he'd been drafted. He appeared content and happy. What could be so great about staring at nothing but white?

Blech!

Mustafa rattled on about this and that, mostly bragging about himself. He reminded me of a salesman trying to sell me on a product. I wished I could've shoved a rag down his throat to shut him up, but I knew that was a pipe dream. So, I'd tuned him out where he mostly sounded like white noise. Sharing chitchat wasn't on the list of duties as far as I was concerned.

After several corners, I questioned if we were going to reach our destination. The corridor didn't seem to end. Hallway after hallway, we took winding turns that seemed to stretch forever. I got the impression that this military base held a massive amount of soldiers. I swallowed alarm. I expected the Illuminist would have legions of armies, but seeing this place with my own eyes made me understand just how doomed we were.

I counted each corner we turned, left, left, then right. The hallways were identical. No numbers or symbols marking the doors. It reminded me of a white maze. I wondered if anyone ever got lost.

We turned down another hall, and as we neared the end, a strong scent of food hit me in the face. My stomach jumpstarted like a car battery kicking an engine off on an icy day of February.

We entered past two metal doors into a large room of soldiers in army-green uniforms, much like the two men we'd passed in the hall on our way here. Hundreds of them sat at long tables eating breakfast. No argument that this was a typical mess hall.

An eerie feeling seethed through me. I recalled the locals' empty faces standing in the food line. The dark circles around their eyes, sagging skin hanging off their bones. They were all dying, even the children carried that same deadpan stare.

Yet these men were different. They appeared alive and animated. Laughter drifted in the air. Such a contrast between the two.

Jarring my attention back, Mustafa tapped me on my shoulder pointing to an empty table. It was small, nestled in a corner by a window. A little too cozy for my taste. Hell, a million miles apart from Mustafa wasn't far enough for me. Despite my feelings, I had to comply.

It helped to envision Dom and Jeffery alive and well, back home in the Garden District. Dom would be working in his garden, and Jeffery would be reading his favorite magazine in his private cubby hole. A smile touched my lips.

I took my seat as Mustafa fell in line. I assumed he was getting our food. I didn't mind. It was one more minute that I had alone and less of his company.

I peered through the thick windowpane. As far as my eyes stretched, I saw nothing but white. No land markings to spot, only the dense snow. It was a complete whiteout. Blind like darkness only a solid sheet of white. The wind howled with no mercy, battering the rooftop.

If I had to guess, I'd say we were in Antarctica. The southernmost continent, a virtually uninhabited, ice-covered landmass. Wherever the location of this ice kingdom was, I had a strong hunch we were far from civilization. No human could survive this harsh climate without the proper gear. The wind alone can flash freeze your skin instantly.

I noted all the crowded tables and the constant hum of chatter. The mess hall was buzzing with human traffic. Military soldiers coming and going. I wondered how they were functioning in this uninhabitable land.

When Mustafa returned, he carried a tray with two plates of food and piping hot coffee with loads of cream. I reckoned the breakfast was the usual soldier's morning brew: scrambled eggs, limp bacon, and two pieces of toasted bread with butter on the side.

I watched in silence as Mustafa pushed my tray in front of me and seated himself. He slightly groaned as he sat in his chair.

I grabbed up my coffee and doctored it with cream and sweetener. I couldn't remember such a luxury of condiments. I started blowing on it. The last time I'd had coffee was at the Cajun's house. Straight up black. Better than nothing but when we had run out there was no promise of replenishing our supply. I'd been needing my caffeine fix for some time now.

Mustafa cleared his throat as if he was about to give me a parental lecture. My eyes lifted from the brim of my cup before I'd taken a sip. "I am guessing you are suspicious of my intentions?" His eyes homed in on my gaze.

I set my cup down and took a bite of my lukewarm eggs and mulled around in my head what excuse I should use. "Yes. I'd thought about it." I briefly looked up at him and then dropped my gaze back to my plate. I knew my evading eye contact irritated Mustafa. My mind and heart warred with each other that if I'd just make nice with him, my life here would be easier, but I never was one for pretentiousness. Straight to the point seemed to fit my true nature. "Why don't you just get it over with and tell me what you want from me?" My mouth spun the words like a spider's poison.

"My child, you are so young and you have little experience to offer. I have been in existence for many centuries. If only you could set aside your incredulity and allow me to teach you the heavenly wisdom of life."

I took a sip of my coffee and drew back a bitter smile. The coffee was too stout. I reached over and snatched up several more sugar packets, adding them to the coffee and stirred. Not bothering to glance up, I spoke, "Is listening to your sermons one of the duties that I'm required to endure?" Sarcasm filled my voice. "If so, you are in no position to give me advice. We may share DNA but you will never fill the shoes of my father. Not in this life or any other." I leaned back in my chair, gathering the cup of coffee, sipping it as I stared out the window. At this point, I'd lost my appetite.

"I know you must hate me. If I were in your shoes, I'd feel the same way. However, if you must learn anything at all, a creature like yourself and I will always obey his or her true nature. It is inevitable. There is no avoiding it."

I cut my eyes back at him, yearning for my knives. "Are you saying that you can't help being a child killer?"

Mustafa's eyes gleamed as though he favored my blistered face.

"Perhaps if you will allow me to explain, I can clear up your misunderstanding."

"I saw you murder my child," I whispered, on the hinge of exploding. "What excuse are you trying to shove up my ass… the devil made you do it?"

"You know so little about my origin and how I came about in this life."

I figured he could say whatever he liked. I didn't have to agree or for that matter even listen. So, I silently drank my coffee.

Mustafa briefly flashed a faint smile and proceeded. "Thank you, Stephanie!" He pushed his tray aside. "As you know very little about our kind, let me begin. In the abode of God, all firstborn angels like myself were given a position, a *duty*. We were to accept and obey our positions without question or protest. My father gave me a duty that bothered my conscience. Much like a child, though I was fully grown as I am now, I wanted nothing more than to please my maker. My duty was a very difficult task. It was never my decision nor my desire. When my father gave me my instructions to end a mortal's life, I had no choice but to carry out my duty."

"Wait! You're saying that God turned you into an assassin?"

Mustafa folded his hands together and placed them in his lap. "Please allow me to finish before I am showered with questions."

"All right," I shrugged.

"Before the birth of Christ, Moses emerged as the leader of the Hebrews. His people were slaves under Pharaoh's rule, known as Ramsey. As the story is told, the Pharaoh ruler was quite pertinacious and wouldn't release his slaves. His gods, although man-made images of stone, advised him to rebuke Moses' warnings. But the most-high God had a point to prove and a prophecy fulfillment for the Hebrews.

When the Pharaoh of Egypt refused to let Moses' people free, a death sentence of each firstborn was set in motion. Though the plague came from the mouth of Ramsey, he was too magisterial to understand the woes he'd brought upon his people. Hardheartedly, he turned his back to the warnings of Moses and the Hebrew God.

The angel of death was commanded to carry out the mission. It was *I* who had spread the kiss of death upon each firstborn. The only ones saved were the houses marked with blood. It didn't matter if they were nonbelievers or believers. The bloodstain signaled the angel of death to pass over. It wasn't an easy task to follow. I didn't want to kill innocent people who were misled or blinded in this battle of gods. Did I feel the battle was just? My opinion did not matter. Furthermore, I wasn't allowed to think for myself or question the Almighty's actions. To my creator, it may have been righteous, spreading death among the sons of man, but it made me heavy in heart. I hated myself for what I had to do."

I sat there with my shoulders stiff. I realized something… he was sharing a vulnerable side of him. Yet I wasn't buying it.

Mustafa continued with his spiel. "Appointed as the death angel, it was my duty to follow through with commandments handed down to me. I had no recourse. For centuries, I followed orders from my maker, never questioning his judgment. He was righteous. *Always*."

"Are you saying it was righteous to murder my daughter?" I was confused. What did my daughter's death have to do with his duties?

He sighed. "I am saying when you come to crossroads which way is right?"

I glared at him, not answering.

"Either road is correct," Mustafa answered his question sharply. "There is not a right or a wrong. It is simply a choice of roads."

I narrowed my eyes. "You think you were right to take my child's life?"

"I'm saying just like back in ancient times when Ramsey refused to heed to Moses' warnings, innocent people died. They were the price for disobedience. The deaths were a necessary consequence whether I agreed or not. It was a very hard lesson to learn, but it stuck with me down to this modern time. It is a difficult truth to swallow but death at times is incumbent. Another example, Christ's death. It was an imperative death for mankind to have a chance at everlasting life. Christ's perfect blood was the wage for man's sin. An obligatory price."

"So, you're telling me that my child's blood had to be spilled to save *you*?" Anger colored my face.

"No, not her blood. I needed her essence to gain favor with my maker. I became pure once again after receiving her untainted spirit. She was the forfeiture I had to take to regain my former position."

He was crazier than I'd thought. My daughter's life was not his to take. "If you think I'm going to accept your selfish excuse due to your misgivings, you are out of your ever-loving, fuckin' gore!" I bolted to my feet, hurling my hot coffee into his face. I couldn't stand to look at him any longer. Without another word, I stalked past him.

By the time the mess hall doors slammed behind me, I was halfway down the corridor with tears pouring down my face. I felt like someone had taken their steel toe boot and stomped my heart into a million and one-pieces. I hated Mustafa. I hated him so much it hurt.

When I reached my room, I flung the door open and rushed inside. I stopped dead in my feet combing the room over. "Did I miscount my door?" It was difficult to discern since the rooms were not marked. How did they expect anyone to tell which door was whose? Where was the logic in this ice hell?

The small space had transformed into a utility room. Even the bathroom had vanished. I peered down the corridor trying to determine if I'd miscounted. I couldn't be certain.

Since I had nowhere else to go, I shut the door and slid down the wall, planting my butt on the cold floor in the dark. I laid my face in my palms and sobbed.

I had no idea how long I'd been there when I heard a click. My gaze popped up when the door crept open. An older woman stepped in with a tray of food. It looked like a burger and fries and a bubbling cold drink in a tall paper cup with hearts. My mouth began to water. I didn't realize how thirsty I was until my eyes landed on the cup. The woman remained silent as she placed the tray of food beside me left me to myself. The food smelled wonderful and my stomach started to churn. I scooted the tray closer and wasted no time picking up the drink. I drew the cool liquid through the straw as I closed my eyes letting it slip down my parched throat.

After nearly polishing the drink, I swept up the burger and took a huge bite, and chewed, savoring the delicious juices. It tasted great and I found myself devouring it in nothing flat. The fries, dripping in ketchup, were next.

After I'd polished off my food and finished the drink, I still felt hungry. I couldn't remember the last time I'd been famished like this. I was used to missing meals. Which led me to believe that I'd gone without eating for some time.

I set down my cup and lay on the floor drawing my knees to my chest. After an unknown amount of time had passed, the door swung open. It was Mustafa, the last person I wanted to see. I rose to a sitting position, not uttering a word but watched him cautiously. I expected him to yank me to my feet by my hair and beat me to a pulp. After all, I did splash hot coffee in his face in front of a whole platoon.

"Come with me," Mustafa said in a gentle voice. "I have your room prepared." His eyes skimmed the darkroom. "I promise you will be much more comfortable in your new quarters." The fallen angel flashed his syrupy smile. I'd memorized every dimple on his face down to his chiseled chin. I despised it too.

Without a word, I climbed to my feet and followed him. We went in the opposite direction from last time and boarded an elevator. We stepped off onto another white hallway. Only this one had double doors every so many feet, like a hospital. When we passed through the last set of doors, we entered an area much different.

The walls were rich with dark wood. A white leather couch, contemporary style, and funny shaped accent chairs stood off in a corner to the side. An oversized glass coffee table with gentlemen magazines spread carelessly about. A strong scent of cigar lingered in the air.

Van came to mind and I nearly gagged.

We continued down a long hall, around two other corners. Midway down another hall, we finally stopped. The room number read, 222.

Mustafa stopped, pulled out a card and swiped it through a small device on the door. I heard a clicking noise with a small green light following and the door opened. He waved his hand and said, "Ladies first!" he smiled.

I slipped a sideways glance at him, still not uttering a word. With caution strapped to my heels, I paused, peering in the room before entering. I didn't trust this place and I trusted Mustafa even less. With a huff, I stepped inside as Mustafa stopped at the threshold, his palm rested on the doorknob.

I padded to the middle of the room and combed my eyes over the fair size room. Eh, decent enough. A pleasant aroma of roses taunted my nose. Suddenly, I recalled Aidan once giving me a rose.

The day I lost my life.

I blew out a long sigh. Memory lane was never good for me.

Moving on, the room was plain. Nothing special. Although, most of the hotels Sara and I stayed at were much worse than this. I spotted a twin bed on my left up against the back wall. An army green blanket, and white sheets were folded neatly on the end of the bed with a pillow.

A bathroom was off to the right and a large picture window that hid behind dark, green curtains. There wasn't a television. No surprise. Out here in the middle of ice land, I doubted they had satellite. I did have a desk placed under the window with a pad and pen. Note to self, possible weapon… *pen*.

I reckoned this was one of their guest quarters. They might be treating me as a visitor, but I knew the reality of my stay. I followed orders or my family died. It didn't exactly make me feel warm and fuzzy. Regardless, I wouldn't complain. I'd struck a deal. Me in exchange for Jeffery and Dom. I intended to keep my end of the bargain as long as Mustafa kept his.

"I hope our guest room is satisfying?"

I was suddenly jarred from eyeballing the pen. I whipped my head around, catching Mustafa's gaze. "Yes, it'll do fine." I averted my gaze.

Mustafa's lips tightened as he stalked over to the desk and swiped the pen, sticking it in his pocket. "The house services will bring you your things, clothes, toiletries, whatever you need." He began to make his way to the door but I halted him.

"What about my family?" I rushed my words.

He snapped his eyes at me as though he was growing tired of my constant asking. "Your family is safe as we speak."

"Safe? Where are they?" I barely held my patience.

"I'm afraid it is a need-to-know basis." His face showed no glimmer of emotion.

I threw my hands to my hips, my face scarlet rage. "I should've known you wouldn't keep your promise."

"My child, you have put words in my mouth."

"Clearly, we have a difference of opinion."

"You have forgotten! It is my opinion that takes the front seat," he flashed a smile that said it all.

I'd been duped!

"Do you even know where Jeffery and Dom are?"

"Yes, but if you think you can reach them, you are wrong. Try stepping outside in this whiteout. You'll die from hyperthermia in minutes. There is nothing you can do. Your mates are in a place that is impossible to reach. Not even a wingless angel can touch."

"Oh, geez! Are they dead?" I threw my arms over my head ready to have a meltdown. Tears swelled.

Mustafa stepped up in my personal space and reached to wipe a tear that had fallen down my cheek. I stepped back. "Don't touch me!" I hissed.

"I wish to comfort you." His brows dipped into a vee as if my feelings were foreign to him.

"I get that it's too human for you to understand my animosity toward you. On the flip side, *I* do understand!" I snapped. "I know exactly how it feels to have lost. I reckon that's the human in me."

Mustafa began to pace around me slowly as if he were an animal encircling his prey. "Perhaps you are correct." His eyes glistened an eerie glow. "However, whether I do or not doesn't affect my decision. You shall obey my orders or else your *nom-de-plume* family will meet *their* maker," he paused. "Are we clear?" he stopped abruptly, glaring, stone cold.

Chills skirted down my spine but I kept my stance. "Very!"

"Very good! I shall leave you to yourself, then. You may ring for service if you need anything." He pointed to the phone on the nightstand. "Or if you prefer to go down to the mess hall, you may. I trust you will not try anything foolish." He dazzled a triumphant smile that made me vomit in my mouth.

Without another word, Mustafa left. I collapsed to the floor, knees drawn to my chest. I wrapped my arms around myself, resting my forehead on my knees, sobbing.

My suspicion was right. Mustafa had never intended to honor his promise. I placed my hope into malevolent hands. Hands that I should've never been trusted. I knew what I had to do next.

Escape.

STRANGER THINGS

*T*he next morning, the same gray-haired lady who'd brought my food yesterday, returned with clean clothes and fresh towels. The threads were identical to what I wore yesterday but I had no qualms with that. The military garments were clean and comfortable. It served its purpose.

With only a gentle smile, she left my room quietly. I suspected that I needed to get moving. Good chance that Mustafa would be starting my duty assignment today. I had to play along with his charade until I had a good escape plan.

First, I'd have to earn his trust. Make him think he had me under his palm. A task that wouldn't be easy and if I wasn't careful, very dangerous. I intended to be one step ahead of him. It was going to take a saint to pull this caper off.

At this point, Mustafa thought he had me over a barrel. He was correct. Even still, I planned to change that minor detail. If he lied about our agreement, then he'd most likely lie about keeping Jeffery and Dom safe? My gut churned over that terrifying thought.

Deep down, my gut also told me that the biggest chance of the guys' survival would be me ditching this iceberg and finding them on my own. If I kept my ears to the ground and my eyes peeled, I might catch wind of where Jeffery and Dom where imprisoned. Bleak as my chances might be, I held tight to hope. It was the only thing keeping me standing erect.

After getting dressed and nothing more than idol hands to keep me busy, I paced the floor, plotting different scenarios of how to break out of this fridge. I needed to familiarize myself with the compound. Before my plan went into effect, I should make a list of things to reassure my chances of survival. Starting with warm clothing and proper shoes. Resorting to stealing wasn't beneath me. I think this would be an exception. It'd be foolish to attempt fate without proper gear.

I remembered reading that Antarctica was the coldest place on earth. The temperature was as low as −128.6 °F. I had a hunch this place was more than just an icecap island. I wondered if the visibility was any better than yesterday morning.

I padded to the window and thrust back the dark curtains. I stood there blinking back the white abyss. How could anyone in their right mind want to live here? It was more than a little unnerving to think that past the glass pane, a hazardous climate promised a faithless future... *hyperthermia and death.* Even wearing the state-of-the-art gear made no promises of keeping a person safe.

On the other rabbit's foot, I wasn't *anyone*. A genetically engineered angel might have a slightly higher survival chance, at least in theory.

Before I put any of my hopes in one basket, I needed to scope out the compound. Maybe make a friend or two. That meant I had to mingle, make nice.

Blech!

I stepped off the elevator onto the ground floor. I walked down a couple of hallways, through the doors to the bright white section. After coiling several more corners, I arrived at the mess hall.

Once I entered past the doors, loud chatter hit me in the face, along with a strong whiff of bacon and biscuits. The hall was bouncing as much today as yesterday. I went through the line and filled my tray with scrambled eggs, a biscuit, OJ, and black coffee with an extra side of sugar and creamer.

With my tray in hand, I skimmed the room for a place to sit. The mess hall was nearly full. All men. Come to think about it, I didn't recall seeing any female recruits. Then I thought of a snarky remark. They probably kept their women in places like the gentlemen's club. I thought about Gina. I hoped she got away and was safe.

My eyes landed on the same table where I had sat yesterday with Mustafa. It was the only table directly by the window and no one was sitting there as if it had been reserved.

I delighted in the idea of eating my breakfast alone. It'd give me a chance to observe the soldiers and even maybe ask some questions without drawing suspicion. You know, like how was the weather? How did a person escape this icebox?

I took my seat and smiled to myself. I let out an easy sigh and separated my food from the tray. I pushed the empty tray to the other side of the table and grabbed my fork.

I had just taken my first bite when I caught a shadow in the corner of my eye. I glanced up. A young woman stood only a few feet from my table, staring at me like she'd seen an alien. By the looks of her baby face, she wasn't much younger than me. It appeared the girl had a fixation on me for some odd reason. I didn't mind a little conversation. But sheesh! Did she have to stand there gawking?

Trying to disguise my irritation, I nodded, faintly smiling. In reply, the girl's brows furrowed as if I'd offended her. After a moment of awkwardness, she spoke up, "You're the new arrival."

Did the girl ask a question or was she stating a fact?

"Umm, if you're asking, then yes," I answered.

"You care if I sit down?" She popped a squat across from me before I could protest. "It's not every day I see someone like you visiting the camp. It gets pretty lonely being the only female." The girl tossed her long brunette hair over her shoulder and smiled. Eh, mildly attractive with a slight overbite.

"I'm Wendy Smith and you are?" She extended her hand.

"Stevie Collins," I replied as I shook her hand.

"I suppose you're one of the new trainees."

"I reckon," I answered curtly. But I was more interested in *her* position. I'd bide my time and then I'd ask a few questions of my own.

"I've been here for only six months. When they recruited me, I had to go through the standard test and transition. You shouldn't have any complications. You look pretty healthy enough." Her eyes traveled over me.

Though not caring for the eye groping, my ears perked. Wendy Smith just might become my next best friend. "Transition?"

"They ain't given you the routine shakedown yet?" Her surprise laid heavily in her large blue eyes.

"Nope, not yet. I hear it's a killer," I smiled sweetly. If I were a gambler, I'd bet that all those years of my schoolyard lying was about to pay off.

The girl tossed a curt glance over her shoulder and then leaned over the table, lowering her voice to a mere whisper. "The physical training was a cakewalk compared to the change."

"A change! That sounds scary," I whispered back, my elbows on the table, giving her my full attention.

"It was worse than getting your toes crushed." Her eyes clouded a moment, seeming as if she was taking a trip down memory lane.

"I can't imagine."

"Where did they recruit you?" the girl asked. Suddenly her interest shifted.

"Hmm, a small town in Louisiana. What about you?"

"They found me in Georgia... Clayton." That explained the soft drawl and twang in her voice.

"Never heard of it," I said nonchalantly.

"So, did you volunteer?" Her bright blues sparkled with curiosity.

"Yep, I reckon you can call it that. And you?" I took a sip of my coffee.

"I didn't have much choice. We were livin' worse than swine." Her southern accent was smothered with anguish.

"It must've been terrible for you."

"We were homeless. No neighbors or family to take us in. Our neighbor, Bo, lost his two daughters to the silver soldiers. He got a thrashin' for trying to stop 'em too. He died in my pa's arms. His wife didn't have any better luck. She ended up murdered right in front of her girls. Nobody know'd where they took the daughters." She shook her head. "Those gals weren't no more than twelve." The girl picked up a napkin and started shredding it into tiny pieces. "My family and I lost our farm. Shortly after Bo's family got raided, late in the night, the silver soldiers came for us. They burned our farm to the ground. Pa and my little brother barely escaped. My ma didn't get away." She paused but when she spoke, her words turned my blood cold. "I ain't never heard no grown woman scream like that before. I still hear her in my sleep. I won't ever forget it neither. No ma'am, not ever." She chewed on a fingernail with a faraway look in her eyes.

"Wendy, how did you end up here?"

"The silver soldiers spared my life. They brought me to their leader, an angel," her eyes gleamed. "The nice angel said if I behaved myself that he'd reward me with clothes and a nice place to live." The girl shifted in her seat. "I ain't never had clothes or even an education neither. The angel set it up for me to have a tutor and I'm learnin' real good too."

"That's very generous." My throat went dry. I envisioned the worse possible scenario happening to this gullible girl.

Wendy dropped her gaze to the table as her eyes moistened. "It was awful what happened to my family but my angel guardian told me that they's in heaven and they have a real nice home like me. He told me that they were happy about my job here. They don't blame me fer nothin'."

I felt an onset of sickness. There wasn't any end to what Mustafa would do to gain his kingdom. "Blame! Why would your family blame you?" Listening to this girl's story and how blind she was to the truth made me see blood. Mustafa's blood.

"Well, the locals think I'm the devil for taking the new rulers' bribe. I ain't believing nothin' those stupid folks say. The angel says they just jealous cuz I gotta nice place to live and good food to eat. And one day, I'm gonna be famous. My name will be written in history books when this is all over. It's a real pleasure to serve The New World Order." Her chin tilted upward in pride.

"Why have the town's folks turned against you?"

The girl laughed but it sounded like she'd gone off her rocker. "I think they believe that I've been begotten by the devil."

"Wow! What a bummer," I gave pause. "So, what happened?"

The girl's eyes darted around the room nervously as she continued to explain. "The men in white jackets started experimenting on several gals like me. At first, we had to just lay there on these small cots while they drew blood samples. The white jacket men took so much blood from some gals, they died. I nearly died too, but somehow I managed to stay alive."

"Why so much blood?"

"The best I could tell was that they were running tests to see who would fit with whose DNA?"

"Did they tell you why?" I had to know. Maybe all this insanity might make sense.

"The scientists were trying to find the most favorable matches. They started injecting us with this blue liquid medicine. It was real frightening too. Watching my friends dying and how the silver guards dumped their bodies in a trash bin just like they were an empty milk jug spooked me something fierce. I thought I was going to be added to the pile, too." The girl's body suddenly shivered as she glanced out the window. No doubt, that the atrocities she had witnessed would haunt her forever. My heart went out to her.

"Do you know what they were injecting into you and the others?"

The girl reached over, jerking another napkin from its container and began ripping it apart, one strip at a time. She kept her eyes lowered. "I do, but..." The girl cut her eyes at me. "It's pretty bad."

"I've seen some pretty gruesome things myself." I smiled back.

She shrugged, "I doubt you've seen anything like this."

"Try me!" I challenged. Then I softened my voice as I reached over and lightly touched her hand. "You might feel better getting it off your chest."

"Okay, but don't say I didn't warn you." She let out a long sigh. "Once they got done testing us, we were divided up by our blood type. The dividing had something to do with antibodies in the plastic."

A fine line appeared between my brows, "Plastic?"

"Yeah," she rolled her eyes. "It's a word that sounds like that. I'm no scientist."

"Do you mean plasma?"

"Yeah! That's the word." Her blues brightened. "It had to do with anti-something in the blood."

"You mean antigen in blood cells and the antibodies in the plasma."

"Wow! You're kinda smart."

"Oh, I don't know. I liked science in high school," I shrugged. School had been such a long time ago that I was surprised I still remembered.

"Anyway, all that stuff determined what type of treatment we got."

My brow arched. "What step did the scientist do next to your group?"

"They divided us up according to our blood type and gave us blood." As if she feared someone listening, she raked her gaze over the room and then turned back to me. "It ain't normal human blood," she whispered.

"What do you mean?"

"Some gals received fey blood, others were given Nephilim and another group remaining were given angel blood."

Holy hell! Suddenly mad scientist came to mind as I blurted out, "Why were the scientists giving you alien blood?"

The girl's innocence suddenly vanished and arrogance took reign. It was as if I was speaking to a completely different person. "Isn't it obvious?"

I bit back what I wanted to say but instead replied, "I reckon I'm not as smart as you think."

She twisted her lips into a frown. "Sorta hard to keep up with current events since this world turned upside down," she laughed, darkly.

"I have been lost. Why don't you update me on the current news?" Despite her personality change, I wanted to push further, hoping to get some inside information that might help me to escape or even better to hold over Mustafa's head. Any information would be beneficial.

"The new rulers need an army," she whispered.

Ice shivered down my spine. It was perfectly clear to me. "The scientist finally found a vessel?"

"Yep!" she answered confidently.

Mustafa and The New Order were creating an army. "You agreed to this experiment?"

"Of course! Wouldn't you?"

"I don't know," I simply admitted. "What did they give *you*?"

She snorted. "Fey!"

Fey wasn't good. I swallowed hard realizing what I'd invited to my table. Fey was temperamental, unpredictable, and plumb crazy. "Did it change you?"

A grin crept across her face. A predatory look I'd seen *on Sam*. My shoulders stiffened. If she was anything like him, I better watch my step. "What do you think?" her voice was almost hostile.

I held my cool. Getting ruffled might trigger her. "I see."

"Ain't you smart." The sudden change in her eyes set off a warning… *I was no longer in the BFF zone.* Typical fey. Always expect the unexpected. It was like dealing with schizophrenia. One minute, they're happy-go-lucky and the next they're the hulk ripping up the neighborhood.

"What's the real reason you sat down at my table?" I hated playing mind games. Just say what you gotta say and be on your way. I had my own set of troubles. I didn't care what this girl's problems were.

"I don't know. Curiosity, I guess," she shrugged. "We're the only females. It seems odd that they'd bring you to my camp?"

"That's a question we both would like to know." Seeing the line between her eyes deepen, I knew this conversation was going downhill fast.

"Not sure what they want you fer, but I've been assigned to bear children. I'm pregnant now." She rubbed her tummy, showing off a small bump.

When her words hit me, I spewed my sip of coffee all over the table. Did I hear her correctly? "Say what?" I choked out.

She glared at me while snatching several napkins from the holder and then wiping her face. When the girl finished, she laid them down and replied in an angry tone. "I said I'm pregnant."

"I'm sorry. I-I …"

She interrupted me. "It ain't nothin'."

"I'm confused." This girl's story kept getting weirder by the minute.

"Injecting fey blood only affected the soldiers for a limited time," she explained. "Once the blood ran through their system, the men would return to their former state… *human*. The scientist needed lasting power. Most of us had trouble holding up. When we came down off the blood, it took a toll on our bodies. After a few times, the others couldn't handle it. Like I said, those gals died. I was different," she smiled. "All that hard work I'd done on the farm made me tough. I was special. The fey blood didn't kill me. It changed my DNA. I survived the change without any problems. They call me Eve around here." I could see the pride in her eyes. Did she not know how sick this was?

"You mean the babies you give birth to are not human?"

"Correct. They're magical. I'm only pregnant for three months. The real magic is when I give birth to sextuplets."

I swallowed my shock. I raked my eyes over the mess hall, counting all the heads, nothing but males. Had she given birth to all these soldiers? Appalled, I kept my feelings to myself as I pushed further. "You're okay with the scientist experimenting on you?"

"I've never felt better!"

"And you don't see any problem being their baby factory?" It seemed her reality was in an aoristic limbo where she didn't realize the serious effect of her bleak future. Fey or not, eventually her body was sure to give out. Unlike Eve, she was flawed.

She shrugged, dismissing my disquiet. "It's a real honor to be a breeder. Afterward, I get rewarded, something nice like clothing to wear or a steak dinner. Real cow too! Angus." She held her head up high as if she was proud of her insidious *duty*. I sat there shocked, staring at her gleeful face.

"Why are you here?" she asked, brows dipped into a V.

"I'm here for other reasons."

"I've killed before," she confessed. Strange how she wanted to make that point clear. I'd suspected she was dangerous and my hunch was just confirmed. She went on to say, "I could do it again real easy."

"Thanks for the warning." A hint of sarcasm flavored my voice. "I'm sorry for upsetting you. I'm still adjusting to The New Order." Although her *duty* was cringe-worthy, I didn't have a beef with this crazy girl. It was her life and her decision. I couldn't help her. Maybe if she'd still been human but she wasn't. The girl was fey.

She paused a moment studying me. "If they're not treating you, then why are you staying at this camp?" she asked with cautious curiosity. "There ain't one breeder to a camp and that's me." Her voice wore ire.

"Well," I drew out. "I'm something slightly different." I didn't want to go into my life's history. If I gave her the scope of what I was and with whom I share DNA, her insecurities might skyrocket.

The girl continued to prod. I could see her sugarcane brain churning. "How are you different?"

"One could say I'm not human." I didn't offer any other information.

"Were you turned?"

Geez! She was making it sound like a vampire had bitten me. I wish it had been that easy. "Nope. I've never been human."

Her eyes orbed, staring at me with wonder. "Wow! For real?"

I laughed. "That's what they tell me."

"Then what are you?" She leaned back eyeing me skeptically.

I was starting to tire of this conversation. Although I had to give her credit for her persistence, it was time to let it go. "Hey, I've enjoyed our chat." I looked around for a clock. I'm meeting someone in just a bit. Maybe we can meet for dinner." I forced a smile. To be honest, I wasn't interested in becoming best buds. Fey were incalculable. I learned my lesson with Sam.

"No, I think we need to finish this talk right here and now."

I had a nagging feeling things were about to go unhinged. "I don't want any trouble." I itched for my knives and felt lost without them.

"If you tell me what sorta creature you are, I might let you off with a warning."

I scoffed to myself. She was warning me. *Really?* I shook my head, pushing off from the table. "Look! I have no ill-will against you. I came in here to have breakfast." But *then came Wendy and the baby carriage.* I snatched up my tray, holding back my ire. "I'm no one you need to concern yourself with. Take care of yourself and your baby."

Shock fluttered through the girl as she stumbled to her feet, knocking her chair to the floor. "Devil be gone!" She gasped, full of fright. "Your eyes blazed like fire."

An impish grin curled my lips. I thought a returned warning was in order. "I'm not your run of the mill genetics," I tightened my gaze. "I don't want to hurt you," I paused. "All the same, if you come for me, I will return the favor."

"You're an ink freak!" she squealed. "You even stink like them." A black curtain of hate veiled her face.

Crap! I reckoned it was too much to ask for a little breakfast without incurring the wrath of the umbrageous. "Hey, you can screw the whole freaking camp if you like," I bit out, lips tight with anger. "Just stay out of my way and I'll stay out of yours. *Deal?*"

In less than a blink, the table went airborne and with a solid quick punch to the jaw, I went flying two tables over, landing in the center of an occupied table.

The recruits scattered, feet flying and food sailing in every direc-tion. The whole room cleared as the attack of the fifty-foot woman charged straight for me. "Holy hell!" I gawked. This bitch was a Neanderthal, with protruding brows and a heavy jaw. I quickly felt for my knives and remembered that the regulators had taken my steel. *Damn!*

Not a breath to waste, I swiftly snatched up a butter knife, gripping its hilt. I sprang into action, rolling off the broken table landing on my feet. I looked up and the girl was charging straight for me. I knew I had to react fast before she got in the next punch. In one swift motion, I jumped on a table and lunged with all my might into the air at her face level, stabbing her right eye. When my feet hit the floor, a hallowing scream bellowed from the creature as she stumbled backward, palming her bloody eye.

I paid dearly for that knife stab as her fist collided with my jaw, sending my body hurling into the concrete wall. I slid to the floor with a loud thud, blinking back the sharp ache.

Though time didn't grace me a moment to recover. My gaze lifted spotting the fey girl, knife still embedded into her eye-socket, tossing tables and chairs from her path, making a beeline for me.

Round two.

I sprung to my feet, fists to my side, ready to fight. In battle, Val taught me to never become the man on the bottom. Moving swiftly, I encircled the creature, using her blindside to my advantage. She spun in a crazed twirl, swinging at me. I ducked barely missing her fatal blows. With each quaking step, she threw a mighty punch, left hook, right, left hook again. Her thrusts were massive and annihilated everything in her wake. Though the girl's size was her downfall. Yet I wasn't much better off. Despite my quickness and light-footedness, I knew all it'd take was one good clock from her and I was dead meat.

I raked my eyes over the room trying to spot some sort of weapon that might even the playing field. Though I had my magick, it was unreliable. It was too risky to try. I needed a dependable source.

When my eyes fell upon a broken chair that had been crushed into pieces, I dodged the girl's left jab and dove for one of the broken legs. My fingers clasped the metal, ready to come up swinging. It was light, not much punch. I doubted it would kill the girl, but it might help to knock her silly enough for me to escape. Then again, she did have a knife stuck in her eye that hadn't slowed her down.

Damn, fey!

Before I knew it, the giant girl had snatched me up by the nape of my hair, swinging me like a carousel on warp speed. I dropped the chair's leg as my mind filled with anguish. I punched at her solid fists hoping she'd let go.

When I thought I couldn't take anymore, the creature released her grip, sending me into a tailspin across the mess hall. I collided into a crowd of soldiers that had gathered off into a corner, watching the fight unfold.

Hands, so many hands, grabbing at every part of my body, and then thrusting me back at the girl as if I were a basketball. Clearly, they were rooting for the hulk-like girl.

When I landed into her hands, she swathed her thick meaty hands around my throat and squeezed for my last breath. My face blistered, spit oozed, I pounded my fist at her grip but she didn't flinch. I knew it was a matter of seconds before I'd meet death. The room began to grow dim as my lungs burned for oxygen.

Unexpectedly, the essence deep within my core whipped through me. Tears welled as if I'd seen a long-lost friend. More than ever before, I was grateful for my powers as I quickly took advantage of my magick.

A radiant heat lubricated my body like burners to an open stove. The giant girl quickly dropped me as she squealed at her swollen fingers. My butt hit the floor with a loud clonk as a sharp pain shot up my spine, but I was able to breathe. I sat there staring up at the girl as I drew in oxygen greedily. At this point, I needed to step up my game or this girl was going to kill me.

"You bitch! You burnt me," she yelled, her face scarlet red with misery. Glancing at her hands, large, pus-filled blisters covered her palms and fingers.

I scurried to my feet, stepping back, keeping my eyes on the mammoth girl. "I don't want to fight you," I bellowed. "You brought this on yourself."

"You started this fight the minute you set foot on this compound," she snarled.

"Then let's cease fighting and we both walk away alive."

She flashed a lopsided grin. "Nah, I think you have to go. There can only be one girl to this compound and that ain't you."

"Listen, Wendy! I don't want to be here anymore than you want me here, but I'm not free like you. I'm a prisoner." I hoped my words would sink into her thick skull. I glanced at the crowd of soldiers huddled in the far-right corner like spectators, egging on the fight. A shiver rolled through me. Hooking up with one of these incestuous soldiers creeped me out on a whole different level.

"I'm not sharing my men with you!" The girl grated through her teeth.

"No problemo, sweetheart. Who'd want those freaks anyway?" As soon as my statement left my mouth, I knew I'd made a big mistake.

As if steam shot through her ears, the Herculean girl backhanded me, flipping me into the air. I hit the floor hard, landing on my back. "Damn! That hurt," I gasped, biting through the raw agony.

A flash touched the corner of my eye as I lifted my gaze. The giant was nearly on top of me. With quick reflexes, I shot fire from my hand, blasting the giant off her massive feet and crashing through a concrete wall. I paused, hoping one blast would quiet her. To my detriment, I couldn't have been more wrong. This cray-cray bitch wasn't backing down.

All at once, the ground shook with great force as the giant creature emerged from a pile of rubble. Cold terror gripped me in its icy embrace as I stood frozen watching the creature crouch into a predatory stance, snarling. She had transformed into a monster with protruding horns and jagged teeth. Those scientists really fucked this girl up.

I had to do something and do it fast. Not allowing my attacker to gain momentum, I reached deep within my essence and beckoned my powers to rise.

Once again, I returned fire. My hands shot a searing blast at the creature, knocking it off its feet. The beast collided to the floor, shaking the ground like a monstrous earthquake.

I forged on. Standing firm on my feet, I shot another blast of a fiery net, backing the creature into a protective cocoon. Soon the fire consumed the giant, keeping her contained. The monstrous girl struggled, gnashing her teeth, trying to claw at the magickal net.

In a quick flash, she turned into her normal, human size. Even still, I found no comfort. The girl still had the strength of twenty men. Now that she was equivalent to me in size, she could move as quickly as I could. I might act like a badass at times but I shivered knowing that I could end up as this bitch's snack. It was time to put a stop to this nonsense.

Somewhere between wall crashing and smashing, I noted that she'd pulled the butter knife out. The eye had swollen from what I could tell from under the congealed blood. "You took my eye out, bitch!" she roared. "You're dead now!" The girl's face took on this deranged gleam.

I hated fey!

"We didn't have to come to blows," I scoffed. "It's still not too late. Do us both a favor and walk away. Like I said, I have no beef with you."

"I ain't done with you yet!" The girl growled as she ripped open the magickal net and vaulted for me. Geez! Not again! I ducked and rolled, clipping her foot, knocking her down to the floor with a heavy thud. I'd hoped she would've clocked herself unconscious.

As luck flew over the crazy ward, I underestimated her strength. The girl flew to her feet with a butcher's knife tightly gripped in her hand. Lord knew where she got that. I suspected one of her children/boyfriends must've handed it to her.

Ew!

I flashed a scowl at the fey girl sending her a message that I was done with playing. Time to get serious. I stretched my arm out, demanding all sharp, blunt objects to obey. In a flash, I spotted a large metal pot hurling through the air, coming straight for me. I snatched it from the air and quickly blocked her violent fist. I gaped at the dent in the industrial pot. That little girl had a powerful punch.

Although I'd been forced to defend myself, I didn't hold her accountable. Wendy's toxic behavior wasn't her fault. The Illuminist turned her into a raging savage. I had a hunch that once her blood was clean, she'd return to the kind girl she once was before. Now in her crazed mind, she was protecting *her* turf like a grizzly bear with cubs.

I thought if I could get a pan to soar through the air, why not other objects. Once more, I stretched my arm out calling upon every knife in the mess hall to entrap the girl.

In a flash, strong winds began to howl whipping through my hair. Just as I commanded, hundreds of knives from a clever to a butter knife soared to my call, entrapping my attacker. The cold steel was like a fortress holding her prisoner. I withdrew a weary sigh. Even still, my heart ached for her. It just wasn't fair. But what else could I do? If she didn't take heed to my threat, this would end badly for her.

Once again, I attempted to reason. Shouting over the high winds, I pleaded, "Can we call this a truce? I don't want to end your life." I stood firm with my shoulders straight, ready to spring into action if she tried to burst out of her cell.

The girl edged forward but the knives moved forward, nicking her in every crevice of her body. "Let me out of here!" she screeched through gritted teeth.

My patience was running thin like melting ice over a fire but I couldn't back down. I had to make her stop. "I will if you yield. Do we have a deal?"

Then I heard a familiar voice drop on the back of my neck. "Well, well! Are we making nice this morning?" I didn't bother looking over my shoulder. I'd recognize Mustafa's robotic voice anywhere. It was too perfect for any human.

"Does it look like we're making nice?" I bit out, still holding my focus on the steel entrapment.

"What is going on here?"

"Your breeder thought I was moving in on her legion of lovers."

Mustafa laughed and turned to the girl. "Wendy, is this true?"

The girl seemed calmed as she said, "Yes, Master. She is the only other female stationed here. I was protecting my home."

In a rush of anger, Mustafa waved his hand at the hovering knives that had imprisoned the violent fey. Immediately, the steel fell to the floor landing with a loud clank. The dark angel then addressed the now seemingly calm girl. "It is not for you to protect or make decisions. You do as your told." He reared his hand back to strike.

Swiftly, I lunged in front of Mustafa, prepared to fight. "Don't you dare hurt Wendy!" My eyes gleamed with justice. "She doesn't know any better. You and your allies have made her into a monster. The least you can do is have mercy on this innocent child." I stood with my feet planted to the ground. I wasn't budging.

Mustafa paused for a moment as our eyes locked. I didn't flinch and neither did he. The dark angel smiled as if he was proud of my stance. "You are quite amazing. This girl was going to kill you, and now you are defending her life. Angel, you make no sense."

"The girl would not have killed me," I countered with confidence.

"Oh, forgive me. I stand corrected." Laughter danced in the dark angel's eyes as he turned to two soldiers that had joined him. "Take the girl to her quarters. She will be dealt with accordingly."

I held out my hand blocking the soldiers, "Wait!" I demanded. "I need to do something first." I didn't wait for permission. I faced Wendy and said, "I can heal your eye. It won't hurt."

The young girl, although a bit shook, nodded yes. I smiled as I laid my hand over her bludgeoned eye and soon a soft golden light spread its healing warmth deep into the wound. In only a few minutes, her eye was restored, leaving no evidence of her injury.

She touched her eye and smiled shyly at me. Her cheeks flushed a bright red. I smiled back, thinking how much she reminded me of a toddler. One minute she was dropping to the floor having a temper tantrum and the next she was playing in her sandbox.

I cut my eyes at the dark angel. "Give me your word you won't hurt this innocent!"

"Why should I show mercy?"

"The child cannot be held accountable for her actions," I argued. "For God's sake, she's been injected with fey blood. Fey are unpredictable and dangerous. This girl is human! You made her into a senseless animal. If anyone should be held responsible then place blame on yourself and these goons you call scientists."

"You think she wasn't aware of her actions?"

"Not entirely, no. She acted on instinct as you have created her to do so. How can you ostracize this child for doing what she has been designed to do? She's a mother protecting her young."

"You are wise to be so young," he paused eyeing me with openness. "Very well. You have my word, daughter."

I suddenly realized that it was more than just Mustafa and my mother having a casual affair. There was something meaningful that he and my mother shared intimately. Could he have truly loved Sara? Was he capable of real love? I didn't want to know. I'd made my mind up a long time ago about him. He was a cold-blooded murderer and my mother wasn't much better. I hadn't mentioned my mother's death to him. If he wanted to know, he could find out for himself. "Thank you," I said flat.

Mustafa stared at me as he waved for the soldiers to take Wendy.

I stood there for a moment until my stomach roiled with sickness.

My loathing of this creature was getting the best of me. "May I be excused as well?" I stared at him keeping my face unreadable.

"Of course," he said. "I certainly don't want to end up with a knife in my eye." He smiled as the hall laughed at his ill-mannered joke.

Without a word, I held my shoulders straight and exited the mess hall. After I was out of sight, I sprinted to my room wanting to put as much distance between me and this whole ugly morning.

AURORA

he next morning, I'd awaken with a startling clank of dishes. Heavy of breath, I sprung from my pillow to a sitting position. Beads of sweat collected over the bridge of my nose as my eyes darted over the subdued room.

When my gaze landed on the housekeeper, I relaxed, exhaling a long sigh. I watched as she busied herself dusting and picking up after my mess.

To avoid another encounter with Wendy, last night I'd eaten dinner in my room. I wanted to steer clear of the fey girl's tantrums nor did I wish to see Mustafa. I reckoned I ought to avoid the scheduled mealtimes and go on off-peak times. Or maybe I'd order in. I liked the idea of eating alone in peace.

My gaze followed the gray-haired lady as she busied herself with the usual tasks of cleaning. Despite her age, she moved fluidly. I was taken by her vitality, though her silence made me wonder. The last time she had come to my room, she'd been quiet as well. Not even an utter. Had Mustafa forbidden her to speak? Or worse… *removed her tongue*? A diabolical act that he was more than capable of committing. For whatever reason, I was certain she was a prisoner like me.

"Good morning," I smiled shyly, watching her pull the curtains back. The light was almost blinding from the brightness of the solid white outside. Cuffing my hand over my eyes, I went on to ask,

"What's your name? I'm Stevie." Gosh! I craved conversation. "I've never seen snow like this. You must miss the sunshine. Nothing here but a relentless solid white."

The gray-haired lady stopped and lifted her gaze at me for a very brief period. Her brown eyes glistened with kindness yet she didn't speak. With only a smile, she exited my room, leaving behind a set of clothes and a breakfast tray. I watched as she shut the door behind her. I stared at the pile of clothes and food. I should probably eat but I couldn't stomach the idea.

I lay back into my pillow feeling disappointed. I reckoned she had her reasons for keeping silent. Even so, it would've been nice to talk to a normal person.

Despair weighed heavily on my heart. I missed home. But where was that special place? With the Cajun? The Garden District? I shook my head no. I might as well accept the hand that life had dealt. I was a misfit and didn't belong anywhere.

I shouldn't whine. Dom and Jeffery could be dead for all I knew. The thought of it tore at my insides. I couldn't think like that. I had to believe they were alive and well.

I prayed that Aidan was bluffing. He might've changed but he loved Jeffery and Dom. He only took them to hurt me. As much as Aidan despised me, I felt that he'd spare Jeffery and Dom. They were his family. I had to believe that. I couldn't accept anything less.

After I'd showered and dressed, I heard a faint tap at the door. With a dreaded sigh, I slid off my bed and answered. I cracked the door open slightly as my mouth twisted into a bitter frown glaring into Mustafa's face. "What?" I asked, not bothering to hide my distaste.

"Good morning," he flashed a tight smile. "I hope you are in the mood for a short tour of the compound. Shall we?" He stepped back, extending his hand.

I huffed to myself and obliged his request. Apart from the fact that I hated spending time with Mustafa, this was the perfect opportunity to scope out the compound without the cloud of suspicion hanging over my head. The more I knew about this place, the better chance I had to escape.

Rather than taking our usual early route, this morning we had ventured down a different passage. Though the pathway appeared the same as the others... a pungent smell of chemicals and bleached white with innumerable unmarked doors. It was enough to give anyone a headache. At this point, I had grown to despise this strange land.

After several minutes of miserable silence, I decided to strike up a conversation. If the dark angel thought I was trying to make nice, he might start to let his guard down. So I asked, "What part of the compound are you taking me to see?"

Mustafa's eyes lit up like a child keeping a naughty secret. "We are headed to the Freeze Zone."

"Freeze Zone?" My brows puckered. "This entire environment is a freeze zone."

"True, the climate is quite brutal here, but this is a special sector of the compound," he smiled. "I wish to show you our work. I think you will be impressed."

"How is Wendy?" I asked, changing the subject. "I haven't seen her in the last couple of days." My opinion about Wendy hadn't changed. I merely wanted to know if Mustafa had kept his word. Other than that, I preferred to keep my distance from the fey girl.

"Wendy is in isolation undergoing treatment. We pinpointed the problem with Wendy's outburst. Certain characteristic traits in her DNA had not been properly extracted from her chromosomes. We are making sure her outburst doesn't happen again."

"So you're not planning to kill her?"

"Of course not. She is very valuable to us. We are helping Wendy to become a more manageable servant. Therefore, a much happier person."

"Don't you mean that you intend to keep her as your whore? Wendy mentioned that her pregnancies only last three months and she's birthing six at a time. I can't even think about the sordid creatures she's bringing into this calamity."

"You are free to judge as you wish, but I advise you to keep it to yourself." Mustafa's eyes grew despotic. "I hope we have an understanding."

I understood but I wasn't going to let him scare me. "Duly noted, King Mustafa," I snarled at him. "It's still pathetic what you're doing to that girl. How do you sleep at night? Is there no end to what you will do?"

"I know you are young and have so much to learn. One day you will see my vision and agree."

True I was young but I would never agree to this madness. One day he would see how wrong he was about me but for now, I'd be patient. "Only the future holds the answer," I replied and didn't discuss it any further. The rest of the way, we walked in a stiff silence. I started to hum just to take my mind somewhere else.

Moving along down several corridors, we came to a sudden halt in front of a door leading outside. I stared out the small window, trying to swallow the knot jammed in my throat.

Mustafa's robotic voice pulled me back to his presence. "We have to dress before we head outside." He nodded to a massive steel door. "Here, put this on," he tossed a one-piece suit that looked similar to what the astronauts had worn.

"Thanks!" I said, nearly dropping the suit. No wonder. The garment was heavy, thick with a wall of insulation.

"Put these tall boots on and the mittens too." He tossed at me. "You can't have any exposed skin. Angel or not, the cold wind will burn your skin right off in a matter of seconds."

A sudden bout of fear clung to my chest. "Where did you say this place is?"

"I didn't." Mustafa scratched his stubble chin, laughing. "We're in another dimension. This uninhabitable land is called *Aurora.*"

"Since no one can live here why do you use this niveous waste-land?" I peered through the window staring at the wind whipping up the snow. The visibility was zero out there. Even with the brightest flashlight, a person would be blinded by the dense white. This place was the polar opposite of hell but worse.

"We wish to prevent unwanted visitors from raiding our camp. We have too much to lose. If an intruder discovered our advanced technology, it could be disastrous. Our scientists have made groundbreaking progress. Therefore, we must protect our work at all cost."

"Good to know," I replied curtly. Whatever he had in store for me, I should brace myself. This project he held with great esteem could be just as sadistic as Wendy and her baby factory. I needed to watch my back. I was limited in this no-man land. Which made me realize that escaping Aurora wouldn't be an easy task if even possible. A dimension… *where*? I doubted it was the same dimension Aidan had taken me to. Nonetheless, I could only assume it was far from earth.

We stepped outside onto a port. I spotted a pole with a rope anchored to it that stretched several feet past the white abyss. Since my visibility was limited, I could only assume that the rope led to a separate part of the compound.

Mustafa looped his rope to mine, using a coupling link with a safety closure to allow the rope to run freely, and then hooked the carabiner to the long rope that connected to his belt. It reminded me of something a rock climber used.

Fettered to Mustafa wasn't my favorite idea but this was one time I'd make allowances. Getting lost in this frozen desert would be suicide.

After double-checking our gear, we proceeded. Even with all this protective clothing, the bitter wind penetrated my suit. I'd never experienced the cold like this. My teeth began to chatter, making me feel like a walking popsicle.

We slowly trekked our way across the opaque blizzard, forging against the powerful winds that thrust us backward. Each step was a painful struggle, fighting the slapping ice and the burning cold. After several feet of mind-numbing misery, I could make out the faint tails of a metal building. It encouraged me to push forward. I was more than ready to get out of this subzero deluge.

Once Mustafa and I entered the metal building and passed through the first entry, a flurry of warmth all at once bathed us. The feeling in my toes and fingers began to slowly return as I welcomed the heat like a soothing cup of hot cocoa. Following Mustafa's lead, I shook off the snow that clung to my suit and hung it on the hook next to the other suit.

When I looked up, I peered down a long dark corridor. Such a contrast to the usual white. Red lights lined the wall, though it didn't shed much light. I wrinkled my nose confused. "What is this place?" The steel walls echoed my words.

"You shall find out soon enough, my dear. Come." He pressed the small of my back, urging me forward, down the dark corridor that seemed to stretch forever.

My heart pounded my chest as we advanced. The building was as creepy as it was plain. It wasn't much more than concrete and metal. It carried the facade of a military facility.

Finally, we reached two metal doors with black and yellow stripes. Bold letters that read, *Authorized Personnel Only*, was plastered across the doors. Mustafa placed his hand over some kind of detector. A bright blue light rolled down the panel, humming, as it scanned his hand. It jogged my memory of a time when computers operated on dial-up. The two sounds were indistinguishable. Once the scan finished, the double doors clicked, releasing the lock.

"Shall we?" Mustafa held the door for me. Although my heart was pounding in my ears, I entered past the threshold but waited for him to take the lead. I followed behind him down another hallway. I eased my breathing, trying to calm my erratic pulse. For all I knew, this place could be a gas chamber for their defected minions like me. Whatever he was running in this building, it carried the stench of death.

Once we reached the end of the hallway, we halted at a glass door. Mustafa turned to me and said, "We need to suit up again but we need to sanitize first. We don't want to contaminate the lab." He made his way over to one of the three, stainless steel, side-by-side, sinks. Soap and clean paper-towel dispensers were placed at each sink.

"First we have to wash." He nodded at the one next to his.

I tucked my hands into my pockets and disputed, "I washed my hands earlier." I was being snarky but what did he expect? I refused to behave like a willing prisoner and this dungeon-like facility made my skin crawl.

Though I had no clue to what Mustafa was scheming, I was certain it wasn't good. I despised his grandiosity. It was as if he anticipated validation from me... like a pat on the shoulder, a handshake, or perhaps a knee bend. Did he honestly think that he could persuade me to his way of thinking? Every time I looked at his smug face I imagined myself strangling him until I'd squeezed his last breath from his dead body. I loathed the dark angel and looked forward to killing him.

Nevertheless, as if Mustafa had turned a muted ear to me, he ignored my comment, pointing to the sink next to him.

Angrily, I rolled up my sleeves and began to scrub my hands and arms under the scorching hot water as if I was trying to rip my skin off. I welcomed the pain. It seemed to distract my rage.

When I finished drying my hands, Mustafa grabbed two blue uniforms and handed one to me and a pair of latex gloves and surgical booties. Not uttering a word, I complied with his orders.

After I'd finished with my ensemble, I stood waiting for Mustafa to take the lead. I knew the moment was at hand that I'd soon witness his prize project. Setting aside my discontent, I kept quiet, behaving as if unfazed. But if the truth was told, I was shaken to my core. What horrible surprise did he wish to show me? I had to collect myself and get my panic under control. After all, I was a genetically engineered angel. There wasn't anything I couldn't face. Yeah, right! My angel-hood was overrated.

We entered into a vast warehouse, nothing but concrete flooring, overhead lighting, and aluminum walls. A strong odor that smelled like industrial glue struck my senses. I cuffed my hand over my mouth and nose, not that it did much good preventing me from inhaling the fumes. Even my eyes burned from the toxin.

As we moved farther inside, I saw nothing unusual until we hung a corner and entered another sector that had been tucked away, hidden.

All at once, my feet froze, panic seized my limbs. My eyes raked over the area as my heart pounded my ribs. "What the hell?" I whispered, cutting my eyes at Mustafa.

"There is nothing to fear. Come. Allow me to show you," he smiled.

There had to be at least a hundred human-like creatures floating in glass cages filled with glowing, green water. The foreign beings were thin-skinned, almost transparent... similar to a fetus in the womb. They were male and uncharacteristically tall with lanky arms and legs. Their eyes were black and void, alien-like. Apart from their strange heartbeats, the creatures displayed no signs of life.

Eerie crept over my skin as I stood there staring. "What is this place?"

Mustafa spread his arms apart as though he was introducing his family. "We are creating super soldiers."

I glared at him as if he'd lost his mind. "Who are you fighting... *humans*?"

"We have many enemies."

"People can't defeat your infrangible faction. You already have them under your control. So why play God?"

"Because there's a rebellion growing." Mustafa's face had hardened as if I had insulted his child.

My lip curled in disgust. "Rebellion!" I shook my head trying to make sense of this. "What rebellion? People are starving and dying in the streets. They are too weak to take up arms!" I screamed.

"You must not have heard the latest."

"What are you talking about?"

A forbidding shadow grew over the dark angel's face as he answered, "We have discovered there is a rising revolt. The rebels are destroying our regulators and properties. We are under attack and must fight back."

A sudden burst of hope fluttered through me. This was the work of the Cajun. If anyone could stir up trouble, it was that crazy Frenchman. I wanted to rejoice but I didn't dare show my joy.

"So," he twirled on his feet. "I am happy to present Wendy's children." His face beamed with eerie pride.

"Of course!" I mumbled to myself. It all made sense… *Wendy's short term pregnancy*. She gave birth to these aliens and these glass cages served the purpose of an incubator. An enclosed apparatus providing a controlled environment for the care and protection of a premature alien. I cut my eyes at Mustafa. "How long does it take for them to fully mature?"

"Since they are a far more advanced race than mundane humans, it only takes about three months for them to complete their incubation."

"In other words, Wendy gives birth to premature fey-like aliens."

"Correct. She cannot carry the embryos full term. To complete their growth, we set them up here as they become fully developed into adulthood."

"I'm guessing that these creatures don't have any kind of childhood?"

"Correct. Certain chromosomes have been extracted to avoid a waiting process. We simply do not have the time to waste on foolish children." Mustafa came off as if he had the right to decide for these creatures.

Whata self-entitled prick!

My eyes narrowed. "Does Wendy know about this?"

"No, she wouldn't understand. If you hadn't noticed, she's not the sharpest rock in the pile."

"That should've made it easy then," I sneered.

"I'm not following you."

"I mean, if the girl is too stupid to see through your bullshit, it was probably easy to brainwash her."

His brows arched. "The girl is agreeable." He held no shame. "I know you do not understand the magnitude of what we are doing here."

"You're right. I don't understand how you can justify any of this," I hissed.

One side of Mustafa's lip tipped up into a contemptible smile. "We are creating a stronger human race. A healthier species."

"You mean aliens!" My brows slammed into an affronted frown, holding my tight fists to my side.

"Weak men do not have a place in our society."

"I think you're afraid that the humans will wake up and see that you're poisoning them," I disputed.

"Don't be absurd!"

"Are there other angels part of this grand scheme?" I asked.

"Humans are limited but they will serve a purpose. At least for now."

"You're insane, you know?"

"This is logical," Mustafa reasoned. "Mankind has proven they are unfit to inhabit the earth. They are each other's worst enemy."

I swallowed the burning lump in my throat. "Who died and made *you* God? What right do you have to decide if one lives and another dies?"

"If we don't take control, man will destroy his race with disease or war. We are saving the world from extermination." Mustafa wore arrogance like a nice crisp tux. I think he honestly believed he was entitled to decide for mankind. But he failed to see the true reality of his insanity. As I stared in the face of a mad angel, there was no question... I had to stop him.

"Have you seen those poor folks, the women and children standing in the food-line? They are nothing more than an empty shell. As if they hadn't a cell in their brain! They come back every day to stand in that damn line. Your food is essentially killing them. Every time I close my eyes, I think about the small children with dark rings around their eyes and how hollow and empty they look. It's as if they're dead people walking! You're using that stupid ink to control those poor people. You steal their livelihood away and force them to eat your poisoned food. You're not helping mankind, you are torturing them by changing them into braindead zombies!" By now, tears had streamed down my face. Mustafa reached out as if to console me, but I flinched. "Don't touch me!" I hissed. "I will never see the good in what you're doing. You and The Order are demented, and I want no part of this atrocity." I looked into his cold eyes. "I'm not your daughter. I have a beating heart!" I suddenly felt as if I was going to implode. My insides burned like molten rock. I wanted out of this place and far away from this depraved angel.

"You will come around. After all, it is my blood that runs through your veins." Mustafa sounded so sure of himself.

"Your blood doesn't control me. I'm in the driver's seat of my own destiny."

"Are you so sure of that?"

My eyes narrowed. I needed to clear this up. "I know you and mother were having an affair," I inhaled a sharp breath. "Is there any way you're my biological father?" I so didn't want any part of Mustafa.

A twinkle in his eyes danced. "The rumors are true. Your mother and I had an affair. I loved her. She was as wild as beautiful. As far as your concern for me being your biological father, I'm afraid that is an impossibility. You see, after the flood, God prevented the angels from procreating. We are unable to impregnate the daughters of man," he paused, sadness glimmered in his eyes. "However, if you will find a place in your heart, I'd like to think that I am your father in every other sense of the way."

I laughed, darkly. "Even if you were my biological father, I'd still want you *dead!*" I bit out the last word sharp as a doubled edge sword. "You killed my daughter for your own greedy reasons. You and that vile Family robbed my child's life before she had a chance to live. And you took Dawn from me before I even had a chance to get to know her. Every time I look at you, I want to thrust my knives in that cold black heart of yours. I hope I'm there when you fall to your death. Who knows, maybe I'll be the one sealing your fate." I was breathless with rage. I couldn't believe this vain angel believed his own words.

I was done with the tour as I spun on my heels and darted out of the lab.

⁓

For the rest of the day, I hid in my room. I skipped lunch and dinner. My appetite was the least of my worries. I think my days were numbered after blowing up at Mustafa. At any minute, I expected the regulators to charge through the door.

I sat in the window staring out at the relentless white. How did people stand this forsaken land? Never a glimmer of sunshine or warmth to caress your face. Only an eternal wall of ice, promising a cruel death.

It was pure luck that I made it back to the compound. White-blinded, I pushed through the biting blizzard. Thankfully, I didn't go off the path.

It had been hours since I left Mustafa standing in the lab, gaping at me. The shock of those freaky creatures was too much for me to bear. What Mustafa and The Order were doing was beyond the pale. Diabolical even. I couldn't stand by and watch them carry out their sinister plot. Yet, how could I go against minions? For a counterfeit angel, I was useless. In a fit of rage, I threw the desk chair across the room. It had busted the lamp by my bed and shattered into hundreds of pieces as it dropped to the floor. I wished that had been Mustafa's head. "Grrrrrr!" How I hated him.

Without warning, I heard a click. My door opened and my breath caught in my chest. In stepped the caretaker. The same elderly woman. She was carrying a tray of food. The aroma jump-started my stomach, giving me a swift kick in the gut. I had a bad habit of missing meals. All those years drifting from town to town with Sara, there were many times I'd gone a day or two without eating. Life was so different then. In some ways, it was easier.

I watched as she laid my tray on the edge of the bed and proceeded to clean up the shattered glass that covered the carpet. Guilt suddenly washed over me. "No, leave it. I'll take care of it. I'm sorry I broke the lamp." I bit my bottom lip. "Thank you for your troubles."

For the first time, the elderly lady interacted with me. With a bright smile on her face, she padded the bed waving for me to come. I smiled back as I climbed into bed. Still not an uttered word, she reached over me and fluffed my pillow. The elderly lady placed the tray in my lap and began to unwrap my flatware. Once she finished, she glanced up at me and smiled. A kind, gentle smile that traveled to her soulful blue eyes. My throat suddenly ached with tears. I couldn't remember the last time someone had been genuinely kind to me.

The caretaker did something out of the ordinary. She leaned over kissing my forehead and patted my head as she turned to leave the room. I watched in quiet as my heart sunk wishing she could stay. I longed for conversation. Sobs poured as I picked at my plate. With slowly mounting terror, I realized what I had to do. Before I could even think about escaping this frozen hell, I first had to stop Mustafa and The Order's baby factory.

NO MERCY

*T*he next deary morning, my eyes fluttered open to Mustafa hovering over the bed. His face was broody and harsh, far from his usual saccharine smile. "Get dressed!" he barked, turning to the door.

"What! No breakfast?" I smarted off, full of my typical sarcasm.

"You'll eat when you've earned your stay." He shot over his shoulder as he stomped out, slamming the door behind him. I sat up in bed trying to gauge his grim mood. Why was I surprised? I'd hurt his fragile ego. And since I'd ridiculed his incestuous spawn, my stay here was about to get gnarly. I didn't just rock the boat, I flipped it over. I blew out a long breath as I slid out of bed and scooped my pile of clothes off the floor.

Mustafa had taken me to the far end of the compound to a facility I was certain its use was for training recruits. I noticed all the weaponry hanging on the walls… knives, swords, and various types of guns. Not to forget the roped-off ring in the back. This place reminded me of Val's gym, the smell of sweat and musk but most especially, his collection of weapons. I wondered if this was an angel thing or for a better description, a war thing. "What is this place?" I asked.

"Welcome to our arena," Mustafa boasted proudly. "This is a good spot to blow off a little steam."

"Yeah, I see all the weapons." I pointed behind me.

"We like keeping things interesting," he smirked, tossing me a camo tank and a pair of baggy pants that matched. "Change into these," he ordered, turning his back to me.

"Where do I dress?" I combed my eyes over the vast arena.

"Right here," he snarled over his shoulder. "Hurry up!" At least he was giving me some privacy. Though I couldn't say the same for the onlookers standing around. I didn't have a choice but to suck it up.

"I don't see the big deal why I have to change," I mumbled under my breath as I angrily ripped off my clothes. Once I finished, I tapped him on the shoulder. "All done," I bit out.

The dark angel turned to face me. "Good." His eyes roamed over me, drawing back a snide smile. "Shall we get started?" We proceeded to the far back corner of the arena to the fight-ring. I spied a huge man standing in the center of the ring with an abnormal amount of hair growth except for his bald head that glinted under the yellow light. My guess that he weighed more than three-hundred pounds. Judging by his height and mass, I concluded that he was Nephilim. His feral gaze collided with mine and in that terrible moment, fear seized my breath.

"Climb up there," Mustafa ordered, crossing his arms over his chest. I shot a quick daggered glance at the dark angel. I saw no point in asking about his intentions. He was punishing me. I slowly turned to the giant. Sweat beaded across my forehead as I felt numb from fright. Unlike my fight with the Zop, Raz, I didn't have Val's protection to make sure the fight was fair. Of course, who was I kidding? There was no such thing as a fair fight. Especially when it was a fight to the death. "Stop stalling!" the dark angel growled.

Grabbing the rope, I hoisted myself up and entered the ring. I caught sight of the repugnance on my opponent's face and terror came gasping up my throat in cold, panting fear. I was in trouble.

I recalled the fight with Raz and how he dished out some pretty hard blows. I gave it back just as good. The Zop was stout but he wasn't near as big as this creature. Compared to this ape, Raz was a cakewalk.

I stretched my neck and straightened my shoulders, chin up, disguising my unease. I edged my way to the center of the ring, halting directly under the light beam and facing the hairy beast. I noticed how tiny balls of sweat had collected over the Nephilim's body and that he smelled worse than horse piss. Instantly, I wanted to cover my nose.

Hands to my side, I made no advancement but stood there staring back into the face of pure evil. Unless fate had other plans for me, I was doomed. Patiently, I held my gaze level to the creature as if I had a fighting chance.

Mustafa started his spiel. "My stubborn daughter, I think it's time you learn the hardships of disobedience." His musical voice was sharp as a sword. "Meet, Narkissos. He is the deliverer. The hand of death for those defiant."

The beast stepped into my personal space, heavy-brows shadowing his beady eyes and grunting like a brainless ape. I glanced at the hostile giant and then cut my eyes back at Mustafa. "Do you think this fight will change the way I feel about you and your precious ploy?" I spoke loudly with firm conviction.

"You complex me in every way, child. I do not understand. Why do you resist me so?"

It was as if he was incapable of insight. How did I make an angel with a black heart understand the harm he'd caused? I flexed my fists and spoke through gritted teeth, "You murdered my child. There's not a day that passes that I don't grieve over her. I reckon that's the human in me, like *my* real father." I was aware that my admission would incite Mustafa's rage. Any effort to appease this vile angel was pointless. He wasn't going to spare Dom and Jeffery. He'd never had any intentions of honoring his word. How could the fallen angel show honor when he was void of such?

It was time for me to face reality and come down from my optimistic cloud. I'd been set up for failure. The chances of me winning this fight were none. The creature was going to kill me. Mustafa's purpose was clear to me. He wanted me gone. If I wasn't with him, then I was against him... *an enemy he couldn't risk having around.* "Since you wish to punish me for my defiance," I challenged. "Why don't you be a brave angel and stand in this Nephilim's place?"

Mustafa grinned at his feet. Then his heated eyes shot straight at me. "Do you take me for a fool? I prefer to leave my hands clean of your blood. That's the sort of father I am."

"A father! What child has a father that would set her up to die?"

"It won't be a set-up if you survive." His voice swirled with virulence.

Away from the spotlight, I noticed spectators were assembling around the ring. Then it hit me. Mustafa had planned this fight all along. I smarted off, full of enmity. "Oh look, Daddy! You brought an audience to watch."

"Taunt me if you wish, my daughter." Mustafa's shoulders shook with laughter. "However, there is no exception to the rule." Abruptly, his voice darkened. "I must make an example of you. I'm afraid I cannot pardon your betrayal. Therefore, I am stripping your magick. As long as you are in the ring, you will not be able to call on your powers."

"So then be it!" I spat. "Take my magick and my life too! At least I can hold my head high with honor. Honor that I am nothing like you!" My eyes fired with fury. "Let the battle begin!"

"As you wish," Mustafa flashed his golden smile and shouted, "Only one rule. No mercy!"

A bell sounded off and the burly creature began his dance, left foot, right foot, fists doubled up and drawn to his chest. I twirled in my feet keeping my eyes pinned to him. Someone off to the side hurled at him a weapon. When he came back up, he was swinging a flail, a chain wrapped in leather with a spiked steel ball at the end. What was this… *medieval times*? Damn! And I was having such a lovely day.

The Nephilim moved swiftly on his feet charging at me as he raised his weapon high above his head into the air, threshing the steel ball in a circular motion. With great skill, he brought it down, striking. I ducked and rolled to the far left corner, keeping my eyes on the giant.

I figured if I stayed on the move, it would make me a harder target and tire him quickly. I might have a fighting chance then. He was packing a lot of body, barrow chest, and thick legs. I suspected he had to take down his opponent fairly fast before he lost his speed and strength. Even still, my chance of winning was slim. With no magick, the odds were against me. One punch from this beast and I was dead.

Again, he returned another death-dealing blow. I dodged the spiked ball by only inches as it plowed a hole into the mat. Keeping on my toes, I eyed the Nephilim's footing. He always moved his left foot before charging.

Once more, my attacker stormed, left foot first, arms high above his head, swinging the deadly ball. I swerved from his fatal lash, sliding under him and jabbing my fist into his gut. He flinched but not enough to keep him from grabbing at my hair. Lucky for me he missed as I scurried from his reach. I sneered at the beast and scoffed at his blistered face filled with vexation. I reckoned he didn't cotton to the idea that a little girl moved faster than his massive duck-like feet.

In a trice, the spectators started cheering. Something wasn't right! I looked up and the Nephilim had changed weapons. Now gripping in both hands, he held a large steel blade and was gnarling at me. It seemed my opponent had an array of weapons. I only had my bare hands. Like I said... *no fight was ever fair*. The way I saw it was that I had two choices... die or get dirty.

Here we go!

It was as if the Nephilim had recharged. He kept coming for me as though he possessed the strength of ten men. Warp feet pounded the mat as he expertly launched each attack, moving side to side, up and down. Each strike was as fast and deadly as the next. I back-peddled as fast as my feet could go. With each rushing step I made, he advanced a powerful swing, missing my head by a fraction. The damn beast was trying to decapitate me!

Suddenly my feet went out from under me and down I went. I'd slipped on the beast's sweat, smacking my head hard. The Nephilim moved in for the kill. Looming over my body, he lifted the sword over his head, fingers gripping the hilt, ready to deliver the final blow when I saw an opening.

Mustering all my strength, I rammed my foot up his groin. He bent over squealing like a pig. Swiftly, I flipped my body sideways slamming my foot into the back of his knee. He screeched from pain as his body hit the mat with a loud clunk, shaking the ring.

Quickly, I nose-dived for the flail. Clinching it in my hand, I leaped onto his hairy back and thrust the chain around his thick neck. With no time to waste, I pulled back with all my might, strangling the Nephilim. But he was much stronger than I had anticipated.

Like a pesty nat, he jabbed me with his sharp elbow in the face, hurling me off his body. I landed flat on my back with the sense knocked out of me as I shook my head. A sharp throb got my attention as I touched my lip, drawling back blood. "The bastard busted my lip!" Now I was pissed. I shot bullets at the beast as I pushed to my feet.

All at once, the crowd roared, egging the fight on. I suspected that the Nephilim might be these freaks' only entertainment. I reckoned I was the sidekick.

Not for long!

The violent pound of the mat snapped my attention back to the giant. The Nephilim had caught his second wind and was charging for me.

Not a minute to waste, I stretched my arm out and called for the bowie knife on the wall. Mustafa had avouched that he'd vanquished my powers, but I had to give it a shot. It wouldn't be the first time he'd been wrong.

All at once, I felt my powers surge deep within. The knife began to wiggle free of its sheath. A half-second later, the cold steel obeyed my command, twirling through the air coming straight to me. Its hilt landed swiftly in my palm just in the nick of time.

As the Nephilim came down hard with his sword, I jammed the blade into his heart. His beady eyes filled with shock and then faded into a blank stare. The creature was dead before his limp body dropped on top of me.

Blood gushed like a water fountain, spraying my face and clothes. I spat the foul-tasting blood from my mouth as I squirmed out from underneath the beast.

Gasp spread like a dark plague over the spectators. Wobbling to my feet, heaving for air, I raked over the arena looking for Mustafa. The crowd began to stir. Some started to boo, others cheered and whistled.

Unexpectedly, my eyes landed on the elderly caretaker. She was standing in the back with just enough light that I could spot her from the crowd. Sadness filled her eyes. And a quick stab of guilt struck me. I wished she'd not seen the bloodbath. Maybe I'd get an opportunity to speak with her again. I should apologize, explain what I was. At best, I hoped she'd forgive me.

I lifted my gaze to the other side of the arena and collided with Mustafa's wide smile. He was standing tall and proud. Beaming like a happy father as if I'd won the gold medal. His approval sickened me, making me want to vomit. I heaved in the air as I waited for him to announce his next endeavor for me. I hoped I'd satisfied his bloodlust enough that he'd end this madness. I never cared much for killing another living being even if the creature was despicable. I blamed the dark angel for this. The blood spilled here today was on Mustafa. He started clapping and the crowd followed his lead. "Bravo! My child, bravo!" He chanted above the merry.

When I looked back for the caretaker, she had disappeared. Relief washed over me that she no longer had to watch this barbaric match. I imagined she'd had her fill. To be truthful, I had mine too. I wasn't proud of myself.

It seemed I wasn't much use for anyone. I got myself captured in hopes that I'd find Jeffery and Dom but I failed them. I was a fool to listen to Mustafa's lies.

Funny... he didn't steal my magick after all. I think Aidan had something to do with that. Infusing our powers together might have saved my life. I reckoned next time I saw him, I should thank him.

Grabbing Mustafa's attention, I spoke over the clatter of the spectators. "I think I've given you enough sideshow for the day." I was beside myself, boiling with anger. The cruelty of Mustafa knew no bounds, but I was about to draw the line in the sand. It was time I came up with a plan.

DEATH COMES

*B*y orders from Mustafa, two soldiers snatched me into their abrupt embrace and hurriedly whisked me away. Not a word shared between the two men but only silence and the clacking of their heavy boots echoed down the hallway.

When we reached my room, the two men shoved me inside and locked the door. I spun on my feet shooting darts at the barrier that now held me a prisoner. My guest's invitation had been revoked. I flopped down on the bed, slumping my shoulders and releasing a sigh.

I should be grateful. Mustafa could've tossed me into the blizzard to die or locked me in a dank dungeon, with the promise of never seeing light again. But regardless of his leniency, the fact remained that I was a prisoner. My freedom had been eliminated. Now I was confined to my quarters for an undisclosed time.

Verklempt with anxiety, I tapped my lip, wondering what plan Mustafa had for me next. Did he intend to let me sit here until I cooled off or until I came around to his way of thinking? I'd rot first before I'd give him what he wanted.

Still, I had to admit… I'd ruffled Mustafa's angel feathers and I had myself to blame for this miserable predicament I was facing. If I'd just placated him, given him some sort of validation, praised him even, I wouldn't be under house arrest. I bet he had guards standing at my door. I could kick myself a thousand times. How stupid could I be? I'd openly defied Mustafa and snarled my nose at his homemade soldiers. In his mind, I was a traitor. And now he probably wanted revenge. I bet he was coordinating some event that involved a rope and my neck. Oh, how badly I wanted to slam my fist through the wall.

I wasn't a traitor. I was on the other team. The ones that stood for righteousness. How could anyone in their right mind support this act of savagery? I shivered remembering the strange creatures staring like dolls, lifeless, floating in those glass cages. Mustafa and the Illuminist were monsters playing God. I didn't know how but I had to stop them.

I glanced down at my stained clothes devoured in dried blood. I touched my caked hair and quickly drew back my fingers, feeling repulsed. It was all over me, my hair, face, arms, and clothes, covered in sticky crimson. A sudden bout of sickness struck and I sprung to my feet ripping off my garments. I had to get the blood off my skin.

Leaving the soiled pile on the floor, I rushed to the bathroom and turned the water knob as far over as it would go. I desperately needed scalding hot water to wash away the blood and the painful guilt down the drain as well. I stepped into the beads of water and scooped up the soap and began scrubbing the soil away. As I collapsed into a tear flurry, I watched as the bright red swirled down the drain. I scrubbed and scrubbed until my skin was raw. I worked the suds into my hair and repeated it again and again until the water turned cold.

After I'd finished, trembling with dripping wet hair, I wrapped a towel around my body and climbed into bed. Slipping under the covers, I drew my knees to my chest, squeezing my eyes shut, hoping to block the images of the day from my brain. I let my mind drift to the past when my mother was alive and when Aidan was... *different*. I had so many regrets. I wished I had been kinder, more trusting of him. We didn't get enough time. I still loved the old Aidan and desperately missed his touch, his kisses, his consoling arms. The man that would've moved heaven and earth for me. How I wished I could thank him for his generosity. But that person no longer existed. Still, it didn't change my heart. I would always love the old Aidan and miss him terribly.

Time had slipped away and somewhere in between, I had fallen asleep until I heard my door jiggle. I sat up startled. When I saw the caretaker enter, tears flooded. I feared she must think of me as a monster. Still... I was elated to see her kind face.

She carried a set of fresh clothes folded over her arm and a tray of food. The aroma of eggs and bacon wafted in the room as my stomach began to rumble.

I sat up in bed and watched as she did her routine, fluffing my pillow and setting the tray over my lap. She unwrapped my flatware and sat it down on the tray. Steam curled into the air as my mouth watered. I found myself eager to eat for the first time since I'd arrived at Aurora.

The caretaker sat down beside me and smiled, patting my foot. I took the fork and paused, smiling back. A strong urge came over me... a need to clarify. "I'm sorry about yesterday. I didn't have a choice," I blurted out. "It was me or the Nephilim. I had no choice but to defend myself. People are depending on me. They're held prisoner by a very powerful Druid," I paused, diverting my eyes to the window. "I thought I was saving them by surrendering. But I discovered I'd made a fatal mistake. The dark angel had never intended to keep his word." The caretaker patiently listened, still not speaking a word. Though she beckoned me to eat and I obeyed.

After thinking about the guys, my appetite began to wane. I worried if they were well and being fed. It seemed unfair. Here I was eating a warm meal and for all I knew, they could be starving or worse... dead. Tears rolled down my cheeks as helplessness squeezed my heart. I was at a loss. I may have defeated a three-hundred-pound killer but I lost the battle. Now I had no freedom to carry out my escape.

The caretaker, as if she'd read my mind, leaned over and pointed to a napkin on my tray. I looked up at her confused. She nodded at the white napkin. I slowly removed the cloth and shock flitted through me. My magickal knives! I gaped at the caretaker. "How did you... " She stopped me by placing her index finger on her lips and winked. In shocked silence, I watched the caretaker leave, shutting the door behind her.

Quickly, I went to hide my knives under my pillow then I remembered the spell Ms. Noel had taught me. The cloaking spell. I recalled the esoteric room she had taken me to. Ms. Noel was quite clever and I missed her terribly.

I finished my meal in a rush. I needed all the fuel I could get. I was about to pull off something that just might be the end of my life. Oh, well. I'd been down that path more times than I cared to count. Toe to toe with death was starting to become a bad habit of mine.

~

I paced the floor waiting for 2 a.m. to strike. I had nine minutes and fifteen seconds to go. This was the night. I had my beautiful knives tucked in their sheath hidden on my person by Ms. Noel's cloaking spell. And when the caretaker left out this morning, she left the door unlocked. Whoever this mysterious person was, she saw that I was in trouble and risked her own life by helping me.

To prevent anyone from suspecting the caretaker of being an accomplice, I decided to break the doorknob. Hopefully, that would divert any suspicion of her.

The whole day had been quiet. Not a stir. No signs of Mustafa or any of his creepy recruits sniffing around. That was good and bad. Good, because my unlocked door had gone unnoticed, and bad because I suspected the dark angel might be preparing my execution. All the more reason why I needed to take this compound down.

On the dark side of this idea, I feared I might be sending innocent people to an early grave. There was nowhere to escape in this freezing hell. I blew out a ragged breath as I raked my fingers through my hair. I hated myself and I hated the Illuminati and the dark angel even more. It was their fault and their prodigious greed that was forcing me to become a mass murderer. To my biggest regret, I was living up to my past criminal charges. If I wasn't a killer then, I certainly was now.

Looking back before I'd discovered my true identity, I never thought in my wildest dreams that I'd end up in a place like this, facing a life and death situation. A rush of rage coursed through my veins. If I thought my death would end all the evil in the world, I'd gladly give my life.

Though if I were a coward, it would make things much easier. I'd simply end my life with something like drinking poison. I'd just close my eyes and never wake up. No more pain, guilt, fear, and regret to face. Just the dark silence of sweet nothing sounded so delightful. I laughed to myself. Here I was an angel and I questioned if there was life after death. And today, I might get my answer.

Bringing me back to the present, I heard my clock ding. It was time. First on the list… finding the mother of the freaky spawn.

I cracked the door open and peeked down the corridor. It was quiet. Not even a breath wafted in the air. I withdrew a deep sigh. If I got caught, I could count on Mustafa having my head chopped off. That was a chance I was willing to take. I stepped out into the hall, looking both ways. I bit my bottom lip, debating on which way. I decided to go left. It seemed as good as any and that was the direction my gut told me. It made no sense but instinct was all I had.

Down the corridor and hanging a right, I kept my eyes peeled for any guards or signs leading me to Wendy. The compound was still, not a soul in sight. Most everyone was asleep in their bunks at this time of the morning. Easier for me to slip past anyone's notice but I was at a loss finding Wendy. My guess, they'd have her under protection. After all, she was their only breeder. If they lose their babymaker how would they make supersoldiers? That was precisely why I had to stop the girl. I didn't have another choice.

Wendy's unwillingness to reason put me in a very precarious situation. She took pride in her position. Like she was the mother goose that laid the golden egg. Her lack of insight threw me for a loop. All Wendy was doing was paving the way for Mustafa and The Order to take over mankind. I couldn't stand by and watch. If I had even the slightest chance to stop this madness, I had to act. I'd do anything to save my friends and family, even Gina.

Once I found Wendy, I'd make it a swift kill. With my magickal knives' deadly precision, she wouldn't see me coming. And no one would miss her until breakfast. I should have plenty of time. That was if I located Wendy's whereabouts before daylight. But I wasn't going to think about what I couldn't do but what I *could* do. Bottom line… I had to find the girl and put a stop to this madness.

I hated the notion of blood on my hands. That was another reason why I hated Mustafa and his black heart. His ambition got in the way of his humanity. Maybe at the beginning of his creation, he might've been decent. Then something happened, twisting him into a psychopath. Regardless of the reason, he had to be dealt with as well.

My plate runneth over. After I rid the world of Mustafa, I had to figure a way to smoke out those who laid in secret… *the Illuminati.*

They were the true instigators. The ones financing these atrocities. I had to stop them.

I needed back-up. Destroying the almighty was a task that even I couldn't do alone. The Cajun was human, he was powerless against the forces of this vile entity. Aidan was too devoted to his family and their antics. He was on the enemy's side. Val was off fighting the spiritual war and that left me. I raked in a burdensome sigh. That was why I had to destroy this place, which meant setting this place ablaze.

I continued to scurry down the hall, quietly, tip-toeing, not making a peep. The lights were low, easier to hide in the shadows as I made my way down the corridors.

I expected guards and monitors at every corner but so far, the halls were empty. I held my breath that my good luck continued.

I eyeballed each white door. "They're identical!" I groused to myself, feeling the brunt of my frustration. I had no idea where to start looking for Wendy. Should I start knocking? Yeah, that'd get things riled!

When I hung a corner, I spotted the caretaker pushing a cart. She glanced up, flashing her usual, kind smile. Strangely, as if the elderly woman read my mind, she signaled to one of the doors. Still not speaking a word, she started rolling the cart in the opposite direction, disappearing around the corner.

I froze, taken aback. Was she pointing to Wendy's room? How did the caretaker know? I cracked the door and listened. I heard a faint sound of feet shuffling and a female voice humming. Then Wendy appeared, dressed in a housecoat headed for the bathroom. I eased the door shut as I stood in the shadows gaping. I'd be damn! That was the fey girl's room all right.

I raked my eyes over the door to see if I spotted any mark. I saw nothing, not a scratch or a scuff. How could I tag this door without it becoming conspicuous? Then it dawned on me. Quickly, I ripped off a long piece of string from the hem of my shirt and spooled it around the doorknob. I stepped back and examined my clever trick and smiled. It was small enough that no one would detect but me.

First, before I took care of Wendy, I had to warn the caretaker. She'd been a bright light in a very dark place for me. I thought if it hadn't been for her visits, I would've gone mad. I couldn't leave without telling her.

I darted off down the corridor in the direction the caretaker had last taken. Swiftly, I moved, keeping a watchful eye on any surprises. I coiled a corner and there the caretaker stood, taking toiletries from the cart. I approached her from behind and tapped her on the shoulder. She inhaled a sharp breath and spun on her heels as her faded blue eyes locked with my face. I quickly stepped up to her and gently placed my hands on her shoulders. I motioned with a finger to my lips for silence as I glanced both ways down the hall. Then I faced her and whispered, "You have to get somewhere safe. A place that will protect you from the explosion. I'm about to do something bad." The caretaker touched my cheek and smiled. I released a sigh. My guilt eased knowing that I'd had a chance to warn her. "Go now. Don't wait," I smiled. With no time to waste, I darted back down the corridor. Though I regretted what I was about to do, there was a little peace in my heart that I had at least saved one innocent.

When I got to the corner of the hall, two doors down from Wendy's room, I checked to see if any signs of a guard were coming. "Whew!" I whispered under my breath, wiping the sweat from my forehead with the back of my hand. My shoulders were tense and my heart was jumping in my throat. Spilling blood never came easy for me despite the reason. I drew in a deep breath to calm my erratic pulse and checked again for any signs of life. Still, the coast was clear.

Quiet as a mouse, I pushed the bedroom door open and slipped inside. No sign of Wendy but I heard water running. She was showering, and oblivious to my presence. I eased my way to the bathroom door and hung back, pressed against the wall. This was almost too easy. The door was cracked open just enough for me to spot my target. As I signaled for my knife, it quietly took position, hovering over my shoulder.

I observed Wendy washing her hair and humming some silly song, still unaware of my company. Thanks to the thick steam, I had the element of surprise but it was essential for me to attack fast. If the fey girl got wind of me, she'd go hulk and wake the whole compound. My mission would be ruined and I'd be dead.

It was time. No backing out now.

Keeping my eye on the target, I motioned for my knife to charge. Without hesitation, my deadly steel attacked, striking her between the eyes with a loud splat. In one death-dealing instant, Wendy's lifeless body slid down the tile. I watched as a rivulet of blood trailed down the girl's body and swirled down the drain.

It was a quick death... painless. At least I gave her that much but there was no time for regret. I had to keep moving as I called for my knife to return to its sheath with the others.

I started to exit the room when I spied matches on the nightstand. In a rush, I scooped the box up and exited.

My next move... *the Freeze Zone.*

When I entered the gear room, I expected to find the suits. But to my horror, I found the room empty. It was as if Mustafa had seen me coming. I started digging through every cubbyhole I could find but found not one single item. I spun on my feet, fingers raking through my hair in a panic about what to do next. Was this a waste of time? Did I take Wendy's life needlessly?

I peered through the small window eyeballing nothing but the dense black. Exposing myself to the hazardous cold without the proper gear would be suicide. I'd be a dead popsicle in seconds. "Oh what shall I do?" I mumbled.

Leaning against the exterior door, I gulped down a truckload of air to muster up the courage. Or for a better word... *insanity*. Could I do this? Could I make it to the other side without protected gear? But going back wasn't an option. The only choice I had was to finish what I came for. I gritted my teeth and mustered all my strength and with one quick shove, I was standing outside into the formidable elements. With every breath, my lungs burned like I'd ingested fire. I began wheezing and coughing, fighting for air. The pain was unbearable.

My vision was hindered by the ice sticking to my face and my fingers felt like frozen sticks. I knew if I didn't move fast, I was going to die. I forced my brain to concentrate, moving one foot in front of the other, thrusting each foot into the deep snow. I hoped luck was with me in this brumal darkness. But just in case, I held tight to the rope. If I wavered an inch off course, it would mean death.

I plunged forward through the bitter wind. It was almost impenetrable. With each step, I gritted my teeth shoving with all my might against the high winds that propelled me backward.

Between the blinding, white swirls of ice that smothered me, I caught a glimpse of a silhouette holding a bright light. "What the hell?" I thought I was the only crazy person tempting fate. I homed in on the glowing outline. As far as I could tell, it appeared he or she was headed for the Freeze Zone. "Why go there?" Unless the person was on to me. Or maybe I was seeing a mirage. But that was impossible in this darkness. Mirages were not a beam of light.

I forged closer, keeping my eyes on the mysterious person ahead. What if it was Mustafa? Then that meant he knew about Wendy. But if that were him why wouldn't he have captured me by now? Could this person be a soldier or a guard? There was only one way of finding out… confront this mystery person.

All at once, I halted gaping at what stood before me. I rubbed my eyes, thinking I'd seen an illusion. But when I looked back, the *caretaker* was standing beside me. She was signaling for me to follow. I couldn't believe my eyes! Was it truly her? Then she reached up and touched my iced cheek. I was lost for words. Shocked. What was she thinking? Did she not know the dangers of exposure in this brutal dimension? But I obeyed. We both needed shelter and fast. I pushed forward, staying behind her as she led me to the Freeze Zone.

Once we shoved past the doors, I rushed to hug her. The caretaker returned the embrace briefly. Then she pushed me away nodding toward the lab. I smiled at her, knowing exactly what I must do next. I rushed my words, "Thank you for your help. I don't know how you knew but somehow you did. I have to stop them. You understand?" I took her hands into mine and urged, "You have to stop following me. Get somewhere safe. Best you get as far away from here as you can. If they find out that you've helped me, they'll kill you."

The caretaker's faded blue eyes glistened as she touched my cheek. I smiled back as we shared a minute of silence. Then in a breath's moment, she vanished. Did I just get ghosted by the caretaker? I stared at the blank wall where she stood only seconds ago. Had I been imagining her all this time?

Whatever she was, I had to worry about it later. The clock was ticking and soon someone would find Wendy and the cat would be out of the bag. I had to forge on and finish what I'd set out to do. I turned for the lab and ran.

When I reached the doubled doors, I recalled the scanner. I paused briefly examining the black screen. I wondered since I shared Mustafa's DNA if the scanner would mistake me for him. A stupid idea, but it was worth a try. Setting off the alarm would alert the compound. Not good for me. If there was a more efficient way, then why not take it. It beat having a rush of soldiers tackling me.

Without further delay, I matched my palm against the red print of a hand on the scanner just like Mustafa did that day I was with him. I held my breath, keeping still as possible. The blue light popped up and hummed, rolling down my hand. When the scan finished with a sharp click, the doors parted way, slowly sliding open. A rush of excitement struck and I did a quick jump for joy. I honestly thought I'd have to break the lock, but I never was one to look a gift horse in the mouth. I hurried inside and bolted down the last corridor, heading straight for the lab.

At the entrance, I stopped, hiding back in the shadows, peering through the glass for any signs of a guard or even the men in white jackets. I struck out! No one was in there except the caged freaks.

When I entered, I instantly scrunched my nose. I'd forgotten about the chemical smell that nearly knocked me on my backside. It reminded me of formaldehyde and alcohol. Whatever it was, it stung my eyes. I cuffed my sleeve over my nose and mouth. Not that it did much good.

I hated this damn iceberg. I desperately wanted to set this place ablaze and put an end to this terrible nightmare. I wished I had it easy like Dorthy. Just click my heels and I'd wake up in my own bed! I laughed. Where would I put a bed? I didn't even have a home.

I eased my breath and got a hold of my temper. Having a temper tantrum wasn't going to get things done. I stretched my neck and focused. My meltdown would have to wait for later.

I darted to the far side where my eyes locked onto countless rows of glass cages. I paused, gawking. "Jesus! Wendy sure has been a busy girl!" I snarled my nose with disgust. I suddenly had to vomit. I bent over to the side and purged this morning's breakfast.

After I finished, I rose to my feet, wiping my mouth with the back of my sleeve, glaring at the myriads of cages. How many men did she have sex with to produce all these creatures? The fruit of one's loins... I was certain the person that made that idiom up didn't have these freaks in mind. "How pathetic!"

Was there any limit to the length Mustafa and the Illuminati would go? Talk about a demented bunch. I hoped my efforts here today would put a wrench in their diabolical plot. Maybe they'd all go up in flames. "The sick bastards!"

I curiously approached one of the cages and paused, tapping my finger against the glass. The offspring made me think of a statuette frozen in time. The only indication that it was alive was the ventilator, slowly rising and falling. I rushed to step back. The thing creeped me out worse than anything I'd ever encountered. Seeing this hideous creature confirmed my purpose for the day. All this mad scientist crap had to be destroyed.

I better get cracking. Daylight would soon be peeking above the horizon and Mustafa and his soldiers would discover that I was missing. Not to forget the incredible Wendy. Once they caught sight of her dead body, they'd come looking for me.

I had only a short minute to destroy this monstrous lab. I was torn between anticipation and dread. This wasn't going to be an easy job. The lab's size must be larger than Central Park. I squared my shoulders, saying, "I got this!" I fingered the matches in my pocket, pulling them out. I opened the box and drew back a scowl. They were soaked and useless. A storm of rage trampled my heart. I'd gotten this far, I wasn't accepting defeat. No way! "Sorry fellas this is the end of the line for you," I whispered under my breath.

I cleared my mind from any disturbance and concentrated on the four elements: earth, wind, water, and fire. In my Zop voice, I called out, "I call to the four elements to hear my plea!" I continued, "I invoke the power of fire!" I felt my lethal essence churn as it clawed to the surface. I pushed harder, louder. "I invoke the power of fire!" I bore down with all my might from my deepest depth. Sweat poured from my temples and down my face as I repeated, "Hear me, almighty! I invoke the power of fire!"

When I opened my eyes, a small fireball hovered at eye level. I smiled as a spurt of joy rushed through me. "Well, I'll be damn! My magick worked," I eased out a breath. "Now it was time to get serious." I gave it one command. "Go!" Immediately, it shot forth, unfurling its deadly wrath. The blaze spread its doom throughout the lab. With a whumph, the fire missile devoured everything in its path.

In a violent thunder, an explosion erupted, shaking the building and ground. In a flash, I ducked under a table, tucking my head under my arms. The offsprings screeched as the fire ate through their cages.

Hearing their agonizing screams, sickened me. Their wails were unnatural and yet human. My stomach suddenly roiled from guilt. Had I made a mistake? Was I any better than Mustafa and The Order? I looked back one last time as the fire blazed in a fury. Though my heart ached, it was too late to change my mind. There was no way I could save them. I had to accept my decision and get out of here before the fire consumed me as well.

The fire took no mercy. Its lethal flames continued to spread. Smoke spilled into the lab, sucking up all the air and blinding my vision. To protect myself, I held my shirt over my mouth and nose, staying flat to the ground, crawling. I couldn't make sense of which way to go. The smoke was so thick. I just prayed I wasn't sinking farther inside. Everything was crazy mad. My mind was flooded with confusion. Sirens blasted in my ears to the point that I couldn't think. But with the will of steel, I forged on. All I could do was to keep moving.

Then I spotted the doors. I was only a few feet away to safety. I scurried past the glass and wabbled to my feet, greedily raking in clear air, filling my deprived lungs.

After the dizziness passed, I took flight. I ran for the blizzard. Daylight was breaking and by all the screaming and alarms going off, I imagined the whole camp was in an uproar by now. It wouldn't be long before they were on to me.

I shoved past the last set of doors, exposing myself to the perilous climate. For a second, the cold soothed my scorched skin but only briefly. Soon my lungs burned like I'd inhaled a thousand needles. I had no time to waste. I had to get to the other side.

In the next split second, another explosion ignited, tossing me into the air several feet. I landed on a hard sheet of ice, banging my head. For a minute, my mind blanked but when my gaze lifted, I saw a huge blaze of fire licking the white sky like a beacon. The whole building was plunged into flames. Everything was gone, engulfed by fire.

Relief caressed my lips as I lay there watching the fire's rage. A bittersweetness filled my heart. I did what I had to do, though it was no fault of those creatures. They had no say how they came into this world. Taking their lives seemed cruel. But war wasn't pretty.

I stammered to my feet. I'd deal with my actions later. I had to return to the compound. Where else could I go? Even a genetically engineered angel couldn't survive this hostile land. Facing Mustafa might be less painful.

From a near distance, I heard men shouting, hidden behind the white dust. Feet shuffling in an incensed flurry. I decided to take it like an angel and face my punishment as I headed back to the compound. If this was the end of the line for me then so be it. Whatever my fate had for me I'd gladly accept. Triumph flickered through me. I set out to do a job and I succeeded. I managed to destroy their army. I might've not stopped Mustafa and The Illuminati entirely, but at least I slowed them down. I couldn't have done this without the caretaker's help but that little tidbit I'd take to my grave.

Before I'd reached the other side, two soldiers seized me. I didn't fight them as they wrestled me to the ground handcuffing me. The larger guy took the pleasure of striking me over the head with the hilt of his gun. A sudden sharp pain struck and everything went black.

NO GOOD DEED

*W*hen my eyes popped open, I found myself laying on a cold stone floor in a locked cell, surrounded by a single candle burning in a small window. The smell of mold and musk drifted heavily.

My head was drumming with a headache. Pain shot through me as I sat up with great effort and slowly scooted to the wall. Breathless, I leaned against the stone and watched as puffs of air shot out from my mouth. "You'd think they'd at least heat this old dungeon," I snidely remarked between the chatter of my teeth. I wrapped my arms around my waist hoping for a slither of warmth. Not that it'd do much good. My clothes were still wet, the cloth stuck to my skin.

I blew out a cold breath, guessing this was my new quarters. I touched the back of my head and flinched. I couldn't count all the times that I'd ended up with a good bump on the noggin. It was a fair assumption that I was hardheaded. A good thing, too. I snorted a wincing laugh.

A sudden sound of feet stomping echoed down the dark corridor. Whoever was coming, they were marching in sync. I could feel the vibration through the stone. I supposed Mustafa was sending his super soldiers. Possibly a troop. Funny, he had to send half his army to handle a small woman like me. My reputation must've preceded me.

Good! Let the dark angel wallow in his loss. After all, the apple didn't fall far from the freakin' tree. I guess that was the dark angel in me.

Amid the darkness, I heard keys jingling, I lugged myself up to a standing position. Bracing against the stone, my limbs trembled, straining. I reckoned all that excitement had worn me out. But I better find some strength somewhere. It was time to face the firing squad.

The door swung open and in stepped two soldiers, tall and broad-shouldered, dressed in formal uniform. Of course, they were here on official business. Not a good sign but I wasn't expecting anything else.

The soldier with the shackles stepped up, barking orders. "Place your hands to your back, prisoner." Why fight the inevitable? Like a good, obedient child, I followed his orders. It was pointless to resist. I was guilty of my charges. Why deny my crime? And when I stood before Mustafa, I planned to hold my chin high and look him straight in the eyes. If he hadn't realized it before, he certainly was aware now that I was his mortal enemy. And by the looks of this smelly dungeon, I think he'd gotten the memo.

Once the two soldiers had finished manacling me in chains, they dragged me into the corridor where a platoon of soldiers stood at attention, like marble statues, shoulders straight, chins up, eyes looking forward, not making a move.

The two soldiers and I fell in line with the others. Two lines of recruits in the front, then the two soldiers holding me in the center, and finally two lines of recruits bringing up the rear.

Though this felt like a procession to my death, there was a little pride bubbling inside me that I must've rattled the mighty Mustafa. Good! He deserved much worse. I turned to the soldier to my left and asked, "Where are you taking me?"

He answered, keeping his eyes forward. "Your trial, ma'am." His voice vibrated like someone with a tracheotomy.

Strange.

"Judged by twelve, hey?" I asked with a slight smirk.

"No, ma'am. Only Commander Mustafa will decide your fate."

"What? No jury?" The use of sarcasm had become a habit of mine. Besides, why not make a joke? It was all I had.

One of the soldiers behind me slipped a mask over my face. I guessed Mustafa didn't want me to see any other secret projects. I stifled a giggle.

After climbing several flights of stairs from the bowels of hell and walking down several corridors, we reached our destination. The same two soldiers hauled me up some short rickety steps and shoved me between two ropes.

When they pulled the mask off my head, I was standing in the center of the fight ring under a beam of light like they expected me to carry out some sort of performance.

I reckoned I was.

As I stumbled, trying to hold my balance, I heard a large crowd of spectators rousing ...whistling, shouting, behind the blinding light.

A thrill of frightened anticipation taunted my spine. Did Mustafa intend for me to fight again? Somehow, my gut told me it was much worse.

Off to my right, I saw a thick man in a black mask gripping a heavy sword with a thick blade. My breath seemed to have solidified in my throat as I eyeballed the man. This didn't look like a fight, it looked like an execution.

Mine!

A tense silence enveloped the arena. Not even a mere pin dropped. My pulse began to beat erratically as the man climbed inside the ring. His arms flexed with brawn as he swung his sharp blade this way and that, growling like a feral animal.

I choked back a cry, terrified, electrified.

I searched beyond the light among the spectators. As if someone had slipped a coin in the slot, they came alive. Fists held high, faces flamed with rage, bouncing in rhythm, shouting profanities. "Kill the traitor!" they chanted. "Burn the bitch!"

I expected this, but how did one truly prepare for such a brutal, violent death? It was overwhelming watching these strange creatures' faces twist with rage. I think I'd much rather deal with a sword severing my head than thrown to this angry bunch. I felt the color drain from my face as I imagined how agonizing it would be when they ripped my limbs apart.

Suddenly as if I'd been given a drop of water in a desert, I spotted the caretaker. I blew out a breath of ease. It was a relief knowing they had not arrested her. Good! They weren't aware. I was so grateful to see her. I focused on her sweet face though her eyes glistened with sorrow. I smiled to myself, relieved that she was well.

I promptly averted my eyes from the caretaker. I didn't want to draw attention to her. If Mustafa caught me in an eye lock, he might put two and two together. One execution was enough for this blood-hungry crowd.

Out of nowhere, I heard the familiar musical voice. Mustafa bellowed above the hostile crowd. "It pleases me to see everyone is here to watch justice handed down." He made himself known as the spectators parted.

I cut my eyes at my adversary as he reached the top step of the ring. I glared at him meeting his icy gaze straight on as he ambled toward me. I felt nothing but hate for this creature. We might share the same bloodline but we were nothing alike.

His spool of lies and his abomination of a race that he created disgusted me. If I had any questions about my actions, I didn't now. I had done the right thing. I had to stop this atrocity. Innocent lives were at stake. I did a good thing. And for my deeds, the world was a better place for it. There was no replacing the girl. Their babymaking factor was shut down. Wendy and her offsprings were destroyed. Even the DNA specimens, all gone. I did that. Me! The little girl from nothing. Mustafa might end my life, but I ended the *apocalypse.*

Unexpectedly, Mustafa halted. He stared, complete surprise colored his face. Gasp spread throughout the spectators. One corner of my mouth tipped into a snide smile. He didn't know that I had druid powers. My fierce eyes blazed, fixated on him. "You have me where you want me. Get on with it and stop making this into a circus."

Mustafa's vexation was apparent. "My daughter, I have always had you where I wanted you. Do you remember your high school friend?"

Holy hell! I hoped he hadn't killed her. I drew in a distressed breath and spat, "What about her?" I held an even stare. I wasn't going to give him the satisfaction of seeing my fear. Not in this lifetime.

"My naive daughter, Jen never existed. She was an illusion." There was an edge of arrogance to his voice.

"What are you talking about? Of course, she was real. We went to the same high school. I had classes with Jen. We hung out at her house. You're lying!" I bellowed.

Though his voice was velvety, his eyes were dour. "When was the last time you saw your friend?"

I didn't answer. I remained silent glaring at him.

"I was the one who sent Jen to your house. I had accompanied her in the beginning. I hypnotized both your living companions and I used the hologram, Jen, to get information out of that gentleman with the squeaky voice. He was quite easy. He followed my orders like a puppet on a string. After everything was set, I excused myself."

"You were the one spying!"

The lively twinkle in his eyes only incensed me more.

"That was then and this is now," he paused. "I'm afraid you've been a bit of a problem, my daughter."

"And you selfish bastard, you've ruined mine." I reacted hastily. I lunged at him, teeth clenching but my attempt was futile. The iron shackles held me prisoned. I felt suddenly weak and vulnerable in the face of his insolence.

Laughter shot out through the spectators. Even Mustafa found humor in my failed retaliation.

"You. Are. Not. My Father. You demented son of a bitch!" My chest heaved as I glared with murderous eyes.

"It pains me to hear such contempt. If only I could have persuaded you to our side."

This was an act. Lies. More lies! He only wanted me for my powers. "Get on with my punishment. You're starting to bore me."

A sudden thin chill hung on the edge of Mustafa's words. "I'm afraid you don't understand the scope of your bad behavior."

"Yeah," I rolled my eyes. "I killed your baby's mama." Acerbity laced my tone.

In a fraction of a breath, the dark angel stood before me, fisting my hair, forcing my head back. His face, a glowering mask of rage, was only an inch from mine. "You are a disgrace to me and the Zophasemin." He released his hold abruptly.

I met his accusing eyes without cowering. "I didn't ask for any of this!" I qualified. "Before I had met Aidan, I'd never heard of the Illuminati nor did anyone mention a blood contract between the Order and my parents. I wasn't even aware you existed. And why would I? My very existence was unnatural. I was my own mother's cash cow and my daughter paid the price for my lineage to you. If punishment should be rendered, it should go to you and my mother! You killed my child for your own selfish gain. I warned you once, and I'll warn you once more. You will pay for taking my daughter's life. Even if it's after my death, I will come for you." I glared at him with open hostility. "So get on with your little sideshow!"

Then without warning, my essence started to surface. A heavy breeze began to stir as it tousled my hair. I could feel its strength bubbling forth. The ground began to rumble. The fire in my eyes deepened.

Panic flamed the crowd, as they staggered, trying to grab onto whatever they could to steady their feet. Many scattered, like scared little mice.

Then all hell broke loose. The arena started to erupt. Brick, wood, nails, and metal began to reign like hail. The brute with the mask stumbled backward, tumbling over the rope and landing on his blade slicing his chest in two. Blood gushed from his limp body, puddling the stone floor in a bright crimson red.

Alarm surged within me as my breath caught in my throat. I was trapped, sure to meet my death if I didn't break free. I fought against the shackles, pulling and tugging.

Then my eye caught the caretaker. She stood there staring back. The whole arena was falling around her and she appeared unaffected. She lingered in the shadows with intense eyes. Panic shot through me like a speeding bullet. I had to save the caretaker. I couldn't let her die on my behalf.

I peered around to see if I could spot Mustafa. I caught a glimpse of him darting out the door. Just like the coward to leave when things were getting interesting. I'd deal with him later. I strained against the chains but the shackles were stronger than me.

Then I heard a voice drop on my shoulder. My head snapped up and I couldn't believe my eyes. Was it an illusion? I gasped. "Hey Freckles, let me try and unlatch these restraints," he smiled as his eyes gleamed.

"Oh, my god! Val, is that really you? How did you find me?" Tears choked my voice.

"Yep, it's me." He snapped the locks freeing me. I leaped into his arms hugging him tightly.

"Wait!" I stepped from his embrace. "We can't leave the caretaker." I spun on my heels, combing my eyes over the arena. I stopped, eyeballing the caretaker swathed in a radiant light. I froze, shocked. How could I have not known? As our eyes locked, love coddled my heart. "Ms. Noel!" All this time, it had been my dear friend hiding under the disguise of a caretaker. My deceased friend. Tears streamed down my face as I silently shared my farewell with my precious friend. I'd love her forever, even in death.

SELFLESS

*W*hen I opened my eyes, we were back on earth but in an unfamiliar location. I pushed from Val's arms, observing the landscape. I was disoriented to where we had landed. I was inclined to think Val had dropped us off in the middle of a deserted island. Only the white sanded beach and blue water were MIA.

Of course, when were beaches enwreathed in a dense forest surrounded by Cypress trees and low hanging Spanish moss?

I counted several ragged tents dotting the grounds and the aroma of burning wood irritated my eyes. People were roaming about, chattering, gathering wood... busy as bees.

The day was near its end. The golden sun was slipping behind the trees and twilight had blanketed the forest. I closed my eyes and drew in the warm air. It smelled like honeysuckle on a lazy summer day. I couldn't remember the last time warmth caressed my face.

All at once, my mood veered sharply to anger. "Why didn't you let me go after Mustafa?" I shoved Val's chest hard, yet he held tight to his footing. "I could've killed him and this whole mess would be over!"

"Are you crazy? With all his minions surrounding him, it would've been the death of us both." Val's tone was relatively civil despite his angry eyes. "You have more pressing problems right now than going off half-cocked after that bastard."

I opened my mouth to speak but...

Val held up one finger, halting me. "Wait!" he insisted. "I promise you will get your chance but not right now."

Suspicion crept into my mind. What was he not telling me? I crossed my arms over my chest, brows pinched. "Okay, cough it up!"

He paused rubbing his day-old stubble, a jaw muscle twitched. He was annoyed at me. "First, you need to be updated on the current events. The new rulers are throwing their virulent weight around. Folks have gone underground. By the orders of the Illuminati, the regulators are destroying every house in the Parrish. They're dragging folks from their homes and setting everything ablaze. People are taken captive and thrown into concentration camps, forced to be their lab rats. Those that haven't been caught are hiding and starving. The world has turned into a cesspool of evil.

"Geez! How long have I been gone?"

"Freckles, it's been five months."

"Five months!" I shrieked. "That's not possible? I've only been gone about six weeks."

"Sweetie, time works differently in dimensions."

My attention drifted to a pretty corn-silk blonde stirring a large pot over a fire. I cut my eyes back at Val. "Who are these people?"

"They're folks that managed to escape the regulators. They're all hiding."

"I thought you weren't coming back. Are you back for good or is this just a short visit?"

Derision and sympathy mingled in his gold eyes. "I'm back for now."

"You made it clear that you wouldn't be returning? What happened? Did you and your Zops win the war?"

"I didn't lie to you." Exasperation coated Val's face. "I wasn't coming back. But when Nick sent a distress call, I decided that my men and I were needed more on earth."

"A distress call?" Ire coruscated through me. "What? Did you have a cell phone in heaven?"

"Are you trying to be funny?" His thick brows collided.

"You gave the Cajun your information, but you left me in the dark." I stepped up glaring at Val. "That hurts me. It really hurts."

He shrugged. "If you recall, we were no longer together. Remember you broke up with me."

"Oh, I haven't forgotten. I had good reason to dump your ass. It had something to do with sharing me with the other Zops."

"You know I'd never allow such a thing. I… I did what I thought was best. You needed to move on. To forget about us."

"So you decided for me. Don't you think I'm old enough to decide for myself?"

"No. Not at the time." His angry retort deepened the lines between his eyes. "You were quick-tempered and impetuous."

"Then why bother? I was so much trouble."

"Because…" he bared down on his lips. "Because I loved you! I still do."

"Well, you have a funny way of showing it," I replied in a low voice, taut with anger.

"Freckles, don't be like that. Right now it's sort of hard to think straight. Let's revisit our issues after the dust settles. But for now, we gotta keep our heads straight. Set aside our personal feelings. Let's focus on the people that need our help."

"Speaking of, have you heard anything about Dom and Jeffery's whereabouts?"

"Time's been a bit of a crunch. I haven't been able to look into it."

"Yeah," I scoffed. "I see how busy you've been… setting up a cozy camp for *strangers*."

"Stevie, at the time, my hands were tied. I may be an angel but I can only do one thing at a time. These folks were homeless and needed immediate help." He shoved his hands in his pocket.

"Fine!" I stood there a minute kicking the dirt. Maybe Val was right. We had no idea where the guys were located. Aidan could have them in ten-fucking-buck-two. People were destitute and needed medical care, food, and shelter. Not to forget protection. Val and his clan could provide those things. As much as I hated to admit it, there were a lot more folks here on earth that needed immediate attention.

When these people were settled, somehow Val and I had to find a way to lock down Dom and Jeffery's location and rescue them. We had to. I won't rest until they were safe with me.

I decided to pick another time for this discussion. So, I changed the subject. Perhaps after dinner, I could speak to Val. He'd have a full belly then.

"Hey! How did you find me?" I asked.

"You won't believe me if I tell you."

"Try me," I challenged.

"Jeffery's aunt appeared to me in a dream."

"What?"

"Ms. Noel led me straight to you."

"Oh, my God!" I suddenly felt faint, balancing my footing by leaning into Val's sturdy shoulder.

"You okay, Freckles?"

"Huh hmm," I nodded. "It's just so wild these past few months. Val, if it hadn't been for Ms. Noel, I wouldn't have destroyed their lab. She revealed herself to me right before you appeared."

"Wow! I believe that's when she came to me. It only took me seconds to reach you."

Val and I shared a stark silence and then I fell into his arms and sobbed. He didn't say a word but held me tight. I remembered the last time I cried in his arms. It was when I lost Dawn. The flood gate opened and tears poured. Val stroked my hair, whispering soothing words of… love.

Could I love this man? Could I love two men at the same time? I loved the old Aidan. That will never change but did my heart have room for another? Only time would tell. The present Aidan… there was no way I'd consider him for a second. I reckoned I could love both since one was dead to me.

After a few minutes passed, I stepped out from under Val's arms, wiping away the tear stains with my sleeve. I had to not act in haste. I didn't want to get hurt. If Val left again, it would rip my heart into a million pieces. No thank you!

I suddenly shivered, wishing I had a stiff drink to warm my bones. And then I thought of the Cajun.

"Where's Nick?"

"He's hunting."

"Do you know if a girl by the name of Gina is in the camp?"

He rubbed his fingers over his stubbled chin. "There's a lot of folks here. Possibly. I noticed Nick hanging out with a blonde. But I hadn't had time to meet her. Could that be her?"

"Maybe. I guess we'll find out when Nick returns." I eased out a breath. "Well… are you going to show me my new home or what?"

"C'mon, let me give you a tour," Val smiled as he pressed the small of my back.

We made our way through the busy camp as folks began to notice us. One by one, they began to draw around Val and me. Curiosity colored their faces.

I recalled the last crowd that I'd encountered wasn't such a pleasant experience but after seeing the various smiles, my unease lessened.

A sworn of children quickly encircled Val, jumping on his arms and tugging on his sleeves. Their laughter and small voices filled the air. I smiled, giggling. It was obvious Val was a big hit with the young ones. And by seeing all the smiles of the grown-ups, I'd say that he was well received.

As everyone seemed preoccupied with Val, I stood back and searched through the crowd. My eyes landed on one familiar blonde that stood out among the rest. Some things never changed. Even at the worst times, Gina managed to look like a model. She was breathtaking, cornsilk hair, long and shiny. I liked the less makeup look. It carved years off her age, giving Gina a babyface. Who would've thought? There was something different about her, a glow. She appeared happy. Something I'd never seen.

Our eyes locked and a smile spread across her face. I pushed through the crowd, making my way to Gina's side. "Oh, my gosh! You're back. You're alive!" she said as she wrapped her arms around me and squeezed. We stayed in each other's embrace like long lost sisters. When we pulled apart, tears streamed down our cheeks. "I can't thank you enough for saving my life," Gina sniffled.

"I'm happy you got away and you're safe," I smiled. "You look well and happy."

"I worried about you. I was terrified that those lizards killed you. It's a miracle that you survived. I desperately wanted to come back and save you." She wiped a fallen tear.

"If you had you would've gotten yourself killed. I'm glad you didn't."

"Nick found me huddled under a bush. I was so frightened. Thank God too!"

"I'm glad you're both safe."

"Nick and I are a couple. It was love at first sight," she giggled.

"You're kidding," I laughed. "Nicks a great person once you get past him speaking in third person."

We both laughed.

"Yeah, at first I thought he'd been eating the government's food," she snorted, laughing.

"Government's food? Are they calling themselves *the government?*"

"As far as I know they're called *The Order*. But they might as well. Same thing. They own the entire world."

"Ain't that the truth," I agreed.

"We're wanted felons. The Order has posters posted of Val and Nick. Even me. I'm an escapee. We're rounding folks opposed to the Order. We're real rebels. Some call us Freedom Fighters. I'll certainly fight. I ain't going back to that gentleman's club and let them brainwash me and violate my body."

"That's not going to happen. You're safe here."

"Hey, I feel I owe you an apology. I was terrible to you in school." Her soft browns filled with remorse.

"Gina, it's all water under the bridge. I think we both have changed. Hell, we're in the throes of Armageddon. Why drudge up a few trivial tiffs from high school?" I laughed. "Besides, I think we humans should stick together."

"Humans? But you're not human, are you?" Gina's voice swam in confusion.

"You caught that, huh?" I paused, glimpsing away. I spotted Val's head sticking out among the campers. "You're correct. I wasn't aware of my nature until Aidan..." I couldn't finish the sentence.

Gina touched my arm, tenderly. "I get it. You and Aidan were tight. What happened to him?"

Crap! I didn't want to answer that question. "Umm, I'm not sure," I shrugged. Aidan was a sensitive subject for me. The present Aidan, I hated. The former Aidan, I loved and adored. I missed that Aidan and longed for his touch. I missed him so much that it hurt. But I had to move on and forget him. I looked over at Val. His head stood out from among the crowd. Why should I dwell on the past when there was Val right there and he loved me. Aidan was gone. The present Aidan was nothing like the man I'd fallen in love with. I shifted the subject. "Hey, where is the Cajun?"

"Nick's on his way. He caught a gator. I'm sure you know how he likes to barbeque?" Gina laughed

"I do remember. Damn good barbeque too," I said.

This was a good sign… Gina and me, friends. I had a good feeling about this camp. If only we had Dom and Jeffery back, things would be almost perfect.

A year ago, our lives were so different. Now we lived in constant uncertainty. Forced from our homes and living in tents, our lives appeared to be in complete utter turmoil. Seeing the end of the rainbow might be an impossible feat. Despite everything that has gone wrong, I just had to believe that better times were ahead.

Out of nowhere, a French voice shot out from the line of trees. It was dark and only a crescent moon to light the way. "Holy hell! She has returned!" I knew that French voice anywhere. Nick came up and dropped a bloody gator by my feet, taking me into his smelly arms and nearly squeezing the life out of me as my feet dangled. I laughed out loud for the first time since I'd been gone.

"I never thought I'd see your derrière again." He looked over at Gina and the others who had gathered to our sides, "This girl has *des couilles en acier* (balls of steel)!" He called out to the rest. The Cajun grabbed me around my neck and kissed me on the cheek. I was relieved that he didn't go for a deadlock kiss. God forbid for the past to repeat itself. I didn't need or wanted Gina's wrath, especially now that we'd made peace.

Thankfully, my worries soon faded when he dropped me and snatched Gina, planting a whopping kiss on her. Even under the soft glimmer of the moon, the sparkle in his eyes glistened at her. It touched my heart. And strangely at the same time, a taste of bitterness struck.

My problem wasn't seeing their affections for each other. I welcomed their happiness. What tugged at my heart was that I realized how lonely I truly was. I glanced at Val. He was speaking with an older man off to the side out of earshot. Val appeared to be the one in charge of things. He was a reliable guy that people depended on. I understood that. He had a pure heart.

I drew in a sigh. I loved Val but things had shifted between us. After he'd left me standing alone, my feelings had changed. He didn't owe me an explanation of his whereabouts. Though, I did feel hurt that he didn't include me in on his contact information. Maybe by his seeming lack of consideration of my feelings, I should just accept the fact that he and I were at different places in our lives. It was clear to me that I wasn't his priority. Actions speak louder than words. I frowned, eyeballing him for a minute. His eyes caught mine but I quickly looked away. I didn't want to face my feelings about him right now. I needed to focus on saving my family. It was easier putting others first. Focusing on someone else kept me busy and my mind off my own troubles. I exhaled a deep sigh.

The Cajun drew my attention back. "Your return could've been at a better time. We have so much work to do."

"How did you end up here? Did you lose your house too?" I asked.

"Merde!" he cursed. "The regulators beat me to the punch. After you and I parted, I went back to my house. I had to see if the old place was still in tack. I regretted going. Those sick bâtards had burned it down to the ground. All my guns and supplies in the shed had been taken. That's when I headed for the woods, deep in the bayou. I found a couple of neighbors on the road and they joined me. Before I knew it, more people joined our camp. We all have lost our land and family."

"Nick, I'm so sorry."

"I lost my family too," Gina spoke up. "The lizards shot my parents in cold blood and then poured gasoline on their bodies setting them on fire. The house was next. They held me down and forced me to watch. I'll never forget that horrible night as long as I live. I hate those lizards and The Order. They murdered my family in cold blood. My parents were good people. Dad was a pharmacist. Half the time, he gave medicine away to folks who couldn't pay. Mom was a homemaker. She'd take me to cheerleading practice and made me eat all my greens. You know, a normal mom. My parents never hurt anyone. The lizards didn't even give me a chance to bury them. That's when they took me to the gentleman's club."

"Gina, I'm sorry to hear about your parents. They can't get away with this monstrosity. We gotta find a way to stop this insanity," I said

"Oui! I agree. But how?" the Cajun asked.

"I don't know," I took a quick sharp breath. "Killing the leaders would be a good start."

"Oui! F'sure," the Cajun laughed.

"Have you heard from any of the gang?"

"They're dead." Sorrow danced in the Cajun's eyes. "When we

were held up at the plantation, Toe and the fellows went looking for us. They attacked the regulators but lost the fight before it started."

"Nick, I'm so sorry." I blamed myself for their death. If I had not convinced the Cajun to go with me, they might still be alive. At that moment, I hated myself.

"Famine has spread throughout the world. Food rationing is only through the Order and that is if you get that merde tattoo, six six six, stamped on your wrist."

"Ah… the food rations. You're smart not to eat it. It's poison."

"Rumor has it that millions have died by starvation and the count is endless of folks being killed. The world is a fucking disaster. If we don't start fighting back, we're all doomed."

"I know. It seems they have the upper hand. We have to fight. Do you have any more moonshine?"

"Oui! But not enough to kill all those reptiles."

"Can we make more?"

"I have a stilt but we need supplies like cornmeal, yeast, sugar, and clean water."

"Damn! And you don't know anyone that has these ingredients, right?"

"Oui," the Cajun answered curtly.

"We need to tap into our resources. We have an angel that can enter any dimension. Maybe Val can help."

"That's a great idea," Gina intervened. "It'd be great if he could find some soap. I sure do miss good smelling soap," she smiled.

"I hear you," I said. "That would be a nice treat. Clean water too."

"Did Val tell you the good news?" the Cajun asked.

"Huh, what news?"

"Val found Dom and Jeffery's whereabouts."

I think my heart stopped. "Are you sure? Val told me he didn't have any information on their location."

"My bad." The expression on the Cajun's face was like a kid getting caught with his hand in the cookie jar. "My misunderstanding. Pardon." It was clear to me that the Cajun was covering for Val. I hate liars.

I cut my eyes over at Val. He was still in a conversation with the older man. I couldn't think of a better time to impose. I stomped over to his side and interrupted. I fisted Val's sleeve and swung him around to face me. "Why are you lying to me? You know where the guys are at." My green eyes clawed at him like talons.

Val stared, complete surprise on his face. "I wasn't ready to tell you."

The older man excused himself and disappeared.

"How dare you hold information from me. That's my family! What do you know?" I demanded.

Val dropped his gaze at his feet and drew in a deep breath. My scouts think they have located the guys but..."

I caught the torn glint in his eyes. Terror blighted my mind. "Oh dear, God! Please don't tell me they're dead."

Val hurried his words, "No! Well, I'm not sure but we have located them."

"Then let's go get them!" I shouted.

"It's not that simple," Val swallowed hard. "They're at the floating castle."

"I don't understand. We've been there before."

"It's not where you think. The castle has moved." Val's jaw tensed. "There may be a problem locating the exact spot."

"Then let's start looking! We will never find them sitting on our thumbs."

"It's not that easy to track! Not only is the castle invisible, but it never stays in the same place twice. It drifts through different dimensions aimlessly. No one can predict its course."

"Oh, dear God!" I murmured as my head spun with sheer fright. "They're lost to us forever?" I choked on a sob.

Val caught my arm, forcing me to look at him. "Not all is lost."

"What do you mean?"

"We have a small window. Straight up midnight, we can enter the castle's relative velocity time dilation."

"You mean tonight?"

"Yes," Val answered.

"When did you intend to tell me?" My hands flew to my hips, chin tilted in defiance.

He sighed. "I wasn't. I'd plan to go without you knowing."

"Why would you not include me?"

"You've been through so much that if things went badly, I didn't want to..."

249

"That's bullshit! I'm going with you!"

"Freckles, no. I have one of my men accompanying me."

"Like hell! I'm going and that's final!" Sometimes, saying no to me meant a hesitant yes. He wasn't leaving earth without me. Even if I had to magickally superglue myself to his ass, I was going.

～

Later that evening, pushing through the busy chatter of the camp, Val jumped up on a log and whistled to get everyone's attention. The camp quieted, drawing their attention to the Zop leader. "Hey everyone," Val called out. "We need to have a discussion. Come, gather around the fire," he continued to announce. "Those who have cooking duties can sit this pow-wow out." I could see how everyone looked up to him. His towering stance emphasized his competence. The very way he stood there told me he was a man of admiration. This was where he belonged.

I combed over the camp trying to spot other Zops. They were easy to pick. They carried a particular aura, a blue or purple. Val's aura flurried in a deep blue and red mixture. Funny, I didn't see any signs of his men. Since I was considered impure and unaccepted by my race, it didn't surprise me if they decided not to show.

I made my way to Val's side and sat on the log next to him. An easy smile flushed my face as I stretched my hands close to the fire, wiggling my fingers. The warmth soothed the numbness, melting it away.

I noticed others began to join us, a great deal more than I expected. I imagined if conditions kept getting worse, there would be even more refugees. I feared that the regulators would eventually find this camp and people would die. I suspected there wasn't one corner of this world left that one was safe. It seemed nothing was out of the reach for the infamous Illuminati.

After everyone settled by the campfire, Val started with his speech. Gina and the Cajun joined me, having a seat on the log. Val started with the introductions. I was inclined to think the campers were wanting to know who I was. After all, I was new and they didn't know me from Adam.

"I want everyone to meet our latest member." Val's voice rose above the crackling fire. "Everyone, I'd like to introduce the newest member to our camp, Stevie Ray Collins." He gestured to me as I stood up. Val began his speech. "She has been held captive by *the Order* but managed to escape. Ms. Collins is not human. She is special. Much like myself, she has a set of unique abilities." The crowd began to stir, chatter wafted in the air. Val called out, raising his voice. "She is not a super-soldier! This young woman is different." Val's drilling eyes washed over the disconcerted assemblage. "Ms. Collins and I are about to embark on a deadly mission. Our goal is to rescue two humans. They are caught in another dimension and we have only a slim chance of finding them."

One scruffy man cut in, his voice, coarse as his clothes and unshaven face. "Will the girl and these strangers be returning?"

"Yes. That is if we survive." His solemn face carried no hint of hope.

A younger man, slim with dirty brown hair, shouted out amidst the crowd. "We do not know this woman," he hesitated, measuring me for a moment. "Can she be trusted?"

Then Gina bounced to her feet. "I can vouch for Stevie! She saved my life from the hands of the Order and sacrificed her life for mine. She put herself in harm's way for my sake. She is our friend!"

"You may take your seat, Gina," Val commanded. "Anyone else would like to voice their concerns?"

The Cajun rose to his feet, mounting the tree stump next to Val. "This is coucou (crazy)!" he bellowed. "Val, you know this girl better than anyone." I could see the irritation spilling from the Cajun's shoulders.

"It's true. I do know her. Setting aside the past, I have to be honest. She was with the enemy for five months. I worry that they have poisoned her abilities. Used some advanced technology on her. What if they controlled her simply by the touch of a button? Are we going to wake up one night to have our camp slaughtered by this seemingly innocent girl? Ms. Collin is a genetically engineered angel. She is very powerful."

I gaped at Val's confession. His admittance struck me like a swift kick to the head.

My face flushed with anger. "Hold on a minute!" I bit out. Had Val turned against me too? I didn't see this coming. I slowly coasted my gaze over the many disgruntled faces. Mistrust and fear laid heavily among them. Somehow, I had to gain their trust or at least ease their concerns before their antipathy spread like gangrene and things turned violent. "Look! I get your skepticism," I admitted. "I won't lie… there is a chance I might have an implant." Hard whispers rolled in waves amidst the refugees. "If I've been infected, it happened when I was an embryo. Regardless, it doesn't change my stance against the Order. I am *not* your enemy. I am the person who is willing to die for you and anyone else who wishes for freedom!"

A woman holding an infant yelled out. "How do we know you ain't gonna bring troops in her' and have us all killed? You could be one of those aliens." Her voice grew sharp and terse. "They're buffooning as humans now. I *seen* it with my own eyes!"

I paused, as the crowd grew restless and fidgety, whispers stirred. I glanced at the Cajun and shot darts at Val.

I turned my attention back to the people. "Despite what all you have heard, I will stand with you fighting the wicked!" My heart was beating so hard against my chest I could hardly hear myself think. I pushed on. "While I was held prisoner by the Order, I set their lab on fire. Nothing is left but ashes," I paused. "I knew I had sealed my fate after their thousands of super-soldiers burned to the ground along with their advanced-alien technology and their rocket-scientist formulas. Years of their vile work had been destroyed in only a matter of minutes." My voice ripped through the camp. "We should rejoice!" I declared above the growing arousal. "Victory is upon us! We *will* take back what is ours!" I shouted into the crowd, my left arm reaching for the stars.

The people stood whistling and clapping to my speech. As my eyes skated over each weary face, I hoped I'd succeeded in raising their spirits. Val grabbed my hand and we rose our arms together cheering everyone on. Even I sensed hope.

Yet with victory came blood. No doubt, we had a long hard road ahead and the blood was only the start. Deep down, I feared for mankind. A defeated sigh escaped my lips. Not even Alexander the Great could beat this one.

Shaken from our celebrated moment, behind the shadows, came a burst of feet simultaneously stomping, much like marching. Whoever was approaching, appeared countless and encroaching fast. Quiet enfolded the refugees as mothers ushered their children close to their sides. Fear spread its wings as each person stood frozen. I didn't understand why no one was running for cover. Then again, where would they hide? My eyes peered into the darkness through the stand of trees. I spotted nothing. I glimpsed up at Val. Fear danced in my eyes, though, Val's face was unreadable. Even the Cajun showed no indication of concern. Frustrated and teeth on edge, I cut my eyes back to the forest, probing for any signs of the enemy. I secretly called for my knives as they hummed to me. My mind rushed with alarm. I continued to stand still next to Val, hiding the trepidation that swelled inside my gut. I waited for what laid in the dark shadows. If the regulators had come for us, we were as good as dead.

As everyone watched, the sound intensified. Then suddenly, a legion of silhouette figures cleared the trees. As the intruders came into the moonlight, everyone let out a gasp of relief, except for me. It was my race …*Zophasemin*. My shoulders went rigid. I was still an outcast.

An impure.

I assumed Val could sense my sudden tension. He gently squeezed my shoulder for reassurance. I slipped him a sideways glance and asked. "Is your clan here to kill me? After all, you mistrust me."

Val's nose crinkled keeping his eyes on the approaching army. "They've been on a mission. I'm hoping I won't be disappointed by their findings."

I merely nodded, holding my thoughts to myself.

I saw this from two scenarios. First, if one of them attempted to take my life…well, he might have a fight on his hands. The second one, if they *all* came for me, I wouldn't have a chance. But what jabbed my heart was that I couldn't trust Val to have my back if the Zops threatened my life. After hearing the doubt in his voice tonight, I wasn't too sure about which line Val stood on. Such an awkward feeling how quickly our friendship had veered.

Once the army entered the camp, Razz fell out of line and approached Val.

"Permission to speak, Commander?" The Zop still was as burly as ever and I had my doubt that his personality had changed either. I remained silent watching his moves cautiously.

"You have the floor to speak freely, warrior." Val concurred.

"We entered the Freeze Zone as ordered. Thanks to the *impure* we were able to penetrate the compound and explore any further activity.

It pleases me to report that the Order's operation is completely eradicated, Sir."

Razz turned to me, acknowledging me for the first time. "If it had not been for you, my kind," he paused, "Excuse me. I mean, our kind, would not have been able to fulfill the mission with success. You made it possible."

I stood there tongue-tied. My mouth popped open and shut. This was something I'd never expected in a million years especially coming from Razz. The Zop hated me. Val gave me a little shove, pushing my shoulder. "Umm, thanks."

Razz smiled as his dark eyes pranced with humor. He stepped up closer to me, then he did something I'd never thought possible... he bent down on one knee and bowed his head.

Val leaned over and whispered in my ear something that only I could hear. I looked up at him wide-eyed, but I complied with his suggestion. "You may rise, soldier," I said shyly.

Razz obeyed and continued, "For your bravery, the *Zophasemin* declares you are a warrior highly reverenced. You are accepted among my race as one of us. Indeed, a true and pure Zophasemin!" he hesitates. "One more thing, I hope you will accept my deepest apology for my ill-treatment toward you. I was out of line for disrespecting you. I beg for your forgiveness." The glint in his eyes displayed a true mark of repentance. All the resentment I had carried in my heart had disappeared and here I stood with reverence by only blowing up a few little old super-soldiers. If I'd known that was all it took, I would've done it sooner. I smiled. A few tears misted my eyes.

"Thank you and I accept your apology."

In my next breath, the whole clan of Zops rushed in, sweeping me off my feet, hundreds of hands had uplifted me, passing me along as deep male voices shouted, "hip-hip-hooray!"

At that moment, I went into shock. I'd never thought the Zops would ever claim me as one of them. But I'd take it. For once I belonged. A joyous feeling, I would never forget. It was like a lost child returning home. I couldn't help it. I sobbed like a baby. A happy sobbing baby.

GLASS MOUNTAIN

The time was near for our departure as Val tapped his watch reminding me of our travels. It was bittersweet. I finally gained acceptance among the Zops, and I was having to leave before I had a chance to let it all sink in.

It was just as well. I had to give all my undivided attention to this new dimension. The Zops would be here when I returned. That was *if* I survived, a big if.

Pushing all doubts aside, saving Jeffery and Dom was my primary goal. Thinking about my death was not the time. I had to believe we all would return in one piece. After all, I couldn't forget we were on the verge of a bloody battle. And I still had unfinished business with the dark angel. No question. Mustafa had to die. If my worth was anything, it was putting an end to that monster and this uprising.

Two minutes before midnight, Val donned on his backpack and joined me in the center of a chalk-drawn circle. The Zops and refugees were giving us plenty of space. Val gathered me into the circle of his arms, with our heads bowed, I called for my essence and Val chanted. It was count down as restlessness settled amid the camp.

In sync, the clock struck midnight, the earth shook with great might. Val and I were swept into a tailspin. Spinning and spinning. The gravity pull was powerful and I felt like Dorothy in the Wizard of Oz, spiraling like the unpainted house. Only we were free-falling.

When we abruptly stopped, I pushed from Val's clasp. Hands braced on my knees, I dragged in stale air and came up gagging. My head spun like the last call for alcohol.

After a moment, my stomach settled and everything stilled. I glanced at Val and even he looked a little green around the edges. I guess the ride was a humdinger for him too.

After my erratic heart settled, I stood up, observing our surroundings. I whistled as I ran my fingers through my disheveled hair. I thought Aurora was a sight for sore eyes, but this dimension won by a long shot. I peered over the land, stunned at what laid before my eyes. Only one word came to mind... *death*.

It was as if we'd landed in the middle of a graveyard, only no grave markers. This place was void of color. The sky was a bruised gray and the dead, leafless trees took on a char black. Everything appeared diseased. Even the air carried a strong odor of decay.

My lungs burned from whatever toxin filled the atmosphere. The land was uninhabited, lacking oxygen. I held my breath and then I realized... "Whoa! Angels don't breathe!"

Val chuckled. "You didn't know?"

"I reckon I didn't get that memo."

Then the excitement of my newfound discovery diminished when I saw the stress lines across Val's forehead as he surveyed the land. A sudden dread came over me. "What's wrong?" Out of habit, I inhaled the nasty smell of rotten eggs and started coughing. I threw my palms over my mouth and nose hoping to block the odor and ease the sting.

"Watch out for this place," Val warned, "And by the way, breathing here isn't a good idea in this death trap." His eyes were sharp and unyielding. "It will take a minute or two, but you'll get the hang of not breathing. Better sooner than later. The atmosphere's gases will make you sick or kill you if you ingest too much." His voice dipped into ice. "If you get sick, you'll be on your own. I won't be able to carry you back."

The shock of his words hit my face. "Thanks for the heads up," I shot back, disliking him at the moment.

"In wartime, life isn't as treasured. Remembering that will keep you alive."

"Duly noted!"

He went on with his instructions as if I was one of his soldiers.

"This place is nothing like Earth. You're going to tire out a lot faster here. In this atmosphere, the gravity pull is five times stronger. So, pace yourself. Don't breathe because it will only make you heavier and hold you to the ground like a magnet to metal."

"Alrighty, Captain. No breathing. Pace myself. Got it." I looked up, past the dark, low clouds, spotting the tip of a castle on the mountain's highest peak. I assumed it was the tower. "Is that our castle?" I asked, not taking my eyes off the distant mountaintop.

Val's gaze followed mine, "Yep, that would be the one, Freckles."

"The shape is different. Weird. I don't get it. Why would anyone want to live in this dead land? This place is worse than *Aurora*. Are all dimensions hostile and dangerous?"

"They each have their own set of dangers. Take fairyland for example."

"Did you just say fairyland like in fey?"

He laughed, shaking his head. "Aidan didn't teach you anything about the other worlds did he?"

"He spoke of some. But I don't think educating me on the other-worldly was on his mind. Why would it be Aidan's responsibility? He wasn't an angel. And until recently, I'd been an outcast."

"It's not. And you're not an outcast any longer."

"True," I smiled as my eyes raked over our surroundings. "Though something tells me that being an outcast isn't as bad as this place."

"Yep. And get used to it. The castle takes different forms, depending on the dimension. Since this one is about death and gloom… "

"I get it!" I interrupted. "What do they call this place?" Fog was starting to grow around our feet as if it had a life of its own. I rubbed my arms, trying to knock off the shiver that seeped into my bones. I just wanted to get the guys and leave this death trap. This place was starting to creep me out. There was something sinister about it.

"It's called the Shadow Sphere. Stay close to me. This place is conta-minated with vapors. That's what you smell."

"Did you say vipers, like snakes?"

Val's eyes had an edge of ire. "Little angel, it's time you stop thinking like a human. A vapor is a ghost, only much deadlier. They come here to prey on the lost souls."

"Oh! That's a relief." I wasn't feeling his short tone. "Since we're not lost nor souls we should be safe."

"You wish!" he scoffed bitterly. "Since we are of the heavenly body we are candy to their insatiable appetites." Val's eyes scanned over my body, "Did you bring your knives?"

"Of course!" I snapped.

"Hope you remember your training. You're going to need it here."

My brows shot together. "Why didn't you warn me about this place?"

"Would it have mattered?"

"No. I would've come regardless. Still, it would've been nice if you had given me a heads up." A sudden slurp of emotions rolled through me. "Back at the camp, apparently by your speech, you don't trust me. Have I betrayed you in some way?"

"Freckles, this is wartime. I have a ton of duties weighing on my shoulders. I'm here to help you. That should say enough."

"Fine!" I hissed. "Could you knock it off with the attitude, then? I'm a bit stressed too."

"Attitude is what's going to keep us alive," he curled his lips into a gnarl. "Of course, no one has ever had an issue with *your* attitude."

"Well, your attitude is about to get you kicked right where you live, bucko." I held my stare evenly with his.

The corners of his lips twitched as if he was holding back a laugh. He wasn't fooling me. His gold eyes frolicked with humor.

It seemed hours treading through the sharp rocks, climbing the steep glass mountain. Talk about uncanny and challenging. Val practically scaled half the mountain, signaling me to catch up. Having to find my legs and learn not to breathe which was a bit difficult, while trying to climb a razor-sharp alp seemed to be outside my scope of skills.

Val bellowed down at me, "Pick up the pace. It's going to be dark soon. We don't want to get caught out here at night."

I glared at him as if I wanted to cut his throat. "I don't see why we can't materialize inside the castle."

"Have you ever heard of the *element of surprise*?" He shouted over the strong gust of wind.

I glared up at him, a little more than annoyed. "I still don't understand why we can't just buzz up there." My muscles ached and my feet
were heavy like lead. Each step grew increasingly harder. I stopped,
unable to take another step. "If we just use our magick, we'd save so
much time and conserve our strength."

"Get up soldier! That's an order."

Oh, the hell he didn't! "Don't order me around. You have no rank
over me. I need a break if you don't mind."

"Fine!" Snappy eyes shot down at me from his windblown hair.
"But you're going to regret not staying up with me when you
encounter a vapor."

I pushed off the rock onto my feet mumbling how much I hated this
dude right now. "I'm coming already! Don't get your panties in a wad,
okay." I sneered as I levered myself up on each painstakingly ugly,
black sharp rock. I didn't dare look down. One slip and it was death.
The rocks were long protruding shards of glass that one slip could slice
a person in two. I certainly didn't want to die in this place.

I forced myself to catch up with Val. He certainly wasn't going to
coddle me. He didn't consider my shorter legs to his long muscular
legs which pissed me off even more. Despite the bloody cuts on my
hands from the glass, I managed to stop complaining and stayed on
Val's heel. After hours of climbing, I thought my arms and legs were
going to fall off.

Val broke my moment of sulking, clearing his throat. "We'll rest
here for a minute. Then we have to move fast, no more breaks. Darkness will soon come. We won't make it to daylight if we get stuck on
this mountain."

"No argument from me." I dragged myself over to a flat rock,
groaning as I planted my butt down. I huffed a sigh of relief or at least
in my mind since breathing was a fatal no, no.

Val leaned back against a rock and stared out at the mountainous
region of black and gray.

My gaze lingered, studying him. It was hard ignoring his good
looks, six-foot-five, and a perfectly lean physique. A faint smile
touched my lips. Val was undeniably beautiful. Hair of wheat, chiseled
chin, strong and determined, wide shoulders, and slim waist. A little
spurt of memory lane fluttered over me. I surprised myself. After all
this time, I was still attracted to him. But so much had happened since

we'd been together. I wondered if rekindling a relationship would be wise? Would it be fair to Val when my heart continued to yearn for Aidan? The old Aidan. I didn't know why I worried about this. The old Aidan was like a memory of the past. And I didn't expect that to change. So why did I feel guilty? Shouldn't I move on and be happy? Or as happy one could be under the circumstances.

I started rubbing my foot. I didn't think angels could ache this much. "I gotta start working out," I mumbled as I nursed my throbbing feet, totally wrapped up in my soreness.

I'd forgotten about our surroundings and apparently so had Val. He'd bent down to reach for his backpack when I caught a faint glance at something hovering just above eye level off the cliff.

Startled, I froze.

Hairs on my neck bristled as I slowly lifted my gaze. Quickly, I realized that our situation became formidable.

We had company.

An apparition, almost translucent, only a thin film, loomed a couple of feet from where we sat. The creature was like nothing I'd ever encountered. It was faceless. Yet, I sensed it was amused and entertained by our presence. Though my gut told me to be cautious.

I was scared as I slowly eased over and gave Val's shirt a good jerk without taking my eyes off our unwanted guest.

When Val's eyes caught our visitor, he drew in a brusque breath and mumbled darkly one word, *"Ghoul!"*

That one word set everything in motion.

I mentally called for my knives. Their soft hum soothed my rising alarm. I slipped a sideways glance at Val as he'd drawn a narrow blade. Unexpectedly, I inhaled a sharp gasp. I recognized the saber that Val clutched in his hand, the enchanted *Sword of Destiny*.

A wave of apprehension pulled through me. What was he thinking? Like a siren going off in my head, Val had made a very careless mistake, but I had no time to confront him.

Val and I slowly rose to our feet, edging closer, pressing against each other, back to back. This was one of those times when covering each other's back, meant literally. By now, others had joined and we were quickly outnumbered and surrounded.

We slipped each other a heedful glance. Neither Val nor I could deny that we had been ambushed. Weapons drawn, we stood in a battle stance, teeth on edge, waiting to engage. I gritted a whisper to Val. "Can't we buzz out of here or throw fireballs at these mist-looking-*motherfuckers*?"

"When we get back," he flung over his shoulder, "We really need to talk about your language."

"Whatever!" I rolled my eyes.

"Don't waste your energy. The fireball will shoot right through them. They're nothing but vapor."

"Then why the freaking weapons!" I gritted through my teeth.

"Haven't you ever faked it 'til you make it?"

I scoffed. Now he decided to make stupid jokes. "Funny. Really, funny big guy!"

Then one of the ghouls glided out from amidst the others. My limbs stiffened, and Val braced as the strange creature began to speak. "State your *purposssse*?"

Val answered, "We are searching for someone who lives in the castle above."

The creature drifted closer. Yet, I didn't detect any hostility. These ghouls might favor Casper the friendly ghost, but I got a strong sense that this ghost and his comrades were far from friendly. I wasn't taking anything for granted. Our volatile situation could change at any instant.

"Why are you *ssss*earching for lost *sssss*ouls?" the ghoul asked.

"Not lost, alive," Val replied, keeping his voice calm and empty of emotion.

The creature without warning turned his attention to me. He said, "You!" He floated closer. A sudden spurt of tension rolled off Val's shoulders, pressing tighter against me, "He weep*sssss* for you. I hear his crie*sssss* when dark consume*sss*." The ghoul's words were strangely hopeful.

My heart did a sudden leap. I wanted to rush to the castle.

The ghoul went on to say, "He love*sss* *you*. An emotion my kind does*sss* not posses*sss*," The ghoul paused. "This*sss* *sssss*trange emotion is*sss* unknown to us*sss*. Go. Retrieve your kind. Never return," the ghoul sternly ordered.

In a flash, they had vanished and I stood frozen, blinking back shock. A sharp clang of metal suddenly jarred me back as I cut my eyes at Val.

He'd puffed out a long breath, taking his free hand and roughly wiping sweat from his face. His other hand still clutched the hilt of the sword. "That's the first," he murmured. "Ghouls never speak and they damn sure don't let visitors go free."

"What the hell are you doing with t-t-that blade?" I stuttered pointing to the steel.

"I didn't have a choice. You wanted to rescue the guys and this sword was our only protection."

"You're sealing your own death!" I erupted. "That damn blade is cursed!"

Val stepped up, toe-to-toe, eyes darting testily. "In case you haven't noticed, our lives are already sealed."

"Why would you risk bringing the spear? You said yourself if the Illuminati ever got their hands on it, our world would be doomed." My eyes bounced between Val's face and the blade.

"Relax! The Illuminati is not getting their hands on the spear!" Val gritted through his teeth. Then he pulled back a brief moment. I assumed he was cooling off. "I did it because I wanted to help you."

"Why would you take such a facetious risk? That's not like you." I was flattered that he cared but not at the risk of losing his life.

"I know what this must look like to you." Val's mouth tightened. "I did it because…" His face blistered as he turned from me and then cut his eyes back at me. "I realized something about myself and my life."

"About your life?" I slugged his upper arm. "What? That you're committing suicide?"

"Not exactly!"

"Then tell me!" I snapped. "Help me to understand."

I saw that Val was struggling with some sort of inner demon. It wasn't like him to stammer over his words. "Val, tell me. You know you can tell me anything." I bunched up his collar into my fist and forced him to look at me.

Our eyes hitched

"You know that I love you, and I want to marry you." He rushed his words.

A hard silence fell between us.

"Val, *no!*" My heart lurched. "I-I don't know what to say." I shook my head, taken aback. This man took a death wish for me by bringing that sword and I couldn't give him an answer. "Val, how can we think about marriage right now? The uprising, the war."

He gripped my shoulders, his fingers bit into my skin. "Freckles, I know I haven't done right by you, but I want to make it up to you."

"So, you think marriage will fix that and to add a bonus to it all, by cursing yourself to death with that damn sword?" I searched his face to somehow understand his reasoning.

"It was the best method of defense we had. The sword is our ally."

"Val, how can you be so illogical and-and *stupid?*" I screeched. "You said yourself the sword is cursed."

"How else did you think we were going to capture Dom and Jeffery against Aidan's army?"

I tossed my arms into the air. "How am I supposed to know?" I shouted. "I'm still trying to figure out all this angel stuff."

"In case you're unaware, you are pretty hell-bent on getting your way and not listening to anyone!" Val had a valid point. "Regardless of what I say, you would've found a way to get here. It wouldn't have mattered if it killed you."

"You damn right I would've!" I fired back so loud my voice echoed across the mountaintop. "Even if it meant sacrificing my own life for Dom and Jeffery." Anger curled from my body. "Say what you want, but I didn't ask you to sacrifice *your life!*"

Val opened his mouth and then shut it quickly. His jaw twitched as he loomed over me, hurt hid behind his glint. I couldn't stand by and let him destroy his life.

I snatched the spear from Val's hand.

SWORD OF DESTINY

*N*ever in my wildest dreams did I ever expect *this*. When my eyes flitted open, Val and I were inside the castle's walls, standing in the center of Aidan's smoking-room.

The room was just as I remembered. The round gambling table, the stench of cigar, the bookcase, and the secret passage that Jeffery led me down to escape that stormy night.

I whistled to myself as I slowly turned, inspecting the old parlor. My gaze caught Val's stunned face as I whispered. "How did you know about this room?"

Val's brows shot together, "I didn't. I've never laid eyes on this place before."

"How is that possible? The only places you can materialize are destinations you've traveled."

"You're right," Val's eyes glistened. "Freckles, I didn't orb us."

"If you didn't then who did?"

Val just made a pointed glare.

I gasped. "*I* orbed us?"

Val rubbed his stubble chin. "I think so, Freckles." He carefully reached over and took the spear from my hand. "I think I better handle this. I don't want to end up on the moon," he winked.

Suddenly, faint voices disrupted our conversation. Val and I hushed, sharing a direful glance.

"Follow me!" I spun on my heels. "There's a hidden passage behind the bookcase." My eyes washed over the shelves as I fingered the books. "Damn! I can't remember which one." My gaze rushed over the books once more. "It has to be right here. I distinctly remembered Jeffery pulling down a book somewhere in this spot, right above my eye level." I kept fingering the books. "Grrr, I swear, it's one of these!"

"We don't have time guessing! Start grabbing books!" Val ordered, leaping over me and snatching up every book he touched. "One of these has to be the lever!"

I rushed beside Val, pulling book after book from its slot, "Not that one!" I rushed down the row. "Nope, not that one either. Damn, it's not here!"

Time had come to a halt, heels were clacking at a speedy pace against the stone floor, voices echoed off the walls down the corridor, increasingly getting louder.

Swiftly, Val and I dove for cover behind the door, backs pressed against the wall. Our cover was about to be revealed. So we acted before they were aware of our presence.

They entered the room, slamming the door behind them. Val and I shared a curt glance and went into action.

Stepping from the shadows, we drew our weapons on the two men. Val had snaked his arm around Mustafa's neck as the mighty blade pressed against his jugular. All four of my knives hovered over Aidan.

Both men drew in a shocked gasp and froze.

"Hello gentlemen," I smiled, darkly.

Val tightened his grip on Mustafa.

"Sorry to intrude."

Aidan gritted through his teeth. "How the hell did you find us?"

"It doesn't matter. I'm here now and I've come for Dom and Jeffery." My anger was tight and needed to be unleashed, but I had to hold on to my wits. The castle had hundreds of nooks and crannies. We still had to find the guys and figure out how to leave this dimension with our heads still attached.

Mustafa had to add his two cents, his voice muffled from Val's tight grip. "Must we be foes? Let's sit down and discuss our differences and somehow end this maddening war." He flinched when Val nicked his throat.

I stepped up into Mustafa's face. I wanted him to understand that I meant business. "It's so easy for you to say that when you have a blade pointed at your neck, but I do agree that this uprising needs to end. I want peace for my people and to live a normal life."

"My daughter, we both desire and seek the same goal." Mustafa cunningly tried to spiel his lies. "Can't you see that everything I have done, it has all been for your benefit? You and I are not so different."

I choked out a bitter laugh. "We are nothing alike, *Father Dearest*."

Aidan stood quiet, not uttering a word. His shoulders slumped and his ashen face carried a sheen of sweat. He'd leaned against a chair for support, but I expected him to collapse to his knees at any given minute. By the wheezing of his breath, it didn't take a pulmonologist to see that he was struggling for air. I fretted that the oxygen in the castle was low. Oddly, Aidan traveled dimensions all the time. Why would this place be any different?

The dark angel reeled me back in as he released a knavish laugh. "Do you honestly think a mere knife can kill me? Daughter, I truly thought more of you." He flashed a sadistic smile. "Extracting your daughter's powers made me invincible," he scoffed, arrogance exuding from his whole demeanor. "No human weapon can touch me." As though Val's blade held no threat, Mustafa stood tall with his shoulders straight. Apparently, his lust was his pride.

Suddenly, it came to me and the impact of understanding nearly knocked me off my feet. It was all too clear to me why Val had taken the sword. Of course, why didn't I see it? Eyes wide, my gaze collided with Val. The one weapon in the world that could end Mustafa's life for good was *The Sword of Destiny*.

I knew what I had to do next and that I couldn't allow Val to die. I remembered a scripture my father read to me often. I'd forgotten it until now.

Matthew 26:52 *for all those having taken the sword shall perish by the sword.*

I stepped up to Val and gently placed my hand on his. "Val, please give me the sword." My eyes pleaded. "This is not your vengeance."

Val's eyes moistened. "He is not worth your death."

I spoke just above a whisper. "Nor is he worth yours either. Val, give me the sword, please." Tears gathered in my eyes too.

THE RIDDLE

or a split second, Val and I had taken our eyes off Mustafa when he made his move. In a shot, the dark angel shoved both Val and me with such force that we went sailing across the room, slamming us into the bookshelves. Books toppled onto Val and me, knocking us loopy. By the time we regained our wits, Mustafa had vanished.

In the heat of the moment, Val grabbed the sword and in one long stride, he darted after Mustafa. I had to act fast. No one wanted the dark angel dead more than I did, but I couldn't let Val die in my place. Swiftly, I tackled him to the ground. The sword went sailing across the floor, a loud ding hit the wall.

In haste, Val threw me off of him and leaped to his feet. "Zop, what the hell are you doing? I could've caught Mustafa and ended this madness forever." Val threw his words at me like stabbing daggers.

"I want Mustafa dead too, but you're not using the sword to end your life as well." My chest heaved as I gathered to my feet.

"My, my!" Soft clapping floated in the air. "Are we having a lover's spat?" Aidan's raspy voice snapped our heads up in his direction. We'd almost forgotten his presence.

Almost.

I turned my cold eyes on Aidan. "Where are Dom and Jeffery?"

He'd flopped down in one of the wingback chairs. His breathing had worsened; his face had grown even more ashen than before. "They're in the dungeon. Just follow the stench. They haven't bathed since I brought them here." Aidan waved his hand, excusing Val. "Before I go, I'd like to have a little chat in private with Ms. Collins," Aidan glared at Val.

Not bothering to answer Aidan, Val caught my gaze and asked, "I don't like leaving you alone with him."

"Val, look at him." I tipped my chin in Aidan's direction. "He can barely sit up." I forced a tight smile. "Go get our guys!"

Val hesitated, cutting his harsh eyes at Aidan and then back at me. "Very well. I'll be back shortly. Don't try anything funny."

"I can handle myself. Don't worry. Go!"

"All right then." Our eyes locked for a brief second and then he flashed a deadly glare at Aidan before wheeling on his heels leaving us to ourselves.

Aidan didn't waste any time getting to the point. "You surprise me with your human traits. I didn't think you were clever enough to find me."

I crossed my arms, remaining silent. I wanted to hear him out.

"I have to say I am pleasantly surprised. I thought you'd never find me. You must care an awful lot to risk your life. I'll never understand why you waste your time on such useless humans. You never were one for logic."

"And you were?"

"You must know that the moment I laid eyes on your ordinary face that I hated you. A little girl dressed in rags with all that magnificent power within her reach *wasting*," He spat out the last word as if its taste was foul. "Such a shame too!" Abruptly, he went into a fit of coughs, deep wheezing, his whole body shook. I watched as he struggled to gain his breath.

I recoiled listening, yet I remained silent waiting for him to gain his composure. He was a shell of a man he once was. I almost didn't believe my eyes. But there he was… frail and weak as a human dying.

"I needed your powers," he rasped out. "And no matter how hard I tried stressing to my nephew the urgency, he ignored my pleas and betrayed me by falling in love with trailer trash." Aidan had another bout of coughing. This time, he coughed up blood as it spilled onto the floor.

"Nephew?"

"Yes," he choked out, "You stupid twat!" He drew in a singeing breath. "When you infused your powers with my nephew, it enraged me." He suddenly pounded his fist against the chair. "My blessed nephew didn't need your powers, no more than you needed them," he paused, "But I needed your powers. *Me!*" He pounded his chest like an ape. "I wanted," he briefly stopped to swallow. It was clear he was struggling to breathe. It wasn't the elements of this dimension stopping him. Inside the castle, there was clean oxygen. Strange. Why would he need air to breathe? Then there was Dom and Jeffery. Maybe he was providing it for them. I eased a breath. That was a good sign that they were still alive.

"I *needed* your powers to cure my illness."

My brows furrowed, "Illness?" Whoa! Wasn't he immortal? Why would he be sick? Did Mustafa curse him with a hex? That didn't make sense either.

Aidan's blood-shot eyes gun-fired at me. "You still aren't getting it. Must I spell it out for you?"

"Why not just say it? I can't read minds."

Aidan scoffed. "Of course not. I suppose that would be expecting too much from you."

Suddenly, Aidan's body shook like a wound-up toy, at warp speed. When he settled, I swallowed my breath, gawking.

Van?

"Holy hell!" I stepped back, eyes wide with unfathomable shock. "You're not Aidan! How is that possible?" I whispered as my mind raced with confusion.

"Startled are you?" he laughed, wiping the blood from his mouth with a napkin pulled from his jacket's pocket. "My nephew knows nothing about the weaknesses of the flesh. *Sickness.* Yes, it seems my love of smoking has cost me dearly. I'm dying as we speak. I have lung cancer and it has metastasized to other organs of my body. I should've died years ago. I suppose I'm on borrowed time," he coughed.

"Did you kill Aidan?" The cruelty of Van's hatred knew no bounds. He'd kill his own flesh and blood just because he hadn't gotten his way. Tears knotted in my throat but I refused to let him see me cry.

"I thought I'd found an answer to my sickness. I discovered injecting Sam's blood gave me strength more than I'd ever imagined.

Although, to my great disappointment, my cure wasn't permanent. Once the blood left my system, I returned to the pathetic sick man I was. After that dreadful discovery, I made a promise to myself that I'd never run out of blood. I commenced, withdrawing quantities of Sam's blood," he chuckled wickedly. "I had stocked a fine collection in my wine cellar as if I were collecting the world's finest Pinot Noir wines."

I thought I was going to be sick but I forced myself to hear him out.

"For me, Sam's blood was the fountain of youth, keeping me alive. However, the most tantalizing discovery of it all, was that I'd developed the same abilities as Sam. I held that little secret to myself and it paid off dearly, until now, of course."

I eyed the spear on the floor. My knives continued to hover over him. considering all things, I wasn't so sure of myself at this point. I'd been deceived but I wasn't certain how long Van had been masquerading as Aidan. For now, I bided my time and listened.

"My life was looking up with Sam's generous blood donations. I was certain that I could live a long life as long as I continued the injections. Until I realized that the effects of the fey blood had weakened and my lung cancer started to spread. Needing more supply and out of sheer panic, I damn near drained Sam of his blood trying to stop the illness. But despite my feeble attempts, I couldn't stop it. Sam's blood only slowed down the process. It wasn't a cure as I had hoped. Oh well, I suppose I should thank my lucky stars. I'd lived a rich, full life. I'd accepted my mortality. Then you walked into my life and I believed God had answered my prayers. If I took your powers for myself, I would be free of cancer and even better." He broke off for a moment, reaching for a cigarette and a lighter. He stuck the cigarette in his mouth and held the small flame to it and dragged in a shallow breath. The cherry flamed as his lips puckered around the butt, drawing in the nicotine and then blowing out a thin stream of smoke. How pathetic could a man be? Dying and still craving the very drug that was killing him. Van continued. "As I was saying, I would gain astounding powers. No longer would I require Sam's blood!" He drew in another puff and withdrew the smoke. "Of course, as a mere mortal, I couldn't perform the incantation. It was going to take a very powerful druid to work the enchantment." Another coughing bout struck, rendering Van from speaking. Once the fit of coughs passed, he wiped his bloody mouth with his napkin and furthered his story. "I approached Aidan to join me but he refused. The bastard turned his back on me," Van laughed to himself. "He thought I'd grown mad. Perhaps I had. That's when I blackmailed Aidan. If he wasn't going to help his dying uncle then I will force him. That's when I gave him the ultimatum. Either I go to the councilmen and report his crimes or he assists me. Oh, he was quite livid, I have to admit," Van drew in a raspy laugh.

"What crimes did Aidan commit?" My heart sunk to my ankles. Aidan had lost his life over this psychopath's greed. I was furious and all I wanted to do was end Van's miserable life. But Van was dying. All I had to do was hear him out.

"Yes, you caught that," Van smiled. "Long before I was around, when Aidan was a young lad, only eight, his parents asked him to do an unthinkable act. The act really was not so unusual for an Illuminist. We often used extreme methods to condition our children for hard times to come. Considering we plan to take over the world, one must prepare, make sacrifices, even murdering loved ones."

I remembered asking Aidan what Van was holding over his head, but he refused to tell me. I think I understood why he didn't wish to speak of it. It must've been terrible for him.

Van furthered his story as I listened quietly. "Aidan's parents demanded him to strangle his beloved dog. When the lad refused, his parents carted him off to the river, planning to drown him. That's when he discovered his gift as a druid. Either we, the *Illuminati*, are born with the gift of magick or we are born as mortals. Aidan happened to have been blessed with many gifts. However, it was also a curse. Naturally, a struggle commenced. Nescient of his abilities, Aidan set his parents ablaze. Both parents died, leaving nothing but ashes to the wind. Of course, Aidan, a young lad, knew nothing of his powers."

I suddenly recalled Aidan disposing of Sam's body by flame. I couldn't imagine how he must've felt. It had to have brought back painful memories of his past. No wonder he struggled with opening his heart.

Van went spieling his confessions. "Scared and half out of his wits, Aidan did the only thing he knew and that was to run away, fearing he'd be punished. Soon, a distant relative, his uncle, an outsider of the Family, discovered what had happened. He set out in search of Aidan. Weeks of endless searching had passed when his uncle finally located the lad, starving and begging for scraps. Once the uncle's sister heard about Aidan's story, he realized the lad wouldn't be safe with him. The child's magick was unpredictable and far too dangerous to take such a risk. One hint of Aidan's magickal abilities, not only would the lad face the torture of a burning stake but the uncle and his whole family would face the same fate. Witchcraft was forbidden back then, and anyone found guilty of such demonic acts would be sentenced to death."

My stomach churned listening to Van. The story had a ring of truth and hearing Aidan's tragedy made my heart hurt.

Van went on to say. "The uncle took Aidan to a secret monastery. There among his own kind, the druids could teach him how to harness his magick."

"Excuse me, but how do you know all this? These accounts happened way before your time," I asked.

"Young lady, I may be a mortal but I do have a very cunning nature. Get a man to trust you along with a little liquor, a tape recorder and you'd be surprised how resourceful one can be." He shot a baleful glare from under his heavy lids. "As I was saying, if the councilmen found this buried secret, Aidan would be sentenced to death. Knowing this delicious little tidbit, I proceeded with blackmail."

I stood at a stance, letting Van confess. I wanted to know every detail for my peace of mind before I smothered the man with a pillow.

"I thought everything was going as planned until he met you. When he laid his lustful eyes on you, he began having second thoughts."

I scoffed. "How dare anyone deny your selfish request."

"Yes, call me what you like." The cavalier in his voice preceded him. "I certainly could do a far greater task with your boundless magick than you," he snarled.

"Really? I can only imagine."

"You're such a simple girl," he sneered. "I would've set out to accomplish the new world, ridding this earth of leeches like yourself and your dead father." Van fell into another bout of coughs.

I laughed to myself. How ironic. The man cursed me with his last breath. Who was pathetic now?

Van sat up as much as he could, his chest fighting for oxygen. I knew he didn't have much longer. He pulled from the bout and proceeded. "I thought my blood supply was plenty and I could manage my cancer until Aidan murdered my son, Sam, cutting my supply off. I was certain to meet death. I'd run through most of it and Sam wasn't making enough blood for me as it was already." Van bit out the words like venom. "It was not until the next morning did I discover that Aidan and you had mated and infused your powers, leaving me without a chance in hell to cure my disease. That's when my second plan went into action."

"Second plan?" A sick feeling suddenly came over me.

"That morning when he left the cottage, Mustafa and I waited for Aidan and jumped him. We managed to wrangle him down and dispose of him. I suspected that you were with child. I figured if I couldn't get my hands on *your* essence then I'd take your child's. That's when Sally came into play. I had her go to the cottage and distract you while I drugged you."

"Oh my God!" Shock knotted inside me. "You were the one at the cottage. All this time I thought it was Aidan but it was you. The ring on your finger… My dreams were real."

"Your dreams were visions, child. Angels don't dream nor do they need sleep like humans."

"Thanks for the heads up," I scoffed.

"As for your mother's boyfriend, he was coming around and demanding more money. If we didn't cater to his demands, he threatened to go to the authorities. I couldn't allow him to fuck up my plans. I feared it might get back to the councilmen. Having no other choice, I had one of my men in black snuff his life out. I hardly remember the twat's name."

"Francis!" I bit out. "Francis was his name."

"After we managed to clean up the mess, I knew a few high officials that owed me some favors."

"That's how you framed me for the murders?" I asked.

"Yes, that's when you went to stay at Haven. After the birth of your child, I wanted you dead, but Mustafa wanted you alive. He was positive that you'd come around and see the light of the Order. Mustafa was the one that got you out of Haven and had the charges dropped. Once we had the child, I didn't see the harm. You were of no more use to me or the Family at that point."

My jaw twitched. I wanted to wrap my fingers around his throat and squeeze. "You're a jolly good fellow aren't you?"

"You should say that about Mustafa. He's a back-stabbing bastard. Your daddy decided to take the child's essence for himself. When I realized during the ceremony that he'd betrayed me, I was going to expose him for the trader he was but he had a guard knock me out."

"Another lie. Why am I surprised?" I didn't think I could take much more of this. I just wished Van would hurry up and die.

"I didn't exactly lie. I was going to stop Mustafa but only to take her essence for myself. Is that what you mean?"

I fisted my hands to my side, burying my nails into my palms. I couldn't kill him just yet. I had more questions. "When you ran out of angels to kill, why did you continue to pretend to be Aidan?"

"As strange as this may sound, I hated you as much as I wanted you in my bed."

I vomited in my mouth.

"Now you know why I became enraged when I found you in Val's bed. I knew if I showed my true self, you'd murder me or worse, allow me to die as I am."

"Is that why you killed Sally?"

Van choked out a bloody laugh. "Yes, when Sally realized that I was using her, she threatened to go to you. I couldn't have her spoiling my surprise."

"Since it doesn't really matter now can you tell me if Aidan and Sally were married?"

Van broke into sick sadistic laughter. "Yes, but it is not what you think. Aidan found Sally in a village about to be burned at the stake for witchcraft. She had cast a spell on a lord's wife and was caught in the act. Aidan the weakling stopped the sentencing by marrying her. He promised to take Sally and never return. I think he dumped her in some brothel miles away. Perfect for a whore. But you can ask him yourself." He fought with another bout of coughing.

I stood there staring, swirled in confusion. Van must be hallucinating. Aidan is dead. "You want me to ask Aidan? Sorta hard since you murdered him."

"You think I killed Aidan?" He battled breathing, choking out laughter. "Sweetheart, Aidan isn't dead. I couldn't kill him without killing you. And even if that were not a factor, neither Mustafa and I or a whole fucking fleet of super-soldiers could take Aidan down. That bastard will outlive the cockroach!"

I stood surprised and more uncertain than ever. "You said you disposed of *him!*"

"Yes, when Aidan returned to the castle that morning looking for his two gay employees, Mustafa and I ambushed him with a spell, binding him to his castle," he laughed. "How ironic, the only enchantment that Mustafa could think of was a love spell. A bloody damn love spell. Only true love will break the spell. I suspected that Mustafa never thought you'd love the Druid." Van snorted, going into a rage of coughs.

My eyes narrowed. "How do I know you're not pulling one of your tricks again?"

"Do I look like I can pull another scheme? My blood source is out and Mustafa won't allow me to use any of his fey that's under his lock and keep. What do I care? I'm a dying man."

All of a sudden, Aidan's riddle rushed through my skull. *"Believe in only half of what you see and none of which you don't."* My eyes snapped up at Van, "Where is he?" I demanded.

"Where he's always been, *in the tower.*"

I ALWAYS HAVE

spun on my heels and darted out the room and down the corridor. I could hear Van breaking into another one of his violent coughs. Although this time, I knew it was his last, and I didn't feel an ounce of sorrow for his death.

If my memory served me well, I recalled something being mentioned about the stairwell to the tower located in the east wing. I figured that I'd run east. Surely, I'd find the stairs leading to it.

I turned the corner and collided with Val's chest. When my eyes lifted, I caught sight of Dom and Jeffery. Immediately, I flew into their arms and we embraced each other as tears streamed down our faces.

"Are you guys okay?" I pulled from their embrace to eye them over. They looked pretty ragged, disheveled hair, beards past their chins and uncombed. Their weight had dropped thirty pounds or more. Both could use a good meal.

Dom nodded his head, speaking, "We are much better now that you are here," he smiled behind his overgrown mustache.

Jeffery barged in, still full of life. "I look like the Unabomber. I need a bath and fresh clothes. A mani is a must. Hell! I needs a whole body wax. I'm too beautiful to look like this! Food sounds good too! I sure could chow down on a fat steak."

I laughed at my beloved friend. Jeffery always knew how to put a smile on my face. "Boo, we're gonna get you guys back and take care of all your needs.

Dom spoke up urgently. "Stevie, Van is masquerading as Aidan. He's been ingesting Sam's blood…"

"I know. Van is dead. He just took his last breath. I know everything," I smiled. "Aidan is alive!" I teared up, choking the words out.

Val stepped up and broke our conversation. "Say that again!" His voice filled with surprise and disdain.

I turned my eyes on Val and answered, "Van has been fooling all of us into thinking that he was Aidan. He had taken on Sam's abilities by ingesting Sam's blood. Fey blood transformed him, giving him powers. That's how he'd been replicating Aidan. I've been so blind, Val. Aidan is alive!"

Val grabbed up my arm and dragged me off to the side. His face was angry. "You don't intend to go rescue him do you?"

"How can you ask me that? Of course, I am."

"Leave him be! Just let the dog lie in his own fleas. He's caused you enough heartache. Why keep punishing yourself?" His eyes were drilling me.

I jerked free of his iron grip. "If you were needing rescuing, I'd come for you! Why would I not do the same for Aidan?"

Val bit down on his lips and then he just said it. "I don't want you to get involved with him. He's trouble. Everywhere he goes, he leaves a trail of mayhem. Have you forgotten my sister? She's missing because of that son of a bitch!"

"If this had been six months ago, I'd believe he was guilty. But now that I witnessed Van's sideshow, I'm not sure what to believe. And I think everyone is entitled to a fair hearing."

"Don't go." Val grabbed my upper arm. "Leave him here. We can make a life for ourselves. Just you and me." There was a plea in his voice. My heart went out to him but he was asking the impossible. If I'd been stuck in the tower, Aidan would've rescued me. The man in that tower was the man I fell in love with. I couldn't turn my back on him now.

"You don't want me to go after him because you're jealous. You're afraid if Aidan comes back into my life, I won't take you back."

Val's jaw twitched. "So? What's wrong with that?"

"Lots of things! Val, we had a good run, but it didn't work out.

Even if Aidan wasn't around, I wouldn't go back with you. I love you, but I'm not in love with you. We wouldn't work. You must know that deep down."

"If we gave it a fair shot, we'd have a good chance as any. Even my men have accepted you. You're one of us now," he argued.

"One thing you're forgetting… I belong to Aidan. He and I are infused, and I am in love with him. I won't betray him again. I should've known there was something wrong when he didn't return to the cottage. I was so stupid and blind." My mind twirled in circles of realization. "Val, I'm going to get Aidan. He's in the tower here in the castle. You can wait or leave. It's up to you, but I'm getting him. He's trapped in the tower under a spell. I'm breaking that enchantment if I have to blow up this whole damn castle."

Val's face appeared stricken. "Fine! Do what you must. I don't plan to let you go that easily. I'll fight for you. And I won't leave you here alone with him. I'll wait but don't take too long. Dom and Jeffery are running out of oxygen." His expression reminded me of someone who had lost all hope. The pain was apparent. I hated myself for hurting Val, but it would've been much worse misleading him.

"I'll hurry!" I nodded to the guys and darted off.

Down the hall, hooking a left turn and then down another hall and taking a right, I came to a quick halt. A wooden door that had been sealed tightly. This had to be the enchanted door.

I band my fingers around the latch and called to my essence. This time, I used something that I'd never used before… *love*. I closed my eyes and with all my might, I called for my magick. Suddenly, I felt a warmth enshrouding my body. I opened my eyes and I was glowing. I could feel my magick surging through me.

I wrapped my fingers around the knob and pulled it back. The door opened with a swish. I gasped with glee when my eyes landed on stairs going up. The steps were narrow and steep. I could see well enough, thanks to my glowing body.

With no hesitation, I took two steps at a time. The stairs spiraled narrowly as I rushed, gripping the course wall, climbing to the top.

When my foot touched the last step, I nearly dropped to my

knees. There he stood gazing out his balcony. After all this time, Aidan hadn't changed a bit. His compelling blues, the confident set of his shoulders, sent chills over my body. He was so perfect, so symmetrical, that any more delicacy would have made him too beautiful for a man. He was dressed in a T-shirt, jeans that hung low on his hips, and barefooted. I almost giggled, seeing him casually clothed. I stood there frozen, unable to take my eyes off him, fearing I was dreaming.

Then he turned facing me and stilled for a moment. Our eyes locked and a faint smile touched his full lips. "Princess!" he barely murmured. "Is that really you or am I dreaming?"

"Aidan!" My voice broke. "I ask myself the same question." I stood motionless standing at the threshold and suddenly my whole being became filled with yearning.

"If we are dreaming… then I shall never open my eyes again," he whispered gently.

Not wasting another second, I rushed into his consoling arms. His hands locked against my spine, bringing me closer as he buried his face into my hair. "I have missed your scent, your touch," he whispered against my hair, kissing it.

"Aidan," I drew back, capturing his eyes, "Van has been pretending to… "

"Shush, my love." He gently placed a finger to my lips. "I have waited so long for this moment. Nothing matters anymore. I have all I need right here with you." His lips slowly descended to meet mine and I couldn't deny my desires any longer. I drank in the sweetness of his kisses. When he pulled away, he gazed into my eyes and spoke three small words, "I love you," he smiled. *I always have.*

I knew things were going to be better. Dom and Jeffery were alive. They were a bit worn but nothing that couldn't be mended.

Val stopped speaking to me and stayed busy with his men. Though from time to time, I'd catch his glance. I sensed his silence wouldn't last forever. Sooner or later, he would confront Aidan concerning his sister.

Aidan and I had a lot to discuss. There was so much to tell him. I wasn't sure how he'd take it. The loss of our child, my involvement with Val. Before we could move forward, I needed to explain.

Mustafa continued to be on the run. When the camp settled, I intended to hunt him down and finish him off. He would pay for his crimes.

At least Van was dead. He'd choked on his blood, died of cancer. His death was like a weight lifted off my chest. That was one less bad guy that had to be dealt with.

The uprising continued. So much had happened since I'd last seen Aidan that wondrous day at the cottage and then it ended so abruptly. When the time was right, I'd sit Aidan down and tell him about our child, Dawn, and I reckoned I needed to come clean about his sister, Helen too. But for now, we'd just take one day at a time.

Only time would tell as we ventured off into our next chapter of thrills and chills and a rollercoaster of life.

ABOUT THE AUTHOR

Jo Wilde lives on a small farm in Waskom, Texas, right on the border of Louisiana, with her husband and their three children. She is a stay at home mom and is earning her BA in English.

Growing up, Jo lived in a time when women were to be seen rather than heard. This notion didn't sit well with her. She often found herself in a pickle, speaking her mind, attending outrageous concerts, hanging out with the cool kids, and pushing the limits of what society deemed as acceptable. Now that she's settled down and has a family of her own, she saves her inner rebel for her books. Jo loves writing stories about strong, spunky female-roles that don't take any bull and makes no excuses. She is best known for her young adult book, The CROSSING. And she promises there are more coming soon!

To learn more about Jo Wilde and discover more Next Chapter authors, visit our website at www.nextchapter.pub.

The Angel Series Collection - Books 4-5
ISBN: 978-4-82417-598-4
Paperback Edition

Published by
Next Chapter
2-5-6 SANNO
SANNO BRIDGE
143-0023 Ota-Ku, Tokyo
+818035793528

1st June 2023